BURDENS
OF
PROOF

Also by Chester Oksner:

PUNITIVE DAMAGE

BURDENS

OF

PROOF

A NOVEL

Chester Oksner

KNIGHTSBRIDGE PUBLISHING COMPANY
NEW YORK

Published in the United States by
Knightsbridge Publishing Company
255 East 49th Street
New York, New York 10017

Library of Congress Cataloging-in-Publication Data

Oksner, Chester.
  Burdens of proof : a novel / Chester Oksner. — 1st ed.
    p. cm.
  ISBN 1-877961-13-2 : $18.95
  I. Title.
PS3565.K7B87   1990
813'.54—dc20

90-30078
CIP

Designed by Stanley S. Drate/Folio Graphics Co., Inc.

10 9 8 7 6 5 4 3 2 1
First Edition

For my father, Bojas

I

THE FACTS
OF THE CASE

1

Peter Saunders left his Ford at the Texaco station for its regular seventy-thousand-mile service, picked up a six-pack of Coors, and started hiking up the hill. Gloria did not care for beer, and, he suspected, did not care much for him drinking it, either. She usually forgot, she said, to buy it. His brisk pace made the bottles rattle.

Gloria's house was a steep mile and a half into the Hollywood hills overlooking the Los Angeles basin. Saunders had not really wanted the exercise so much as time alone to think before he reached Gloria's, his home for the past three weeks.

Gloria Brewer was the secretary-treasurer of Mothers for Peace. By her own admission, the closest she had come to motherhood was an aborted six-week pregnancy, and she was the most unpeaceable woman he had ever known. She was at least willing and often eager to argue about anything.

Fortunately, Gloria had no interest in remarrying. Her alimony alone exceeded Saunders's modest income from his navy pension and savings. Saunders reminded himself that she had recently expressed early-morning anxiety that living with him was jeopardizing her spousal support payments. Perhaps she would be relieved to learn he was moving out.

As Saunders cleared the last rise, he was aware that he was still breathing easily. Not bad for a fifty year old with contam-

3

inated lungs. Gloria's small redwood and glass house clung to the hillside, as it had tenaciously for thirty years. The oleander was overrunning the front wall. He must remember to prune that before he left.

The carport was empty. Time for one or two peaceful beers before Gloria returned. Out of habit, Saunders headed for the side door inside the carport. Only guests used the front door. There was no back door. The rear wall and deck cantilevered into thin air 300 feet above the winding street below.

Saunders swung the door open, eyes downcast as he struggled to free his key from the lock. He looked up to face an apparent giant—bigger and wider than himself anyway, which was generally considered big enough.

Instinctively, Saunders's left hand dove for his jacket pocket as if to fire a concealed handgun.

The hulk hesitated . . .

With his right, Saunders swung the six-pack into the side of the man's head with everything his back and shoulder could put into it.

He was just beginning to enjoy the satisfaction of seeing the man slump against the clothes dryer when the world exploded inside his head.

An immense man stood holding a piece of firewood like a club over Saunders's prone body. "Sullivan, you okay yet?" he asked his groaning partner.

Sullivan shook his head but was not ready to move anything else. "Yeah. I think it's only my jaw that's broken."

"Good. That's the part that's always getting you into trouble anyways." The huge man threw the log into a corner and drew his switchblade. The blade flicked open.

"Jeez, Doblonski!" yelled Sullivan as he wobbled to his feet. "The boss said no killing." At six-feet-four and 240 pounds, he was only a little smaller than Doblonski.

"He saw you, Dumbo."

"You clobbered him so good he won't remember anything. If you off him, Magnasunn will have your ass. I wouldn't give a fuck except if you go down for this you'll take me with you. Come on, we did what we came for."

"Shit," said Doblonski, but he snapped the knife shut as he headed out the door.

2

The ringing telephone brought Saunders back to consciousness. It was a climb up Mount Everest, but he managed to pull the receiver off the wall phone before slumping back to a sitting position. He pulled a beer bottle out from under him before answering. The cold glass felt better applied to the back of his neck. The room swam into focus. Everything seemed normal except for a floor full of beer bottles.

He meant to say, "Hello, this is Peter Saunders." He had started answering the telephone that way since moving in with Gloria. It reduced complications. What came out was, "O, thusPeerSaunerz."

Jesus, his head throbbed.

"Mr. Saunders? Good. This is Herbert Furness, special agent, Federal Bureau of Investigation. Say, are you all right?"

Saunders was confused. He hadn't even called the police yet, had he? God, what a headache. "Excuse me." A wave of nausea overtook him. He took a moment to fight it down before explaining what had happened.

"I'll be there within thirty minutes," Furness said. "Do you want me to call an ambulance?"

"I think I'm okay. Come to the side door. I'll just sit here until you show up."

Furness made it in twenty-three minutes, a commendable showing in the face of afternoon traffic between Wilshire and Hollywood.

The young agent stuck his aviator-style sunglasses into the breast pocket of his seersucker suit as he surveyed the scene.

Saunders was still sitting on the utility-room floor, surrounded by beer bottles. "I haven't touched anything," he said.

5

"I noticed," said Furness, as he replaced the dangling telephone receiver. He helped Saunders to his feet and steered him
to the living-room couch. "Jesus, you must weigh close to two
hundred. Mr. Saunders, I telephoned because I'm investigating
a report that a substantial amount of plutonium is missing
from the Point Anacapa Nuclear Power Plant. I had intended to
make an appointment to come out and talk to you about it."

Saunders tried to nod, but even that hurt the back of his
head.

"What do you remember happened here?"

"There had to be at least two of them. The one I hit was
wearing gloves, the plastic disposable kind."

"Can you describe any of them?"

"The one I hit, but I only had a glimpse of him."

"Is anything missing?"

Saunders shrugged. A mistake. Pain stabbed the backs of his
eyes.

"Mr. Saunders, it would be helpful if you would cooperate."

Saunders ignored that. "I mean I haven't had a chance to
check."

Furness nodded. "What time did this alleged assault occur?"

"Alleged? How do you think I got this bloody lump on the
back of my head?"

Furness was not there to answer questions. "I'll have to
report this to L.A.P.D."

Saunders did not dare nod or shrug again. "Sure," he said.

"You don't seem too concerned, Mr. Saunders."

"Look Mr. . . . Jesus, I can't even remember your name. My
head is bursting. I promise to get goddamned pissed off as
soon as I can think straight, okay?"

"Maybe I should just look around a little before I ask more
questions. Give you a chance to rest a few minutes. I'd like to
sweep for radiation first. I brought a Geiger counter. All right?"

Saunders's brain was not too muddled to comprehend the
implication. If the agent brought a counter, then Saunders was
a suspect. He waved permission. He did not feel like talking
any more. According to Gloria, he never felt like talking.

The pain was coming down to a dull ache but he was not yet
enthusiastically mobile by the time Furness returned with a
report.

"There is radiation in a cube of butter in the refrigerator door. The rest of the place seems clean."

Saunders sat upright in spite of the burst behind his right ear.

Furness let him finish wincing before he asked, "Know anything about that?"

Carefully, Saunders leaned back against the couch. "No. But I'm beginning to get some ideas."

"Good." Furness volunteered his first information of the day. "I can't tell specifically what radioactive material or how much with this equipment. I telephoned for the tech squad. Be here in a few minutes. Nothing seems to have been disturbed in the rest of the house. I've got a lot more questions if you're up for it."

"Shoot."

Saunders answered all the questions tersely but candidly. Other than his denial that he had taken radioactive material from the Point Anacapa plant owned by Consolidated Utilities, he had little useful information, only suspicions.

His suspicions came easily enough. His uninvited visitors must have planted the deadly stuff.

Furness raised an eyebrow. "And who would do that?" he wanted to know.

Consolidated Utilities, obviously. Why? To discredit him, of course. He was lecturing, publicly saying things that could hurt the company. What do you mean "hurt?" He meant, "hurt financially." Saunders explained that the reforms in safety standards he was advocating could cost Consolidated Utilities hundreds of millions, if people listened and acted, he meant.

"We'll have to impound the butter," Furness said with a straight face. "It's evidence. I'll leave a receipt."

"Can you arrange to take the whole refrigerator?"

"You mean the contents?"

"No. The refrigerator, too. I can't decontaminate it here. It's dangerous."

The same crew that came for the butter handled the disposal of the refrigerator. Only a rectangle of dust remained.

Furness was totally noncommittal. No, he could not tell Saunders what would happen next. The investigation would continue was all he would say.

"Thank you . . . for your cooperation," Furness said, as if he did not believe he was getting any. "Sure you're all right?"

"Yeah, great." *He probably doesn't believe one damn word I've said. Cops.*

3

"**C**ops," Saunders snorted as he walked slowly into the kitchen and stared at the dusty patch where a refrigerator once stood. "Cops and thugs." His rage erupted.

He picked up a beer bottle to throw. Still cool. *You too,* he told himself. *Stay cool.* He used the bottle opener instead, temporarily compromising on a long, calming draft.

The bathroom had two mirrors he could adjust to view the back of his head. Just some dried blood and an abrasion. He patted the spot with a damp washcloth. Another mistake. The pain surged. Bastards.

He blinked hazy blue eyes. At least they still focused properly. The front of him looked the same as it had for twenty years. Thick blond hair kept close at the sides in military fashion. Okay, maybe receding some and a little gray at the temples.

Saunders returned to the couch with his beer. His head felt better in horizontal mode. Had he left out anything in his answers to Furness? Better start at the beginning and think it through again.

Where was the beginning anyway? *I was born in 1937 in Boulder, Colorado, of modest . . .* no, not that beginning. Saunders supposed it was when Rickover picked him as engineering officer for one of the first nuclear submarines.

In 1978, when Consolidated Utilities offered Lieutenant Commander Peter Saunders a supervisorial position in the construction of its first nuclear power plant at Point Anacapa, Saunders was grateful on several counts.

He had been drained empty by the death of his wife, Rachel, the year before. Her last terrified, pain-ridden months pervaded his memory. The doctors had a catalogue of diseases and symptoms, but it was obvious they had not even been able to diagnose her. The death certificate said congestive heart failure, but that was the effect, not the cause.

Saunders did not think his naval career would continue to advance. He had been commissioned through NROTC training in college, not the Academy. He had a Russian father. He had never held command.

Consolidated Utilities was offering four times his navy pay. Besides, Saunders thought, he was probably the only sailor in the world who had never seen California.

Life would begin anew.

When construction and preliminary testing at Point Anacapa were completed, Saunders again faced alternatives. The navy urged him to return with no loss in grade and command of a new nuclear testing facility. Consolidated Utilities, ready to go on-line twenty-four hours a day, offered his choice of the three production shift supervisors' jobs and another salary increase.

Saunders decided to stay. He had grown comfortable, living in San Luis Obispo, a small central California town twenty miles from the plant site.

Everyone but Saunders worked graveyard shift for the 15-percent bonus paid for inhuman hours. Saunders chose it because of insomnia and because his boss worked days. Insulated from the plant manager, Isaac Karrasch, Saunders enjoyed his job. San Luis Obispo was a good place for a solitary man, which is what he had become, isolated by an invisible wall.

The first breach in Saunders's wall was so subtle, he had not realized it occurred. Only a minor accident on his shift, really. A pressure relief valve had stuck open but the control-room gauge showed it closed. The alarms did not register until the containment floor was covered with several inches of deuterium oxide, heavy water, highly radiocative.

Saunders had supervised the cleanup. It was no big deal. He had worn protective clothing and was cleared by the lab afterward. The plant health physicist assured him that the amount of xenon and krypton gas that he might have inhaled was insignificant. What you breathe on the 101 Freeway is worse, he had said.

Saunders had been complaining about that valve for months. Karrasch had promised him it would be rebuilt, then assured him that it had been. And Saunders had believed him.

And then, only a few months later, that twenty-eight-inch pipe burst in his face. He had saved the plant and the public from disaster, but at a terrible price. He was walking around with lungs full of radioactive contamination.

Soon the cancer would get him. He had already been sentenced. He was just hanging around for the execution.

Of course, Karrasch's stooges had again assured him he was fine. That bastard, Karrasch. He would sell his mother a soiled carpet and throw in a certificate that the stains were Scheherazade's tears.

Before this afternoon he had been content to quit Consolidated and walk away. There had been no thought of revenge, but after this . . . Karrasch. Consolidated. Thugs. Those total, complete bastards.

What would he feel first? How long before . . . ? He closed his eyes and saw Rachel's terrified face bathed in sweat.

Mercifully, the unmistakable sound of Gloria's ancient Mercedes diesel sounded in the carport.

"Peter," he heard her yell. "Come and help me, please. I bought a lot of things that have to go into the freezer right away."

He hurried, but she was already standing in the kitchen doorway, arms full of groceries, staring at the empty dusty rectangle on the kitchen floor.

Saunders took the groceries and explained. It was the first time he could remember that she could only say, "But . . ."

Saunders did not yet feel much like driving, but that seemed the least painful alternative. His quick run to the supermarket in the Mercedes produced an inexpensive ice chest and enough ice cubes to keep the provisions intact. On the way back, he decided a replacement refrigerator would make a nice farewell gift. His head stopped throbbing.

Three glasses of Chablis with ice cubes, and the promise of a morning refrigerator shopping trip, calmed Gloria to the point of reminding Saunders, "We promised to show up at Vanessa's thing tonight. You feel well enough, don't you?"

"Only a dull ache, but I'm not up for another fundraiser tonight. Those bastards could have killed me. And the FBI probably thinks I stole . . ."

"Come on. It's for the sea lions." Gloria's cherub lips pouted. "You like sea lions, don't you? She'll have hors d'oeuvres. You won't even have to talk. Congressman Cummings will do that."

"Paul Cummings? This part of his senatorial campaign?"

"I suppose. He's such a hunk. Say, tell him about what happened this afternoon. Maybe he can do something. Come on. It will make you feel better."

Saunders doubted that. He was furious at what he was sure was Consolidated Utilities' scheming. Maybe Cummings really could help, though. Wasn't that something congressmen did?

He was also annoyed by Gloria's lack of concern for his injury, but, hell, this might be his last night with her anyway. One fight a day was enough.

4

Tables and chairs had been scattered about Vanessa Armour's rear yard, but many guests preferred sitting at the edge of the pool, dangling bare feet, dipping raw vegetables into unidentifiable mixtures.

Over by the diving board Congressman Paul Cummings III stood surrounded by layers of admiring constituents. Most were women.

"Isn't he just a hunk?" Gloria asked rhetorically.

Saunders could never completely adjust to the thirty-eight-year-old woman talking like a teenager, but he had to admit the man was unforgivably handsome. It seemed hardly possible to be that tan or have hair that white.

Since the Point Anacapa accident, Saunders had acquired a minor, if morbid, celebrity of his own. At Gloria's urging he had already given his first lecture on "Our Need for a Responsible Nuclear Power Industry."

Public speaking was hell for Peter Saunders, for whom not even idle conversation came easily. But he was compelled by determination that the brief remainder of his life count for something more than just a metaphor for bad luck.

It was after that first lecture that Gloria had persuaded him to come home with her. What a night. The thrill of having actually forced himself to stand up and speak to 153 women. Gloria's adoring green eyes. Stars above. City lights below. The bottle of Piper Sonoma. Everything sparkled that night, three weeks ago.

Now, in Vanessa's yard, he and Gloria were soon surrounded by a small group.

"Mr. Saunders, there are so many safe alternatives. Shouldn't nuclear power simply be banned?" an extremely large, possibly blonde, woman wanted to know. She looked as if she might accomplish it single-handedly.

This was the only cause dear to Saunders, but he just did not feel like getting into it. He gave the polite, oversimplified response. "No, ma'am. There is no feasible alternative. There are other technologies with promise for the future, but they have their problems, too. Within ten to fifteen years, demand will be for even more nuclear power. What we need is to make it safe."

"Isn't that an oxymoron?" another asked. "I mean safe nuclear power?"

Cute, thought Saunders. Oxymoron. "No, ma'am. There is no inherent technical obstacle to resolving the safety problems. The only serious question is whether we have the political will to take the necessary action."

Saunders continued to answer questions while Gloria watched for an opening around the congressman. "Excuse us, ladies," she finally said. "Peter darling, there's a lull. Come on. I'll introduce you."

Congressman Cummings listened patiently and frowned with apparent concern as Saunders told his story. "I think

Mrs. Ferrara may do you more immediate good than I. Fortunately, I brought her along. Where . . . ? Oh, there, on the other side of the pool."

He grasped one each of Saunders's and Gloria's elbows, leading them toward the woman in the shadows at the far side of the pool. She started to rise as she saw them approach. Saunders wondered how he could have missed her, even in the dark.

"Lucrezia, I've brought you a new client," the congressman bellowed. "Counselor, this is Peter Saunders. He has a most interesting story. Peter, this lady is the best 'people's lawyer' I know. Of course, you read about the case of the raped policewoman versus the City of Los Angeles a couple of months ago? And last year, the four-million-dollar verdict against Ford Motor Company?" Cummings excused himself to carry on the campaign.

Lucrezia Ferrara's silver hair was pulled back in sort of a chignon. She wore a simple knit dress of some subdued shade of red.

The dress covered her from neck to wrists and knees, but seemed only to accent her sexuality. As she shook his hand she smiled at Saunders without opening her mouth. It made him wonder what marvelous secrets she could tell.

Gloria noticed his awe. She searched the corners of Lucrezia's eyes for tiny wrinkles. *With that hair she has to be at least forty-five, although there is nothing else to suggest it*, Gloria mumbled to herself. *I hate her.* "Hi. Gloria Brewer," she said.

Lucrezia Ferrara not only listened to Saunders, she asked a lot of questions. Many were on the order of "What proof do you have that . . . ?" Saunders tried to answer accurately. He didn't mind questions in general. Only the personal ones.

It was beginning to sound to Gloria as if Lucrezia Ferrara thought he might have a case. Gloria, who had indirectly promoted this meeting, began to feel the compulsion to shoot it down. Whether it was the third glass of wine or merely jealousy, Gloria could not desist. Hell, she had spent a year in law school, hadn't she?

"Sure," she said. "All you have to do is prove Consolidated Utilities intentionally misrepresented the condition of the plant, fraudulently covered up the extent of his contamination, and that it is, in fact, lethal. Then keep him alive long enough to get to trial while Consolidated, meanwhile, is trying to kill him."

Vanessa came up bearing a tray. "Piece of cake?"

"Precisely," said Lucrezia.

5

"All right if I drive?" Congressman Cummings asked as Lucrezia's new Lincoln LSC Mark VII was brought up.

Lucrezia shrugged to hide her annoyance and climbed into the passenger seat as the red-jacketed attendant held the door. They had left his vehicle at his downtown office and taken Lucrezia's because, he had said, he loved driving her new car. Lucrezia knew the real reason was that he considered his white Eldorado with personalized CONGRES license plates and the PC III gold-leaf-monogrammed door sills as too visible. It was imprudent for the leading senatorial candidate to be seen driving the streets of Los Angeles late at night with a handsome woman other than his wife.

"What do you think of Saunders's claim?" asked Cummings as he peeled rubber off Lucrezia's brand-new tires to prove how much fun he was having.

"I let that little bitch girlfriend of his provoke me into bragging about what a cinch it would be, but I don't really believe that. I really feel for the poor bastard, but he has serious burden-of-proof problems. You were a pretty fair lawyer before you decided to become a star. What do you think?"

"A lawyer should not indulge her feelings. I should get a healthy contribution out of Vanessa. Maybe one of the others. Anyone home at your place tonight?"

"Just drop yourself off where your car is parked. I've got an eight A.M. settlement conference."

"Lucrezia dearest, I am truly sorry. I know you're disappointed. I know I said I'd be moved out by this week, but now Barbara's taken sick. She's going in for tests tomorrow. I can't walk out on her right now. They would make me look ruthless. That could cost me the *Times*'s endorsement." They drove in silence for several miles before Cummings spoke again. "Lucy, you know I love you."

Yes, she knew that. In his fashion he really did love her, but never so much as he loved the idea of becoming senator. He was bright and could be fun. Lucrezia thought she probably loved him, too. She was certain his burning ambition hid a warm, caring man.

Lucrezia said, "All I know tonight is that I hate this sneaking around. You're not even consistent. Sometimes apparently it's all right to be seen with me. Sometimes it isn't. I don't even understand the criteria. I'm not adamant about marriage but I will not continue being the other woman."

Cummings parked the Mark VII behind his Cadillac and started around to help Lucrezia out, but she was already backing into the street. He jumped aside. The Lincoln stopped, then leapt forward to where he stood.

Lucrezia lowered her window. "Call me after you've solved your marital-political problems."

The rear tires smoked as she backed the car onto Flower Street, executing a perfect 180-degree skid, which pointed toward home.

Lucrezia's house was modest by Beverly Hills standards. Master bedroom, two guest rooms, and bathrooms upstairs. Living, dining, kitchen, and what real-estate agents call a powder room, downstairs. Some of the fifty-year-old varicolored roof tiles were cracking, but they were irreplaceable, and Lucrezia refused to substitute commonplace homogeneity. The rest of the place was impeccable classic Spanish, purchased at a bargain price from a desperate commodities trader with her first big fee. She had added the expensive swimming pool, but, as morning laps were her only serious exercise, that had been easy to rationalize.

Lucrezia ignored the chicken molé casserole and avocado salad left by Carmen, her housekeeper. She chose instead a tall glass, into which she splashed equal parts of brandy and soda. Carmen was absolutely right. She did drink too much.

Lucrezia toyed with the idea of swimming a few laps but decided to postpone that until morning. She walked up the curved mosaic-tiled staircase to her bedroom backwards because she felt like it.

She turned and threw her husband a good-night kiss.

He smiled back. There he was, resplendently uniformed in the silver frame from where he had smiled for the past seventeen years.

Didn't I warn you to be careful, John? Two tours of duty without a scratch and you have to get yourself run over by a drunken chaplain. I really loved you, you careless son of a bitch.

Lucrezia drew her red-knit dress over her head and laid it carefully over the back of a chair out of respect for its beauty. The rest of her clothes she left carelessly on the rug, a puddle of rose silk on snowy Berber wool.

In the shower her empty brandy glass filled with soap suds. Toweled and tooth-brushed, she reached into a bureau drawer for white silk pajamas. "Naa," she muttered, slammed the drawer shut, and crawled under the quilt.

6

Peter Saunders waited in Ferrara and Associates' reception room, angry with himself as well as Consolidated.

While moving out of Gloria's house he had discovered her ring behind his spare tube of toothpaste—a small sapphire surrounded by tiny diamonds in a gold mounting.

Gloria had reported it stolen the day after the attack. She

thought she had left it on the kitchen counter. Surely that was simply a mistake. She had mislaid it and would be grateful if it was found.

He had slipped the ring into his shirt pocket. He would pretend to find it in her ear. His sleight of hand always lightened her mood and would ease the parting.

He thought she only pretended to be disappointed that he was moving out. Some sort of vague arrangement for dinner next week accompanied a desultory kiss.

"Anyway, I'll see you Monday at the lawyer's," was the last thing Gloria said as Saunders drove away, entirely forgetting about the ring.

He had intended to return it this morning but had forgotten to bring it. His doctor had said that distant metastases in the brain were not uncommon as early evidence of lung cancer. Had the doctor said loss of memory was one of the symptoms? He couldn't remember that either, and that angered him.

When Vanessa and Gloria showed up, the group was immediately ushered into Lucrezia's office. Except for a profusion of wildflowers and houseplants, the room looked starkly functional. Case files strewn about all available horizontal surfaces, law books packed too tightly into the shelves.

Saunders was impressed and Vanessa was disappointed. She had expected glamour. Gloria was indifferent, still obsessed by the thought that the woman was much too . . . what was the polite word. . . ? mature to be attractive to Peter.

As soon as they were seated, Saunders's angry questions boiled over. "Couldn't Consolidated be charged with attempted murder? Immediately restrained from molesting me again? Is suit going to be filed today? No? What do you mean, No? Don't you understand those bastards aren't content with having killed me? Now they want me shut up."

Gloria had never heard him talk that much.

Lucrezia was sympathetic, but direct. Sorry, but Saunders was going to have to wait for answers until she knew more.

"As executive vice-president of Mothers for Peace I consider that you'll be doing a great public service by exposing this conspiracy," Vanessa said.

"Ms. Armour, I respect the goals of your organization and would be honored to be of service, but I must tell you we have no evidence suggesting conspiracy. We have pitifully little evidence against Consolidated Utilities alone. If this turns out to be a case at all, it will be Mr. Saunders's case for fair compensation for his injuries and perhaps punitive damages to assure no further harassment."

"Call me Vanessa, please. At least his cause will generate sufficient publicity to raise—"

"Vanessa, I hope not to sound rude, and I am not ungrateful for your interest in Mr. Saunders's case." Lucrezia knew her words could be offensive. She tried to keep the tone conciliatory. "But you are raising questions concerning your role in this case that had better be addressed early."

Vanessa was not foolish. "Of course, we realize that our contribution toward your fees will be for your representation of Mr. Saunders as well. But I'm sure you recognize that his case is only one battle in the war against an irresponsible nuclear-power-industry–government complex."

Lucrezia shook her head. "Please, everyone. Be patient while I explain some basics. If I decide to take this case, my only client must be Peter Saunders. Again, if this is a case at all, it is only Peter Saunders's case. Mr. Saunders may welcome the financial and moral support of Mothers for Peace, but the organization cannot be a party to this lawsuit."

Gloria said, "I understand that Peter's claim against Consolidated is his alone, but can't you also represent the cause Mothers for Peace stands for? Isn't a responsible nuclear-power industry worth fighting for?" She did not care for the idea of any relationship, even lawyer-client, exclusively between Peter Saunders and Lucrezia.

Lucrezia answered no. "Two reasons. The first is simply my policy. I only represent people, not corporations or organizations. Just individual human beings.

"The other reason is specific to this case. There are obvious conflicts between the interests of Mothers for Peace and Peter Saunders. Your organization, quite understandably, wants publicity that will help in its drive to bring the nuclear-power industry under control. I don't oppose that goal. But Peter's case only involves fair compensation for his injuries.

"For example, I must be given authority to settle this case in Peter Saunders's interest even if that would deprive the cause of attention.

"Peter may stand for the same things as your organization, and I am sympathetic to those aims, but that is not what this lawsuit will be about."

"I'm more interested in justice than the money," Saunders said.

"As refreshing as that is, it's also, pardon me, naive." Lucrezia smiled and Saunders smiled back, before she continued. "In our civil-law system, money is just about everything. Even justice. That's all the law can give the injured or damaged person. The law cannot undo the injury. Money is all the justice there is."

"I reckon you're right. I am naive. Start educating me."

"From the cold-blooded point of view of your chances of winning, you have already weakened your case somewhat. It was a tactical mistake to quit if there was a chance you were going to be fired. You would have had a much easier case for wrongful discharge. You would only have had to show emotional disturbance. Now you are going to have the added burden of proving physical injuries, which will not be a cut-and-dried thing if you are still asymptomatic."

Gloria thought that was extremely insensitive.

Lucrezia continued. "You also have the burden of proving that Consolidated's wrongful conduct caused your injuries. And not just simple negligence on its part, either. That would be covered by workmen's compensation. We will have to at least establish that Consolidated has fraudulently misrepresented, concealed, or acted with reckless disregard of your safety. I've got to do some research before I am even sure myself. Right now, I'd say we are pretty thin on proof."

Saunders nodded. "You're saying I'm screwed."

"No, I just want you to be realistic. I would like to take a shot at negotiating a settlement first."

"If I've got such a lousy case, why would Consolidated be willing to settle?"

"I would be dealing with their lawyers rather than management. The lawyers might have a more enlightened view of the benefits of settlement. After all, at this early stage they have a much clearer sense of their potential vulnerability in a lawsuit than we do. They know where their skeletons are."

By the time the meeting ended, Lucrezia was fully convinced

that Saunders was telling the truth as he knew it. There remained the difficulty that honest people's perception of the same event often differed. Lucrezia agreed to take on the case after repeated warnings against unrealistic expectations.

Saunders elected a contingent-fee arrangement, privately reasoning that he could not afford the alternative. Mothers for Peace offered to advance costs so long as they were satisfied with the progress of the case.

Gloria took two aspirin. Losing anything made her head ache.

Lucrezia chose to open settlement negotiations by letter rather than telephone. That was slower, but it invited a measured response. The letter permitted the opportunity for internal investigation and it avoided the temptation of instant defensive reaction.

Lucrezia's letter objectively stated the factual basis of Peter Saunders's claim and politely demanded one million dollars in full settlement. It mentioned the desirability to both sides of avoiding the risks and expense of litigation, and requested the courtesy of a prompt response.

The office of Consolidated Utilities General Counsel and Vice-President Estes Lousaire was smaller than he would have liked, but he had done his best to make it impressive. He thought the oiled walnut wall made a perfect background for the thirty-seven diplomas, certificates, licenses, and awards that covered it.

Lousaire passed copies of Lucrezia's letter to his visitors. He had summoned Point Anacapa Plant Manager Isaac Karrasch for a conference before responding. Karrasch had suggested the presence of Assistant Vice-President and Security Chief Rod Magnasunn.

General Counsel Lousaire hummed to himself and sipped coffee while the others read. Slowly and painfully, he had learned that the less he said, the more respect he received, or, at least, the longer he retained it.

Lousaire was the son and grandson of Tipson, Grumm & Nuttzer partners, and himself an alumnus of TGN, the largest, oldest, most prestigious law firm in the state of California. Early in his career it became apparent that, even with nepotism in his favor, he was not TGN material. The senior partners had struggled to rationalize a partnership for young Lousaire, but his inimitable combination of ineptitude and laziness had been too much to overcome. In the end, even his own father voted against him, recognizing that his appointment would have demoralized the entire firm.

But the firm's honor could not countenance the son and grandson of partners being thrust into the street. He was foisted off on Consolidated Utilities as house counsel. It was easy. There was a TGN partner on Consolidated Utilities' board of directors. Young Lousaire had been not only subsidized, he had been placed in a position from which he could assure continued referral of legal work to the firm.

In spite of his shortcomings, Estes Lousaire was not without talent. He had raised avoidance of sole responsibility to a minor art form.

"So what do you think we should do?" he asked as Karrasch finished reading.

"Tell the bastard to stuff it." Karrasch smoothed both ends of his broad black mustache, then patted his briefcase with an extraordinarily hairy hand. "I can prove that our plant was in complete compliance with Nuclear Regulatory Commission regulations at the time of both accidents. What happened was the sort of minor breakdown that occurs in any complex system. Some accidents are unavoidable."

"What about his claim that he has been lethally contaminated?" Lousaire asked. "That could expose us to a large verdict."

"He claims to have independent evidence of that," Karrasch

tapped the briefcase again. "But our lab reports show he only incurred insignificant quantities of radiation. Everybody that works in the plant is occasionally exposed to some minor extent."

"Jesus. Don't go around saying that." Candor always made Lousaire nervous.

"Besides," suggested Magnasunn with a smile, relishing Sullivan and Doblonski's success, "it looks like he contaminated himself outside the plant with stolen plutonium. The FBI found some when they searched his house, and they are still investigating."

Lousaire liked that. "So you gentlemen don't think he has much of a case against the company?"

"How long would it take to get Saunders's case to trial?" Magnasunn asked.

"In Los Angeles County, four to five years," guessed Lousaire.

Magnasunn stood as he tapped a Camel out of the package. The man was bigger than Doblonski or Sullivan. "So even if the bastard really has a lethal dose, he'll probably be dead before he can get to trial. Anybody got a match?"

8

Lucrezia cleared a pile of books from one of her office chairs so Saunders could sit. He leaned over to help. Would heaven smell like her?

"Stonewalled," Lucrezia explained. "I was counting on Consolidated's house counsel referring your claim over to Tipson, Grumm & Nuttzer. I didn't believe the little weasel had the guts to turn it down on his own. TGN would have at least opened up negotiations with us just to build up billable hours, if nothing else. More coffee?"

He lifted his cup to show it was still half-full.

Lucrezia continued. "I think Lousaire has been conned into believing they can show you somehow contaminated yourself while in the act of stealing plutonium. For whatever reason, he has definitely been convinced by management that they are impregnable on this one."

"Or that I won't last long enough for the case to get tried," suggested Saunders.

"You're learning fast. There is no way this case is ever going to be settled without filing suit. I'm sorry, Peter."

Saunders got the idea. Obviously, a lot more proof was needed. Not only proof that he had been fatally wounded, but that Consolidated was the cause, and that its conduct was something worse than merely negligent.

"I'm shafted then?"

"There may be a way you have a chance. We could file suit now, and—"

"I don't understand. You've been saying we don't have enough evidence, and now you're suggesting we solve that by suing?"

Lucrezia smiled. "You don't have enough evidence to win is what I've been saying. And even if you won, you don't have evidence of substantial damage. By filing suit now, even though your case is extremely weak, we gain methods of possibly producing the proof needed to win."

Lucrezia went on to explain the things that could be accomplished through formal discovery only after suit was filed. Depositions of witnesses under oath, even hostile witnesses against their will. Inspection of Consolidated records. Inspection of the plant.

"Filing suit on a weak case could be the strategic move that gives you at least a shot of obtaining the proof you need to win."

"And if we don't get any breaks? If the proof does not develop, then what?"

"You lose the case. You've spent a lot for court costs, including Consolidated's. There is even the possibility that they would then sue you for malicious prosecution, although I'm inclined to think they would be content to let it lie without dredging up more dirt. And of course, there is the worst consequence of all . . ."

"I'd lose my credibility. No one would listen to me. My chances of getting any reform would be zip. And what has happened to me wouldn't count for a damn thing. I guess the future's in your hands, Lucrezia. Call it."

"We don't seem to have much choice, do we?" Lucrezia picked up the intercom. "Molly, get someone drafting on the *Saunders versus Consolidated* complaint. Let's try to have it ready to file by Friday."

As Peter Saunders stepped into the empty elevator, he punched the down button, setting it and God knows what else, he wondered, into motion.

II

PREPARATION
FOR TRIAL

9

Almost two years after filing the complaint in *Peter Saunders v. Consolidated Utilities of California, et al.*, Samuel Coleridge Corbin stood before the managing partner of Tipson, Grumm & Nuttzer.

"So how long have you been with this law firm, Corbin?" asked H. W. Morgan, without bothering to say good morning or even glance up.

The son of a bitch, thought Corbin, motionless in buttery carpet before the seven-foot, hand-carved, American walnut desk. *I can see my open personnel file. Isn't he going to ask me to sit down?*

Sam resisted folding arms by locking fingers behind his back. He concentrated on the peeling pink spot at the apex of Morgan's otherwise deeply tanned skull.

Sam braced against the crushing weight of being the firm's most senior associate. If he was not made partner within three years, he would be encouraged to resign. The firm policy was immutable. He would be a has-been at thirty-five. Dumped by the most prestigious law firm in the state.

In spite of his resolve, Sam's throat constricted. He managed to answer, "Thirty-three months, sir."

Then he thought, *Jesus, Sam, unemployment looms perhaps seconds away. Be assertive, man. Say something brazen. Say . . . something.* So he said, "Three months left, sir."

"Eighty-six days, actually," said H. W. Morgan, glancing at the open file. "Have a seat."

The smug son of a bitch. Sam reaffirmed the thought as he folded his underweight, six-foot-three-inch frame into a too-low, minimally cushioned captain's chair.

When the senior partner's intercom buzzed, Sam gratefully used the interruption to gain composure. As Morgan addressed his handset in low monosyllables, Sam sat politely for a few moments, brushing dark-brown hair out of light-brown eyes, then struggled out of the low chair and walked to the north window.

From the forty-second story he could see from Bunker Hill to the Los Angeles County courthouse, beyond that the Hollywood Freeway interchange and, finally, vaguely through yellow smog, the San Bernardino Mountains.

Ordinarily, the muted moss-green carpet, soft leathers, and hunting prints mounted on paneled walls would have conveyed quiet elegance. Today, they only mocked Sam's inadequacy and emphasized his distaste for the managing partner. H. W. Morgan's specialty was acquisition and merger. He was what Sam scornfully thought of as a takeover artist.

In a typical transaction, Morgan's corporate client would borrow the funds to purchase and absorb a vulnerable company, repay the borrowed money out of the sale of the acquired company's assets, pocket the profits, and spit out the decimated remains. Morgan had led the rape and pillage of so many companies he had been nicknamed "The Pirate" by the Los Angeles office of the Securities and Exchange Commission. Through the mere shuffling of paper, credit, and money, Morgan and his clients amassed millions. Sam did not consider himself particularly virtuous, but was offended by their total lack of social productivity.

The managing partner hung up the telephone and beckoned Sam back to his uncomfortable seat. "At yesterday's executive committee meeting, the vote did not produce a majority in favor of offering you a partnership. We all agreed that your credentials held great promise. But frankly, in spite of that, some don't think you have what it takes." Morgan paused in order to give Sam Corbin time to contemplate what it took to qualify as Tipson, Grumm & Nuttzer material.

Sam availed himself of the opportunity. *It takes,* he thought, *a record of success. If you're a litigation attorney like me, that's easy to assess. More wins than losses. But, if you've defended a losing case, a loss for less than you had offered in settlement is a win, isn't it? It takes producing income, either by earning fees or generating new business. It takes a team player. Does the firm's interest come before even—*

Morgan decided Sam had contemplated long enough. "I'm not suggesting you resign now. The committee will vote again within three months. Obviously, your performance between now and then will be crucial."

Sam hoped locking eyes with Morgan would mask his relief. He was tempted to argue the merits of his performance. But dammit, Morgan would just perceive that as groveling. And nothing Sam said now could change the vote already taken.

Why not just tell Morgan to stuff it and quit right now? Because, dummy, Sam told himself, *the entire California bar will assume you were forced to resign because you failed to make partner. There is also the matter of fiscal responsibility to your wife, stepchild, the Bank of America, and other creditors too numerous to mention. Shit man, you could grab a senior deputy DA's position in a minute. Yeah, at half what you're making now. And you can't even get by on that.*

Sam's curiosity took over. *If I'm not being asked to resign now, why the hell then has he called me in?*

"Let's get to why I called you in here. You will take charge of the *Peter Saunders versus Consolidated Utilities of California* defense. Lawrence's illness will not permit him to return in time to try the case."

Sam and every other male in the office was aware of Lawrence Levenson's sexual propensities. Levenson had been coming on to them for years. Knowing his reckless promiscuity, it was not difficult to guess the nature of his illness. His wasting away had become obvious.

For the past two months, Sam had been preparing the *Saunders v. Consolidated Utilities* defense virtually single-handedly. He had not minded. Lawrence Levenson was one of the few partners with human tendencies, reasonable, a good teacher. Poor Larry. No one would say the name of the disease, but Sam was sure Levenson was dying.

Morgan went on. "Firm policy normally requires a partner to be in charge of a case of this magnitude, but there isn't time left before trial for another partner to prepare. You're the only trial lawyer familiar with the case. Therefore, you are now lead attorney for the defense."

"I'll need help."

"Obviously."

Sarcastic son of a bitch. Sam decided to let the taunt pass.

"I shouldn't have to remind you," Morgan reminded him, "that Consolidated Utilities of California is one of our oldest and most valued clients. The defense of this case is vital to the interests of our client and of this firm. Do you entirely understand what that requires of you?"

Yeah, Sam thought. *Maybe I'm beginning to.*

"Yes, sir," he said. Sam decided he could risk one bold question. "Do you mean that I'll be offered a partnership only if I win this case?"

"I'm suggesting that how you handle this defense will be a significant factor in determining your future, if any, with Tipson, Grumm & Nuttzer."

He means do whatever is necessary to make the firm look good. Sam concluded he had to tough it out with TGN. A partnership was his only door to financial and professional independence. "Who do I report to?"

"Head of litigation, of course. You're substituting for a partner. At least try to think like one."

In spite of the chastisement, Sam tried. "Right, H.W.," he said, daring the familiarity for the first time.

"This is your last chance," Morgan waved dismissal. "Corbin."

10

The seven senior partners of Tipson, Grumm & Nuttzer, comprising the executive committee, sat at the round ebony table in identical Cordovan-upholstered chairs. Except for cleaning people, no one else was allowed in the executive conference room. A little sunlight forced its way through the closed Flemish draperies.

They were the heads of the seven departments into which the firm's functions were divided, such as litigation, probate & trusts (never probate and trusts), international law, and four others.

There were 348 partners, but it was the executive committee that effectively controlled the firm. The remaining partners, sometimes referred to as junior partners, even if with the firm for forty years, had only one means of voting. With their feet.

The managing partner, H. W. Morgan, acted as chairman of the committee. Their average age was sixty-one. All of the members were men.

"I gave *Peter Saunders versus Consolidated Utilities* to Corbin this morning," said Morgan. "Not an easy case to defend. Keep an eye on him, Bart."

Bartlett Pringle, head of litigation, nodded. "Of course, he may be washed up here even if he does well."

"If he blows it we'll have to dump him for sure just to placate Consolidated," said Whipple Ewing, who was credited with the Consolidated account. He had inherited it from his grandfather.

"We may lose Consolidated anyway if he blows it."

"At least we won't lose a great rainmaker. Corbin has not brought in an impressive amount of new business."

"I can't understand that. Look at his credentials. Good family background. Brilliant scholastic record. Clerked for Supreme Court Justice Willard Bronson. Married General Fremont's daughter. Jesus. The General himself ought to be a great contact. Former ambassador to Spain. Chairman of the Board of United Southern Mutual Insurance. Corbin couldn't have better social connections."

"His wife drinks."

"Everyone's wife drinks."

"Never mind. She really drinks. She has alienated everyone she comes near."

"Speaking of alienation, won't we blow the United Southern account if we dump Corbin? His father-in-law could dump us in retaliation."

"Not so likely as it sounds. United Southern Mutual has been with this firm for sixty years. On the other hand, the General has only been Corbin's father-in-law for four years, and from what I hear, Corbin's marriage is pretty shaky. The way I figure it, old Richard Ortega Fremont is not going to take his business elsewhere merely because of a second son-in-law who may not even be that for long."

"Corbin's done a good job on his cases," said Bartlett Pringle. "Favorable results on what he's handled alone, and good reviews from Larry on those cases in which he assisted."

"All except *Mott versus Channing Industries.* We had it on a contingent fee. He invested six months' work and lost it."

"Hold on. We insisted he take that on to pacify old Smith Varney. Threatened to pull his account if we didn't. None of us thought it was much of a case. In spite of that, Corbin negotiated a pretty fair settlement proposal, as I recall. But our client rejected it, so he was forced to trial. And we still have the Smith Varney account. Be fair."

"We don't have to be fair. We're the executive committee."

"His billings are way off. Hard to forgive that."

"That's because he's taken on ridiculous cases like *Bridges versus Fresno.* There's no money in those violation-of-civil-rights cases. What are we, in the social benefit business? To me it raises the more important question. Are his instincts right for Tipson, Grumm & Nuttzer?"

"Good litigators are not common. It's a rare talent," said Bartlett Pringle. "It may be short-sighted to force him out."

"The lad looks like a proper lawyer. Like Jimmy Stewart in . . . oh, hell, I can't remember the name of it, you know, with what's her name. Wouldn't it be a shame to make him the scapegoat?"

Morgan answered that. "Not if there has to be one."

11

Sam left the office at a reasonable hour, a rare and refreshing event, and one of the advantages of thinking like a partner, he told himself. Sam had rationalized that he wanted quiet time to plan strategy for the *Saunders v. Consolidated* defense, but what really was bothering him was his disappointing performance with the firm. He had gone seriously wrong, but how and why?

Sam believed the rationale for requiring associates to make partner or leave within three years was valid. Over-ripe associates don't feel complete or accepted and older associates often resent younger partners. On the other hand, partners are motivated to work together with a minimum of friction. They have a capital investment to protect and a share in the profits. It is their firm. Associates are mere employees, and probationary ones at that. If a lawyer is not good enough to be a partner within three years, something is wrong enough so that he should not be permitted to hang around indefinitely, Sam agreed.

Sam's last year's Buick was where he had parked it, third level down. The top two levels were reserved for clients and for partners, of course. As he climbed in, he managed to bump his knee on the steering wheel, as usual.

He really disliked the car. He disliked the synthetic velour upholstery, the imitation wood, the imitation Euro-look. He even disliked that the manufacturer called the color cabernet. It was dark red, dammit.

Sam wheeled the Buick into the Figueroa Boulevard lineup and waited his turn for the use of the northbound Harbor Freeway onramp. Even when he braked hard, the Buick bounced enough to brush his head against the roof.

He had never liked the car, but Buicks, BMWs, or Volvos were appropriate for Tipson, Grumm & Nuttzer associates. That was unspoken gospel. He had already bought the Volvo station wagon for Allison. They could not afford two of those overpriced hulks. He would have preferred the BMW anyway, but they couldn't afford that either. Hell, they couldn't afford half of what they had.

Sam wondered how much better off he would be financially if he made partner. Partners drove Cadillacs or Mercedes, except senior partners, three of whom had Rolls. He laughed. The unwritten Code for California Lawyers. Lincolns were too liberal. Chryslers too plebeian. Jaguars and Saabs were radical. Ferraris, Lamborghinis, and Maseratis were downright irresponsible. Next it would be skydiving and then where would it all end? It was all unspoken, but everyone knew what was acceptable, just as worker ants understand what is acceptable. Oh, a partner in otherwise really good standing might pioneer with a Peugot and get away with it, but why take the risk?

What does any of that have to do with my inadequacies, except demonstrate my ability to concentrate on them? Sam cleared the interchange and headed northwest on the Hollywood Freeway toward the San Fernando Valley.

Justice Bronson had been so pleased with Sam's clerkship that he insisted Sam stay a second year, a unique exception the judge never made before or since.

After that feat, Sam was sought after by every major California law firm and a few East Coast ones that ordinarily only looked to Harvard and Yale.

In fact, it was during that second year that Sam was invited to the Justice's birthday dinner party and introduced to Allison Fremont. Allison came with her father, she fresh from her divorce and reversion to her maiden name, the General just returned from his ambassadorship to Spain. He had urged Sam to take the Tipson, Grumm & Nuttzer offer. After all, he argued, the firm had represented his family's insurance business for sixty-two years and they had yet to receive a bill under a thousand dollars. How could Sam help but become successful with a firm like that?

The firm was initially delighted with its catch. Sam's marriage into one of Southern California's oldest, most established families was icing on the cake. The lad was "a find."

So where, thought Sam, as he turned onto the outbound Ventura Freeway, *where have I gone wrong? As a rainmaker, I've produced pitifully little. Why is clear enough. Because all the social contacts have dried up. And why is that, Mr. Corbin? Aren't you still married to the only daughter of the former ambassador to Spain and the chairman of the board of United Southern Mutual Insurance Company?*

Yes, but they don't invite us and we don't invite them to parties anymore. People get embarrassed watching Allison putting me down.

I don't accept golf dates anymore because I hate the game and I can't afford to lose. Tennis bores me. I'm addicted to running. It's just about the only thing I do well, but no lawyer ever made any money running, except maybe for office.

Sam guided the Buick south across Ventura Boulevard and started climbing the hills of Encino, locally and generously referred to as the Santa Monica Mountains. Even though the grades were not particularly steep, the Buick's performance was barely adequate. *About equal to mine*, thought Sam.

Sam's house was near a cul-de-sac marking the end of a one-block-long street on a terraced ridge of one of the middle mountains, a sprawling ranch house with thick cedar-shake shingles and gray, distressed siding, indigenous to Southern California. Allison, when asked, could never decide whether to describe it as a single-story or split-level. After all, one did step down two risers from the entry hall to the living room and down two more to the informal dining area.

The garage door had been left open. As Sam approached, he

could see Allison's white Volvo wagon. He let himself into the pantry from the garage. Great garlic and butter smells greeted him. Lord, the lady could cook. Sam supposed that the $1,800 three-day French chef's seminar at the Beverly Hilton last year hadn't hurt.

As Sam entered the kitchen, Allison turned from closing the refrigerator door and half-tripped over nothing. Sam caught her and converted to a hug.

"Sorry, love." Her speech was barely slurred. "I'm afraid I started a little early. Do some martini. There's still some in the fridge. It's also fettucini Alfredo and poached salmon, but not for half an hour."

"Thanks. I'll have a Coors." Sam opened the can and leaned against the refrigerator door as he took a long drink. It still lifted him to look at her, unchanged in four years. Sam had learned early that girls seemed to like him, so he had never felt a shortage, but Allison had been extraordinarily attractive from the first moment. Even in a tank top and faded denim shorts, even at thirty-three, she was still one of the best-looking women in Los Angeles County, if not the great Southwest. Long blonde hair parted in the middle. Green-gray eyes far apart. Small, straight nose. Perfect teeth. Sam was eternally grateful that they at least had been paid for before they met. Oh, a little hint of spread behind, but only enough to accentuate her waist. Sam put down the beer, and still leaning against the refrigerator door, grabbed her for another hug.

"Excuse me," interrupted Carrissa Elizabeth, as she came around the corner. "I'm sorry to break this up but I need a Coke fix desperately."

Sam tried not to be annoyed at his stepdaughter as he freed up Allison and the refrigerator door. Allison shrugged and mouthed J-E-A-L-O-U-S.

Having accomplished her purpose, Carrissa started back to her room. "Oh, there was a telephone call for you."

"Thanks," said Sam. "Who?"

"John Somebody. I forgot to write it down. Sorry." She was gone.

"John Somebody. That narrows it down. I've told her a . . ."

"Relax. She is only thirteen. Have another drink before dinner. I'm going to."

"You explain it to her. Maybe she will listen to you." Sam headed for the master bedroom and a change into cool clothes. He opened his middle dresser drawer, stared, slammed it shut, and stalked back into the kitchen.

"Allison, three of my T-shirts are gone. I know they are not in the laundry. When I left this morning, there was a red, green, and blue one in my dresser and now they . . ."

Carrissa came back around the corner bearing a blue T-shirt. "I borrowed your red one this morning and accidentally tore it on my bicycle so I threw it into the rag drawer. Then I borrowed your green one because I couldn't wear your red one anymore, after all, and I spilled yogurt on it so it's in the laundry. So here. Sorry."

"Carrissa . . ."

She was gone again.

Sam tried to stay cool. Every time he tried to follow and explain to her, she locked her bedroom door against him. He would stand in the hall, yelling, "Open that goddamn door," and feeling like an idiot.

Perhaps he could get Allison to seriously discuss it over dinner. The only hope he had of disciplining the brat was with Allison's cooperation.

He thought he would cool down faster if he went into his study and read the mail or perhaps the paper before dinner. The mail was mostly bills for things they didn't really need and could ill afford . . . like house payments. They could not have bought the place at all if Allison's father had not given them the down payment as a wedding present. Pool maintenance. Nobody had used it since its installation summer before last. The electricity bill was enormous. The air conditioning was running constantly. Monthly bill for boarding Allison's and Carrissa's saddle horses. He had just finished paying for the animals. Tuition: the Briton School for Young Ladies. That was doing a lot of good. Telephone bill: $1,830.25. Eighteen hundred dollars! Sam stormed into the kitchen.

Allison met him halfway into the dining room with a steaming platter in her hands. "It must be a mistake, love. I'll take it up with the telephone company in the morning. Sit down. Dinner's ready."

Allison uncovered the platter of fettucini and salmon. A large wood bowl brimming with green salad and a bottle of Monterey Chardonnay were already on the table. There were only two places set.

"Where is . . . ?"

"Carrissa's having dinner at Mary K.'s. They're studying together."

"It's getting worse between Carrissa and me all the time. Neither of us feels that I have the right to discipline her. I can't even get her to stay in the room when I'm talking to her. Without your help, it's hopeless."

"It's just her jealousy, love. She's afraid you're winning me away from her. Pour me some more wine, please." She held out her glass.

"Why does it have to be a competition?" Sam thought he got enough of that at work. He refilled her glass.

"She is still only a child, in spite of the way she looks," said Allison, as she drained the glass in one draft.

Sam wondered if there was a little jealousy there too. "I was hoping the Briton School for Young Ladies might teach her something, considering what I am paying each month."

"You're bringing it down to the level of money again. The telephone bill, the tuition bill. Why does everything have to be discussed in terms of money? Besides, earning enough money is your problem. More wine, please."

"Don't you think you've had enough?" Sam poured it anyway. "Even as an associate, I already earn more at Tipson than most lawyers ever make. It's the way you two consume it that . . ."

"If you buckled down and made partner, you'd earn enough to properly support us without this niggardly quibbling about a few household expenses. Morgan told Daddy that your billings are way below . . ."

"Daddy? What the fuck is Daddy doing sticking his nose into my business?"

"He was only concerned about you because I had to borrow money . . . maybe I didn't mention that. Anyway, if it weren't for Daddy, we wouldn't even have this house and. . . ."

". . . If it weren't for this house we wouldn't have half these fucking bills. Tell your daddy to butt out of . . ."

"Keep my daddy out of this."

"I will if you will."

"I'm taking a bath." Allison started to leave the room, turned back to grab the half-empty wine bottle, and stalked out.

Sam knew his billings were low, 20 to 30 percent below the average of other associates, even though he put in long hours and cranked out more than a respectable amount of work. He knew why, too. When he worked in a new area of law, he could not bring himself to bill the full hourly rate for his education. He had difficulty charging the full rate for travel time, much of which was spent daydreaming, eating, or snoozing. He could not bring himself to pad his time sheets as some of the others between themselves admitted they did routinely. Several of them consistently turned in twenty hours of billing time per day, always being careful, of course, not to bill more than six or seven hours to any one client.

One associate even argued seriously to Sam that this was not dishonest. He could, he claimed, regularly work on three cases simultaneously, devoting full attention to all three. So why shouldn't the clients pay for that?

Sam sighed and changed into running clothes. He started walking the quarter mile up to Mulholland Drive. It was too steep to run. He had not even warmed up. By the time he reached Mulholland, Sam was breathing heavier and sweating a little. He did a few stretching exercises at the roadside. He ran a few easy miles before returning home.

I'll try again, he resolved, *without mentioning money*. But Allison was already asleep in the king-size bed. Or was she passed out? The empty wine bottle and a glass lay on the floor.

Sam showered and crawled into his side. Well, tomorrow he would try again. Carrissa had to be made to understand that he was not fighting for her mother's sole affection. Allison had to realize they could not keep up with Daddy, and they could not have Daddy keeping them up. *Maybe now with the extra work I have on* Saunders versus Consolidated, *I can get my billings up.* Sam fell asleep.

Allison's caress awakened him. He was as hard as diamond. He had no idea what time it was. He thought he could see gray pre-dawn light behind the fluttering drapes.

"Let's not quarrel again, love," she whispered as she snuggled into him. He could smell the wine, but it was not unpleasant and the rest of her smelled delicious. She drank too much but she was his. She was on him now, her lips kissing his neck, her nipples brushing his chest, her nails raking his hard abdomen. She spent too much, but she would learn. He grabbed her behind. It didn't feel oversized. Sam pressed into her and rolled her under him. He kissed her bruisingly hard. She locked her long legs around his back. She was a spoiled bitch, but she was his spoiled bitch. And he loved her.

12

"**M**r. Pringle will see you now, Mr. Corbin." The secretary had not even looked up from her typewriter. Sam was surprised she called him mister.

"Thank you for seeing me so promptly," Sam said to the head of litigation.

"Sure. I realize *Saunders versus Consolidated* is coming up on master calendar, and I don't see another decent chance for a continuance. Have a seat."

Every time Sam saw him he was reimpressed with how aptly Bartlett Pringle had been named. The spread of hips and broad bottom, tapering up to narrow shoulders and a mostly bald, pink scalp gave Bartlett a strong resemblance to a pear.

Pringle was an incongruity. He liked litigation, but not trial work. Appearing before a jury or even a judge made him stutter and perspire. But he could analyze key issues of a case faster than anyone else Sam knew and was a superb strategist. What more perfect job for the man who could not try cases himself than head of litigation?

"I may have something better than a continuance. Here, take a look at these, please," Sam said. "These are both treaties between the U.S.A. and the European Economic Community countries."

"The Common Market?"

"Right. This one is the English version of the 1958 Treaty of Florence, and this is the Paris Convention of 1962. There are just a few relevant paragraphs. I marked them."

Pringle put on his half-glasses and read. He looked up. "Do you have the French versions?"

Sam was impressed. He handed them over.

When Pringle finished reading, Sam went on. "The combined effect of the two treaties is to give the Common Market country concurrent but preferred jurisdiction in tort cases related to breach-of-warranty actions between Common Market country corporations, provided that the Common Market country corporation is a proper party to the related action."

"At least arguably." Pringle leaned back and clasped his hands behind his head. "I'm listening."

Sam continued. "The named defendant, Consolidated Utilities of California, is a wholly owned subsidiary of Conglomère Française de Energie, the French conglomerate. That's public knowledge, although not widely publicized. The *Saunders* complaint alleges that plaintiff's injuries were proximately caused by a defective pressure relief valve that is part of the reactor cooling system. That pressure relief valve is manufactured by the Belgium company of Fabrique National d'Saupape. Belgium and France, of course, are Common Market countries, and signatories to both treaties—"

"I don't get the point," interrupted Pringle. "You're not suggesting that Ferrara and Associates will attempt to remove the case to Belgium or France, are you? After all, they filed suit in California. They could have brought the suit in a European court, right?"

"Of course. What I'm suggesting is that Consolidated Utilities and Conglomère Française de Energie, the parent company, file suit in Belgium against Fabrique Nationale d'Saupape, the manufacturer of the allegedly defective valve. The suit will be for indemnity in whatever amount Saunders recovers against Consolidated as a result of the defective valve.

"Then we file a motion to transfer *Saunders versus Consolidated* to the Belgium courts, on the grounds that the treaties require it. We have a good chance. And if the California case does get switched, the benefits to Consolidated are fantastic. New complexities cloud the issues. Everything in Flemish and French. Astronomical additional expense. The case could probably be dragged on forever without ever going to trial. . . ."

When Sam saw Pringle was shaking his head he stopped and waited.

Pringle let him wait a little. "Corbin, how can you manage to be so fucking smart and so naive, all at the same time?" His wet black eyes could become quite steely.

Sam could not contain his exasperation. "But it is you who have always advocated that causing the opposition maximum expense, sowing confusion and delay are legitimate defense tactics. This tactic has everything—"

"Corbin, where are our foreign offices?"

"London, Beirut, Tokyo, and Panama City," Sam answered. "Oh."

"That's right, Corbin. No Brussels office. Not even a Paris office. If the case is removed to Belgium, a Belgian or French law firm takes over . . ."

". . . and collects all the fees." Sam acknowledged. It was clear Pringle had killed the idea. Sam figured he might as well go down in flames. "Still it would be good for the client, dammit."

Pringle raised an eyebrow at Sam's audacity. "Maybe. But what is good for Tipson, Grumm & Nuttzer is what's best for the client."

13

"**I** can't believe you did this." Sam glowered at Carrissa, who stared sullenly back. Allison alternated between sipping her vodka on the rocks and repairing her nails with an emery board.

Carrissa had confessed to Allison that afternoon. She had copied Sam's credit card telephone number from the card in his wallet, then sold the number to three friends for ten dollars each. The telephone company had traced one of the calls placed from a number Allison recognized as one of Carrissa's friends.

Carrissa's friends had called everyone they knew on Sam's account. Fortunately, none of them were acquainted with anyone out of state.

"She has promised to pay it back, haven't you, dear?" said Allison. "Why don't we go to parties anymore?"

Sam was livid as he faced her. "What is she going to do? Borrow the money from your daddy? And we don't go to parties anymore because we are no longer invited, which has nothing to do with the topic under discussion."

"Oh, Sam, the child used poor judgment, I admit, but the telephone person said they may not charge us with the full amount, and they are issuing a new number to you so that it can't happen again."

"So long as we buy a wall safe. I would like to feel that I can leave my wallet laying around my own house without taking security precautions against other people who live here. I would like to hear from Carrissa's own lips that this will not happen again." Sam turned back to Carrissa.

She was gone again.

"Why don't we give a party, Sam? I'm so bored with bickering about money. We haven't been out for a month."

"Sure, let's forget about how your kid is turning into an embezzler and get down to the important stuff. We don't get invited, and we don't give parties anymore because on either occasion you get obnoxiously drunk. Last time at your father's, you went around pleading with everybody to please bring me their legal business because I couldn't bring in enough on my own to be made a partner. Do you remember that one?"

Allison finished her drink. "I apologized, didn't I?"

"And the time before, when I was balking at buying you a Volvo station wagon, you were telling everyone what a skinny, stingy bastard I was."

"And you are," snapped Allison. "I'm going shopping with Claire."

In his study, Sam settled down to work on the next day's round of depositions. He heard the Volvo backing out of the garage. At least the house would be quiet for an hour or two.

Twenty minutes later, the telephone rang. "It's Allison. You'll have to come and pick me up. I've had a car accident. . . ."

"Are you all right?"

"Yes, I think so. It's just the car. All the cars . . ."

"God. How many were involved?" Sam got the location and promised to be right there.

By the time he arrived, most of the crowd had dispersed. Three vehicles were involved. Apparently Allison had rear-ended the car in front of her, which had slowed for another car. Allison had swerved to her left in an effort to avoid the collision. The Volvo had careened off the rear-ended car, across the double line, and into the oncoming traffic lane, where it was broadsided on the passenger side. Fortunately, Allison had not yet picked up Claire.

Miraculously, no one involved claimed any injury. The police, although called, had never shown up. Essential information was exchanged by the parties. Sam removed Allison's bulky sweater from the front seat of the Volvo, arranged for the Auto Club to tow the car to the dealer, and drove her home.

They drove in silence for a few minutes before Sam spoke. "I'm glad you weren't hurt. You were lucky."

"Some luck."

"Considering what you'd had to drink, it's also fortunate the police didn't show."

"Oh, come on. One vodka and tonic before I left."

"Oh, come on yourself." Sam unrolled Allison's sweater and removed a quarter-empty bottle of vodka as they rolled into the garage.

Allison grabbed the bottle and stalked through the house into the bedroom, loudly slamming doors behind her.

If that's a hint, Sam thought, *she needn't have bothered.* He grabbed a beer and turned on the late show. *Return of the Jedi.* Perfect. He needed escape to another galaxy.

The sun streaming through the window woke Sam. The television was displaying black-and-white snow. He glanced at his watch. 0610. Just as well. He needed an early start to get it all done. He massaged his neck, stiffened from his night on the couch. The shower helped. Before he left, Sam left Allison a note reminding her to call the insurance agent, check with the dealer, and suggesting that she rent a car.

Later that morning, she telephoned Sam at his office. "The dealer says the Volvo is totaled. Our insurance adjuster has already looked at it. He says to get two other estimates but he thinks the dealer is right. How could that be? It's a Volvo."

"Not a Sherman tank." Sam sighed. "Jesus, Allison, you were broadsided by a one-ton pickup."

"He's got an executive seven-forty turbo, he will warranty as a new car, we can have for twenty-nine thousand dollars. Sam, it's white with the softest chocolate brown leather . . ."

"Please don't buy a car alone, Allison. Please. We'll talk about it when I get home. Didn't you rent something?"

"Yes, and guess who I met at the rental agency? Ashley Woolworth. Remember he was on "Dallas" until they killed him?"

"Allison, what did you rent?"

"I found a darling pink Cadillac convertible. Don't nag me about it. I wasn't being extravagant. The only other cars they had immediately available were a Land Rover and a Daimler."

"Jesus. Where did you go? Rent-a-Cars for the Stars?"

"Cheap bastard." She hung up.

14

Every time Ferrara and Associates took another deposition of a Consolidated employee, that witness made an allusion to additional Consolidated records.

This always produced another Ferrara and Associates' request to inspect records, and that request always resulted in someone from the defense searching files in Consolidated's Century City or Point Anacapa plant office.

This time it was Sam's turn. At the Century City office, the deputy controller had passed Sam off to the chief of operations accounting section, who had lateraled to the accountant, senior, supervising. Reba Hanst was an essentially straight up-and-down lady whose excessive verticalness was interrupted only by large horn-rimmed glasses and a prim mouth.

Miss Hanst's sniff suggested what an imposition she considered Sam's requests to be. The file room contained stacks of file cabinets, a shredder, and a photocopy machine. One wall was stacked almost to the ceiling with cardboard transfer cases. The window wall also had a wall-mounted telephone. Everything was some shade of green.

Miss Hanst spread the Ferrara and Associates Request for Inspection on the plastic-topped table, and reviewed the list of requested documents. She began to noisily open file cabinets, remove folders, and stack them with a slap, simultaneously emitting long sighs. Sam was reminded of air escaping from a blown-out tire.

Sam started thumbing through the files. But, of course, Miss Hanst could stack faster than he could thumb.

The wall phone rang and Miss Hanst answered it, making notes on the wall-mounted pad. Sam took a moment to stand and stretch. He wandered to the opposite wall stacked high with transfer cases. One marked with a broad red marking pen caught his eye: *Pt. Anacapa. Inter-office memos/desk cals. Post and discard.*

Sam pulled it down and lifted the lid. It seemed to be filled with exactly what had been described: old inter-office memoranda and desk calendars. Sam was absorbed in flipping through a stack of last year's memos, when Miss Hanst snatched the case out from under him.

Sam was startled. "Hey. I was about to read something in there."

Miss Hanst replaced the case on the stack, before turning to Sam. "Nothing in this stack concerns you," she said sweetly.

"That box is marked Point Anacapa. Look." Sam turned to point and saw she had reversed the case so that no label was exposed. "That box is full of inter-office memos on the Point Anacapa project. Here, I'll show you." Sam moved to pull the case back down from the stack.

But Miss Hanst was prepared to sacrifice her shriveled virginity if necessary. She spread her tubelike body across the wall, defying Sam to take one step closer. "You are mistaken. Nothing on this wall has anything to do with you. Nothing."

Sam made another effort. He reached for the box. "Let me just show you . . ."

"Are you trying to get me fired? Don't you understand?" Miss Hanst screamed.

Sam was beginning to. He left Miss Hanst quieting her hysteria as he marched back to the assistant controller's office. Sam was angry. It was finally in the open. Consolidated was definitely concealing evidence from its own attorney.

Sam was kept waiting another five minutes by the controller's secretary, which made him even angrier. He paced the reception area.

Finally, the secretary's intercom buzzed. "Mr. Morticoi will see you now."

Sam was furious. "I am the attorney for this company. I am

defending it in a lawsuit exposing it to a very large amount in damages. I am trying to prevent that, but I cannot be successful unless this company begins to cooperate with my investigation. Miss Hanst just refused . . ."

"Miss Hanst just telephoned from the file room. She explained the misunderstanding."

"Misunderstanding? There is no goddamned misunderstanding. You are concealing data from me that I can only conclude must be damaging to the . . ."

"Mr. Corbin, I don't understand you. You say you are trying to defend this company, and yet you seem determined to dig up something damaging against it. How the hell will that help our case?"

Sam tried to calm down enough to explain. "Obviously it won't help our case if there is damaging evidence. But it is a hell of a lot better that I find it first, instead of the other side discovering it and ambushing me with it at the trial. At least I can be prepared to explain it."

"Why don't you let us worry about what the other side might discover, and you concentrate on winning this case. Isn't that what you are being paid for?"

"You must show me the documents in that box."

"Miss Hanst told me what's in the box. You are obviously mistaken about what you think you saw. Get on with defending this company's interests. Whose fucking side are you on, anyway?"

15

When Sam got home that evening, Carrissa was in the kitchen spreading peanut butter and strawberry jam on apple slices. "Hi, Sam," she said. "Mom's in the bedroom lying down . . ."

Sam was surprised at her friendliness and to learn that Allison was home. The pink Cadillac was not in the garage.

". . . because of the headache she got since the accident," Carrissa finished.

"But the accident was three days ago."

"No. I mean today's accident." Carrissa popped an entire slice into her mouth and rolled her eyes.

Sam hurried into the bedroom. Allison lay on the bed with an ice pack on her head, reading *Vogue*. She looked uninjured.

"What happened?"

"Please don't get angry and start yelling. I have a shitty headache already. There was a little accident with the Cadillac."

"Well?"

"I went to vote. I parked on the hill in front of the polling place, you know. I'm sure I put the car in 'park,' though."

"And?"

"And when I came out it had rolled down the hill . . ."

"And?"

Allison sighed and adjusted her ice pack.

Sam heard himself almost scream. "And?"

"Two parked cars and a garage door." Allison sighed again. "Plus, of course, the front and right side of the Cadillac."

Sam persuaded Allison that they could not immediately afford to buy or rent another car. It was a temporary victory, he realized. But she did seem to understand that the cost of the recent mayhem had to be assessed before Sam could determine what they could afford. Sam already knew they couldn't afford anything. The question was how to go on buying things they couldn't afford.

He had pacified Allison by giving her his Buick and found a twelve-year-old MGB for eight hundred dollars. That was less than two weeks' rental on the Cadillac. He could drive the MGB to work. Allison would have to trade whenever he had to transport clients. The firm would have to forgive his temporary aberration. He assured Allison that when they knew how much of the disaster was going to be financed by their insurance, they could decide about permanent transportation.

Allison reluctantly accepted, sensing that two accidents within three days weakened her bargaining position.

16

"Lucrezia, look. Finally a lead that might pay off." Molly Moscowitz, one of Ferrara and Associates' two paralegals, rushed in waving a letter. "I've found L. Ronald Boden. He's doing time in Lompoc."

Lucrezia was miffed at the interruption.

Molly ignored that and continued. "I'm talking *Saunders versus Consolidated*. Ronald Boden was a health physicist, whatever that is, at the Point Anacapa plant. His name and last-known address were among those listed in the answers to our third set of interrogatories, you know, like 'state the full name, or names, of each person employed by Consolidated Utilities of California, on, or in any way related to, the con-

struction or operation of the Point Anacapa Nuclear Power
Plant project, that person's present or last-known business and
residential address and telephone numbers, job title, and description, between the date of commencement of the project
and—' "

Lucrezia held up both hands. "Please. Spare me."

"Anyway, their answer listed him as a former employee
during part of the critical period, and I just found him."

"In a federal prison. What's he in for?"

Molly scratched her auburn pixie cut. "Smuggling."

Lucrezia's interest mounted. "Really. Plutonium from the
plant?"

"No. Cocaine from Baja."

"So you feel that Mr. Boden may now be free of Consolidated's constraints. I suppose it's worth following up. So far, we've
discovered damn little except how impenetrable Consolidated's stonewall can be. We can take his deposition if we get
permission from the director of federal prisons, right?"

"Right. Lompoc is sending down an application form. It will
take some extra work, but it could be a break."

"We are about due, aren't we? Health physicist. He might
give us a better I.D. on that other health physicist, Clyde, who
Saunders says cleared him for contamination, or he might even
establish that Consolidated's lab reports on Saunders were
falsified. Get on it, Molly. We are running out of time."

When he received the notice scheduling the deposition, Sam
walked down the corridor to another associate's office. "Doug,"
he asked, "you have a client in Lompoc, don't you?"

"Yeah, as a matter of fact I'm going up to see him next week
about his appeal." Doug grinned. "Doesn't have a prayer."

"Would you mind asking him to pass along a message?"

"Message?"

"Yes, it concerns another inmate's civil rights."

On the date set for Ronald Boden's deposition, Lucrezia
drove a half-hour out of her way to pick up her deposition
reporter. That was a nuisance, but she felt more comfortable
using a reporter whose competence had been established.

Lucrezia took her silver Mark VII out the Santa Monica
Freeway to Pacific Coast Highway. The route was about ten

minutes longer than the 101 Freeway, but Lucrezia hungered for the sight, smell, and sounds of the ocean.

Lompoc Federal Penitentiary looked more like a sprawling rural high school. Lucrezia parked in the visitors' section and waited while the reporter retrieved her stenotype machine and briefcase from the trunk.

In the outer office, they filled out the visitors' roster and waited while a guard checked cases and handbags. Both were issued passes in plastic to be worn on their persons. After being let through two electrically locked steel doors, both women were seated on a wooden bench to wait again. Finally a guard led them to a small conference room containing nothing but a small wooden table and four chairs.

Sam was already there thumbing through a file. He glanced up and smiled, as always, at seeing Lucrezia. He would have had trouble disliking her if he had a reason, but there was none. All their dealings throughout the tedium of trial preparation had been courteous. If anything, Lucrezia had been too easy but had given away nothing substantial. Sam respected her competence.

He considered her amazing-looking. Only her silver hair pulled softly into a chignon suggested she might be over forty. But those high cheekbones, clear skin, that swimmer's figure.

He had not been able to resist the temptation to look up her biography in Martindale and Hubbell. He knew she was forty-eight. *How would his wife, Allison, look in* . . . Sam did the mental calculation . . . *fifteen years?*

At last, thirty minutes later, Ronald Boden was led in, a spare man, thinning blond hair and frameless glasses. Sam was surprised by his mild appearance. The guard asked if they wanted him to stay in the room. Neither Sam nor Lucrezia thought that necessary. The reporter was not that sure, but kept it to herself.

"I'll be just outside the door," the guard said. "Rap on the glass when you're finished or need anything."

"Let's have everything on the record," suggested Sam, "since it's unlikely that Mr. Boden will be coming to the trial. No offense, Mr. Boden."

"Mr. Boden," the court reporter asked, "will you please raise your right hand and be sworn?"

Ronald Boden put down his cigarette and raised his right hand.

"Do you swear to tell the truth, the whole truth, and nothing but the truth, so help you God?"

"Sure," said Mr. Boden, picking up his cigarette.

"State your full name for the record, please."

"Lamont Ronald Boden."

"Mr. Boden, I'm Lucrezia Ferrara, the attorney for the plaintiff Peter Saunders in the case of *Saunders versus Consolidated Utilities*. You are not named as a defendant in this case. You are simply a possible witness to some events that occurred at the Point Anacapa power plant while you were employed there. We just want to ask some questions about that."

"Lady, I'm doing ten years in this country club. Why should I tell you anything? What are you going to do, have me held in contempt?"

Lucrezia did not give up easily, but Mr. Boden remained adamantly silent.

Lucrezia was becoming apprehensive. One more deposition that gained nothing.

As they walked out to their cars, Lucrezia turned to Sam. "Did you somehow manage this fiasco?"

Sam tried to look shocked but all he felt was embarrassment.

17

Sam dreaded going home. There had been another terrible fight last night. Sam was almost certain that Carrissa had stolen $40 from his wallet, but she denied it. Allison defended her. Then Sam learned that Carrissa had borrowed, she said, his calculator and, she said, lost it. When Allison assured him that Daddy had a lot of them and she would get him another tomorrow, Sam had exploded.

As much as he detested another confrontation, Sam was determined to achieve some resolution. The situation had become intolerable. Allison's drinking and Carrissa's plundering had to be brought under control. Sam was not precisely sure what the best way to achieve either was, but as he drove home he listed alternatives to himself. None would be easy, but there was going to be a start.

First, Sam realized, as he turned off the Ventura Freeway and headed for the Encino hills, he had to bring himself under control. No matter how great the provocation, no matter what, he would remain cool, patient, even kind. Neither Allison nor Carrissa was stupid. They could be made to understand how destructive they were being. He could do it. He would.

As he rounded the corner he could see the garage door open and the Buick absent. Allison was not yet home. Good. He could take a shower and really collect his thoughts before dinner.

Perhaps, if Allison didn't have anything cooking, he would take them all out to dinner. Let Carrissa pick the place. That way, a calm discussion would be easier to manage.

Sam had a Coors out and opened before he even noticed the buff-colored envelope addressed, "Sam," on the kitchen counter. The flap was unsealed. The brief note in Allison's brown ink even bore her scent.

Sam,
I have gone off with Ashley Woolworth. We will all be better off.
My lawyer will contact your lawyer.
Allison

Sam's first reaction was that he didn't have a lawyer. There was another sheet of paper sticking partly out of the same envelope. Ruled three-ring binder paper, folded four times. Sam unfolded it. Large block letters were scrawled in blue crayon.

ME TOO. FUCK YOU

Sam sighed. Some anonymous note. He left the beer on the counter to die and went slowly into the bedroom, stripping off jacket, tie, and shirt as he went.

In the bedroom there were half-opened drawers, a suitcase taken down from a shelf but on the floor unused, empty hangers on the bed.

Sam removed the rest of his clothes and stepped into the shower. Wasn't that what he had planned to do first?

Who the hell was Ashley Woolworth? Oh yeah, the actor. Sam tried to remember his face. It had been some time since he had been killed on "Dallas." All Sam could think of was a golden retriever.

As the warm water washed over him, so did emotions, but too fast and slippery to grasp. Shock. Anger. Remorse. Hurt. Shame. What was that, relief? Slipped by before it could even be identified. Love? Still? After this? Come on. Fear? Fear of what, for Christssake? Could he possibly be getting lonely already?

Sam realized he was shivering. He had run out of hot water.

18

Sam did not have to throw himself into his work in order to cope with the loss of Allison. His workload was already overwhelming before she left. The demands on his intellect and energy were almost totally engrossing, although he was occasionally aware of a sort of detachment he had not noticed before.

Allison did manage to intrude once or twice during each busy day. In the middle of dictating a trial brief paragraph on ultra-hazardous conditions, Sam suddenly felt his palms underneath her bottom. *That superficial, alcoholic, faithless bitch,* he thought, as he wiped his hands on his shirt. *That beautiful, sexy, faithless bitch.*

The chances of obtaining another continuance of the trial at this late stage were dim, Sam knew. He would try anyway. It had nothing to do with not feeling up to trying the case. Of course he felt up to trying the case. A little thing like being jilted could not put the lead defense counsel off his form.

He would try for a continuance simply because he owed it to his client to delay the trial in any legitimate way, a traditional defense tactic. Memories fade and blur, passions cool, witnesses become unavailable. Very few defendants are anxious to get to trial.

Sam thought Lucrezia might harbor a grudge after the Lompoc episode. He forced himself to pick up the telephone and call. It wasn't so hard if you took two deep breaths first. "Hello, Mrs. Ferrara."

Her voice was clear as temple bells. "Sam, I thought we were friendly enough enemies to call each other by first names."

"I tend to get formal just before I ask a favor."

"Sam, your firm has already had three continuances."

"I know, but with Larry Levenson out, things are really stacking up. Just three months is all I need. Couldn't you use another three months, Lucrezia?"

"Almost always, but I have a client with a time limit. Sam, I don't think you deserve three minutes, but, just as a courtesy, I'll agree to three weeks."

"Two months, Lucrezia. We can't possibly be ready in less than that."

"Sam. Three weeks out of the goodness of my heart, and only because I haven't sent out subpoenas yet. If you can't live with that, you'll have to file your motion."

"You're a hard woman, but thank you. I'll prepare the stipulation and have it messengered over."

After he hung up, Sam thought, *God, a lovely, gracious lady, but what a cream puff. She was right. I didn't deserve three minutes. No one else would have given it to me. Will she let me walk all over her at trial, too?*

19

As Sam stepped off the DeHaviland, the heat slapped him hard. It had been hot in Los Angeles when he boarded the flight to San Luis Obispo. He had hoped for relief two hundred miles up the coast.

Ferrara and Associates had requested inspection of records kept at Point Anacapa, which Sam was obligated to inspect before releasing. The deposition of Isaac Karrasch, the plant manager, had been noticed. He needed a preparatory interview. There were other potential witnesses at Point Anacapa Sam wanted to talk to. He wanted no surprises during trial. The way to avoid that was to learn everything in advance, good and bad.

Even though the overnight trip was completely justified, Sam felt he was on an excursion simply because it was so pleasant just to be out of the office for a couple of days.

The small San Luis Obispo Airport terminal building was mercifully air conditioned. Sam stopped at the ticket counter to confirm his flight back to Los Angeles and inquire about a taxi to Point Anacapa.

"Yes, sir, I'm sure one of those out in front would be delighted to take you out there," the ticket representative said. "Cost you, though. It's almost forty miles. And you might have trouble getting a cab back. You would have to call one and wait. It's completely isolated out there. Frankly, since you're going to be two days, I'd rent a car if I was you. Cost you less than the taxi ride out there and back. Budget and Hertz are right around the corner."

Sam chose Budget. Any compact car would do, he said, so long as it was air conditioned. The plump young lady stopped chewing gum long enough to point out where Sam was to initial and sign. In spite of her directions, Sam finally found the white Dodge Dart at the far end of a lot the size of the Mojave Desert. He threw his nylon overnight bag in the trunk, rolled down the windows, and started driving just to cool off. He fumbled with the air-conditioner controls as he went. He was almost all the way to his hotel, halfway between the airport and town, before realizing that all he would ever get out of that air conditioner was warm air.

Gratefully, Sam stepped into the shade of the Bayside Inn lobby and stood under a ceiling fan, waiting for his eyes to adjust. The place had not changed much in the ten years since he had last been there. New brightly colored floral prints cushioned the old wicker furniture. The cracks in the columns had been filled and freshly painted soft white. Potted plants were all over the place. Contrary to the stereotype of the decrepit old small-town hotel, the place looked better than ever.

A shower seemed urgent, but Sam made himself check out the amenities before settling down. It had been obvious that the air conditioner worked when he had opened the door. He quickly checked the plumbing and the telephone. My God, even the color television worked. Sam would have preferred a different decorator, but the room was clean, light, and spacious.

The shower ran out of warm water before Sam was half-finished. He seemed to be having that problem frequently. At least the weather was right for it. Clad only in blue bikini undershorts, Sam took a cold Carta Blanca from the room refrigerator before dialing the Point Anacapa power plant office. Upon request, he was put through immediately to Isaac Karrasch.

"Good morning, Corbin. Welcome to Central California. I was told to expect you."

The words were friendly but Sam instantly disliked something in Karrasch's voice. He could not pinpoint why. It didn't seem worth thinking about.

"Come on out this morning. We'll be expecting you."

Sam was tempted to exchange his rental car for one with

operational air conditioning, but the airport was fifteen miles in the wrong direction. He opened all the vents and windows. What the hell, so long as the car was moving, the temperature was not intolerable.

North of Morro Bay, Sam turned off U.S. Highway 1 when he came to the diffident black-and-white sign.

CONSOLIDATED UTILITIES OF CALIFORNIA
POINT ANACAPA
PRIVATE ROAD

Consolidated was not actively advertising their nuclear power plant. Certainly, there was none in sight. All that could be seen from the intersection was a two-lane blacktopped road, snaking into a heavily forested area, disappearing over a rise.

A mile along the road there was still nothing more to be seen, except an occasional PRIVATE ROAD PATROLLED sign, and once, possibly the reflection off the lens of a closed-circuit television camera.

Even when Sam pulled up at the guardhouse set into the electrified fence, nothing was visible beyond the gate but more road into thicker forest.

"Samuel Corbin. I have an appointment with Mr. Karrasch."

The guard stepped out and glanced inside the car. "Would you open the trunk, please, sir." It was not a question.

Sam got out of the car and did so. The trunk was empty except for the spare tire and usual tire-changing accouterments.

"Firearms or explosives?" The guard carried an Uzi machine pistol and was extremely serious.

Sam resisted saying "No, thanks," and shook his head.

"Go on ahead, Mr. Corbin. They're expecting you."

Only as Sam's car cleared the crest of the last hill did the plant come into view. He had seen photographs, of course, but these had not prepared him for the awesome scale of the thing. Sam pulled over to the shoulder, set the handbrake, and climbed out for a better look.

For an instant he wondered if he had been foolish. He was undoubtedly standing within sight of an armed guard down there someplace. A trigger-happy rookie could easily pick him off. Then he relaxed, deciding they would have been informed that he was coming.

Several hundred feet below and a quarter-mile straight ahead, Point Anacapa terminated in sheer cliffs rising out of the sea. The Pacific Ocean filled the horizon. Every living thing had been cleared from the land, formed into a plateau as smooth and flat as a vast table top.

Out of this featureless surface rose twin reactors, each encased in a twenty-four-story hemispheric containment. These giant half-spheres were themselves enshadowed and surrounded by four identical high-rise towers, thirty-six-story cylinders tipped with apparently seamless domes. A dozen windowless two- and three-story boxlike buildings were clustered around, but dwarfed by the towers and containments. The entire complex glistened arctic white.

Sam was not sure whether he heard or imagined a low, almost subauditory hum rising. Perhaps it was the sea.

The only feature that looked like anything Sam had ever seen before was the blacktopped parking lot at the road's terminus. He climbed back into the Dodge and headed for that.

At the parking lot entrance, another guard armed with a sidearm and hand-held transceiver directed him first to a space marked "Visitors," and then to the entrance of the nearest building.

Walking across the parking lot, Sam no longer heard the hum, but thought he felt the pavement vibrate through the soles of his shoes. Inside the reception area there was only the whirr of air conditioning and piped music. Another guard examined the contents of his attaché case, took his photograph with a Polaroid camera, and within a surprisingly few minutes issued a badge bearing his picture.

Sam was greeted by a black-haired Japanese receptionist who informed him that Mr. Karrasch's secretary would be out in a minute and offered him something cold to drink. Sam accepted a Pepsi and watched the guard watching the receptionist type.

Mr. Karrasch's secretary appeared to be close to retirement. She announced that her name was Constance Savin and apologized for Mr. Karrasch's absence. He had been called away, but hoped to return in time to take Mr. Corbin to lunch.

Meanwhile, he had instructed her to see that Mr. Corbin had whatever he needed.

Sam thought he would like to start with a look at the personnel records.

Mrs. Savin wondered if Sam could tell her more specifically what he was looking for. That would assist her in finding what he needed. Sam tried to explain that he was trying to antici-pate whatever Ferrara and Associates would look for in order to be sure that there were no unpleasant surprises. He ex-plained that Saunders was alleging that he had been tested and cleared for contamination by a lab technician or health physicist named Clyde. Saunders did not know the man's last name, but his attorney would be trying to identify him in order to get his testimony. Sam needed to know whether any of the records confirmed the employment of such a person.

"A lot of such records are in Los Angeles at the Century City office, you know," Mrs. Savin said. At the Century City office, Sam had been told that all such records were at the Point Anacapa plant. When Sam explained this, the woman gave him a wan smile and directed him to a row of filing cabinets. "These three drawers are personnel files on employees that we keep records on."

"You mean there are some employees that you don't keep records on?"

"Only like, you know, casual labor, or contract temporary help."

Sam spent an hour on the files, reading the names on the tabs, looking for a file on Clyde anybody. Nothing. He started over again, searching those files with first names that might have produced Clyde as a nickname. He got through the N's before being overcome with total boredom. There must be a better way.

He sought out Mrs. Savin and asked if their payroll depart-ment would not have an alphabetical list of all employees, including those for whom there were no personnel files. She was very sorry, but the payroll clerk was in San Luis Obispo and would return tomorrow afternoon. She would be happy to get the payroll records for Sam herself, but she did not know where to look. Besides, they were locked up. Only the payroll clerk and Mr. Karrasch had keys.

Sam repeated the description given by Saunders in his deposition. He was not surprised that Mrs. Savin recalled no one who matched.

When Karrasch thundered in and boomed a greeting to Sam, patting his shoulder and shaking his hand at the same time, Sam confirmed his dislike, although Karrasch was saying the right things. It wasn't necessarily his appearance, dark, fat, and hairy. It was expression and mannerism, that was it. The man sneered and swaggered, even in repose. A man who respected nothing, Sam decided.

"I'll take you to lunch," Karrasch boomed as he led Sam to his Jeep Cherokee. Sam resented that the Jeep's air conditioning worked fine. They drove back to the Golden Tee in Morro Bay and had the crab melt on sourdough. Sam ordered a Millers on draft and Karrasch had ice water. *No wonder I don't like him*, Sam thought.

Sam wanted to explain what he was looking for, but Karrasch insisted on hearing all about the case from the beginning to its present status.

"Gorgeous, another Millers, *por favor*," Karrasch yelled without bothering to ask Sam if he wanted it. "What is this Clyde character supposed to look like anyway?"

Sam again repeated what Saunders had testified to in his deposition. "Blond, light-colored eyes, gray or blue. Thirty or thirty-five years old. Medium size and build. Suntanned. Always wore a T-shirt and white jeans."

"Christ, I've got at least four men who match that description, but none of them health physicists."

"Can I interview your people, the ones you think fit Clyde's description? And those who were on shift during Saunders's accidents. Saunders's attorney may get around to taking their depositions. It's better that I talk to them first."

"Sure, Corbin. We'll set it up right after lunch."

Back at the office, Karrasch produced two of the men. The others, he said, were too busy to interrupt, but he would have them available for Corbin in the office tomorrow morning.

Corbin interviewed the two men. Karrasch was right. They both fit the description. One was a plumbing supervisor, the other an electrician. Sam spoke to them separately. Both had always worked days. Neither had ever worked in the lab. They knew of no one named Clyde who worked for Consolidated presently or in the past. They both expressed a desire to help, but had no information that could be of any assistance. Sam noted that neither displayed the slightest curiosity about Saunders's allegations of unsafe practices and defective systems. He thought that was unreal.

Sam waded through correspondence files, but turned up nothing damaging. There were gaps in the file suggesting documents had been removed. When Sam asked a clerk about it, she just shrugged and seemed in an unusual hurry to leave the room.

Sam asked Karrasch's permission to talk to other supervisors and workers.

"Of course, man. Try not to interfere with the work, though. I've got a production schedule to maintain. You'll need a guide. You could get hurt down there alone. We don't want any more lawsuits. Okay?" Karrasch snorted at his own joke. "Oh, there's the regular weekly thing at my house tonight. Food and drink. You're invited. Constance will give you the address. I've got to get on the telephone."

Sam thanked him and accepted the address, although he had no intention of spending any more time with Isaac Karrasch than duty required. He waited in the reception area for his guide, who turned out to be Karrasch's secretary, Constance. *At least I won't be burdened with more information than I can absorb*, Sam thought.

Mrs. Savin wanted to show him the new Xerox machine and employees' lounge, but Sam insisted on seeing the reactor area. "Show me containment number two. That's where Saunders's last accident occurred."

Mrs. Savin wrinkled her considerable nose. "Hot and noisy," she said, but led him to a storage room from which she obtained two yellow hard hats. She donned hers with obvious distaste.

She led him into an elevator and down Sam wasn't sure how many stories. The digital display was showing numbers like 186, 174, 169. Sam knew there were not that many stories in the structure and pointed questioningly.

"Feet above sea level," Mrs. Savin explained.

Sam grinned. Who said she wasn't a fount of information?

At level 133, they exited into a corridor. It was still cool, but Sam could hear a distant roar now. Deep and continuous, like a faraway waterfall. Through two more sets of double doors and the decibel level suddenly doubled. But that wasn't the only shock. The temperature shot up twenty degrees.

They were standing on the containment floor. The steel-truss- and girder-reinforced hemispheric dome rose more than three hundred feet above. Sam had never imagined enclosed space of such volume.

At the precise geometric center of the vast room stood the nuclear reactor, a massive steel-clad cylinder nearly reaching the ceiling and resembling a scaled-up fifty-five-gallon fuel drum, studded with ladders, plumbing, and electrical conduit. Nothing visible moved, no noise seemed to emanate directly from it. Only Sam's knowledge of what it was suggested the elemental power trapped within the steel wall.

The steam generator, which looked like a giant boiler to Sam, stood next to the reactor. Although Sam had read enough to understand the physical principles involved, he could not begin to trace the functions of the maze of plumbing: orange, gray, gleaming stainless steel. He saw one-inch-diameter tubing and massive pipes large enough for a man to sit up in. Sam could only guess at which shapes were the automatic and manual valves, the pump motors, the filters, the sumps.

Sam deduced from their absence that the steam turbine and electricity generators were housed in another building. Everywhere, steel staircases and catwalks connected the network.

It was surprising to Sam how few men were working inside the containment. He talked to those he could reach, explaining that he was Consolidated's lawyer, defending the company in a suit brought against it by Saunders. He summarized Saunders's contentions. He described Clyde. Nobody had a clue. They all seemed to somehow expect him. Well, Karrasch could have passed the word around that it was okay to talk to him. There was something else, though. Something vaguer. Even though each one appeared to cooperate, Sam sensed reluctance. Could it be that they were simply busy, or did not want to be bothered? Did not wish to become involved? Sam wasn't sure. He was sure it was hot and noisy. Maybe his approach needed improvement. Maybe there just wasn't anything to learn. That was enough. He would give it another try tomorrow.

20

Sam drove back to the hotel. He was grateful there were no messages.

It seemed cool enough now to run comfortably. The tide was low. There was plenty of beach and there appeared to be a strip of hard-packed sand along the waterline. Sam dug his running clothes out of the overnight bag. God, he was pale. He needed sun. Screw the skin cancer.

A sea breeze still blew, even though it was late afternoon. There were only a few sunbathers. Mostly girls, mostly very young, and all tan as tobacco leaves. Sam had not thought about girls at all lately. Not even much about Allison. At night he missed her and was lonely. But the peace was nice, too. And, usually, he was so exhausted he wasn't lonely for long, he was asleep. Anyway, regardless of how he felt, she was permanently gone.

He glanced at his watch as he took off. Four seven-minute miles would be enough. He had not run for a week.

The surf roared, flirting with his feet. The sand had just enough give to absorb the impact. After a mile he increased pace and could feel sweat glands open. His blood warmed, pulse quickened, it felt great. All his negative feelings flushed away by sweat.

A girl ran ahead. No, not a girl like the children of eighteen he had passed, but a young woman. A young woman with a lovely body, it appeared from this distance, and one who knew how to run. Her head was up, her elbows in, her stride smooth. The lady had style.

He was gaining but not rapidly. He could see she had dark hair. Tourist? Foreign or American? Sam grew curious to see her face. He speeded up. As he overtook her, he turned to his left to glance at her face.

Startled by his sudden appearance, she turned to her right as she gazed up at him. They were too close. Sam's toe caught her ankle, it twisted, and she went down.

She was on her back, staring up at Sam. Her slate-blue eyes were big. Her pupils dilated.

Was she on something? Sam wondered. Whether she was or not, he felt mortified at his clumsiness. He reached to help her up.

"No." She raised both elbows to ward him off. Her tone seemed near hysteria.

She stared up. He stood there awkwardly, sheepishly, his hand still extended. Then it seemed to him that she suddenly relaxed, as if the fear had gone out of her.

"I'm sorry," she said as she gave him her hand. "You startled me. Please help me up."

"I'm the one to apologize. That was incredibly clumsy of me. Where are you hurt?"

She balanced against him, her right hand still in his, and raised her left leg, testing knee and ankle. "I think I'm all right. You just scared the hell out of me."

Both feet back on the ground, she tugged to release her hand. "You can let go now, thank you."

Embarrassed, Sam let go. She was walking around him now, testing her weight.

Sam began again. "I really am so sorry. There was—"

"—no room to pass?" She waved at the 200-yard-wide beach.

Sam decided he had better just tell the truth. As he explained, her smile grew. "I understand. Have you seen enough?"

"No . . . I mean yes. No, I mean, I would like to see you again. I'm Sam Corbin. Let me take you to dinner and apologize properly."

She was still smiling, but shook her head. "I'm sorry. I never date men who try to pick me up on the beach at San Luis Obispo."

"Is that a frequent problem?"

"No. This is the only time, but I can't allow exceptions."

Clearly, her mind was made up. Better retreat gracefully and live to fight another day.

"Are you sure you're all right? I can accompany you back to your—"

"No." She faked a cringe, but her smile was genuine. "Just tell me which way you're going."

Sam pointed.

She took off in the opposite direction.

Sam ran another two miles, kicking himself for being an oaf, and trying to reconstruct the girl's appearance.

He could not be sure of her hair under that wide headband, other than it was dark. Her mouth was too wide. Were her eyes blue or gray? Small breasts. Delightful nose. *Forget it*, he told himself. *You blew it with your clumsy curiosity.*

It was early when Sam wandered down to the dining room. A glance convinced him that he would not enjoy dining alone. The desk clerk suggested he try the Silent Woman, in town. It was easy to spot. The carved wooden sign was the shape of an oversized female . . . with her head cut off. Three couples were waiting on the sidewalk. Through the glass front he could see the restaurant was crowded.

Sam was about to settle for pizza when he remembered Karrasch's invitation. Aw, what the hell, he might meet someone who would talk to him about Saunders and Consolidated. He might even learn something.

Karrasch's imitation hacienda was on a gentle hillside of Point San Luis, overlooking Avila Beach, easy to find. A dozen cars were randomly parked around the entrance.

As Sam walked through the open doorway, Karrasch spotted him. "Sam," he thundered. "I had given you up." He guided Sam to the bar and raised an inquiring eyebrow.

"Beer," Sam said to the Mexican barman. He accepted a Corona and managed one swallow before Karrasch herded him to the buffet table.

"Eat," he commanded. "I've got three more guys lined up for you to talk to tomorrow. Eight-thirty, my office."

Sam was tempted to suggest that no one seemed interested

in telling him anything, but decided it could wait. After all, Karrasch was a gracious host.

The food was inviting, his hunger was extreme. He loaded a plate.

Sam found a corner outside the traffic flow. He put his beer on a table and stuffed food into his mouth, proud of his foresight, limiting selections to items that could be eaten with the fingers of one hand.

Karrasch beckoned him over to a cluster of guests. "Sam," he bellowed. "Come over and meet some people."

Sam put down his plate and picked up his beer. As he rounded Karrasch's bulk, she came into view. The girl from the beach. She recognized Sam and smiled.

"This is Sam Corbin, one of the company's lawyers," bellowed Karrasch. "Sam, this is Victor Salinas . . ."

Sam managed to politely acknowledge each introduction, but he could hardly take his eyes off her.

". . . and this is Susan Schooling. Mrs. Schooling is Consolidated's assistant vice-president for environmental planning."

"Good evening, Mr. Corbin."

He would have preferred "Sam," but at least she hadn't said they'd already run into each other.

Her hair was not merely dark, it was raven, long, thick, and wavy. She wore the simplest yellow dress he had ever seen. That and white sandals. Nothing else. No pearls, bracelet, earrings, watch, rings. No rings?

Sam thought she looked terrific. "I'm delighted to meet you, Mrs. Schooling, although I would have preferred Miss, and how is your ankle?"

"Don't be crestfallen. I'm divorced, and it's fine."

Delightful nose. What the hell was he supposed to say next? Oh. "Mine is in the mill."

Susan Schooling looked confused.

"My divorce, I mean. We're separated, though," Sam added hurriedly.

"Got it. You can call me Susan then. Can we get me some more wine?"

Sam thought it would be a sin to deny her. They walked out to the patio and found a bench. It was cool. The ocean smelled good.

Sam learned that Susan had just been promoted to assistant vice-president, dealing with environmental planning for new and expanded plant sites. Her ten-year-old daughter was named Emily. They lived in Santa Monica because the schools were superior to those in Los Angeles. She liked tall glasses of white wine, lime, and soda. And she had a lovely laugh.

Susan learned that Sam was less than enamored of his stepdaughter, or was that his ex-stepdaughter? He liked beer a lot more than wine, and, in spite of his awkwardness, he might be a hell of a runner, based on what he claimed his times and distances were, anyway. He had extremely full, long eyelashes and he was quite bright.

Susan drained her glass. "This has been lovely, but I must get back to my hotel. I am working."

"Do you have a car?"

"No. Isaac will take me."

"Let me drive you down."

She looked at Sam seriously for a long time. "Thank you. I'll just tell Isaac."

When they were settled into the Dodge, Sam asked where to.

"The Bayside Inn, please," Susan replied and yawned.

Sam laughed. "What room number?"

"What? Oh. What's yours?"

They estimated that they were separated by two floors and at least thirty-two rooms.

"However . . ." Sam started to suggest, then decided he was being too forward.

Susan did not answer. He could not see her face in the dark as they wound down the hill. Was she thinking it over? Or had he offended her with a single word? Sam walked her to her door and waited silently as she shuffled for the key.

Finally, Susan fished out the key and turned her face up. "Sam, I would love to jump into the sack with you tonight. But I don't just jump into the sack. Not with anyone. And I don't know whether I want to be involved with you."

Sam started to ask why, but Susan pressed her finger on his lips. "Call me," she said.

"Tomorrow?"

"No, I fly back in the morning. Call me when you get back to Los Angeles, at the Century City office."

She gave him an extraordinarily long, soft, full kiss before leaving him standing in the hall.

21

After Sam finished interviewing employees, he accepted a cup of coffee from Mrs. Savin. He sat in an unused office, sipping and reviewing his notes.

Sam could not get past the suspicion that people were not disclosing what they knew. His gut told him. His head suggested they had been coerced. Why? Of course, because there was evidence of Consolidated's culpability to be suppressed. But not from him, dammit. He had to know to do his job. No, Sam admitted, it was even simpler. It was merely his damned insatiable curiosity. He had to know.

Sam walked to Karrasch's office. He was not sure how to start. If someone was ordering employees to clam up, it was quite possibly Isaac Karrasch. It was not made easier by the fact that Sam did not exactly warm up to the man, anyway. *Hell*, he thought, *I'll just wade in.*

"It's only that I'm surprised," Sam was going to say "appalled," but thought better of it. "Surprised at how little everyone seems to know. It is as if they had never heard of the plant accidents or *Saunders versus Consolidated.* I would have thought Saunders's problems and the litigation would have been a prime subject for gossip, at least." Sam knew he sounded sort of lame.

"Is that what you are looking for? Gossip?"

"No. Of course not. Look, everyone appears to be cooperating with my investigation, but I get the gut feeling they are holding back . . ."

Karrasch gave the right half of his mustache one outward stroke. "Holding back what, Sam?"

Sam shrugged.

"Has it occurred to you that no one can give you any information on this company's involvement because there isn't any? Personally, I think Saunders's claim is one big scam."

Sam tried not to show his annoyance. "Why? I mean, why would he invent claims like this?"

"I dunno. Maybe to bail himself out of a bad situation with the FBI investigation. Maybe because Mothers for Peace or one of those other pinko organizations put him up to it."

Sam tried again. "Look, I cannot successfully defend this company unless it begins to cooperate—"

"Corbin, I don't get you. You're trying to defend us, but you seem determined to dredge up dirt. That helps?"

Sam felt anger building. "Because if I find our weaknesses first, at least I can be prepared to explain them, instead of being sandbagged at the trial by the opposition."

"Let us worry about what the other side might find. You concentrate on this case. Stick to your job, Corbin. Let us do ours. We'll all get along fine. Okay?"

Dammit, the man was hopeless. Sam tried to cool down. "Would it at least be possible for you to explain to your people that I am on your side? If this Clyde character exists it is vital we locate him before plaintiff's side does."

Karrasch's unblinking black eyes looked back with synthetic sincerity. "Yeah, I can see how that could be important."

22

"**C**onstance. We don't want to be disturbed." Isaac Karrarsch turned to his visitors. "Okay."

Jesse St. James, Consolidated's executive vice-president, glanced at his watch before addressing Chief of Security Rod Magnasunn. "All right, what's so goddamned sensitive that we couldn't discuss it on the telephone?"

Magnasunn leaned against the wall, smoke from his cigarette curling around his iron-gray crewcut. "Clyde is out of hand," he said.

St. James looked blank.

"Clyde," Karrasch prompted. "The one who altered Saunders's medical records."

St. James remembered. "Yes, the one stashed in Puerto Vallarta. I thought he'd been made happy for the duration."

"He wanted a condo, we rented him a condo. He wanted a white Mustang convertible. He got that. Two grand a month pocket money. Living like a fucking king." Magnasunn tried not to look embarrassed. "Now he wants a fifty-foot Hatteras sports fisher—"

St. James scowled. "A five-hundred-thousand-dollar boat?"

"—and another two grand per to maintain it. I told him no way. He said he'd give us to the end of the week to change our mind." Magnasunn shrugged.

"Stupid and greedy," Karrarsch said.

"It's only the beginning of the problem," Magnasunn agreed.

"Perhaps you could find a way to eliminate the problem."

St. James glanced at his watch again. "And get me the helicopter. I've got a twelve-thirty speaking engagement before the Sierra Club."

Three men stood at the base of the cliff next to the mangled white Mustang convertible. It was right-side-up, although it must have rolled several times after leaving the highway apparently southbound for Manzanillo.

Both Federales dressed like affluent west Texans. "Everything is just as you found it?" the short one asked the traffic patrolman.

"*Si.*" The Transito wiped his brow with the sleeve of his sky-blue uniform shirt, then dried that on his black leather holster. After all, it was thirty-eight degrees centigrade in the shade.

The thin one used his breast handkerchief to grasp the blond hair of what was left of the driver. He laid the body prone on the broken seatback, then patted its pockets. He removed a wallet.

He read aloud the name on the California driver's license. "Prescott R. Clydesdale." His English was unaccented. He showed the open wallet to his companions. "Empty," he said.

The Transito shrugged.

"It is a miracle the vehicle did not burn after driving over that cliff," the short one said.

"It is a miracle he could drive at all with a forty-centimeter-long incision in his gut." The thin one pointed.

The short one bent over. "You are right. He is still strapped in. The steering wheel is only bent. He was not cut in the car. It had to be a razor or knife. *Buey guero.*"

The thin one grinned as he extended his palm to the Transito. "To share is to be happy."

The Transito grinned back as he handed over two-thirds of the American currency.

III

TRIAL

23

On a Monday morning in late November, two years and one month after suit had been filed, *Peter Saunders v. Consolidated Utilities of California* came on calendar for trial. Sam was late. He'd had difficulty finding parking.

In Department 1, the Assistant Presiding Judge was already calling, "Number Thirty-three. *Saunders versus Consolidated Utilities.*"

"Plaintiff is ready," said Lucrezia Ferrara from somewhere in front. Sam could not see her from the rear of the vast room.

"Defendant's motion for continuance, Your Honor," Sam answered, standing to be heard.

"I'll come back to you after I've finished the calendar call."

Although Sam knew there was no real hope in his standard defense ploy motion being granted, it was possible that all available courtrooms would be assigned to other cases before his motion was heard, resulting in a continuance on the court's own motion.

When the judge re-called *Saunders v. Consolidated*, Sam and Ben Davidoff walked to the front of the huge room.

Lucrezia Ferrara turned and waved as she waited before the judge's bench.

"She must have been a fantastic beauty when she was young," whispered twenty-three-year-old Ben.

"I can't imagine much difference," Sam replied.

Benjamin Davidoff had been *Law Review* editor at Berkeley, but that was not why Sam had selected him as assistant trial counsel. Almost every associate attorney at TGN had equally impeccable credentials. Sam picked Ben because he had more freckles than anyone he'd ever seen, and he enjoyed having him around.

Ben enjoyed Sam, too, although office comedians made innumerable references to Mutt and Jeff. Ben, who outweighed Sam but was a foot shorter, no longer found that amusing.

With all counsel before the judge, Sam spoke. "Your Honor, defendant Consolidated moves for a continuance on the grounds that its lead attorney in this case, Mr. Lawrence Levenson, is seriously ill and cannot be here to defend this case this morning."

"I'm aware of Mr. Levenson's illness, counselor. My condolences. Did you know we were in army intelligence together? Larry was a star cryptographer. But are you suggesting that Mr. Levenson will be well enough to try this case later?"

"No, Your Honor," Sam confessed. "But we need more time to enable another attorney to take Mr. Levenson's place."

"Just a moment, Mr. Corbin. The file shows this case has already been continued three times on the defendant's motion. The last time was while I was on vacation. Judge what's his name was sitting in. Damn, I know it as well as my own name."

"Judge Ginsberg, Your Honor," said Lucrezia.

"How soon we forget," Sam mumbled.

"Mrs. Ferrara, do you have any opposition?"

"Your Honor, this trial has been continued by stipulation one additional time at the defendant's request. The defense has been aware of Mr. Levenson's illness for months. If, for any reason, Mr. Corbin is not deemed competent to try this case, they have had those months in which another attorney could have prepared. Mr. Corbin has been in on the defense of this case since the complaint was served and, in my opinion, is entirely qualified and prepared."

"Mr. Corbin, you seem to have a dilemma." The judge smiled. "If you argue eloquently enough to persuade me that you are not competent to try this case, how can I then conclude that you are not?"

The judge decided to spare Sam the effort. "I seem to recall, Mr. Corbin, that it was you who tried *Parker versus Bell Telephone* before me in Department 58 last year." The judge lowered his voice, "Frankly, I've never seen anyone work a jury better than you did. Is there any reason why you can't defend this case yourself?"

"No, Your Honor."

"Splendid. Your motion is denied. Stand by for second call."

On the second calendar call, the judge told them, "*Saunders versus Consolidated* has a priority because of the preliminary injunction. There is one priority case ahead of you, and at the moment I have no courtroom available. We may be able to send you out tomorrow morning. You will trail until nine A.M. on Tuesday."

Sam had always known the day would come when he would curse that injunction. Without priority, the case would have been too far down the calendar to have any chance of obtaining a courtroom. Over Sam's objection, Levenson had insisted on obtaining an order enjoining Saunders from selling or transferring any plutonium in his possession or under his control. Larry insisted the smoke it raised outweighed any disadvantage. He wondered if Larry would still think so today. His tactic had cut at least two years off Saunders's waiting time.

"Let's go to work, Ben," said Sam.

At the next recess, Sam and Ben walked to the front of the room to see Tom Moyer, the Department 1 clerk, seated next to the vacant judge's bench.

"Morning, Tom. Which departments are likely to open in the morning?" Sam's blatant question would not be answered directly. Both men realized he was not supposed to ask, Tom was not supposed to tell.

"No telling." Tom grinned. "Say, I've got to see the judge for a second. Guard my desk, will you?"

Before Sam could answer, Tom placed a sheet of computer printout on top of a half-inch stack and started toward chambers.

Sam edged around so he could clearly read without touching the paper. "Here it is. Tomorrow's predicted open civil jury trial departments. Departments 44, 98, and 101."

Tom was already coming back. "Sorry I can't help you, Sam." He shoved the sheet back under the stack.

"Thanks anyway, Tom. See you later," replied Sam. "Let's go, Ben."

"How the hell did you work that?" asked Ben.

"A couple of years ago, Tom's wife had a legal problem. He sent her to me. I helped."

"At no charge, I assume."

"Not until very recently."

Ben removed that morning's *Los Angeles Daily Journal* from his attaché case and turned to the listing naming the judge currently sitting in each Superior Court department.

Sam read aloud over Ben's shoulder. "Department 44, Judge Haas. Son of a bitch. Department 98, Robinson. Department 101, Iverson. Let's go back to the office and do some judge-shopping."

24

Sam, Ben, and Branford Dodds sat around a conference table. Dodds, a partner in the probate & trusts department, had been a Los Angeles County Superior Court judge for eleven years before returning to private practice. With two daughters in college, he could no longer afford the honor.

"We have biographical material on each of the three judges," said Dodds, tapping the open *California Court and Judges Handbook*. "We have printouts of our own firm's experience with each of them. We have my impressions as their former colleague and yours as attorneys who have appeared before them."

"Only Haas for me," corrected Ben.

Dodds continued. "Haas first. Everyone knows the man is probably psychotic. The only mystery is how he got elected. Totally irrational, therefore unpredictable. One may as well flip a coin. Faster and cheaper."

"You're right," added Ben. "I won my case before him, but I shouldn't have. A sure loser. We only went to trial because the other side refused to even discuss settlement."

"Are there any grounds for a challenge for cause in that bio material?" asked Sam. He recognized that, although judges are required by statute to disqualify themselves when appropriate, they occasionally have to be reminded.

"I don't know of any," replied Dodds. "You will probably have to exercise your peremptory challenge."

"I've never done that," said Ben. "Do you—"

"As you may know," Dodds interrupted pontifically, "before commencement of trial, each party has a right to disqualify a judge to whom the case has been assigned for trial without proving any prejudice or disqualifying condition. This right may be exercised by each party only once in each case. The affidavit form—"

Sam did not need the law lecture, and doubted that Ben did either. "We all agree Haas is intolerable. What do we have on the others?" he asked.

The data on Robinson revealed that he was plaintiff's counsel in two cases against Consolidated before assuming the bench, and a former associate of TGN, who had resigned after two and a half years.

"Oops," said Ben.

"I think it is reasonable to assume that Judge Robinson may be sympathetic to Saunders's position," said Dodds. "You might be able to live with Robinson, but he is really not desirable in this case. Let's look at Iverson. Ex-justice of the peace from Alhambra, ex-municipal court judge, a simple kindly old gentleman who has come up through the ranks and spent most of his professional life on the bench. Generally thought of as a plaintiff's judge, though, at least in personal-injury actions."

Sam said, "Definitely Iverson is our first choice, Robinson can be tolerated, if necessary, but is undesirable. Haas is unacceptable and must be avoided.

"So," Sam continued, "let's start by assuming we are assigned to one of the three, and that the other two are then
available or will be the next two courtrooms to open. If we are
first assigned to Iverson, the plaintiff can peremptorily challenge him. If we are reassigned to Haas, we would use our
peremptory challenge on him. We would then be reassigned to
Robinson. Having exhausted our challenge, the plaintiff's side
then gets its choice of judge. Of course, they'll want Robinson."

Sam continued. "If we are sent out first to Robinson, we can
challenge him. If we are then reassigned to Iverson, the plaintiff won't dare challenge him because the case might then end
up with Haas, which they won't want any more than we do. If
we are reassigned to Haas, the plaintiff will have to challenge
Haas. We will then get our choice, Judge Iverson.

"If we are first assigned to Haas, and we challenge him, then
plaintiff can challenge Iverson if we are reassigned to him, and
plaintiff will end up with Robinson, their first choice. If, on the
other hand, we are first assigned to Haas and plaintiff challenges him, then the reverse happens and we are given our
choice of judge, Iverson."

"I think you've given me a headache," said Dodds.

"I follow it," said Ben. "If we are first assigned to Iverson,
we'll probably end up with Robinson, and there's nothing we
can do about it. If we are first assigned to Robinson, and play
it right, we should end up with Iverson, our choice of judge. If
we are first assigned to Haas, we have to find a way to persuade
Mrs. Ferrara that Haas is somehow acceptable to us, so she is
conned into using up her challenge on him."

"By George, you've got it," said Sam.

25

Early the next morning, Sam and Lucrezia separately stalked the courthouse, hoping to appear to run into the other accidentally before the master calendar call. They found each other in the ninth-floor cafeteria.

Lucrezia reached the end of the line first with her third cup of unwanted coffee. "Good morning, counselor. I'm surprised to see you here this early," she lied.

"Good morning, Lucrezia. I had an eight A.M. settlement conference in an eminent-domain case," Sam lied. He complimented her on her red suit and she complimented him on his impeccable taste.

Sam got around to the real agenda. "It appears likely we'll be sent out today. Probably Judge Haas."

"I'm glad you mentioned that," replied Lucrezia between sips of inexorable coffee. "I should disclose to you that Haas and I were at Stanford together. I tutored him in Ad Law. We went together for a while. Not grounds for disqualification, but I thought you should know. I don't wish to be accused of sandbagging. . . ."

"Oh, I appreciate your mentioning it, although I agree that it shouldn't matter," said Sam, hoping he sounded indifferent. "Time to get down to Department 1."

Ben found Sam a few minutes before the calendar call.

"The good news, boss, is that the one case ahead of us settled last night and we are now number one on the priority calendar. The bad news is that Judge Haas is the only open department."

"Judge Haas. Son of a bitch."

"You don't seem to be able to say Haas without saying 'son of a bitch.' "

"That's a reflex conditioned by trying two cases before the son of a bitch," said Sam. "The rest of the bad news is that Haas, the son of a bitch, seems to be acceptable to Lucrezia. Apparently, they were law-school buddies."

"Can't we disqualify Haas for bias, then?"

"Even if they were lovers that wouldn't show bias. I'm afraid we're going to have to use our peremptory on Haas."

"Son of a bitch," said Ben.

When *Saunders v. Consolidated* was called, Sam answered, "Ready," but he approached the bench reluctantly. Could Lucrezia be bluffing about accepting Haas? Sam was not sure, but he could not afford to call a bluff.

"Still a three-week jury trial, is it?" the assistant presiding judge asked.

Both sides nodded.

"Assigned to Department 44, Judge Haas."

Sam stood mute. *Come on*, Lucrezia, *cave in.*

Lucrezia turned and started to walk away. She spoke to Sam over her shoulder. "I'll pick up the file."

The judge was waiting for Sam to speak or move on.

I guess that's it. Sam sighed, and spoke loudly enough for Lucrezia to hear. "Affidavit, judge. Move to disqualify Judge Haas pursuant to C.C.P. 170.6."

"I was afraid of that," mumbled the judge. "File your affidavit, Mr. Corbin. There is no other courtroom available right now. You'll continue to trail."

Sam filled in the name of Judge Haas, the date, signed, and silently handed the form to Tom Moyer.

As Sam turned away from Moyer's desk he almost bumped into Lucrezia. She was standing quietly behind him.

She almost whispered. "Thank you, Sam. I haven't been able to stand the son of a bitch since he threw up on my prom gown." Lucrezia smiled and walked away.

Damn, thought Sam. *I've been had. She would have returned with the file and challenged Haas if I hadn't.*

"Mrs. Ferrara snookered us," Ben agreed after Sam explained. "If we're assigned to Iverson, Lucrezia can use her peremptory and probably get Robinson. If we're assigned to Robinson first, we're stuck with him."

"Shut up, Ben." Sam would have to hope he could keep Judge Robinson under control if the judge could not himself restrain his own probable bias.

Thirty minutes later, *Saunders v. Consolidated* was reassigned to Department 98, Judge Robinson. Sam thought Lucrezia practically skipped down the aisle. *Of course, she knew Robinson was coming up just as we did.*

Judge Robinson rose from behind his desk. "Mr. Corbin, good morning. This is Mr. Davidoff with you? Nice to meet you, young man. Sit down, please. Lucrezia, you look smashing, as usual. Obviously, you still swim every day. We must set up a tennis date."

Sam's heart sunk. He tried to appear unconcerned, but not with complete success. Lucrezia was beaming. *At least she's not clapping her hands,* thought Sam.

"People, we may have a problem," said the judge.

Sam raised his head in hope. *Anything at all,* he thought.

The judge continued. "My daughter, Ann, is engaged to be married to Newell Courtland. Courtland is an assistant VP in Consolidated's industrial marketing division." Sam was puzzled. That was not grounds for disqualification.

Lucrezia brightened. "Well, that's not statutory grounds, Your Honor. And I'm sure counsel for the defense will agree that your daughter's engagement does not suggest any prejudice on your part—"

"Let me finish, please. The wedding is scheduled for one week from next Sunday, well within the time estimated to complete this trial. Within two weeks, I shall be Newell Courtland's father-in-law, which will disqualify me from hearing the rest of this case by reason of relationship—"

"—to an officer of a corporation which is a party, by affinity within the third degree," Ben blurted out, then looked around, embarrassed.

"Thank you, Mr. Davidoff," said the judge coldly.

"But," said Lucrezia, "certainly we can stipulate to waive that disqualification." She looked pleadingly at Sam. "After all, it's a mere technicality, isn't it, Sam?"

Sam thought quickly. "Your Honor, obviously there is no question of bias on your part. Personally, I would be delighted to have you hear this case, but if I waive your disqualification and then lose the case, I'll be making my firm vulnerable to a malpractice claim by our client. That would be unfair to Tipson, Grumm & Nuttzer."

Judge Robinson got the point. "Of course. I'm sorry, but I must disqualify myself. Return to Department 1 with the file. I'll call the APJ and explain." The judge rose.

"Thank you, Your Honor," said Sam, meaning every word.

"Call me, Lucrezia. We'll set up some doubles," said the judge as they filed out of chambers.

The assistant presiding judge was not pleased. "I just can't seem to get you people to settle down," he grumbled. "All right. Department 101. You are assigned to Judge Iverson, unless of course you wish to exercise your peremptory challenge, Mrs. Ferrara."

Lucrezia was tempted. She was frustrated and angry. But she had no idea who she would draw next if she challenged Iverson. There were many who could be worse for Saunders's cause. Iverson was not going to help her as Robinson might have, but he would not hurt her either.

She sighed, "No, I'm satisfied with Judge Iverson, Your Honor."

"What should I send Ann Robinson for a wedding present?" whispered Sam.

26

$\mathbf{B}$y the time the lawyers escalated up three flights to Department 101, Judge Iverson was already hearing a two-hour postjudgment motion in a case he thought he had finished last week.

He apologized for his clerk's failure to notify Department 1 of the unscheduled motion and suggested that efficiency, if not justice, would be served if the trial of *Saunders v. Consolidated* commenced at 9:30 the following morning.

Even back at her office, Lucrezia's frustration refused to numb. She had Sam beaten on that play. Losing Robinson was a bad bounce. Well, Iverson would not be bad. It was just that the odds could have been really stacked in her favor.

"Vanessa Armour, a Mother for Peace, on line one."

"I'll take it. Hello Vanessa. I already gave."

Lucrezia spent twenty minutes attempting to persuade Vanessa that scheduling a news conference announcing that *Saunders v. Consolidated* was going to trial was a less-than-desirable media event. The result could be a mistrial before they were barely started. Even if that did not happen, prospective jurors could be adversely affected. The plaintiff's side could not afford jurors to have any reason to suspect the case was being brought for publicity. Vanessa understood and readily agreed. Lucrezia was relieved that Ms. Armour really was concerned about Peter Saunders's welfare as well as her cause. Lucrezia promised full cooperation with a news conference as soon as the case was won, and hung up.

"Congressman Cummings on line two, Lucrezia. Are you in?"

Oh, what the hell, she thought, and picked up the telephone. "Hello, Paul. And how is Mrs. Cummings's health?"

"No improvement yet, I'm sorry to report. They've taken her in for more tests this afternoon. She'll be at St. John's for a couple of days. Say, Lucrezia, I'm not doing anything tonight—"

"Neither am I." Lucrezia hung up.

She allowed herself a moment's seething. *So Paul Cummings is witty, handsome, and pretty good in bed. Is that all, or am I really in love? Or am I so enamored of being Mrs. Senator or maybe even someday, First Lady, that . . . ? Some relationship. Aren't there any ordinary people left out there?*

"Mr. Saunders is here," the intercom buzzed. "I'm sending him in."

Saunders stood in her doorway and smiled. She smiled back, so he beamed. Lucrezia bet if he had a hat he would be twisting the brim.

"Peter, the trial is on. Tomorrow morning. There is a lot I want to talk to you about, but I must clear away things here first."

Saunders smiled and waited.

Lucrezia chewed her pencil for a moment. "Can you meet me at Anna's at seven? West Pico? It's not greatly out of the way home for either of us. I'll buy you some dinner."

"Nope. Other way around."

As Peter Saunders closed the office door, Lucrezia put down her pencil, leaned back, and closed her eyes.

During the months of trial preparation she had seen Peter frequently, of course. Each time she felt . . . something . . . what? Affection? The man was easy enough to like. Compassion, too? Yes, that and worse. Fear—fear of the lurking threats, cancer, Consolidated, failure. She must not fail him.

He looked fit. Tanned. Certainly no sign of deteriorating health. The periodic medical reports had been guarded, but blessedly negative.

They had spent hours together going over testimony, Lucrezia playing cross-examiner, but was he really prepared for the impending ordeal? She would talk to him about that tonight. Lucrezia turned back to her work.

27

Saunders walked into Anna's nearly an hour late. Westbound traffic on the Santa Monica Freeway had been stalled by a jackknifed semi.

Lucrezia waved from behind a candle flickering in the mandatory wickered Chianti bottle. "You're going to have to start helping out. I'm already deeply into Valpolicella." Lucrezia started to pour from the half-empty bottle.

"I'd sooner have a beer, if you don't mind. What are you working on?"

Lucrezia's three-ring notebook was unsnapped. Ruled sheets of paper were spread across the checkered tablecloth. "I'm selecting voir dire notes, jury questions. Want some antipasto?"

"Thanks." Saunders helped himself. "I was reading about that in your waiting room. You want twelve impartial jurors. Can't you just ask them if they are?"

Lucrezia laughed. "I suppose it is simple enough in theory. The difficulty seems to be that everyone's objectives are different. While seeking jurors partial to his side, each attorney is simultaneously attempting to keep the opposition from doing the same thing. At the same time, each attorney is using voir dire as an opportunity to sell himself and his case."

"Or herself. I see it's complicated."

"Not yet you don't. The prospective juror's objective is just as selfish. Usually he has already made up his mind whether he wants to serve on this particular jury. His decision may be based on the type of case or whether a friend on the panel has already been accepted or rejected."

"So the prospect answers questions however he thinks will get him what he wants? Doesn't the judge have any control over that?"

"Often the judge believes the parties should waive the jury and let him decide. In that case, he just wants selection over with as quickly as possible."

"Should we go with a jury or just a judge?" Saunders poured the rest of the bottle into Lucrezia's empty glass.

"Has Madam decided?" the waiter wondered.

"Yes, the jury, the linguini calamari, and another bottle of Valpolicella."

"Mmm, this is good." Conceding the difficulty of communicating verbally with a mouthful of squid, Saunders washed it down with more beer before continuing. "Will you want me there while you pick the jury?"

"Absolupely. Excuse me, too much wine. Good public relations for the jury to see you sitting there through the entire tedious process, looking interested and confident. Besides, you might have an insight."

Lucrezia pushed away the half-eaten platter and drained her glass. Saunders refilled.

This was better than she had felt all day. How good to be away from that scheming Sam Corbin. Oh, Sam was a nice young man actually. Still another goddamned lawyer, though.

How awfully good to be out of the clutches of that selfish bastard, Paul Cummings whatever. In a pleasant place with an ordinary, pleasant man. Well, not that ordinary. Put a ten-gallon hat on him, he would be Gary Cooper. And his eyes were the vaguest blue.

The wine made Lucrezia uncharacteristically blunt. "Trial will be grueling, Peter. Are you still feeling all right?"

"Plum good, Lucrezia. Really. I moved into my own place Monday without help."

Lucrezia rested her chin on one elbow-propped hand. "I'd always thought only brown eyes could be so sad."

"I've already painted the bathroom and the bedroom. Just the kitchen and living room to go."

"I'd like to see it." Maybe Randolph Scott was closer.

"Sure." It took a moment. "You mean tonight?"

"Now." Lucrezia stood up. "Oooo." She steadied herself on the table edge. "You'd better drive."

Saunders's apartment was the lower south quarter of a remodeled Victorian, a block from Venice beach. All the living-room furniture was neatly stacked against one wall, covered with a dropcloth. Cans of paint, thinner, buckets, brushes, and rollers lined up single file behind a wooden stepladder.

The bedroom was as immaculate as a barracks and as simply furnished. Double bed, nightstand with lamp, clock radio, four-drawer dresser with mirror. And one photograph, which Peter quickly turned facedown. "This is the only place to sit," he said.

Lucrezia stretched out on the bed next to him and threw off her shoes. Her red suit exactly matched the new bedspread.

As he bent to kiss her, she pulled him into her arms.

An hour later, Lucrezia lay, stroking Saunders's blond chest hair. "Peter," she whispered, "I thought you were a simple man. Where ever did you learn to do that?"

But he was already snoring softly, only the barest smile on his lips. She snuggled in as close as possible, drifting into wine-soaked contentment.

As the sun lit the open window, Lucrezia came awake with a hard realization. Hard, but indisputable. The gentle, decent man next to her was just the gentle, decent man next to her.

She was still in love with the selfish bastard. Whether it was Cummings himself, his glittering future, or some combination, she was not sure. She was still knotted to the bastard, whatever the reason.

God, the way she had behaved last night was enough to make her sick. After she was, she felt better.

When Peter awoke she would explain. A hell of a way to start the man's day, but she must. There was no future in this relationship. She owed him the soonest possible awareness of that. She must do it without hurting him—make that hurting him as little as possible. He would understand the wine shared the blame.

She used his toothbrush. Was this what it meant to rob Peter to pay Paul?

28

Even back at his desk, Sam still gloated over his good fortune. Judge Iverson had been handed to him by magic. He caught himself feeling a little sorry for Lucrezia. Hell, that was silly, wasn't it? The woman obviously had it made. Gorgeous, smart, successful. She had looked so disappointed, though.

Should he try Susan Schooling again? On Monday, his first day back from Point Anacapa, there had been no time to call.

Gaining responsibility for the Consolidated defense had not relieved Sam of other cases. He worked as late as he could handle, managed to drive home without falling asleep, and fell into bed with no dinner.

He had left messages with Susan's office twice on Tuesday but there was no answer. Maybe that was the answer. He had not swept her off her feet. Oh yes, he had. But only literally. She had not been exactly carried away by passion.

What the hell, I'll grow on her. He tried again and was put through immediately.

Susan apologized for not yet returning his calls. She was swamped, she said. She didn't have to say, "First things first." She was sorry that she couldn't make a date. Too many things going on. Her schedule was a shambles.

"Thank you, Sam, but it will have to be later."

"Of course," Sam replied. "I understand. Later."

His secretary Jean entered, soundlessly dropped a pink inter-office memo form on his desk, and departed.

TO ALL PERSONNEL:
  Partner Lawrence Levenson died today 1:50 P.M. at Cedars of Lebanon. The family informs that no public service is scheduled.

It is requested that flowers not be sent. Cards of Condolence will be available in the reception area for signing by any personnel wishing to participate until 5:00 P.M. . . .

Sam crumpled the note without bothering with the rest. It was already 6:00. He would send his own goddamned card.

Pacing was impossible in Sam's tiny office. One pace in any direction was the limit. Larry had been listed critical for weeks, but still . . . shit. Sam felt lousy.

He tried to go back to work. Impossible. He walked down the hall to Ben's office.

"How about going down to Doyle's Irish Delicatessen?"

"Where else can we get chicken Filipino-style with matzo balls?"

They took the only empty booth, next to the kitchen door. The red vinyl bench was split. A previous customer had half-heartedly tried to carve a swastika into the Formica table top.

Ben was on his fourth beer, Sam had just finished his fifth, or was it sixth? He raised his hand for another.

"Sam, I don't understand how you do that without getting fat."

"It's a combination of physical exercise, mental control over metabolism, and usually being too tired to eat."

"What was he really like?" Ben asked.

"Larry? Smart, funny, kind, patient. Hell of a lawyer. Also the queerest son of a bitch I'll ever know." Sam raised his glass. "Here's to you, Larry. I hope you're well."

Ben clinked glasses. They sat in silence.

"Sam, I guess we're as ready as we ever will be to pick that jury in the morning."

"All we need are twelve citizens who seek justice and truth." Sam toasted them, too.

"Come on, Sam. The jury seldom even hears the truth."

Sam hiccuped. "S'cuse me. You can't hold the jury responsible for not finding facts that never reach it."

"You know how we should do it, Sam? Strip every witness naked. It's not easy to lie in the nude."

Sam downed his last beer. "Take it up at the state bar convention. Let's go. Tough day tomorrow."

Coaxing his tired MGB up the freeway ramp, Sam laughed aloud at Ben's suggestion. Larry would have loved that. The naked truth. But the direct lie was not the greatest evil. The worst deception was withholding the truth. Could stripping cure that?

29

"The judge will see all counsel in chambers," his clerk announced. Sam and Ben followed Lucrezia and Molly. Sam was surprised to see Lucrezia wearing the same red suit she had worn yesterday.

Without the black robe to cover his white suspenders, Judge Iverson still looked like a rural justice of the peace. His body had lost its original shape decades ago, his scalp was sparsely populated with white hairs, but his eyes sparkled and his smile revealed perfect replicas of real teeth.

"How do you want to handle the voir dire?" the judge asked.

"Your Honor, I believe we would both prefer to conduct our own," Lucrezia answered, looking over to Sam, who nodded agreement.

Judge Iverson, being an old trial hand himself, was not afraid to let the lawyers do their jobs. "Good," he said. "I've always felt that the judge picking the jury was like a minister picking the bride. He may know all the right questions, but he doesn't have to live with her."

A panel of forty prospective jurors were seated in the audience section behind the bar. The clerk had inserted forty paper slips into a battered wooden box and drawn twelve at random. As he read the name from each slip drawn, a person would come forward and take the jury box seat indicated.

One prospect had a sister who still worked day shift at the Point Anacapa plant. Another had recently been a juror in the case of *Jaworsky v. Consolidated Utilities*, a personal-injury case arising out of a motor-vehicle accident. Both were excused by stipulation.

Several on the panel admitted reading something about the case in newspapers. Not surprising. It was also not surprising that not one admitted to having been influenced.

Lucrezia excused prospective juror number three, an elderly retired telephone operator. The lady had served on a jury in an invasion of privacy case Lucrezia had tried last year. Lucrezia had won the case, but it was a stingy verdict, and this juror had voted against even that.

When Sam could not base his decision on whether to accept or reject a juror on any specific data, he simply trusted his instincts. So did Lucrezia, only she was usually even better at it. If a juror seemed eager to serve, impatient or inattentive, that was enough to trigger an instinctive rejection.

Sam was particularly enamored of Isadore Steinberg, a recently retired heavy-construction superintendent. Steinberg had supervised several Bunker Hill high-rise projects. Here was a man who would sympathize with the need to operate profitably, and who would recognize that some accidents were unavoidable. He would understand the vast community appetite for electrical power that could only be met by nuclear plants in spite of the public prejudice.

True, the jury book showed he had voted a plaintiff's verdict in an earlier case, but that had been a cinch rear-ender. Only reasonable thing to do. The man had the weight of experience and strength of personality that would make him Sam's ideal jury foreman.

Both sides had already passed him for cause. Sam could only hope that Lucrezia would not exercise her last peremptory challenge against him.

Lucrezia, too, was favorably impressed with Steinberg. She recognized the force of personality that could get him elected foreman. She assumed from his name that he was Jewish, although that was not apparent. She was willing to indulge the stereotype of the generous, liberal Jewish juror. That was confirmed by the jury book, which showed that he had voted an adequate award for the plaintiff in a modest personal-injury case.

She perceived his heavy-construction experience as potentially valuable to the plaintiff's case. The man would empathize with a supervisor's responsibility for safe working conditions and would be comfortable with large dollar amounts. Such a man might have no qualms at all against an adequate verdict he knew a public utility could easily afford.

Peter Saunders had no feeling about Steinberg, but Lucrezia's assistant, Molly, was not comfortable. She could not identify what about the man bothered her but she was eager to check further. Lucrezia could only encourage such dedicated intuition.

Molly was back in twenty minutes. "I found one of the jurors in the other case. She talked to me. I also telephoned his ex-employer. Listen. Steinberg was forced to resign last year because his lousy safety record was costing his company a fortune in workmen's comp premiums. He has been married four times, and he tried to get everyone on the other jury to convert to Muhammadanism. Is he an Arab-loving Jew?"

"He is, at best, a loose cannon. We can't risk him. Lucky we have one shot left."

When Lucrezia's next turn came, she used her last challenge to excuse Steinberg. Sam was disappointed, but not surprised. After all, Steinberg made such a classic defense juror Lucrezia had to see it, too.

At the next recess, several men entered the men's room behind Sam. As the door swung open, he heard, ". . . the work of the Devil."

It was Steinberg, who came up and stood beside him. "I guess you heard me there. It's nothing personal against you, Mr. Corbin. You're just doing a job for a client. I understand. But anybody can see that nuclear power has to be the work of Satan. They even named the stuff after Pluto. Straight out of hell. Allah would have loved to have me stick it to Consolidated for ten mil."

Steinberg shook and smiled. "Lucky for you I got bounced off that jury, huh?"

30

It was Friday noon. Twelve jurors and one alternate had been passed for cause by both sides. Lucrezia had no more peremptory challenges left. Sam had one.

Most of the tough jury-selection problems had been Sam's. Lucrezia had to seek out the right psychological types, but she had not had to worry about jurors with deep-seated prejudices in favor of nuclear accidents. Sam was forced to deal with the reality that nuclear power was not as popular as basketball. A lot of people would not work up much guilt about voting a large verdict against a giant corporate utility.

At Lucrezia's request, the judge had allowed the selection of one alternate juror. This was insurance. If a regular juror became unavailable during the trial, the alternate could be substituted and the trial concluded. Without an alternate, the defense could force the discharge of the incomplete jury and the case would have to be retried from the beginning.

Judge Iverson looked down at Sam. "Mr. Corbin. Up to you."

Sam glanced back to see whether Estes Lousaire had any comment on the defense's last opportunity to challenge. The house counsel was supposed to monitor the trial but tended to drift off without notice. Obviously, he was going to be useless.

Is this my jury? Sam wondered. *Seven women, five men. One black, one Vietnamese, three Hispanics, four overweight, five retired, one smoker. Twelve minds and a substitute.* There was no one left he felt negative about. *God only knows what is on those twelve minds. Can I do any better? How the hell would I know?*

Sam mentally shrugged and rose. "The defense is pleased to have this jury, Your Honor."

The judge rapped his gavel. That seemed unnecessary, but it was as close as he could come to a drum roll. "The clerk will swear the jury."

After the jury was impaneled, Judge Iverson mercifully announced he had a judge's conference that afternoon and three motions that had already been scheduled for hearing before this case had been assigned to his courtroom. *"Saunders versus Consolidated*, therefore, is in recess until Monday morning at nine-thirty." The judge turned to the jury. "You are admonished that it is your duty not to converse among yourselves or with anyone else on any subject connected with the trial, or to form or express any opinion thereon until the cause is finally submitted to you. We'll have opening statements Monday morning. Have a nice weekend."

Sam and Ben rushed back to the office, grateful for the gift of time. Sam had given up on Susan. She obviously had a problem. He didn't know whether it was with men in general, or him in particular. Hell, maybe she was living with someone. It was just not going to happen for whatever reason. He had too much to do already anyway. Friday was half-over, and he was still behind for the week. If he skipped lunch that would help make a dent.

When his intercom buzzed he responded with sincere lack of interest. "A Mrs. Schooling on three," the switchboard operator said.

Sam picked up the telephone. *Be cool and aloof, man. She probably wants free legal advice.* "Hi, Susan. I'm really glad you called." How come he felt so good suddenly?

"Hi, Sam. Can you have lunch? I know it's short notice, but I'm already at Civic Center at a Planning Commission meeting, and we just recessed, and—"

"The Windsor? One o'clock?" He could catch up on his work Saturday.

"That would be lovely, but it's too extravagant. How about the Hamlet in the Tishman Building?"

"Great." *The Hamburger Hamlet. Think of the money I'll save.*

They had bacon avocado burgers. Screw the calories. They were delicious.

"Susan, can I ask you something serious?"

"Sure. But I can't take you seriously until you wipe the ketchup off your chin."

Sam wiped it off. "Are you stalling?"

"Why, no." Susan lowered her eyes. "I . . . guess so." She looked straight up at him. "Yes, I have been."

"Can I ask another?"

"You're on a roll."

"That day on the beach in San Luis . . . when I tripped you?"

Susan nodded.

"You weren't just startled, were you? You were terrified." It wasn't even a question. Sam was certain.

Susan was surprised that it was so apparent, but she nodded again.

"And that has something to do with this . . . your . . ." Sam did not know what the hell to call it. "Your ambivalence. About me, I mean."

"You are certainly entitled to an explanation." Susan cleared her throat and wished she still smoked. "Okay. When I was seventeen, my last year in high school, I was virtually . . . excuse me, this is hard to say . . . raped. I say virtually because the boy who did it was my date, and we had been drinking beer and petting. But I didn't want him and I tried to stop him. Of course, there was no one else there. It would have been his word against mine. So I say virtually, since there is admittedly some room for a different point of view and—"

"It's sufficient for me that you didn't want to," Sam said. "Go on."

It was not easy. She twisted her paper napkin to shreds. Sam gave her his.

She had been impregnated. The doctor confirmed it. Fortunately, it was spring and she was able to graduate without embarrassment. Everett was eighteen and in her graduating class. Their parents pressured them to marry. They lived in a small town in Iowa.

"Estherville, the county seat of Emmet County. Population, 8,388." Susan took a moment off for a feeble joke. "No bonded indebtedness."

Susan realized, even then, that the marriage was at least as much to avoid embarrassment for the parents as it was for her.

She didn't want it, neither did the boy. But they had nothing with which to resist the pressure. The indignity was compounded by a farce of a church wedding.

Everett turned out to be totally no good. That was a whole story in itself. Sam would just have to take her word for right now. As soon as she was physically able, Susan bundled up their daughter and left. She could not go home. She took a 130-mile Greyhound bus ride north to Minneapolis.

It was incredibly difficult—she would tell him about that another time, too—but she worked two jobs, raised her child, and put herself through college.

Finally, she moved to Los Angeles, partly to get warm and partly to get away from her husband, the lump. None of the big architectural firms were interested in a raw female graduate from the University of Minnesota, even if she did have a nice portfolio of renderings. Finally, Consolidated Utilities started her as a junior designer.

"And now I've got a good shot at moving up to vice-president for planning," Susan concluded.

"I understand that you've been badly burned and that makes you cautious, but . . ." Sam still did not understand her terror.

"Oh, I didn't explain, did I? It happened on a beach. It was only Lake Okoboje, not the ocean. But it was on a beach, you see. I was running away. He chased me and tripped me, so . . ." Susan's eyes searched to see if Sam understood.

Sam understood, but he wasn't sure how completely. "And never anyone since?"

"There have been others, but not very successfully."

It seemed to Sam there was more. "Is there something else? About me?"

"Not you personally. It's lawyers. Everett's father hired a lawyer, to advise us, he said. I've learned since that he told me a thousand lies. The attorney I hired in Los Angeles to put through my divorce put the make on me in his office. I had to practically beat him off. He got even by overcharging." Susan looked apologetic. "Those are my only two experiences with lawyers."

Sam was not sure what to say. Hell, he was not even sure what he felt. She was afraid of relationships with men, prejudiced, perhaps justifiably, against lawyers. This might be a good time to gracefully walk away. Sam did not believe he especially needed another challenge just then. But what a delicious nose. And she was obviously attracted to him or she would not have invited him to lunch.

"Have you ever been sailing?" Sam asked.

"Never. Why?"

"You're not talking to just another smooth lawyer. I'm really a pretty good sailor. How about Saturday? We'll just go out for the afternoon and have a picnic." Sam saw the hesitation. "Bring Emily if you want to."

She gave him the most grateful smile he had ever seen.

"Yeah," she said, before kissing him on the forehead, dropping a twenty on the table, and walking out.

Well, he could finish the work on Sunday.

31

Late Saturday morning, Sam, wearing swimming trunks and a Transpac T-shirt, picked up Susan and Emily at their Santa Monica Spanish bungalow. They were sitting on the front stoop when he arrived. Was that promptness or precaution? It didn't matter.

Emily was a ten-year-old picture of her mother, but as warm and open as Susan was cautious. She extended her hand to shake Sam's even before he got his out and said, "Hi, Sam, can I steer the boat?" as if they were old friends.

It was only a few-minutes' drive to Marina del Rey, where Sam had chartered a Columbia for the day. It was a spartan twenty-one-foot fiberglass sloop, but it was clean and a forgiving sailer.

They powered slowly out the entrance channel, constantly passed on both sides by larger yachts. The little outboard only had three knots to give. Sam boosted the mainsail to steady them in the wake of a sixty-foot Chriscraft.

Just before they turned to go out the south breakwater opening, Sam unfurled the genoa. He took the tiller, shut down the outboard, sheeted in the headsail, and trimmed the main in fluid sequence. As the sails filled, the little sloop leapt forward. The only sounds were humming rigging and the swish of the bow wave. The motion was easy, like his softly sprung Buick.

"I love it," yelled Susan.

"Neat," said Emily. "When do we eat?"

It was only a two-hour sail south to Redondo Beach. Sam veered toward shore, heading upwind. He let the sails luff as he stepped forward and dropped a small Danforth anchor. Satisfied that the anchor held, Sam dropped the mainsail and furled the genoa.

A mild offshore breeze kept them weathercocked toward the beach, only a hundred yards off.

"Tuna or ham, ladies?

"One of each, please," said Emily.

"Me too," said Susan, "if there's enough."

Sam had had the foresight to bring six sandwiches. He had dealt with first-time crews before. After lunch, they piled into the inflatable raft. Sam rowed ashore. The surf was minimal. They hauled the boat to a safe distance inside the tide line and tied it to a rock. Half a mile down the beach, Sam bought much-too-large ice cream cones, which dripped to their elbows before they could be finished.

On the way back north, Sam broke out two ninety-nine-cent paper kites and string. Susan's was red and white. Emily's was red and yellow.

"You'll lose them in the water when you reel in, but that's better than them ending up in the LAX traffic pattern."

Before they made it back to the Marina del Rey breakwater, the wind died, and they had to motor the last quarter mile.

Back in the slip, dock lines secured, Susan put on sail covers, Emily hosed down the boat, and Sam packed the inflatable.

As they walked back to the parking lot Susan asked, "Did you bring any clothes?"

"Clean T-shirt and shorts."

"Then you're invited to stay for dinner. You can shower at our house."

"But I'm invited to Kathy's and to spend the night," said Emily.

Susan and Sam looked at each other. Susan practically grinned. Sam tried not to.

Susan's Spanish bungalow was over sixty years old, but the interior was sparkling contemporary. A wall of the old formal dining room had been removed, forming a spacious living-dining area. One of the original three bedrooms had been converted to a second bath with the remainder going to enlarge Susan's bedroom.

The outsides of the kitchen cupboards were white laminate, the insides vibrant blue. The counter tops were deep-red glazed tile. Light flooded in from two skylights. The place was instant cheer.

Sam was impressed. "Did you do all this?

"I designed it all, of course. But I had help with the execution. I'm not enthusiastic about refinishing floors, for example."

While Susan delivered Emily and her overnight bag to her friend's house, Sam had a shower and changed. By the time he came into the living room, Susan had a bottle of Piper Heidseck and two iced glasses waiting.

"Thank you for the demonstration," she said. "I am convinced that you are, indeed, a respectable member of the human race."

"In spite of my profession?"

"You may be a refreshing aberration."

32

Dinner had been nice, but this was nicer, thought Sam, as he stared up at Susan's bedroom ceiling, Susan breathing softly into his chest, clutching his ear.

She had insisted on hearing his post-high school history during dinner. Four years of bumming around, looking for a niche. A lot of crewing on boats. Some commercial fishing boats up to Alaska, but mostly yachts. A couple of Transpac races to Hawaii. Several Ensenada and Puerto Vallarta races. Deliveries of yachts down the Mexican coast, one to Costa Rica. Stuff like that.

Then college and UCLA law school.

Susan was impressed with his Supreme Court clerkship. "Didn't you have to be an honor student to get that job?"

"Second in my class," Sam confessed. "I stayed with Bronson for two years."

"Two years. That's a one-year appointment. You must have been really good. I mean you must be—"

"We got along well."

She seemed to believe he was capable of that. After dinner she led him into her bedroom, peeled off her clothes, and came into his arms.

"This is not the wary Susan I have known."

"Caution is not my usual mode. I've just been trying not to pass through hell again."

Susan had persuaded him. Caution was not her normal condition. She had been playful to the verge of wild.

Afterward Sam thought of how soft, round, and subdued Allison had been. Susan was lean, firm, and strong. He knew the comparison was morbid, but could not help it.

He dozed off.

Susan's caress awakened him. He was hard as diamond.

"Haven't you slept enough?" she whispered as she snuggled into him.

Sam had no idea what time it was. He thought he saw moonlight behind the fluttering drapes.

She was on him now, lips kissing his neck, nipples brushing his chest. Her nails raked his abdomen. *She may not want a relationship, but this is not a bad temporary substitute.* He grabbed her behind. *If she doesn't like lawyers, I am sure as hell the exception.* Sam pressed into her and rolled her under him. *I can't promise heaven.* He kissed her with crushing vigor. *But, surely, I won't put her through hell.* She locked her long legs around his back. *Oh, Jesus, this is totally unique.*

God, am I in love already?

33

"**S**o far, you've only plied me with flattery and played with my knee. You enticed me into this mausoleum on the representation that something serious could not wait." Lucrezia's tone indicated that she was not overwhelmed by the somber dignity of the Los Angeles Athletic Club dining room. "What is it, Paul?"

"That's one of the things I love about you, Lucy." Paul Cummings III lowered his voice. "No bullshit."

Paul's eyes roamed the high, beamed ceiling and profusion of crystal chandeliers, reproaching her failure to appreciate the beauty of his selection. "I asked you here for dinner because I understand your being offended by being compelled to meet discreetly. Here, everyone knows who we both are."

"And will conclude that since we meet in this brightly lit museum of decorum there can be no impropriety in our relationship. Cute." Lucrezia marveled at the inner flaw which compelled her to remain in love with this model of facile hypocrisy.

"That's another thing I love about you. Smart. If I just keep my nose clean, I'm a cinch for the Senate. With one good term under my belt, I'll have the ideal posture to capture the nomination. Lucy, imagine. President of the United States of America. I need someone savvy and attractive at my side. I need you. Think of it, Lucrezia Ferrara Cummings. First Lady."

"And will the invalid Barbara live with us?"

"Honey, that's what I wanted to talk to you about. Those quacks have finally diagnosed her. Mononucleosis. . . ."

"Isn't she a little old for that?"

"Only physiologically. Be serious. She'll only be down for a couple of months, and then they predict she'll be completely cured."

"So what do you want of me now? Get your hand off my knee and I'll rephrase that."

"Please, Lucy, don't toy with me. You know how I feel. I want you now. We'll still have to be a little careful, true. But it's only for a little while. I'll make it up to you, I promise. I swear on the day Barbara is pronounced cured I will leave her. The next day I will file for divorce. I can do it then without repercussions. I've already cleared it with the party. Everyone agrees that marriage to you easily outweighs the divorce."

"Romantic devil. Can the balance sheet afford a brandy for me?"

34

When Peter Saunders came out of the Wilshire Oncology Medical Group offices he should have headed straight for his car. He was already late for court. Instead he walked down Wilshire.

Christmas decorations were up along the boulevard. The stores would not open for another thirty minutes, but the sidewalks were already filled with shoppers.

His doctor had tried to be gentle. "I'm sorry, Peter. Lung cancer can develop insidiously, too unremarkable to be detected last month but grown large enough to be both diagnosable and incurable today."

Saunders took a deep breath. For a long time he'd known this day had to come. "How long, Doc?"

"A decade ago I would not have given you more than two months, but we've made great progress."

"Doctor, how long?"

"Peter, long-term cure remains elusive but a number of patients with small-cell lung cancer live five years or more."

"Not the wishful thinking, just the reality. Please."

"All right, Peter. For patients who respond well to chemotherapy, median survival time is two years."

At the next corner, a miscast Santa, given away by dark Asian features, mechanically rang his brass bell. His placard said something about Pakistan. Saunders dropped a ten-dollar bill into the pot. The man said "Merry Christmas" with a sincere absence of enthusiasm. Saunders tried to smile. We all have our problems.

Saunders kept walking. *I must survive at least long enough to expose Consolidated, maybe even long enough to cause real reforms in nuclear power. No, not maybe. Must.*

He walked another mile before he realized Lucrezia would need this information as early as possible. Not knowing could screw up her presentation. He hurried back to the parking lot. *Be patient, Rachel. I've still got a lot to do.*

35

At 9:23 Monday morning Lucrezia sat at the counsel table trying to concentrate on her notes. She had given no commitment, or even encouragement, to Paul last night, but she knew she would. Knowing that his lust for her was exceeded by his lust for the White House in no way dimmed her attraction. Enough of that. This morning her only commitment was to a strong opening statement.

Lucrezia believed many jurors made up their minds after opening statements, in spite of the court's admonitions to keep an open mind. Once opinions formed they were difficult to change. If she could implant a disposition favorable to the plaintiff's case, she would start with a virtually uncatchable lead.

"Where's Peter?" she whispered to Molly, seated at her side.

"Monthly medical checkup. Said he'd be along right after."

The judge looked around to make sure the lawyers, jury, and court personnel were all in place. "Please proceed, Mrs. Ferrara," he ordered.

As Lucrezia stood, she adjusted her red string tie and pulled down the jacket of her white flannel suit. She glanced at her notes, then left them on the table and walked over to the jury box.

She began speaking quietly, conversationally. Without using the words at all, Lucrezia managed to convey that Consolidated's raw greed motivated it to cover up its wanton disregard for the lives of Peter Saunders and the rest of the public.

She alluded to Consolidated's size and wealth. Every time she said the words "Consolidated Utilities," it was like she was describing some loathsome progressive disease.

"This case is about fear, pain, terror, and death. It is about the living death caused by radiation—slow, agonizing, lingering. That is what the evidence will show.

"They have condemned Peter Saunders with their callous disregard for his safety, your safety, disregard for everything but one thing—profit."

She walked to the other end of the jury box, forcing the jurors to turn their heads. "And how do they claim this happened? Not at the nuclear power plant where Peter Saunders was employed, not where tons of uranium and plutonium and all the other radioactive materials were in constant daily use, but in his own home. They claim he did this to himself. Can you believe that? That somehow, some way, this man brought radioactive plutonium out of that plant and contaminated himself.

"But, ladies and gentlemen, we don't have to prove to you how that material got out of the plant and into Peter Saunders's lungs. The law makes it Consolidated's responsibility to keep those lethal substances confined, to keep all of us, including Peter Saunders, safe from such extra-hazardous materials.

"It is as if Consolidated kept a cage of deadly cobras inside their plant. If those cobras get into the streets and into your homes, and you are poisoned by those fangs, you don't have to prove they negligently let those snakes free. They are strictly liable to anyone killed or injured by those snakes. Unless they can prove you, yourself, let the snake out and permitted it to bite you. It is their burden of proof.

"Please listen carefully to the evidence. They have claimed Peter Saunders did this to himself. But listen. See if you can hear one word from the defense as to how this is supposed to have happened.

"This case is about how Consolidated Utilities has tried to cover up the defects in the design and construction of its facilities. How it has covered up the death sentence its recklessness has imposed on Peter Saunders.

"Now this is not televisionland. You are unlikely to hear some witness get up on the stand and confess all. This is the real world where such nice neat climaxes rarely occur. But there are circumstances, ladies and gentlemen, and you will hear evidence from which you can make your own deductions and draw your own reasonable conclusions as to what has really happened.

"This mindless nonthing we have named a corporation has no mind of its own, it has no father or mother. It owes no allegiance. It has no feeling. Its blood is profit and its soul is money. You cannot live, eat, make any movement without using some corporate product contaminated by—"

Sam stood. "Your Honor, it is not quite time for closing argument." He wanted Lucrezia reined in.

"Counsel, approach the bench, please," said Judge Iverson, who waited until they were out of the jury's earshot, and smiled at Lucrezia. "Just turn down the heat a little, Mrs. Ferrara."

"Yes sir, I might have gotten a little carried away." Lucrezia thought she really had. She cooled it a few degrees as she continued. "The law is powerful, but it isn't God. The law cannot remove contamination from Peter Saunders's body. It cannot cancel radiation that has bombarded him. It cannot cancel anguish and fear. The law has only one feeble way of redressing such awful damage. Money. It may seem crass, but let us get it up front now. The bottom line is that this is a case about money. There isn't enough of it in the world to make up to Peter Saunders for what they have done to him, but your verdict can insure that Consolidated and other giant corporate utilities will act reasonably in the future . . . so that this never happens again."

Lucrezia spoke for another forty minutes, outlining the evidence she intended to put on, before thanking the jury.

She sat down, fully intoxicated by her own rhetoric. The effect would quickly wear off, but at the moment First Lady did not seem like quite enough. She would have to decide between appointment as Attorney General or to the Supreme Court. She could do First Lady on her time off.

"We will take a fifteen-minute recess before hearing from Mr. Corbin." Judge Iverson vanished into his chambers. The jury filed into their jury room. Molly took Lucrezia for a cup of coffee to sober her up.

"Pretty good, huh?" Ben asked Sam.

"Pretty good? She was nothing less than brilliant, you dull clod. You're pretty good."

"Thank you, I think. How are you going to overturn the impression she left?"

"No way. I can only hope to weaken what she's built. Find a few niches, drive a few wedges. Things to keep pounding on as we go."

When Judge Iverson resumed the bench, he scanned the courtroom again, before turning to Sam.

"Do you wish to make an opening statement, Mr. Corbin?" asked the judge, certain that he would.

Like Lucrezia, Sam spoke without notes. "I am not here to discredit the plaintiff, Peter Saunders. It is simply my job to bring out the true facts. If those facts happen to discredit plaintiff's case, that has to be. My job is to see that the whole truth gets to you."

Sam unbuttoned his suit jacket. "You know, Consolidated Utilities is just people, too. I know that a lot of you work for, have worked for, big companies. When you look at all this evidence coming at you, you have to distinguish between counsel's mythical demons and the human beings at Consolidated who are just people trying to do their jobs.

"One of the big issues in this case is how did the plutonium, which the plaintiff alleges contaminated him, get into his home? Plaintiff's counsel has already suggested to you it may be hard to believe that he would do that to himself. But the evidence will suggest some motivations to you. This will be circumstantial evidence, but it will speak loudly and you will have no trouble hearing."

Sam had a typical defense problem. He hoped to develop his case through cross-examination of the plaintiff's witnesses. He could not cross-examine effectively if he recited details in advance. He had to hold surprises.

There were things he could talk about, though. "The evidence will show that the Point Anacapa plant was operated and maintained at a safe level.

"The evidence will show that plaintiff has not sustained any medically detectable injury. He has been regularly examined but shows no medical symptoms. This talk of fatal injury and death sentences is just that. Talk. Talk and allegations written by a word processor in a complaint, not proof.

"The proof will be that the Point Anacapa plant, at all times, was in full compliance with the inspections and the regulations of the state of California and of the Nuclear Regulatory Commission. You will see that this plant was designed and constructed by experts, including the plaintiff himself, and in full compliance with the licensing requirements.

"I am confident Judge Iverson is going to tell you more than once throughout this trial to keep your minds open until you have heard it all.

"Keep in mind this trial is like a detective story. The answers will not be apparent until the end.

"And remember that the burden of proving this case to you is on the plaintiff. He has to prove Consolidated's liability, and he has to prove his injury. If he fails to do either one, remember, you have sworn an oath to reach a verdict for the defendant, Consolidated Utilities. Thank you for your attention and patience."

The courtroom wall clock showed 11:52. "This seems like an appropriate time to recess," said the judge. "We will reconvene at one-thirty."

36

"Come on, Lucrezia," urged Molly. "You have an hour and a half to see if you want this new case and grab some lunch. Leave those files. The courtroom will be locked."

"Shouldn't Peter be here by now? What new case?" Lucrezia finished stuffing files she didn't want anyone snooping at into her attaché case.

"I started to tell you this morning. You weren't listening. He's in County Jail. We can walk and talk."

It was only two and a half blocks, the sun shone, smog was minimal.

Molly rattled off everything she knew and more. "Like I told you, it was in this morning's *Times*. I suppose it wouldn't have been if it had been some unemployed black on South Broadway—"

"As you said, Molly, we only have an hour and a half."

"Yeah. Okay. This guy, Innes Balintin, owns Balintin's Music Company out on Wilshire, you know, pianos, organs, synthesizers."

Molly caught Lucrezia's glance. "Oh. Sorry. Anyway, this guy Balintin shot his wife with a nine-millimeter Berreta. A lousy shot, apparently. Only winged her in the arm. Pistol-whipped his twelve-year-old kid who tried to stop him—"

"Allegedly, Molly. Allegedly assaulted his wife and child. Unless the presumption of innocence was also repealed this morning. Did I miss that, too?"

"All right, Lucrezia. I was just telling you what was in the paper. Anything else?"

113

"Yes, 'winged her in the arm' is redundant. But, please, do go on."

"Jeez. Thank you. Anyway, this guy's story is that he allegedly caught his wife fooling around with his cousin. The paper didn't mention what happened to him. I guess Cuz was fast enough to get out before the shooting started."

"Has he been charged?"

"So far P.C. 245. Assault with firearm. Two counts. It will probably be attempted murder by the time he's arraigned."

"Isn't it fortunate he's a lousy shot? When did he call us?"

"He didn't. His wife did."

Lucrezia didn't think Innes Balintin looked aggressive enough to even own a Berreta. If this nervous wisp of a man had bumped into her on the sidewalk, she probably would have said, "Excuse me."

"Thank you for coming so promptly. I asked Judy to call you. I've heard of you, of course. I know you're the best. Don't worry about your fee. I'll take care of that as soon as I'm out of here. You can get me out of here, can't you? This is so humiliating." Balintin pulled on the "County Jail"-stenciled T-shirt the county had been kind enough to lend him after taking his clothes.

"Mr. Balintin, I'm here to see whether I can help you. Why don't you tell me what happened?"

"I just lost my head when I found them in our bedroom. I . . ." Balintin covered his face with both hands, smearing his rimless glasses.

"Your wife and your cousin? Were they . . . doing anything?"

Balintin understood. "No, they were just standing by the bed. On opposite sides, actually."

"Fully clothed?"

"Fully clothed. Judy swears they were moving furniture. She must be right. I'm such a fool. What will they do with me?"

"Your child was involved?"

"My son. He was just trying to protect his mother. My God, he's only twelve. What will they do with me?"

"Your wife and son, Mr. Balintin, are they ambulatory?"

"Yes, thank God. They are both at home. What will they do . . . ?"

"Mr. Balintin, I'm going now to arrange your release on bail. You will be out of here by mid-afternoon. I want you, your wife, your son, and your cousin in my office at six o'clock. After we have talked, I'll be able to tell you what can be done."

"Thank you. I can't tell you . . . I don't think I can persuade Cousin Shane to come, though. I understand he is rather upset with me."

"All right. The rest of you will do. Please try to be prompt. I'm in the middle of a trial so I have a lot to do and not much time."

37

Peter Saunders sat down behind Lucrezia just as Judge Iverson asked, "Are you ready to call your first witness, Mrs. Ferrara?"

"Yes, Your Honor. Thank you." Lucrezia stood and turned to the rear of the courtroom. She nodded and smiled at Peter, then located her witness in the crowd. "Professor Otto Dreistein, will you take the stand, please."

Ben was a little surprised at Lucrezia's choice. He would have bet she would put Saunders on first, and said so to Sam. Sam shrugged impatiently without answering. He wanted to concentrate on the examination. The impression made by the first witness could be crucial.

Dreistein was ancient but he looked like a professor should look, even to his rumpled Harris tweed jacket and scarred wingtips.

Lucrezia efficiently established the witness's credentials. Professor of nuclear physics at UCLA. Awarded the Nobel Prize in 1939 for his work on the cyclotron. On the Manhattan Project, which developed the atom bomb. Atomic Energy Commission. Consultant to Consolidated Utilities of California on the design of the Point Anacapa Nuclear Power Plant.

Professor Dreistein made the principles of a nuclear power plant sound simple. Steam drives turbines, he said, which power generators, which make electricity, which burns your toast. It is exactly like a conventional power plant, except that the water which produces the steam is heated by a nuclear reactor instead of a coal furnace.

"And also except," he added, "that a reactor produces the penultimate power. The power of atomic fission, atoms disintegrating into energy. Radioactive atoms, including uranium and plutonium 239."

That was the lead-in Lucrezia had been waiting for. "Tell us about the plutonium, please, Doctor Dreistein."

"Plutonium is a manufactured element. We transmute it from uranium. Plutonium emits radiation in the form of alpha particles. These alpha particles move at incredibly high speeds."

"How fast, Doctor?"

"Compared to an alpha particle, a guided missile is a snail. Over ten thousand miles per second."

It took Professor Dreistein an hour at the blackboard to explain what alpha particles were and how each alpha particle struck with a force of five million volts.

"Now tell us, Doctor, what happens when radiation in the form of an alpha particle strikes a cell." Lucrezia turned toward the jury box and spaced her words. "A human cell, Doctor."

Two jurors stopped leaning on their elbows. Judge Iverson stopped doodling on his yellow pad. "Perhaps this is a good point at which to break for the afternoon recess. Fifteen minutes."

"Peter, you were so late, I was worried about you," Lucrezia said. "Doctor have anything new to say?"

Saunders could not bring himself to deliver the announcement of his reduced life expectancy. He patted his breast pocket. "Brought the whole nine-page report. You can read it all after court." He managed a smile.

"Good. Excuse me. Must make a couple of calls now. Maybe we'll have a few minutes to talk afterward."

Lucrezia went to the telephone booths down the hall to check on the state of Innes Balintin's freedom.

"He is being processed now, Lucrezia," the bondsman said. "He'll be on the street in ten minutes."

Lucrezia thanked him and called her office. "I've made a six o'clock appointment with the Balintin family. Oh, you'll have to move him down to six-thirty. Listen, if the Balintins get there before I do, watch them carefully. At the first sign of hostilities, put Mr. Balintin in the library. And telephone our next witness. Yes, that's him. Tell him to show up in Department 101 at nine o'clock tomorrow. That will give us a few minutes to talk. Got to go. Bye."

Sam was in the second booth down, telephone cradled on his shoulder, pencil between his teeth, shuffling paper with both hands. It was obvious to Lucrezia he was trying to keep his workload from sinking him. The problem was not uniquely his. Except for a few superstars, every lawyer dealt with it during trial. Somehow, that did not console her. Sam managed to work in a nod and smile to Lucrezia as she passed.

Portrait of Lawyer as Juggler, she thought, as she waved back. *Nice boy, or at least, could be. Too bad he's locked into that law factory. Lovely eyelashes anyway.*

Lucrezia searched but Saunders had vanished. He returned as Professor Dreistein inched his way to the witness stand. Lucrezia waited patiently as the old man tried to make his bones comfortable and smoothed his wreck of a necktie.

"You were about to tell us, Doctor, what happens when an alpha particle strikes a human cell."

"That is extremely simple to explain," said Dreistein. "It can kill it."

"Perhaps I didn't make myself clear, Doctor. I was only asking about the effect of one alpha particle." Lucrezia knew, of course, that she had made herself perfectly clear.

"Yes. When a single subatomic alpha particle, traveling at a speed of thousands of miles per second, with the energy of five million volts, strikes a human cell, it can kill it. It is like shooting a single high-powered rifle bullet through the brain."

"Doctor, we are all pretty much aware of the devastating effect of a nuclear bomb, but what is the effect on healthy human cells when only a small amount of plutonium gets inside a person?"

"A small amount?" Dr. Dreistein snorted. "Let me try to be

more precise. One twenty-eighth of an ounce is a gram. One billionth of a gram is a nanogram."

Juror number eight was scribbling furiously in her notebook.

"I apologize," continued Professor Dreistein, "but I must introduce yet one more term so you can comprehend the immense power we are talking about. A curie is a measure of the amount of radiation in nuclear material. One curie of radiation is the amount of activity in one gram of radium. A nanocurie is one billionth of a curie."

Juror number seven was scowling with the effort of unaccustomed concentration.

The professor had seen the same look on students. "We are almost there," Dreistein assured him. "Sixteen nanograms of plutonium produce one nanocurie of radiation. That submicroscopic amount releases two thousand alpha particles a minute."

Lucrezia started to ask another question, but Professor Dreistein was too wound up to be interrupted.

"So the answer to your question, Mrs. Ferrara, is that sixteen parts of one billionth of one twenty-eighth of an ounce of plutonium inside a body will be bombarding it with two thousand of those speeding five-million-volt particles every minute of every day of the rest of that body's life."

"And with what effect, Doctor?"

"Effect? Oh yes. Some of the cells, as I said, will be destroyed. But the effect can be even more insidious. Some of our cells contain data banks, little warehouses of information. Such information, for example, as how to grow and when to stop growing. When an alpha particle hits one of those cells, it can destroy the data bank. That cell no longer contains vital information. It no longer knows when to stop growing. That is the beginning of a cancer. That cell continues to grow and multiply millions and billions of times. Then one day the patient's doctor discovers a malignant tumor. But that cancer started the moment one alpha particle struck one cell and erased its instructions. At that instant eventual cancer was guaranteed."

"Professor, are you stating unequivocally that such an infinitesimally tiny amount of plutonium inside the body, regardless of early detection and treatment, will result in cancer?"

"Detection and treatment do not occur until after the cancer has formed. I am stating that once the particle knocks out the cell's information center, the process has started and there is no way to stop it. Cancer has already become inevitable."

Lucrezia glanced at the jury. Without exception, their faces were solemn and transfixed. No one in the courtroom was moving. "I have no further questions. Thank you, Professor."

Judge Iverson nodded and looked at Sam. "Mr. Corbin?"

Sam hesitated for the barest instant. "I have no questions, Your Honor. Thank you for an educational lecture, Professor Dreistein."

Plaintiff's next witness was a nuclear engineer who took the rest of the afternoon detailing the operation of the Point Anacapa plant. Innocuous stuff.

As the jury filed out of earshot, Ben turned to Sam. "Dreistein was a pretty dull overture, huh?"

"Sure. All he did was describe the extra-hazardous, inherently dangerous nature of plutonium without even mentioning the terms. He followed up by establishing the inevitability of Saunders's cancer, and the jury started out with a vivid horror of inhaling even a whiff of the stuff . . . a feeling they will undoubtedly carry throughout the trial."

"If he was that strong, why didn't you cross-examine? Surely you could have nailed him on something."

"The old man's credentials are impeccable. Consolidated has even used him as their own consultant. Every word of his testimony is universally accepted science. What was I supposed to impeach him on? Sloppy dressing?"

38

Lucrezia had to return two emergency phone calls before she could turn to the medical report Saunders had placed before her.

She had been wading through one of these a month. Invariably, each had gone to great length to describe no change in Peter Saunders's condition.

She skipped over *History of patient.*

Symptoms. General health: excellent. Muscle function: excellent. Complains of occasional headaches.

Who doesn't? she thought.

Examination and tests. Chest X-ray: no abnormality noted. Computerized Tomography: negative. Pulmonary cytology. Radionuclide scan.

Meaningless numbers.

Mediastinal lymph node biopsies.

Lucrezia flipped pages.

Diagnosis. Undifferentiated small cell carcinoma with lymph node metastasis. T1, N3, M3. Stage III.

Lucrezia stopped. Carcinoma? She glanced at Peter. He was smiling, wasn't he?

She returned to the report.

Preoperative evaluation. Because of metastases to opposite side of trachea, surgery as primary treatment is contraindicated. A trial of multiple-drug chemotherapy consisting of two or three cycles of antitumor drugs is recommended. Continuation of treatment to depend on patient response to drugs. Palliative radiation may be considered as symptoms of distant metastasis develop.

Lucrezia's eyes started to fill. She tried to keep reading. How bad was this?

Prognosis. The duration of remission varies, but a range of 9 to 32 percent is reported to survive in excess of thirty months.

Oh, Peter. Lucrezia threw down the report.

She held him tightly and tried to control her sobs. He clung and stroked her neck. "All right. All right," was all he could say.

The intercom buzzed. "The Balintin family has arrived for their six o'clock appointment."

"Damn," Lucrezia sobbed. "I'll send them—"

Peter shook his head.

He was right. The world was not going to stop. Lucrezia dabbed her eyes. "This will only take a few minutes. Then I'll cancel my six-thirty. Wait for me. We'll have a drink and talk."

Lucrezia, who was no longer often surprised, had to admit that Mrs. Balintin had done it. She had expected Judy Balintin to be an overly made-up, flirtatious blonde, significantly younger than her husband. But Judy was as pale and plain as Innes and at least as old.

Twelve-year-old Innes, Jr., wore a butterfly bandage on his forehead. He was almost as tall as his father, and looked a lot stronger.

Mr. Balintin polished his glasses and stared at Lucrezia's crimson carpet.

Lucrezia kept seeing that medical report. Maximum survival thirty months? She forced herself to concentrate on the Balintins.

"Mrs. Balintin, since it was you who asked me to defend your husband, and because you're here now, I assume you are not anxious to see him in jail."

"Jail? Oh no, Mrs. Ferrara. Innes just lost his head. He's so jealous." She actually blushed. Lucrezia would have bet she hadn't sufficient blood. "The poor man's already suffered enough. I don't want to press any charges."

"I'm afraid that is no longer entirely up to you, Mrs. Balintin. The district attorney may insist on proceeding." Lucrezia turned to the boy. "Innes, is there anything you would like to say?"

The boy's smile lit up the room. "Dad just flipped. He's okay."

"It's my fault, too," Judy Balintin said. "I should know how he gets by now. It's been fourteen years. I must learn to be more careful when another man is around."

It was hard for Lucrezia not to smile. "The police have taken the gun as evidence?"

Mr. Balintin nodded sheepishly.

"There aren't any more guns around the house, are there?"

Mr. Balintin shook his head. It seemed difficult for him to look at Lucrezia.

"Besides, we really need him. People think we're so well off with that big store and all, but actually, we are mortgaged up to here." Judy Balintin paused to indicate where "here" was. "If Innes had to go to jail, there would be no one to run it. He is the whole business." She found a handkerchief and struggled against the tears.

"Are there any prior arrests or convictions, Mr. Balintin?"

"Oh no," sobbed Judy Balintin.

"Two traffic tickets," said Mr. Balintin. "I paid them."

"I'll speak to the district attorney's office. With no priors, the chances are we will keep you out of jail."

"Bless you, you're an angel," cried Judy Balintin.

"A saint," said Mr. Balintin.

"It's nice to have met you," said Innes, Jr.

As soon as the Balintin family filed out, Lucrezia's receptionist called again. "Mr. Saunders said he was going home. He'll see you in court in the morning. He looked awfully tired."

39

"So listen," Doblonski was saying. "We park across the street. There ain't no light within a hundred feet. We get a perfect view of the 7-11. You're in the car with the motor running. Saunders shows. I go in with the twelve-gauge sawed-off under my jacket. I waste Saunders, the same for the clerk. I boost whatever is in the cash register and we split."

"What if he doesn't show?" Sullivan asked.

"He shows every night we stake out till now, don't he? Between eleven and eleven-twenty. Anyways, if he don't, we come back the next night. Big deal."

"Suppose there's another customer in the store?"

"Jeez. He's the only one every time so far. Okay, if there's other customers we drive away. We do it another night."

"I don't know. Magnasunn said he didn't want any martyrs."

"A guy which gets himself fragged by some junkie in a 7-11 holdup is no martyr. Shit, there's one a week."

"I still think we ought to take it up with the boss. Get his okay."

"Christ, Dumbo. All Magnasunn wants is deniability. You wanna get ahead, you gotta show initiative."

"We split the loot?"

Doblonski grinned. "Fifty-fifty. Hell, I'll even boost a couple fifths of Beam."

"There he is," whispered Sullivan as Saunders appeared around the corner.

"Eleven-eighteen," said Doblonski. "And what the fuck are you whispering for?"

"It's perfect. No one in there but the clerk."

The Ithaca Stakeout Doblonski lifted from the car floor only resembled an ordinary 12-gauge shotgun. Shortened barrel. The standard wooden stock replaced by a fiberglass pistol grip. Everything finished flat black.

He released the safety and pumped the first hollow-point super slug into the chamber. *Click. Cli-click.*

Sullivan had heard that thousands of times. He still thought it was the most intimidating sound he knew. He flicked the key starter. The big V-8 rumbled before settling down to purr.

Doblonski concealed the sawed-off gun under his jacket and opened the passenger door. He got his right foot on the ground before the black-and-white patrol car angled across two parking spaces in the 7-11 lot and screeched to a stop.

Doblonski put his foot back inside and gently closed the door as two uniformed L.A.P.D. patrolmen stepped into the store.

"Nine perfect nights in a row. Then this shit." Doblonski was fumbling to remove the shotgun.

"Put on your safety. Maybe they'll leave before Saunders does." Sullivan switched off the engine.

But when Saunders came out carrying a six-pack and disappeared around the corner, the officers were still inside, sipping coffee and reading some magazine.

"Shit, shit, shit," Doblonski fumed as Sullivan restarted the car and drove off.

They were in place again the next night. But exactly the same thing happened, except that it was only 11:12.

"Can you believe this crap?" Doblonski jabbed the glove-compartment lid as they drove away.

On the third night the patrol car showed up again.

"Infuckincredible," Doblonski muttered.

"Look," whispered Sullivan. "The cops are leaving—"

"But our boy is still in there. Oh man, this is it. Take your time, man. Shop around. Check out the wine labels, man. Please."

Sullivan watched the rearview mirror. The first patrolman was already in the black-and-white cruiser starting the engine. The other started to climb in, then stopped.

He started walking across the street toward them.

He was still a hundred feet away but Sullivan could see him unbuckle his holster and reach for his flashlight. "He's made us," Sullivan yelled as he peeled out from the curb and around the corner, leaving a thousand miles worth of rubber.

"We're clear, Dumbo. Slow it down and turn on the lights. Y'know, that fuckin' Saunders must lead a charmed life."

40

"I call Michael Bagdasarian as plaintiff's next witness," announced Lucrezia.

As the compact young man came by him, Sam could see the pin holes on his right sleeve where the label had been removed from the brand-new blue blazer.

The clerk administered the oath, bade the witness be seated, and asked him to state his full name.

"Michael Victor Joseph Bagdasarian, Jr." He smiled a bright white smile. "Armenian."

Lucrezia had been standing near the rail, patiently awaiting the completion of the ritual. She thought the young man's large hooked nose detracted nothing from his dark good looks. The jury would like him.

"Where do you presently reside, Mr. Bagdasarian?" she asked.

"San Luis Obispo. All my life."

"Are you presently employed?"

"Yes. I take programming classes at Cal Poly mornings. Afternoons and some evenings, I'm a salesman at Central Coast Computer in San Luis."

"And before that were you employed at the Point Anacapa Nuclear Power Plant?"

Bagdasarian testified that he had been a night-shift foreman under Peter Saunders's supervision. A year earlier, he had started work at the Point Anacapa plant as a technician. He had no previous experience with nuclear reactors, and his knowledge of physics was limited to what he had learned in high school.

He had been a good auto mechanic, though. He said an atom only had three parts—protons, neutrons, and electrons—so he knew it couldn't be as complicated to work on as an Italian carburetor.

Bagdasarian's narrative was articulate, if not always grammatical. His syntax occasionally stumbled but kept moving. Lucrezia needed to ask only an occasional prompting question. She knew that to exert tight control over Bagdasarian with many questions could imply to the jury that she did not trust her own witness. Besides, she expected to be pleased with his answers. They had already gone over his testimony twice in her office.

Bagdasarian had been born and raised on an apple ranch in See Canyon, a few miles south of the Point Anacapa plant. He had parked in every corner of San Luis Obispo County. Hunting and fishing, he said, but three jurors smiled.

"Could you locate and describe the Point Anacapa plant for those of us who have never seen it, Mr. Bagdasarian?"

At Lucrezia's suggestion, Bagdasarian pointed out the location of the plant on an easel-mounted map. Point Anacapa, he said, is on the Pacific coast between San Simeon and Morro Bay. The power-plant site is on a bluff on the north side of the point. It is too far to be seen from the highway, and, in any case, is hidden on the land side by tall hills. When approached by sea from the north, it is totally awesome, he said.

He described the twin hemispheric reactor containments, surrounded by four identical cooling towers, as a science-fiction version of the city of the future. What he really thought was that it looked like a giantess's brassiere, surrounded by four huge middle fingers pointing skyward in the traditional gesture.

That control room is something totally awesome, Bagdasarian said. Lucrezia thought two "totally awesome" spectacles within five minutes were perhaps too much, but let it pass in the interest of uninterrupted narrative.

"It is like the bridge of the Starship Enterprise on TV, but about ten times bigger," Bagdasarian continued. "There is a hundred-and-fifty-foot wall—I paced it off one night when it was slow—covered with dials and gauges and warning lights and switch indicators. There are seven hundred alarm lights and over twelve hundred separate instruments.

"I was sitting at the center console facing the instrument wall. From there I can see and run everything. Theoretically. I mean I can when things are running hot and straight, I mean normal. But when there is any little problem, it gets more complicated. Like, I can see all the instruments, but some of them are so far away, I can't read them. Sometimes it takes two guys just to make an adjustment because the meter is sixty feet away from the switch that controls it on the center console.

"Anyway, Pete . . . Mr. Saunders . . . called me into his office. That's just a little glass enclosure at the back of the control room where he can still see everything but get a little peace and quiet to do his paperwork. So I turned the console over to Buck Grimes and went back to see what Peter wanted.

"'Mike, I want you to check out the cable room,' Peter said. 'I can't make out what they're trying to say in this day log. The day shift was replacing ceiling tiles down there that were cracked in the last SCRAM. I can't figure out from the scribbling whether we're supposed to finish the job or it's already done. So hop on down and take a look, Mike, will you?'"

Lucrezia interrupted. "Excuse me, Mr. Bagdasarian, but will you please explain SCRAM to us before you go on?"

"Right. That's the automatic safety feature that drops the control rods into the core and stops the chain reaction. Then everything is cool. Really. It just cools down. All the radioactivity is contained. Okay?"

"Yes, thank you, Mr. Bagdasarian," Lucrezia replied. "You had just explained that Mr. Saunders wanted you to check the cable room. Now please continue."

"Right. So I amble on down to level 160, like Pete asks, which is okay with me because it gives me a chance to stop outside and grab a smoke. Consolidated don't allow no smoking in the control room. They say it's a safety hazard. We're babysitting 200,000 tons of uranium and 30,000 grams of plutonium 239, and smoking in the control room is a safety hazard.

"Anyways, the cable spreading room is about the size of a large closet. It can't be more than eight by eight. It's right below the control room. This is where all the electrical cables and wiring for the whole plant comes together and feeds into the instruments and switches in the control room.

"I put out my cigarette before I go in, naturally, since there is no smoking in the cable room either. The instant I turn on the switch, the light blows out. There is just a single four-foot fluorescent in there. That's all you need in that dinky room. So I go down to level 102 storage room. I pick up a new fluorescent tube and a small stepladder and a flashlight. I try out the flashlight because I been stuck before, and it works fine.

"I haul all this back up to 160 on those narrow steel stairs. There's an elevator but it's at the other end of the building. Back in the cable room, I set up the stepladder and I climb up with the new tube and the flashlight to change the light. It's black as a tomb in there. No windows. So I shine my flashlight up at the light fixture so I can see what I'm doing. No light. Can you believe it? I point the flashlight down, it works fine. I point the flashlight up, it don't work. I jiggle and slap it a couple of times but that don't help.

"So I put the flash down on the top rung and I pull out my trusty Zippo lighter. That was a mistake.

"The instant I flicked the lighter and raised it above my head to see, the whole ceiling was aflame.

"I didn't know this then, but the whole ceiling had been covered with sheet polyethylene. The day shift had not finished replacing ceiling tiles, and somebody had decided that instead of leaving all that wiring exposed, they would temporarily cover the unfinished job by taping plastic sheets up. I don't know why, keep out dust or something. Anyways, when those flames started spreading, I didn't have time to figure out what had happened. In the first place, I was so startled, I damn near . . . excuse me. I nearly fell off the ladder.

"There was a chemical portable fire extinguisher by the door. I tried that but it didn't even slow that fire down. By then insulation on electrical cables was starting to burn, too. I thought all that stuff was supposed to be fireproof, but it wasn't. Then the automatic fire extinguisher system kicked in, and the clouds of Halon that came out of that thing blew me right out of the room. I mean, you can't breathe that stuff.

"I climbed back up to level 172. That's the operating level, where the control room is. As I come through the door I can see the panel is lit up like a Christmas tree. I mean there must be fifty alarm lights flashing and a dozen warning buzzers going. It figures. The fire in the cable room must be blocking and shorting out circuits all over the place. That has to be screwing up the monitor and control systems.

"I run up to Pete and tell him about the fire and he says 'thank you, Mike.' You know, like I just passed him the salt or something. Then he picks up the phone, orders up two fire-control techs, and gives them directions.

"Meanwhile we are losing more controls because the fire is burning up more wiring.

"Buck Grimes was still at the console. He yells, 'Primary coolant pumps are down.'

"I wondered whether that was really true or was it just the gauge that had failed. I was trying to figure out the significance of pump failure, if that's what it was. The pumps carry steaming hot water from the reactor core to steam generators. Then the steam drives the turbines.

"Then Buck yelled, 'We've got turbine trip. Turbine trip.' He yelled it twice. I about jumped through the roof then. I been through this as a trainee in the simulator, of course, but I never really experienced it.

"After the shock of hearing it, it made sense to me that the turbines had switched off without steam to drive them. That's what they were designed to do. Like a car runs out of gas. But that creates a new set of problems. The most serious is that we were no longer generating steam. Steam is necessary to carry off the heat from the water cooling the reactor core.

"You see, if the core continued to overheat, well, that would be like the ultimate disaster. When the core reaches around five thousand degrees, we've got the beginning of what we call meltdown. It will melt right through the steel pressure container. That's twelve inches of forged steel. Then it will keep on going right through the twenty-six-foot-thick reinforced concrete foundation. Probably, it will keep going until it hits bedrock. But the worst is that as soon as it hits groundwater, all that boiling radioactive water in the core will flash to steam and blast out of the ground. That would spray radioactive steam wherever the wind carries it. That's probably what happened at Chernobyl 'cause they didn't have our safety features.

"I don't mean that we were that close to the big one, though. True, heat and pressure were building up in the core, but we still had ways of bringing them down. And we still had the SCRAM. Of course, if the SCRAM kicks in, we still have a hell of . . . excuse me, a big internal mess to clean up and a prolonged shutdown. Management is not too thrilled about shutdowns. That costs the company something like twenty-five thousand per hour.

"Anyway, heat and pressure are still climbing. There is a pressure-relief valve that is supposed to open to reduce the pressure. Some fancy made-in-Belgium deal. It either failed or the solenoid switch that controls it has fried. We couldn't tell which was the cause, but it was a cinch from the mounting pressure that that valve was still closed. Automatic SCRAM should have kicked in then and shut down the reactor. But by then we had lost so many controls and monitoring gauges that we really couldn't tell what had happened. We didn't know whether maybe the system had SCRAMed, we just couldn't tell, or whether the controls had failed and the chain reaction was still heating up.

"Pete is sure in control, though. He sends one crew to the top of the pressurizer to open that relief valve manually. Then he dispatches another crew to check the control rods, and to drop them by hand if we have not already SCRAMed. Next, Pete grabs me and two other guys, and says we're all going down to the containment.

"Now that containment dome is really about the last place I want to go because that out-of-control reactor is sitting smack in the middle of the dome. I know in my head that the danger is no worse standing next to the reactor than if I am in the next building, but my stomach don't know that.

"But I have to go along, naturally, and while we are on the way, Pete explains. We are going to bypass the primary coolant loop and reroute the excess water from the core into a holding tank. That will relieve the pressure in the reactor core which, in turn, will bring down the temperature. That makes great sense, because it buys us time to get this mess under control, and the sooner we do that, the sooner we get the plant back on-line.

"By opening two valves and closing two valves, Pete explains, we can bypass the shutdown pump and gravity feed the excess water down into the tank on level 69.

"Three of the valves are a cinch. The handwheels spin like roulette wheels. But the last one is a bi . . . excuse me . . . a big problem. First, it's high up on this immense twenty-eight-inch-diameter pipe, so you have to climb up rungs and balance yourself ten feet off the floor while you are closing it. There is only room there for one man to work. And second, the valve wheel is missing. That naked valve stem is sticking out and there is no way on earth to turn it without that wheel. Somebody suggests a pipe wrench, but we don't have anything nearly big enough with us. And anyway, trying to balance yourself up there on that narrow rung and swing a two-handed wrench at the same time is almost impossible.

"Then Pete gets a brainstorm. 'Pirate the wheel off the number twelve,' he yells.

"So with a small wrench, I remove the retaining nut from another valve. The nut comes off easy, but I had to use the wrench like a hammer to knock the valve wheel loose. Anyways, I get it finally, and one of the other guys passes it up to Pete, who has already climbed the pipe.

"Pete fits the borrowed valve wheel easily, but it won't budge. From down on the floor, ten feet below him, I can actually see his veins bulging. His face is turning red. Pete is heaving with all his might, but that mother is stuck. The pressure behind it must be enormous.

"Pete yells down for a four- or five-foot length of small-sized pipe. One of the guys chases down a piece of inch-and-a-half steel pipe. Pete jams that between the spokes of the valve wheel and commences hauling. Now, of course, he has tremendous leverage. But he's standing on one leg, and leaning out as far as he can reach to pull on the end of that pipe. If the valve suddenly comes free, he is going flying.

"It didn't seem like that valve was giving an inch. Then I saw a little spray of water and the next instant all hell broke loose. Excuse me, but that is the only way to describe it. That monster twenty-four-inch pipe cracked right behind the valve, and a gusher of scalding water burst out with the force of God only knows what.

"Pete took it right in the face and chest. Of course, it knocked him right off that perch and he fell to the floor. A ton of water was still cascading on him. Me and one of the others pulled him clear as quick as we could.

" 'God, stop,' he yells. 'My back. I think it's broken.'

"Jesus, the man was laying there in a puddle of radioactive water, with a scalded face and a broken back, and he starts barking orders. 'Close number nine. Stop the gusher.'

"The other two guys hopped to it. In a couple of minutes the water slowed to a trickle, then stopped.

" 'I'm calling the medic,' I said. We had one paramedic on duty on night shift. Only problem was that the dispensary was about three blocks away. It would take him awhile.

" 'First, rig the backup pumps.' Pete had more things he wanted done. 'Get an estimate on how much coolant we lost and pump that back into the reactor as soon as we know the relief valve's been opened. We can't have the core uncovered.'

"So I get on the phone and line up some help for that. Then I start to dial the dispensary again, but Pete interrupts. 'Let's jury-rig some wiring to the sensors so we can monitor pressure and temperature while permanent repairs are being made,' he says.

"I sent the other two guys to dig up an instrument technician and help him string wires.

"I was about to get on the phone again when one of the guys yells down from the catwalk. 'Relief valve's working and we got SCRAM.'

" 'Get me to a medic and a shower,' says Pete. 'I'll need a stretcher.' "

Even though Bagdasarian's narration had taken almost all morning, he held the jury. Lucrezia noted that even the jaded bailiff was still attentive. She took a long moment preparing for her next question. She didn't mind the emotional impact sinking in as far as it was able.

Judge Iverson broke the spell. He cleared his throat. "It's eleven forty-five. We'll take the noon recess now."

41

Sam left half an inedible sandwich and stretched. "Bagdasarian was a well-prepared witness. There just may not be any cross-examination of him, either."

"Aren't you the guy who's always saying the bigger lead the plaintiff builds, the harder it is for the defense to catch up?" Ben asked.

Sam knew that Bagdasarian's testimony had impact. It was not realistic to hope that the effect could be destroyed. He could only hope to impair it. But Lucrezia's order of putting on her proof had so far been close to brilliant. She had carefully limited her witnesses' testimony to unassailable points. Sam was being given nothing he could use. The jury would resent an unwarranted attack on Bagdasarian. He had gained too much rapport.

To top off Sam's problems, last night Lucrezia had sent over a copy of Saunders's medical report. The poor bastard. Inoperable cancer, with a lousy chance for survival. That sure as hell strengthened plaintiff's case, though. The defense argument that Saunders could not even prove any injury was down the toilet. Sam knew he would be made to eat some of his opening remarks.

"Stay cool, Ben. We haven't even come to bat yet," he said. "Let's head back to the office. We can still get in an hour's work."

After lunch Lucrezia put Bagdasarian back on the stand and resumed direct examination. "We left Peter Saunders flat on

133

his injured back in a pool of radioactive water. What happened next?"

"Well, we strapped him onto a stretcher and hauled him down to the dispensary shower. Theirs is big enough to lay a stretcher in. I helped scrub Pete down. I needed the decontamination too, although I didn't take on anything like he did. The scrubbing was murder for Pete. Every time we touched his back or shifted his weight, he would spasm and yell. And, of course, we couldn't scrub his face. It was already blistering. All we could do was flush it and pat it with a soft cloth."

"Then what?" Lucrezia prodded.

"Oh yeah. The medic took a urine sample from both of us. You know, to check for radioactivity. There wasn't anyone in the lab to test it until the day shift started at eight o'clock. But that afternoon they reported that we were both okay. They said neither one of us had taken in any unsafe amount of contaminated water, internally, I mean. I knew I hadn't, but I was relieved about Pete."

Lucrezia wanted to know whether a doctor had examined Peter Saunders that night.

"Well, it was morning by then, although it wasn't dawn yet. A doc came up from San Luis real fast. He must have driven like a bat. . . . Anyway, he said he was pretty sure Pete hadn't broken anything, but he wanted to get him into the hospital for X-rays, just to be sure. And he put some goop, some kind of stuff, on Pete's face and chest for the burns."

"Was Peter taken to the hospital that morning?"

"Yeah, the doc had an ambulance take him into French Hospital. I saw him late that afternoon. His face was covered with dressings, but he didn't have no fracture. It was just a pinched nerve or a bruised nerve, I forget which. He said they had given him muscle relaxants, but he still twitched a few times while I was there."

"Did Peter say anything else to you that day?"

"He said cigarette smoking may be hazardous to your health."

Some jurors smiled. The bailiff howled. Judge Iverson silenced him with a look.

"Anything else?"

"Yeah, he said be sure to put that cracked pipe on report."

"Is that when you quit your job at the Point Anacapa plant?"

"Actually, it was the next day. That was the day I quit smoking, too." Jurors smiled again. The bailiff was stone-faced.

"Thank you, Mr. Bagdasarian," said Lucrezia. "You may cross-examine, Mr. Corbin."

"Thank you, Mrs. Ferrara." Sam thought Lucrezia's smile was indecently smug. But perhaps she was entitled. She certainly had not given anything of value away. He would have to proceed cautiously. He stood up. Sam always did that to cross-examine. He thought the jury appreciated the small courtesy.

"Mr. Bagdasarian," he began, "wasn't that the day you were reprimanded for smoking and using the exposed flame of your lighter in an unauthorized area?"

"Yeah. Old man Karrasch let me have it pretty good."

"Mr. Isaac Karrasch is the plant manger, is he not?"

"I guess that's his title."

"Mr. Karrasch pointed out to you that your unprofessional behavior was the cause of the entire incident?"

"He said that, but I still don't think that's so."

"Isn't it correct that if you had not flicked your Bic in the cable room, none of this would have happened?"

"It was a Zippo and—"

"Objection," said Lucrezia simultaneously. "Immaterial and irrelevant."

"I'll withdraw it," said Sam. "And didn't he tell you that you had single-handedly cost the company millions of dollars in repair bills and loss of revenue?"

"I don't think that's fair either."

"And didn't Mr. Karrasch also say that you had endangered the lives of Mr. Saunders and of all your co-workers?"

"As far as I am concerned, Mr. Karrasch is—"

Lucrezia caught Bagdasarian's eye and shut him up.

"Go on, Mr. Bagdasarian." Sam was willing to have the jury hear the rest.

"—wrong," said the witness contritely.

"And right or wrong, didn't he tell you that if it were not for the union contract, he would fire you on the spot, but that he was still considering it?"

"Yeah, he said that."

"And he also said if it came out you were smoking in the

cable spreading room, he would be looking into possible criminal charges against you for arson, didn't he?"

Michael Bagdasarian grew sullen, but he nodded.

Sam made the witness answer audibly before he continued. "And that is when you quit the job, isn't it?"

"Yeah."

"And that is why you quit, isn't it? To avoid being fired and to escape possible criminal prosecution?"

"I quit because," Bagdasarian gulped. "I was scared."

"Because you were afraid of being charged with a felony?"

"Because I was scared that what happened to Pete could happen to me. Or worse."

Thanks a lot, thought Sam. *And why couldn't I quit while I was ahead?*

Bagdasarian was not going to admit his resentment against the company, but Sam thought he had enough so that some of the jurors would infer it. And he could certainly argue that in his summation.

But Sam did not dare let the examination hang on Bagdasarian's last words.

"Mr. Bagdasarian, you testified about Mr. Saunders with obvious affection. He is a friend of yours, isn't he?"

"He sure is."

"And your testimony is affected by the fact that you want to see your friend win his case?"

"I want to see Pete win this case because I think he is in the right. Otherwise, I wouldn't be here."

Jesus, thought Sam. *He is going to shoot me down again.* He tried another way. "You don't think he got a fair shake from the company, do you?"

"Right. I don't."

"Just like you didn't get a fair shake, right?"

"Right."

Lucrezia was coming to her feet with an objection but she was too late. She sat down with a sigh.

"No further questions, Mr. Bagdasarian. Thank you."

Lucrezia had no redirect examination, so Bagdasarian was excused. She was relieved to have him off the stand. It was not desirable that the jury dwell on the moral question, however irrelevant, of how much responsibility Consolidated should bear for the unauthorized misconduct of one of its employees.

Judge Iverson asked to see all counsel in chambers in five minutes.

In the lull, Ben whispered to Sam, "Good man. I thought he had you in deep shit a couple of times, but you ran right over it."

Sam was not that sure.

"Anyway, Sam, considering what you had to work with, that was great. The jury's got a whole new perspective on that witness's testimony."

"Sure. If they don't spend too much time considering that I did not change his version of what happened one goddamned bit."

42

As Lucrezia, Molly, Sam, and Ben settled around the judge's battered desk, the reporter set up her stenotype machine.

Judge Iverson had no jokes to tell. Something was very wrong. The bailiff was standing in a corner. That in itself was ominous. There was no need for a bailiff in chambers. When he finally spoke, Judge Iverson's eyes were flat and hard. "Something extremely disturbing has occurred."

Everyone had already figured that out.

"At the conclusion of our last recess, juror number nine handed this note to the bailiff." The judge waved a sheet torn from a spiral notebook, encased in a transparent plastic envelope. "I'll pass this around. Please do not remove the plastic cover."

He passed it to Lucrezia first. She was closest. Molly, seated next to her, leaned over to read. Sam could not wait an instant. He stood behind Lucrezia so he could see over her shoulder.

Ben held out for another ten seconds. He went to her other side.

The neatly handwritten note said:

Confidential to Judge Iverson,
I am in danger. My life has been threatened if I don't vote his way. I am fearful, but I don't know what I'm supposed to do. Please respond promptly.
Respectfully yours,

Amelia Pennington, No. 9

Lucrezia passed the envelope back to the judge.

"Well?" he asked.

Finally, Sam spoke. "Have you talked to her yet?"

"No, I wanted to give it some thought first. I decided to get your suggestions on how to proceed before taking any action."

"The note says 'if I don't vote *his* way.' At least that lets Lucrezia and me off the hook," said Molly.

"Molly, if that's an attempt at humor, it's feeble," said Lucrezia.

"I have to agree," said the judge. "That could refer to Mr. Saunders."

"Sorry," said Molly.

"How about having her brought in here so we can question her on the record," Sam suggested. "That should give us a better idea on how to proceed."

"But once you've questioned her, won't that disqualify her as a juror?" Molly asked. "She is unlikely to remain impartial after that. At best, she'll contaminate the rest of them, if she hasn't—"

Molly caught Lucrezia's sharp glance. She shut up.

"It seems to me she has already disqualified herself by writing the note," Sam said. "Regardless of what the cause turns out to be, she has already established a bias against one side or the other."

"Sam is right," the judge said. "Her usefulness as a juror is already over. We don't risk that by questioning her. What does bother me is that if we bring her in here to be confronted by all of you, she may be so intimidated that we get nothing out of her."

"I have a suggestion, Your Honor," Lucrezia said. "Bring her into chambers with just yourself and the court reporter present. That way you can question her preliminarily, but we'll all be protected by a record. After you have her statement on the record, you can let us back in to question her. You could even assure her first that you'll have the bailiff present to protect her."

"That makes sense to me, Lucrezia," said the judge. "I would like to proceed by stipulation, if we can. Would you agree to that procedure, Sam?"

"Yes, it makes sense to me too, Judge." Sam trusted the old trial hand to get the facts accurately.

"That's the way we'll do it. Then, after any argument either side cares to advance, I'll make a decision. That may be hard, but my choices appear limited. I suppose I either declare a mistrial or we proceed with the alternate juror."

"Or we could stipulate to an eleven-man jury and still save the alternate," Lucrezia offered.

"That is another possibility," said the judge. "There is one more distasteful thing. It seems obvious to me, but we had better have it out in the open. Not only do we have the question of how to proceed with this trial, there is also the possibility of criminal prosecution and disciplinary action. I may have to turn this over to the district attorney or the State Bar Association. Any comment on that?"

The possibility of a criminal accusation against one of them had already occurred to Sam and Lucrezia. Sam shrugged and Lucrezia tried to smile. What could they say?

Sam knew he had not threatened the juror. *That only left Lucrezia, didn't it? No way. The lady was straight as the golden rule. Saunders himself then? The man was fervently devoted to his cause. Hell, he would not even know how to go about it. Who then? Morgan or Pringle? Neither senior partner would have any scruple against it. It was too heavy-handed and risky, though. Not their style. Consolidated itself?* Sam suspected it had concealed evidence and altered records, although he had no way of proving that. *Would the company go to any length? Damn right. It had to be someone within the company. Jesus. His own client.*

Has to be Consolidated. But who is going to believe I had nothing to do with it? Sam felt himself falling, falling. Fired? Suspended? Disbarred? Shoved over the edge of the cliff by his own client.

Molly and the three lawyers waited in the corridor while Judge Iverson interviewed the juror. Molly and Ben tried to make jokes about it. Neither Lucrezia nor Sam thought they were amusing.

Forced into temporary alliance, Lucrezia and Sam spent the time comparing notes. Amelia Pennington was a sixty-seven-year-old widow, a retired copyeditor. She lived alone at a respectable address in Pasadena. She was well-educated, obviously intelligent, and registered Independent. Her driver's license listed no physical restrictions. She had not previously served on any jury. Everything else they had was equally useless.

When they were called back into chambers, Mrs. Pennington sat alongside the judge's desk, hands in lap, chin high, brave and defiant. So tiny and frail, she seemed to Sam. The bailiff stood behind Mrs. Pennington and the judge. Off in the shadows, the court reporter waited, fingers poised.

The judge looked even grimmer than before. He motioned the four to chairs placed facing, but safely distant from, Mrs. Pennington. "We are still on the record," the judge began. "The attorneys of record and Molly Moscowitz, paralegal assistant to Plaintiff's counsel, are now in my chambers. The court reporter will now read aloud the record of my interview with Mrs. Pennington. Please refrain from any interruption until she has finished. Following that, you will be permitted to examine—" Mrs. Pennington went rigid. "I mean, ask questions." Mrs. Pennington looked relieved.

There was more detail, but it all came down to one appalling fact. Mrs. Pennington had just stated, under penalty of perjury, that Mr. Samuel Corbin had come to her home, last night at 11:00 P.M., and threatened she would die unless she swore to vote for a verdict in favor of Consolidated Utilities. She was certain of the time, she said, because it was right after the rerun of "Hollywood Squares."

Sam seemed dazed. Lucrezia started to reach for him, then caught herself.

Apparently no one else was ready to ask a question, so Judge Iverson did. "Where were you last night, Mr. Corbin?" He sounded sad.

"I worked at my office until around ten o'clock, then went home and crashed . . . fell asleep."

"Can anyone substantiate that?"

"I logged out of the building around ten o'clock. The security guard's record will show that. But that doesn't prove anything. I drove straight home. Didn't talk to anyone."

"Can't anyone at your home confirm that?" the judge asked.

"I live alone."

More silence. The judge sighed.

Sam was not paralyzed, but he was stymied. His mind was in fast-forward, but he just could not think of anything useful to ask. He kept thinking, *set up by my own client.*

Lucrezia refused to believe Sam was guilty. She yearned to say it aloud.

Ben raised his hand. "Your Honor, may I?"

"Please go ahead, Mr. Davidoff." It sounded like "somebody do something."

"Mrs. Pennington," Ben asked. "Did Sam Corbin come to your home last night in person?"

"Well, not exactly, but I'm sure he was live."

Everyone else was stunned. Ben continued as if he had expected the answer. "You mean on television, don't you?"

"Yes, of course." Mrs. Pennington's chin rose another notch. "He was carried on all channels, except thirteen. They were showing *Bedtime for Bonzo.* They are so cute together. You know, the chimp and whatshisname."

The bailiff had jammed his fist into his mouth and was silently convulsing. Fortunately, he was standing behind the judge.

The judge looked at the group. Twitches at the corner of the mouth were becoming endemic. He closed his eyes and pinched his nose. He took out his handkerchief and blew it.

"Mrs. Pennington," he said finally, "I have decided to excuse you from further jury service. If you have no vote on a jury you cannot constitute a threat to any party. Conversely, no party will have any continuing motive to threaten you. In this way we can assure your future safety."

"Thank you, Judge. You're an extremely erudite man. It has been an honor to serve such wisdom." Mrs. Pennington stood up, curtsied to the judge, and walked sprightly out of the room without a glance at anyone else.

Judge Iverson turned to his bailiff, who regained bodily control barely in time. "Stay with her. Make sure she gets to her car."

He turned back to Ben. "Thank you, Mr. Davidoff. You have a bright future at the bar. Now, we still have serious questions to resolve. Any suggestions on how we proceed?"

Relieved of the burden of accusation, Sam's brain began again to function. A mistrial would result in a delay of months or even years. The case might never be retried within Peter Saunders's lifetime. This was a great tactical opportunity. The firm would love the elegance of a pragmatic victory.

"Your Honor," Sam began, "the defendant moves for a mistrial on the grounds that prejudice has occurred which is so irremediable it cannot be cured by an admonition to the jury. It is highly probable that the excused juror's fears have been communicated to some or all of the remaining jurors—"

"Nonsense," Lucrezia interrupted. "There is no evidence that Mrs. Pennington's fears or anything else have been communicated to any other jurors. On the contrary, the record of your own interview, Your Honor, contains her sworn statement that she never did discuss this matter with any of the others. We have an alternate juror ready for just such contingency as this."

"The dilemma," Sam answered, "is we cannot be certain the other jurors are untainted without questioning them. Such examination in itself will necessarily create distrust. Thereafter, it will be impossible for this jury to dispassionately decide this case. It is regrettable, but a mistrial is the only fair action this court can take."

"This is precisely where I feared we were headed," Judge Iverson mused. "You two are obviously never going to resolve this by stipulation. I'm afraid that leaves it up to me."

Judge Iverson frowned, grimaced, and scratched his head. Watching was as painful as the process. He rested a moment. "I am going to call the jury back in. I will question them, in your presence of course, concerning any communication of a prejudicial nature with the excused juror. I will attempt to do this in a manner which does not raise any bias or suspicion against either side. Any objection either of you has to any of my questions will be made to me only outside the presence of the jury. Any questions either of you wishes to ask of the jurors will be submitted to me. If I deem the question proper, I will ask it. Clear, so far?"

It was clear that Judge Iverson was not in a jolly mood. No one answered, so he continued. "After I have completed my examination, I will have the jury returned to the jury room. If, at that stage, either side still believes that any irregularity exists, I will hear further argument. Then I will rule on the motion for mistrial. Any questions?"

Judge Iverson's examination gracefully established that no other juror was aware of Mrs. Pennington's paranoia. The questions raised no suggestion even of what had occurred. The excused juror's departure was explained innocuously.

Sam continued to press his motion on the theory that it didn't hurt to ask, but it was no surprise when he heard the judge say, "Defendant's motion for mistrial denied. Reconvene at nine-thirty tomorrow morning."

"Your Honor, one more thing, please," Lucrezia said. "I have a probation and sentencing set for nine o'clock in Department 152. *People versus Balintin.* I'll ask for priority, but I still may be a little late."

"Thank you, Mrs. Ferrara. Reconvene at ten o'clock then. Call if it looks like you're going to be later than that."

Out in the corridor, Sam finally got the chance to ask Ben, "How the hell did you know to ask if I had come to her home in person?"

"Elementary. My Aunt Huldah had the same problem. Only with her it was Perry Mason, and it always happened right after 'Donahue.' "

43

Almost as soon as he became aware that a juror had been excused and the alternate substituted, Consolidated's Chief of Security Rod Magnasunn began pondering the potential usefulness of such knowledge. What the hell was General Counsel's extension number?

"Lousaire? Magnasunn. We just heard down here that in the Saunders case a juror was excused for illness or somethng. I guess you were there. Is that the straight skinny?"

"Why yes, what you heard is correct. Just today it was, I believe." Lousaire supposed that was what Magnasunn wanted to know.

"Well, what happens next, I mean, as a result of that?"

"Nothing really. The alternate has been substituted for the excused juror, and the trial goes on as if nothing had happened, you see."

"But what happens if another juror gets sick?"

"Oh, the judge could just continue the trial until the juror recovered, or, if it was clear that the juror would not be available for a long time he could declare a mistrial, or, if both sides agreed, the trial could proceed with eleven jurors."

"Yeah. That's what I thought. Thanks a lot." Magnasunn hung up.

Lousaire went back to his Christmas shopping list without another thought. Everyone was always asking strange questions. He was just pleased when he knew the answer.

Magnasunn fumbled for a cigarette as he explained. "No gain in going after witnesses. No single witness is crucial to plaintiff's case. They could easily substitute for anyone. Understand?"

Sullivan nodded. Doblonski flicked his switchblade open.

Magnasunn continued. "Saunders doesn't make sense as a target either. Even if we offed him now, his cause of action survives. That means the trial could go right on anyway. As a matter of fact, if Saunders was iced now that would probably just increase the jury's sympathy and up the verdict. See?"

"Yeah, but it would sure stop his speeches," Doblonski said.

"It would, but he can't keep that up long. His cancer has been diagnosed as incurable. The guy probably only has a few months."

Sullivan said, "Jeez, we—"

Doblonski stared him into silence, turning the five-inch blade to reflect the light.

Magnasunn lit the cigarette. "But if just one juror is eliminated, that forces a mistrial. Long delay before the case gets retried. By then Saunders is long forgotten. Clear?"

"It has to look like an accident," Doblonski said.

"It would obviously be stupid to go after Saunders," said Sullivan."

"Obviously," Doblonski agreed. He snapped the knife shut.

44

In Department 152, Lucrezia sat waiting, flanked by Balintins. She should properly have been sitting in the attorney section forward of the rail, but she feared leaving Mr. and Mrs. Balintin unsupported. From knees to lips, Innes quietly trembled. His wife, Judy, was twisting her lace-trimmed handkerchief into rope. Only Innes, Jr., was composed, tossing Lucrezia an occasional smile that made her wish she'd had one or two like him.

It was already 9:20, and Lucrezia still had two priority cases ahead of her. Well, there was nothing she could do about that. She was lucky to even be here. Making a deal that kept her client out of jail had not been as easy as predicted. After all these years, she should have known better than to make optimistic forecasts to clients.

It had taken almost two hours last night to sweeten that puckered-faced deputy DA. Since the voters, he had pointed out, passed the Proposition 8 referendum, the court's power to accept plea bargains in serious felony cases was greatly limited. Besides, he had argued, probation is prohibited in attempted-murder cases. Even if the charge were reduced to assault with firearm, jail time was mandatory. Obviously, he considered Innes Balintin another John Dillinger.

Point by point, Lucrezia had forced him to concede that without the wife's and son's cooperation there was insufficient evidence to prove the prosecution's case. "Besides, Balintin is an asset to the community, essential to his business and his family. He experienced insane jealousy. It was a stupid mistake and he knew it. Fortunately, no one was permanently injured. His wife and child forgive him. He is contrite. He is no menace to society. What do you want?"

Finally, the DA had agreed to a reduced charge of two counts of simple assault. Innes Balintin would plead guilty in exchange for a one-year suspended sentence, two years' summary probation, a $2,000 fine, and 100 hours of community service. The man had a heart the size and consistency of pea gravel.

At 9:40, *People v. Balintin* was finally called. Lucrezia guided Innes Balintin to the front of the courtroom. His legs were rubber.

The judge accepted the plea bargain without hesitation or modification. In three minutes Balintin had signed a copy of the order granting probation and it was all over.

Once outside Department 152, Lucrezia struggled to free herself from the grateful Balintin family. Judy kept squeezing her arm and repeating, "I'm so relieved, so relieved."

Innes would not release her hand from his sweaty grip. "We can never repay you."

"You've already paid me. Your check was deposited yesterday, thank you. All you have to do now is stay out of trouble. I
must go. I'm holding up a courtroom full of people." Lucrezia
fled into the elevator, relieved to be done with such embarrassing adulation, but feeling good, too.

45

At 10:01, Lucrezia dashed into Department 101, unpacked
her attaché case, and waved good morning to her next witness,
MacGregor Burns.

MacGregor Burns's lantern jaw could probably be used
to batter down walls, Sam thought. The rest of him was un-
imposing.

"NRC," Ben whispered as he dug for his notes and deposition
on the Nuclear Regulatory Commission inspector.

Lucrezia established the inspector's qualifications and experience with compound and leading questions. Sam did not
object. The technical impropriety speeded things up for both
sides. Lucrezia knew the line and respected it.

Burns testified that he had made forty-two field inspection
trips to the Point Anacapa facility and thousands of individual
inspections.

"And why, Mr. Burns, do you find it necessary to make
inspections of such magnitude?" Lucrezia asked.

"Obviously because the consequences of a failure can be
serious."

"Can you expand on what the most serious consequences of
a nuclear reactor accident can be?"

"Objection. Irrelevant and immaterial. We are not here to
determine the feasibility of nuclear power."

"Sustained," ruled the judge. "I think we are all well enough in mind of the effects of a nuclear catastrophe, Mrs. Ferrara. Let's confine ourselves to this case."

"Of course, Your Honor. Thank you. Mr. Burns did you inspect the burst pipe which is the subject of this lawsuit?"

Burns testified that the pipe was cracked for 72 percent of its circumference. The crack was next to a weld on the intake side of the valve Saunders had been attempting to close. At its widest point the crack was .628 inches. He estimated that over 1500 gallons of radioactive water had leaked on the occasion of the accident.

"Do you have an opinion as to the cause of the crack?"

Sam did not object. Burns was an obviously qualified expert witness, and therefore, competent to render an opinion.

"My opinion is that the failure of the pipe was caused by a combination of factors. First, an initially inadequate weld joint at the pipe-valve juncture created an inherently weak condition. Probably there was an internal hairline crack from the beginning. Secondly, the crack gradually enlarged until it penetrated the pipe wall. This was caused by corrosion and vibration."

"But Mr. Burns, surely this joint had been inspected."

"Oh yes, once by me and, according to plant records, three times by the operators."

"Then why wasn't this defect detected and corrected before this accident occurred?"

"The pipes are tested externally with an ultrasonic device. This device is intended to measure internal crack depth. The theory, obviously, is to detect the crack and measure its depth so that the pipe can be replaced before the wall is dangerously weakened. Unfortunately, it has been my experience that this ultrasonic testing technique is a delusion. There is no consistent correlation between actual crack depth and measured crack depth. In my opinion, the actual depth of a crack is invisible to this technique. Pipes can, and all too often do, break without warning."

"Have you communicated your conclusions regarding ultrasonic testing to the management of the Point Anacapa plant?"

"Twice. The first time verbally, the second time in writing."

"When was this done in relation to the date of the accident?"

"The first time was ten months before the accident. The second time was three weeks after the first time."

"Do you have an opinion as to the proper way to test these pipes for cracks?"

"Yes. The only consistent way to accurately test the pipes is to X-ray photograph them during the assembly process. That must be coupled to a strict quality-control program which rejects pipes which are substandard on leak-rate tests and . . ."

Burns went on for most of the morning with explanations of good and bad practices in maintenance, and the pros and cons of various safety testing techniques.

"Mr. Burns, will you please summarize the elements of a proper pipe-testing program?"

"I've already expressed the opinion that all pipe must be X-ray photographed during assembly. A strict quality-control program must be followed in which pipes that are substandard are rejected. Finally, there must be a consistent program of replacement on a conservative schedule before internal cracking approaches the point of pipe failure."

"Did you take any official action as a result of this accident?"

"Yes . . . I issued a citation for violation of Nuclear Regulatory Commission regulations . . ."

Lucrezia heard the hesitation in Burns's voice and saw the uncertainty on his face. Her witness needed some guidance, but she was damned if she knew about what. And she did not dare try to discover the answer while her witness was on the stand. The only safe tactic was to go no further until she understood the problem.

"Thank you, Mr. Burns. Your witness, Mr. Corbin."

I sure hope so, Sam thought. *I'm due one.*

Sam put down his notes and walked over to the foot of the jury box, from where he could observe the witness and the jury simultaneously. Juror number three smiled. He smiled back.

Sam commenced. "Good morning, Mr. Burns. I shouldn't keep you long. I have just a few questions."

First Sam established the enormous volume of Nuclear Regulatory Commission regulations.

"Eighteen thousand, four hundred twenty-four current regulations, you say. Mr. Burns, would it be fair to also say that some of these regulations are contradictory?"

"Yes, that is a valid criticism. There are provisions which are ambiguously drafted and appear to conflict with other provisions."

"You yourself have written memos to the commission pointing out inconsistencies in the regulations and suggesting clarifying changes, have you not?"

"Yes, that is correct."

"And not all of your suggested corrections have been acted upon by the commission, have they?"

"No, they have not yet."

"So it would also be fair to say that it would be impossible for a nuclear-power-plant operator to follow all of the regulations to the letter?"

"Some regulations are susceptible to such an interpretation. We try to apply them sensibly."

"But some regulations could reasonably be interpreted so that it would not be possible for an operator to follow all of them strictly?"

"Unfortunately, yes."

"So if an operator attempted to comply to the letter with all the regulations, nothing would get done at all, would it?"

"I would concede that the operation would be substantially impaired."

"The operation would be substantially impaired. All right, Mr. Burns, I'll accept that. Let's go on. Mr. Burns, you've testified to your dissatisfaction with the ultrasonic testing technique. I believe you said you considered it inaccurate, is that right?"

"I said there is no correlation between actual and tested crack depths. I consider the test to be inaccurate, yes."

"As a matter of fact, you communicated your concern about this testing technique to your head office in Washington, didn't you?"

"Yes, I did." Mr. Burns folded his arms.

"And?"

"They disagreed."

Sam waited.

"They said the present testing procedure is adequate."

"And you don't agree with your head office on that?"

"No, I don't and I have offered to prove my position is the correct one."

"All right, let's leave that between you and your superiors, Mr. Burns."

Sam moved to a position between the witness and Lucrezia. "Tell us please, Mr. Burns, what is the present status of the citation that you issued against Consolidated Utilities after this incident involving Mr. Saunders?"

Lucrezia heard her internal warning buzzer but she couldn't even see her witness. She shifted her chair to get a view, but it was too late to do anything.

Burns was visibly upset as he answered. "The citation has been withdrawn."

"Was that because you were ordered to withdraw it by your Washington office?"

"They said it was unwarranted."

"Thank you, Mr. Burns. I have nothing further."

Ben could hardly restrain his glee. Sam quietly put his hand on Ben's arm and did it for him.

Lucrezia was furious but struggled not to show it. "No questions at this time, Your Honor, although I would like to reserve the right to recall this witness after further evidence is developed."

"We'll take that up as the occasion arises. Now we'll take our noon recess. Back at one-thirty."

Burns came down from the witness stand and Lucrezia cautioned him not to speak until the jury had filed out.

"I'm sorry, Mrs. Ferrara. I didn't—"

"When was the citation withdrawn?"

"Three days ago. It just did not occur to me to mention it to you—"

"Three days ago? After the trial started?" Lucrezia glanced over at Sam, but he was huddling with Ben.

"I didn't realize I would be asked about that. And when I was, it took me by surprise. I didn't know what you wanted me to say."

"What I wanted you to say? What I wanted you to say was what I always want you to say, the whole truth. Withholding part of the truth can be a greater deception than a direct lie. And, if you're caught, difficult for the jury to forgive."

Burns lowered his eyes and started to leave.

Lucrezia put her hand on his. "Mr. Burns, I realize it was inadvertent. I'm grateful for your assistance. Don't worry about it too much. I don't think you've destroyed my case."

"Thank you. You're a very gracious lady."

You bet I am, thought Lucrezia as she marched over to Sam's end of the table. "Samuel Coleridge Corbin, you cute son of a bitch. I have two questions. How did you find out that citation was withdrawn only three days ago? And what did you have to do with it?"

"Privileged information, sweetie. But I'll tell you after the case is over if you buy me lunch."

"If I buy you lunch, you'd better have someone taste it first."

"Lucrezia Borgia?"

"A direct descendant, so watch your step, sweetie."

46

The entire afternoon of trial had been taken up with witnesses testifying to proper pipe-welding standards and techniques, leak-rate testing procedures, and similar boring, but necessary, evidence.

Lucrezia was still a little sore at the way Sam had pulled the rug out from under Inspector Burns's testimony and was happy to be back in her own office.

"The Balintins are waiting in your office," said the receptionist. "I was sure you wouldn't mind."

Lucrezia sighed and entered. Three beaming Balintins stood in front of . . . what? A piece of furniture? As if on cue, the tableau parted, revealing a small electric organ wrapped with a silver satin ribbon.

"Merry Christmas," chorused the group.

"A little early, we know, but we wanted you to have it now," said Judy.

"It's such a great way to relieve stress when you're under pressure," added Innes.

So how come you didn't try it instead of taking a shot at your wife? Lucrezia wondered. "Thank you all," she said. "It's a marvelous gift, and I know I'll enjoy relaxing with it."

"All solid-state electronics," Innes pointed out.

"And it simulates thirty-six separate instruments," said Innes, Jr. "Here, I'll show you."

Lucrezia spent a quiet moment with a cup of tea after they had gone. As much as she enjoyed music, she couldn't get a tune out of a kazoo. Maybe an orphanage would like it, she mused. Still, it was satisfying to be so appreciated. Every once in a while the practice of law made her feel really useful. Lovely feeling.

"There is good news and bad news," Molly walked in and announced before noticing the organ. "Oh. Neat." She strolled over to it and dashed off the fanfare from *Wellington's Victory*.

"Give me the bad news first."

"You have Dr. Myron Shapiro of the Independent Biological Testing Laboratories on call to testify in the morning. He's been run over crossing the street. He was just admitted to Cedars with a concussion. Nobody knows when he'll be available."

"Corbin probably managed that, too."

"It was a twelve-year-old boy on a bicycle. What do you want to do? You have a choice of using his lab technician in his place or reading his deposition to the jury."

"Reading deposition questions and answers to a jury is about as effective as . . . it has as much impact as . . ."

"I don't have time for you to search for the appropriate metaphor. His office is holding on line two. What will it be?"

"We'll use the lab technician. Get his name and ask him to show up about fifteen minutes early so we can go over it before he testifies."

"His name is Camille Maria Fuentes." Molly went for the telephone.

"Just one moment. What's the good news?"

"I lied about the good news. Hello, Miss Fuentes. Thanks for holding . . ."

47

Camille Fuentes was a tiny Hispanic girl with beautiful teeth, who said she was twenty-two and looked twelve. Not your most imposing witness, thought Lucrezia, but ten minutes out in the hall indicated she knew her business.

"Miss Fuentes, you are employed by the Independent Biological Testing Laboratories at 1311 Sunset Boulevard, here in Los Angeles, is that correct?"

"Yes, I am the senior laboratory technician."

Lucrezia thought she saw juror number eight suppress a titter. Ah yes, her notes indicated that number eight was a fifty-nine-year-old senior typist at Bell Telephone.

"What are your duties as senior laboratory technician, Miss Fuentes?"

"I supervise the other four technicians and the assistants, review their results and reports. In Dr. Shapiro's absence I manage everything."

"Yesterday afternon you informed us that Dr. Shapiro has been hospitalized and so will be unavailable to testify here as scheduled, but that you could appear in his place, is that right?"

"Yes. Dr. Shapiro has been admitted to Cedars of Lebanon Hospital. We don't know yet when he will be released. As managing director of the laboratory, he would ordinarily be the one to testify on our report. Dr. Shapiro is a certified pathologist. However, I personally performed the tests and wrote the report on Peter Saunders."

"What was the purpose of testing Mr. Saunders?"

154

"Mr. Saunders telephoned for an appointment to be tested specifically for radioactivity contamination. Do you want me to go on and explain the circumstances?"

"Please, go on," said Lucrezia. She caught herself almost saying, "thank you, child," but she was delighted. This girl had the demeanor of a seasoned professional.

"Over the telephone, Mr. Saunders stated a history of swallowing and inhalation of potentially radioactive substances during the course of two industrial accidents.

"He explained that he had been tested by his employer on both occasions with negative results. Now he wanted independent tests made as a check. A second opinion, in other words.

"Mr. Saunders's request was unique. Our work has always been referred by doctors or hospitals, but Mr. Saunders did not have a personal physician at that time.

"I discussed Mr. Saunders's request with Dr. Shapiro. He agreed that, although it was unusual, it seemed reasonable under the circumstances, and instructed me to make the appointment."

"Tell us what routine was followed when Mr. Saunders appeared for his appointment."

"First, Dr. Shapiro took the patient's history and satisfied himself that the patient's concern was authentic."

Sam did not care much for that bit of hearsay characterization, but it had slipped in too quickly to catch. He decided not to object. That would only emphasize what he hadn't wanted the jury to hear.

Miss Fuentes continued. "Then Dr. Shapiro physically examined the patient and indicated which tests he wished me to perform. The tests and results are listed in our written report."

"I'm going to offer the entire written report in evidence when you are finished, Miss Fuentes," Lucrezia waved a copy. It was as thick as a small-town telephone book. "But for now would you please just state the types of tests performed?"

"Certainly. Hemogram, differential white blood count, those are various blood tests. Urinalysis, PA and lateral chest X-rays, that's front, back, and side . . ." Camille Fuentes was rattling off test names, medical terms, and succinct explanations as fast as she could turn pages.

Lucrezia waited for her to finish. "What was the finding as the result of all these tests?"

"There was measurable radioactivity. Contamination was particularly acute in both lungs to the extent of six nanocuries of radiation."

Sam thought there was something in the girl's tone that conveyed sympathy. He hoped it was only his personal reaction as he anticipated the next question.

Lucrezia continued. "And what, in your opinion, Miss Fuentes, is the physical consequence to Peter Saunders of six nanocuries of radiation in each lung?"

Sam had come to his feet before the question was half-finished. He really did not want that one answered.

Sam knew Lucrezia would have little difficulty in proving Saunders had contracted lung cancer. That was established by the medical report he had already seen. But she still had the burden of proving the cancer was caused by contamination from the plant accidents.

"Your Honor, that question obviously calls for an expert medical opinion. May I examine the witnees on voir dire so that the court can determine whether she is qualified to answer?"

"You may proceed, Mr. Corbin."

Sam had hoped the judge would suggest the voir dire examination take place outside the jury's presence. He would have to be careful not to offend any juror with his questioning of this pleasant and obviously competent young lady.

"Good afternoon, Miss Fuentes. I'm Sam Corbin, the attorney for Consolidated Utilities. The judge has granted me permission to interrupt Mrs. Ferrara's direct examination because the last question she asked of you clearly calls for an expert medical opinion. Such an opinion must be based on reasonable medical certainty and can only be expressed by a qualified medical expert. Sometimes even physicians are not qualified to express opinions on highly specialized areas of medical science, so you—"

Lucrezia grew impatient. "Your Honor, could Mr. Corbin please be instructed to get on with his questions. We are already aware of his reluctance to let the jury hear the rest of this witness's testimony."

"Your Honor, I resent counsel's insinuation. I am obligated—"

Camille Fuentes decided to save everyone trouble. "I understand that Mr. Corbin wants to know about my educational background and work experience. Shall I just go ahead?"

Judge Iverson permitted himself a broad smile. "Miss Fuentes, we would be grateful."

"Four years ago I completed high school. I was a National Science Award winner with an A average. I have been attending University of Southern California and Loyola University night classes for the past three years. I have about 100 credits toward a bachelor's degree in biology and organic chemistry, with a 4.0 average. For the past four years, I have been employed by Dr. Shapiro, first as a technician's assistant and for the last year as supervisor. Of course I don't have a medical degree, but I did consult Dr. Shapiro about his opinion on this matter and—"

Sam objected. "Miss Fuentes's relating Dr. Shapiro's opinion would be hearsay."

"Sustained," said Judge Iverson. "Why don't you two come up to the bench. You know the way by now."

"Your Honor," Sam whispered. "We don't even know yet whether this witness has an opinion to express, but even if—"

"Don't bet any money she hasn't," the judge whispered back. "I am already satisfied that as impressively competent as this young lady is, she is not qualified as a medical expert. Is there any reason, Mrs. Ferrara, why I should not sustain an objection to your question?"

"Your Honor, what I have asked is concededly a medical question but it is equally a biology question, which I submit this witness is qualified to answer."

Nice shot, Lucrezia, Sam thought. He had no answer for that so kept quiet.

But Judge Iverson was not persuaded. "Mrs. Ferrara, I know you've taken Dr. Shapiro's deposition. You can use that. I strongly suspect that you intend to call other medical experts to testify. Do you really want to risk a reversal on appeal just to save a little extra work?"

Receiving no response, the judge continued. "The court rules that Camille Fuentes is not a qualified medical expert, and, on its own motion, sustains an objection to the last question on that ground inasmuch as Mr. Corbin overlooked making an objection himself. Shall we get on with it now?"

Lucrezia excused the witness. Sam had no cross-examination. He was quite willing to quit while he was ahead.

Lucrezia resigned herself to a morning reading aloud Dr. Shapiro's deposition in lieu of the blocked testimony.

In his pre-trial deposition, Dr. Shapiro had said that a substance producing six nanocuries of radiation was more than enough to guarantee lung cancer, so long as the patient did not first die of something else. And Dr. Shapiro had determined that the patient was in otherwise excellent health.

As she read lifeless questions and answers to the jury, Lucrezia found a correct metaphor. It had all the impact of a wet paper towel.

"I wonder what Camille Fuentes thinks of lawyers?" Sam said as he packed a briefcase.

"I'm only sure what she thinks of you," Ben replied. "Male chauvinist pig."

48

"**I** don't know," said Magnasunn. "So he always drives down to the same bar, and he always goes home after on the Hollywood Freeway. Even if you get him stinking drunk, that doesn't mean he's got to have a smash-up."

"The beauty of it, boss, is that it's no risk. Even if he's lucky enough to get away with it, which ain't likely if he's driving six miles of freeway, what have we lost? A couple of hours and a bar bill. We don't stick out our necks at all."

"Okay, Doblonski, but you do it. Sullivan couldn't hold no two hours' conversation without saying something we'll regret."

Stefan Genik, juror number three, usually drove down to the Jewel on the Nile for two ginger and ryes after dinner. Last month the dingy old bar had been called McGillicuty's. The name changed with each new owner, which was every six months. No one could make any money with the place. All the old neighborhood trade was gone. This stretch of Western Avenue was largely populated with East Asians, and they never entered the place. Genik kept coming back only to reminisce about Sophie, and because it gave him something to do until the 9:00 movie. Even though he came in nearly every night, nobody in the place even recognized him anymore. That was nothing new. When he drove out to the rest home to see Sophie, she didn't either.

Doblonski almost blew it. "Hiya, old timer. How you doing?"

"Name's Stefan. I'm only sixty-six, and I'm doing fine."

"Hey, it's just an expression. Let me buy you a drink to show there's no hard feelings."

Booze and conversation quickly warmed Stefan Genik. It was nice to have someone to tell all about the trial. Of course, he wasn't supposed to discuss the case, he knew, but all of them did.

Doblonski was delighted with the easily obtained intelligence. Magnasunn would want to know that a lot of the jurors already felt that Consolidated had given Saunders a raw deal.

Genik stuck around until long after 10:00. He was having a good time for a change. This guy, James or John, or whatever his name was, was buying the drinks and laughing at his jokes. He'd already seen the movie, anyway.

"Don't you worry about me, ol' Jim," Genik said, as he balanced against his bar stool. "I can drive just fine. Done it a million times. I'm just going to pee first, then I'm on my way."

As soon as Genik disappeared into the men's room, Doblonski called Magnasunn, who pulled up across the street almost instantly.

Magnasunn's Pontiac speeded away before Doblonski completely closed the passenger door.

"That cellular phone you got is really something," Doblonski said.

"I just want to get out of here before some cop recognizes us. If he has half the snootful you described, he might pile up within a block. There could be fuzz all over the place."

"The company owes me twenty-two bucks for the drinks."

Only with difficulty did Genik make his way down toward

the corner where he had left his car. It became easier, he discovered, if he kept his hands out of his pockets. But the parking place was empty.

He might have had a lot to drink, but he remembered damn well where he had parked his goddamned car.

"Son of a bitch!" he exclaimed out loud. "Someone stole my goddamned Oldsmobile." Oh well, he had mailed the insurance premium on time. He waved to the oncoming Yellow Cab. "Hey, taxi."

49

Molly stifled a yawn. So far it had been a morning of innocuous testimony and indecisive sparring.

"I'm calling Hesselmann next. The way things have been going all morning, it's time to arouse some attention. Besides, I want his testimony before he gets run over," Lucrezia whispered to Peter.

"Heinie is all right," he replied.

"That's the most ringing endorsement I've heard out of you so far," Lucrezia said. Saunders had been immobile, without comment or even reaction.

Heinrich Hesselmann's suit was twenty years out of fashion and too snug for his beer-barrel shape, but there was neither wrinkle nor speck of lint on it. Every close-cropped hair on his head continued to stand at attention as the retired day shift supervisor sat in the witness chair.

"This may be their strongest witness. We have nothing negative on him, except his Hitler Youth membership," Ben said.

"Hell, he was thirteen years old. Raising that old skeleton might only cause resentment," Sam said. "Is he wearing a hearing aid? There is nothing about any hearing impairment in the notes."

"He wasn't wearing it when I took his deposition, but that was months ago."

Lucrezia established that Hesselmann lived in Leisure Village, raised schnauzers, repaired his neighbors' appliances, and nursed his invalid wife. He had retired a month after the accident as a function of age, not the accident, he said.

Since he worked days and Saunders worked graveyard, much of their contact had been through their respective daily log sheets. Each shift left messages for the others: unfinished work that required immediate attention, warnings of potentially defective equipment, notice of completed maintenance schedules, the never-ending details that needed coordination in the running of a complex system.

Hesselmann and Saunders saw each other almost daily although briefly. When Hesselmann came on shift, Saunders would usually still be tying up loose ends, and they would exchange pleasantries. If a required action was particularly urgent or complicated, Saunders would stay on to discuss it.

That was the extent of their relationship, Hesselmann said. They liked each other, but they had no opportunity to be friends. Hesselmann was intimately familiar with Saunders's work, however. After all, he said, he had to live with the results of it every day.

Hesselmann testified that he had the utmost respect for Saunders's competence. This was demonstrated constantly. Lucrezia had Hesselmann give example after example of Saunders's continuing efforts to improve plant conditions and upgrade safety standards.

"Did Peter Saunders ever make a specific recommendation with regard to the plumbing on the primary cooling system?"

"Yah, on all the high-pressure plumbing. On too many of pipe joints the welds is bad, he said. Many he found bad. Testing procedures not good enough. The ultrasonic is not working. Better testing devices we need. Regular plumbing replacement we should have, he said. On this I always think he is right."

Lucrezia thought she had better clean that up. Corbin would try to make something of it if she didn't straighten it out now. "Then you did not always agree with his recommendations?"

"No, I did not. I think sometimes he is too picky. Too much he expects. This is funny from me, the German engineer, no? Saunders, he is saying always to the manager, 'I know this will cost to correct. A lot it will cost. But otherwise . . .'" Hesselmann shrugged.

"Otherwise what?" Lucrezia wanted to know. "What did Mr. Saunders warn would happen if his recommendations were not followed?"

"The words I don't remember. It is obvious. Without the safety measures we get what we got. A bad accident. It could have been worse, yah? But was enough."

"How long after his accident was it before Peter Saunders returned to work?"

"A week about. On a Tuesday, it happened. He is back the next Monday."

"On that day, Mr. Hesselmann, did you overhear a conversation between Peter Saunders and the plant manager, Mr. Karrasch?"

"Sure. By the control room, all of us. By the east wall they was standing. I was sitting at the console."

"Was anyone else present in the room?"

"No, the graveyard shift had gone already by their lockers, and my shift wasn't here yet."

"Now please, to the best of your recollection, tell us what each man said."

"Saunders said, 'You promised me every one of the high-pressure pipes would be reinspected. You told me that is done. You said all the bad welds had been replaced. But that number twelve weld failed, and you know it could have damn well killed me.' That is what Saunders said."

"And did Mr. Karrasch reply?"

"Karrasch says—he is very red in the face—he says, 'I promised the high-pressure system would be reinspected, and it was. All of the bad wells is replaced. We do everything I said we would. I do not appreciate suggestion that I am liar. What happened was fluke. No matter what precautions we take, there is risk of failure someplace, some time.'"

"Was anything else said by either man?"

"A few times 'round and 'round they went. But it was the same all over again."

"Then have you told us the substance of everything that was said?"

"The substance, yah. Everything."

"Thank you, Mr. Hesselmann. Cross-examine, Mr. Corbin?"

Lucrezia felt well-satisfied, and deservedly. If the jury believed Hesselmann's testimony, it had to conclude that Consolidated's conduct had been far more reprehensible than mere negligence. By promising to reinspect and replace components with interior welds, Consolidated had implicitly accepted that a serious risk existed.

By claiming to have corrected the defects when in fact it had not, Consolidated had engaged in a cover-up of its own nonfeasance. Lucrezia now had a solid ground upon which to argue that Consolidated's conduct was, at best, reckless and wanton. She might even have a persuasive argument that Consolidated's conduct was intentional, a greedy attempt to cut expenses and increase profits.

The chances of obtaining punitive damages were looking up—if the jury accepted Hesselmann's testimony. *Thank God,* thought Lucrezia, *the man is a stone fortress.*

Sam glanced at the wall clock. 11:40. He hoped the judge would declare the noon recess. This witness had done too much damage to let go without some attempt to discredit his testimony. Sam's only problem was that he had not the slightest idea how to do that.

"Go ahead, Mr. Corbin," said Judge Iverson. "You can at least get a start before lunch."

"Thank you, Your Honor." *Thanks a lot,* Sam thought.

He circled Hesselmann cautiously, searching for an exploitable opening. The Saunders-Karrasch conversation was the core, of course. Hesselmann's version had to be somehow discredited.

But no matter how Sam approached him, the old man remained unwavering and consistent. Sam knew he was only reinforcing Lucrezia's case.

Sam walked back to behind the counsel table. That was about as far away from the witness stand as he could get without appearing obvious. "Mr. Hesselmann, I just noticed you're wearing a hearing aid. What make is it?"

"Why, it's a Bosch."

Sam lowered his voice as far as he dared without seeming unfair. "And can you hear me all right?"

"I hear you fine, Mr. Corbin. No problem."

Well, back to the drawing board, Sam thought. It was 12:05. Had Judge Iverson given up lunch?

The judge finally stepped in. "This sounds like a convenient place to break. Recess. We will reconvene at one-forty-five. Take charge of the jury, please, Mr. Bailiff."

"You're striking out," Ben said. "Want to drown your sorrows over a beer and corned beef? We can taxi over to Sam and Gene's and be back in time."

Sam shook his head. "You go ahead. I'm skipping lunch. I have to go see about a hearing aid."

"What the hell?"

"Eh? What's the smell you're referring to, Sonny?" Sam grinned and left.

After the noon recess, Sam's cross-examination of Hessel-mann resumed. "As I recall, your testimony was that this conversation you overheard was in the control room. Saunders and Karrasch were against the east wall and you were at the center console. Have I got it right?"

"Absolutely right."

"And would you agree that the distance between you and the two gentlemen conversing was about seventy-five feet?" During the recess, Sam had scaled the distance off the floor plan.

"From the console to the east wall where they was standing? Yah, at least that. Maybe eighty-five even."

"And it's pretty quiet in the control room, isn't it? There is not much noise from the plant operation, is there?" Sam knew there was not from his tour of the plant before the trial.

"Like a tomb. Completely sound-insulated from the plant."

"Fine. Saunders and Karrasch were speaking in normal tones, weren't they?"

"Yah. Karrasch was getting red by the neck, but he was not raising his voice."

"Didn't one of them have his back turned to you?"

"Karrasch, yah."

"There is no doubt in your mind that you heard every single word of their conversation?"

"Every word. No doubt."

"Excuse me for belaboring this, but isn't it possible that from such a distance you could have misunderstood part of what was said?"

"No. I heard what I heard. As clear as you now."

"Mr. Hesselmann, from where you are sitting to the far rear corner of the courtroom has been measured at fifty-nine feet. Would you agree, Mr. Hesselmann, that the distance from you to the southeast corner of this room is at least sixteen feet closer than the distance was between you and Mr. Karrasch?"

"Yah, it's closer than that even. You would have to go out into the hall." Hesselmann was enjoying this game.

"All right. Now I'm going to take Mr. Davidoff with me and we are going to pretend to be Saunders and Karrasch, talking in the corner of the room, do you understand?"

"Sure. You want to know can I hear you." Hesselmann was grinning. A gold-filled incisor glistened.

"That's right," Sam answered. "Come with me, please, Mr. Davidoff."

Sam guided Ben to the rear of the room, took him by the shoulders and placed him in the far corner facing the witness stand. Then Sam faced the wall, his back to the witness.

Sam turned his head to see if Hesselmann was ready, and just in time to see him reach under his suit jacket for his volume control knob. Sam faced back to the wall and smiled. This might work better than he had hoped.

Then Sam shouted as loudly as he could, spacing each word. "MR. HESSELMANN. IF YOU CAN HEAR ME, PLEASE REPEAT WHAT I JUST SAID."

Hesselmann had stiffened when Sam shouted. Now Sam turned back toward the witness, but said nothing.

Hesselmann pressed his ear and appeared perplexed. He looked at the judge, then the jury. Some jurors were beginning to smile. Hesselmann squinted across the room at Sam, who remained silent.

Mr. Hesselmann reached under his jacket again. "I didn't understand that last question. Would you please repeat what you just said?"

Sam walked slowly up to the front of the courtroom. He waited until his face was inches from Mr. Hesselman's.

"That's all right, Mr. Hesselmann. No further questions."

Lucrezia was puzzled and dejected. Sam had just pulled the

rug right out from under another witness, but she did not have the least notion how. It had to be some trick with the hearing aid she did not understand. She had to do something. She was running out of rugs.

"Your Honor, could I please have a few minutes to consult with my witness before we continue?" Lucrezia hated to ask that. It was amateurish. It was also an implicit admission to the jury that Sam had nailed her witness and she did not know how to deal with it. But Hesselmann's testimony was too critical to just throw up her hands without an attempt at rehabilitation.

Fortunately, Judge Iverson was astute enough to have some inkling. He wasn't sure how Sam had pulled it off either, but he was suspicious that it had been some sort of mere trick. If that was so, it would be unfair to let the defense get away with it without giving the plaintiff's side a chance to expose the gimmick. After all, a trial wasn't a game, was it?

Lucrezia and Hesselmann figured it out in the corridor. In a quiet room, with no extraneous noise, Hesselmann's hearing aid permitted him to hear words spoken softly from an impressive distance. But shouts against a reverberating paneled wall echoed and blurred. And, of course, Hesselmann had made it worse by taking the precaution of turning up the volume on his control unit. That had converted Sam's shouts to pure static.

Lucrezia put Hesselmann back on and went through all that, but she feared the explanation sounded lame.

"Sam," she touched his arm at the next recess, "that was a hard act to follow."

Sam felt himself blushing. Jesus, why was she complimenting him? Lucrezia had too much class to ever pull such a stunt. A goddamned act was all it was. He wanted to be admired by her, but, dammit, they were adversaries. Wasn't his obligation to give his client all he had? So why should he feel so ashamed?

50

Lucrezia was ambivalent about calling Isaac Karrash as an adverse witness. There was no procedural obstacle. But it was usually a futile exercise to attempt to prove a case through the testimony of a hostile witness. Lucrezia did not hope that Karrasch would agree with her main contentions. If she wrung some small admission from him, that would be an achievement.

She was tempted to call the plant manager because she found him obnoxious and believed the jury probably would too. If Karrasch fulfilled her expectations, he would deny her allegations, but would do so in such a distasteful manner the jury would be offended.

Ordinarily, the defense would have been compelled to call Karrasch in order to have him contradict Hesselmann's version of the control-room conversation.

Lucrezia feared that Sam, realizing how unsavory Karrasch could be, might elect not to use him as a witness. Sam might conclude it was a reasonable gamble to rely on his discrediting Hesselmann, rather than risk Karrasch before the jury. That would deny Lucrezia the opportunity to cross-examine. The jury would be deprived of Mr. Karrasch.

Lucrezia decided that the benefit was worth the risk, and that the risk was manageable.

"Plaintiff calls Isaac Karrasch as an adverse witness, pursuant to Evidence Code, section 776."

"The terrible Turk," Ben whispered. "He'll chew her up and spit her out."

167

Sam disagreed. "No, it's the right move. If I were in her position I'd use him."

With his left hand, Karrasch smoothed the ends of his black mustache. As he stared at the ceiling, his right hand drummed the rail before him.

Amazing, Lucrezia thought. *The man has the capacity for being disagreeable without saying a word.*

"Mr. Karrasch," she began, "you have the title of plant manager for the Point Anacapa Nuclear Power Plant, is that right?"

"I am vice-president of Consolidated Utilities for management of the Point Anacapa plant."

"Well, as vice-president of Consolidated Utilities for management of the Point Anacapa plant, would you agree that Peter Saunders was zealous in his efforts to upgrade the safety of the plant?"

Karrasch shrugged.

"Mr. Karrasch, you must respond audibly so the court reporter can record your answer," said Judge Iverson.

"You can put it that way if you like," Karrasch answered.

"Would you prefer to say Mr. Saunders was overzealous?" Lucrezia asked.

"No, I would not prefer to say that."

"Well, would you say that Mr. Saunders's conduct was an irritant to management?"

"I would say that Mr. Saunders's conduct was an unwarranted intrusion into the functions of executive administration and of the Nuclear Regulatory Commission. Design and inspection were not part of his job description. He had no understanding of the problems of revenue and cost. The man had become a nuisance." Karrasch glared at Saunders.

Saunders glared back.

"How do you distinguish between a nuisance and an irritant?" Lucrezia asked sweetly.

"Your questions, for example, are only a nuisance, not an irritant."

"I apologize for subjecting you to my questions, Mr. Karrasch. I'm simply trying to get out the facts."

"Then get to it. What's your point?"

"Please, Mr. Karrasch," admonished the judge, "just confine yourself to answering the questions."

Karrasch nodded to the judge, then said to Lucrezia, "So go ahead."

Judge Iverson put his hand over his mouth and silently counted to fourteen.

"Are you saying that Peter Saunders did not have the expertise to offer any useful recommendations regarding design or inspection methods?"

"Your words, not mine. I'm simply stating Mr. Saunders's qualifications were not so overwhelmingly superior as to entitle him to override the nuclear physicists and engineers who designed the plant, or the Nuclear Regulatory Commission, who established the inspection regulations and safety standards."

"What are your credentials for judging Mr. Saunders's qualifications? Are you a nuclear engineer?"

"It is my responsibility to judge the qualifications of the people working under me. And no, I do not profess to be a scientist. I do know the business of running a power plant, however. I have a B.A. in business administration from NYU."

"Didn't Mr. Saunders tell you that his inspection of the high-pressure plumbing had convinced him that the welded joints should be reinspected and redesigned or, at least in some instances, repaired?"

"On countless occasions, Mrs. Ferrara."

"Thank you, Mr. Karrasch. Finally, a point on which we agree."

Lucrezia smiled. Karrasch stared back.

"And as a result of Mr. Saunders's statements to you on those countless occasions, didn't you promise that the pipes would be reinspected and redesigned or repaired as necessary?"

"I told Mr. Saunders that I would consider a review of the inspection procedures."

"You haven't answered my question, Mr. Karrasch. Didn't you promise the pipes would be reinspected and redesigned?"

"I have no recollection or record of ever making such a statement. This plant was designed by the best people in the industry and under license by the NRC. So why would I promise to redesign anything?"

"Mr. Karrasch, please. I've already cautioned you once," said the judge.

Lucrezia asked, "So why would you promise a review of the inspection procedures? Was it because you knew they were inadequate?"

"I said I would consider a review."

"And why would you consider a review of the inspection procedures if you believed they were adequate?"

Karrasch's dark irises made his narrow eyes turn entirely black. Lucrezia waited for a response.

"Have you decided what your answer is yet?"

"I just wanted to shut him up."

Lucrezia thought it was clear he meant "you too."

"Mr. Karrasch," Lucrezia continued, "let's go to your conversation with Mr. Saunders in the control room. . . ."

"There wasn't any such conversation."

Saunders stiffened. Lucrezia restrained him with a light touch.

"Did you hear Mr. Hesselmann's testimony regarding that conversation?"

"The old man can't hear. Obviously he can't see, either. I was not in the control room that morning."

"When I took your deposition, you said you could not recall any such conversation, didn't you?"

"Now I recall. There wasn't any."

"But you do recall a conversation between yourself and Mr. Saunders on the day he resigned?"

"I remember it very well. In my office."

"And do you recall Mr. Saunders telling you that an independent laboratory had determined that he had been mortally contaminated?"

"No. He never told me that."

"Just a moment, please, Mr. Karrasch." Lucrezia went quietly over to the exhibit stack.

Sam knew what was coming but he was powerless to stop it. He had reviewed the inter-office memo with Karrasch only the day before yesterday, but Karrasch had evidently forgotten. No matter what he did now, Karrasch was going to be discredited. Sam could only hope Karrasch would keep it at a minimum by admitting his mistake.

Lucrezia returned to the witness stand. "I'm handing you plaintiff's Exhibit 42. It's a Consolidated Utilities inter-office memo form. Please read it aloud for the jury."

Karrasch read, " 'Check Saunders claim Independent Biological Testing Labs L.A. reported contamination.' It's initialed 'K'."

"Isn't that 'K' for Karrasch?"

Karrasch was silent.

"Wasn't that memo initialed by you?"

Karrash started to tug at his collar, then realized how that looked.

"Is it too warm in here for you, Mr. Karrasch?"

Karrasch glared. "It looks like my initial. I just don't recall that memo."

"Didn't that memo instruct someone to verify whether Saunders's statement, that the independent report showed him to be contaminated, was true?"

"I suppose so."

"And you would not have written that memo unless Saunders had already told you Independent Biological Testing Labs had determined he had been contaminated, isn't that so?"

Karrasch gave up. He had been caught and he didn't know how to wiggle out of it. The best he could come up with was, "I don't remember."

"Mr. Karrasch, a few minutes ago you testified that you remembered your conversation with Mr. Saunders on the day he resigned very well. Is there any other part of that conversation you are no longer sure you remember?"

"I recall telling him that if he had maintained proper discipline over his foreman the excursion would never have occurred."

"Excursion? You call an accident that almost resulted in a meltdown an 'excursion'?"

"That's just a term for a reactor overheating. There was never any danger of spontaneous energetic disassembly."

Lucrezia thought she was a lot further ahead than she had hoped to be. "Spontaneous energetic disassembly?" She made sure the jury saw her disgusted disbelief. "No further questions."

Ben whispered to Sam, "Why couldn't he have just admitted that Saunders told him about the independent report? That wouldn't have hurt."

"I know. He just got flustered, and he's not used to backing down." Sam badly wanted a chance to talk to Karrasch. He hated leaving a witness so discredited over a stupid lie. "Your Honor," he said, "I could use a moment to look over my notes. Would this be a convenient time to take a recess?"

"Let's finish with Mr. Karrasch first, counsel. Do you have any questions?"

"Yes, Your Honor, just a few." *I will just have to try to lead him into admitting he made a mistake.*

"Mr. Karrasch, referring you once again to plaintiff's Exhibit 42, do you have it in front of you?"

Karrasch nodded. "Yes, I have it here." He seemed composed.

Sam willed Karrasch to understand his mistake and to rehabilitate himself. "Doesn't looking at that memo again, Exhibit 42, refresh your recollection about what Mr. Saunders said to you on the day he resigned?"

"Objection. Leading and suggestive."

"Sustained. Rephrase it, please, Mr. Corbin."

"Yes, sir." Karrasch had to get that hint. "Tell us whether Exhibit 42 refreshes your recollection about your conversation with Mr. Saunders."

"Yes, I recall now. I was right all along. Saunders never did tell me about any independent lab report that day. This memo confused me because it's undated. But I remember now. I wrote this memo after Saunders had filed this lawsuit. I wanted to check the claim made in the complaint he served on us, where it alleged that an independent lab report found him to be seriously contaminated."

Sam thought that was the lamest explanation he had ever heard, but could think of no way to undo it. "Thank you, Mr. Karrasch. No further questions."

Lucrezia didn't think she could do any better either. "Mr. Karrasch is all finished, Your Honor."

Sam and Karrasch waited until they could be inside an attorney's conference room. Neither wanted the anticipated yelling overheard.

Karrasch started. "How did they get that fucking memo anyway? That's our internal record."

"I reminded you about it two days ago. Why the hell did you think I was doing that?"

"I didn't understand they had it too. . . ."

"Jesus. That's what a subpoena is all about, Karrasch. They demand a document. We have to produce it."

"Shit. If you keep giving away inside information, you'll blow everything."

"You mean there is still more information I don't have? You're covering up, aren't you?"

"I just mean you are supposed to be defending us, goddammit. This isn't some schoolgirl game."

"How the hell do you expect me to defend you if you won't tell me the truth about what's happened? I have to know *before* you screw up on the stand, not after."

"I'll try to keep it simple. You are not supposed to be out searching for the truth, like hide and seek. You are supposed to be protecting me. Me. I represent the company. Isn't that what the fuck you're being paid for? Defending the company? Not snooping around to figure out whether we're right or wrong."

51

Sam was sure he would hear from Pringle or Morgan regarding his bout with Karrasch. Sam knew he had been downright rude, but, Jesus, the man had provoked him.

"Here are your messages," Jean said. "How did it go today?"

"Grrrr."

"Oh. Well, let me tell you about my day. First—"

Sam raised both hands. "You win."

Susan had asked Sam to help a friend of hers, Elena Espada. After hearing Susan's horror story of her professional experiences with lawyers, Elena was wary of unknown attorneys.

Elena had signed a contract to have her house sprayed with a space-age polymer finish guaranteed against fading, chipping, or peeling for life, whatever that meant. A surprise for her husband, Orlando, who was out of town, she'd said. She had paid the $1,800 down payment. The house was sprayed.

When her husband returned, he had raised hell about the price. It was just fancy paint, he said. He had forbidden her to make any of the monthly installment payments. But, she admitted, they were satisfied with the quality. It hadn't peeled, faded, or chipped.

They were being sued for the balance of $12,850, including attorney's fees, interest, late charges, and court costs.

It took Sam four telephone calls. He finally settled the Espada case for the amount of the down payment by threatening to rescind the contract on the ground that Elena had been thirteen days shy of her eighteenth birthday, technically a minor, on the day she had signed.

One hour shot to hell. Well, Susan would be grateful.

The winter sun had long since set before Sam was able to place his stockinged feet on Susan's coffee table and sip beer. He told her about the confrontation with Karrasch.

Susan scowled. "Are you in as dirty a business as it seems, or is it just that you have the dirty side of it? How can you have any faith in clients like that?"

"I have to have faith in the system even if not in the client. Doesn't the system still deserve the best I can give?"

Susan shook her head and grabbed his feet. "Hey, how about a moonlight run?"

"You're a terrific person. My stuff's in the car."

"Emily. Watch yourself for an hour," Susan said.

The grass center divider of San Vicente Boulevard was well lit, with few intersections. Although Susan had excellent form, Sam was much faster. Even on the upgrade, their pace was slow enough for Sam to repeat the reprimand Pringle had handed out before Sam left the office. Tipson, Grumm & Nuttzer attorneys do not yell at Tipson, Grumm & Nuttzer clients, Pringle said. It is a law of economics, he said.

"I understand that," Susan panted. "But those people are so rotten." She shook her head again. "I keep forgetting I work for the same company."

She allowed herself another breather as they topped the rise at Barrington.

"Oh, Elena told me how grateful she is for her settlement and how wonderful you are. You were unequivocally right there."

"What I did was take advantage of an obscure technicality to get her out of an otherwise perfectly valid agreement. Where is the good in that? You look confused."

"That's because I'm thinking."

As Sam stepped out of Susan's shower, cleaned and dried, she was at the dressing table, brushing her black hair. Sam was fascinated by the highlights. He kissed her shoulder. "As soon as I get my partnership, let's get married."

He felt her stiffen and saw the mirrored hesitation. "All right. All right. Let's just make rapturous love and fall asleep in each other's arms. I have to be up at six-thirty."

Susan's eyes softened. "Yeah, it is after ten o'clock."

52

"**M**y, it's already after ten o'clock," Ida Tucker said to her cat, Hermes, as she switched off at the conclusion of the "Barreta" rerun. She only had Hermes to talk to. Her husband, Harry, had been snoring on his Barcalounger for the past half-hour. He seemed to drift off every time he heard "and you can put that in the bank and draw interest on it."

Ida went to the hall closet for her coat and purse. It was only two blocks to the liquor store, but it would be chilly now. Her old broadcloth coat was still in excellent condition, but getting much too large. Ida had been losing weight steadily for months. She had never been heavy, but now she was down to ninety-seven pounds. She felt fine, though. The doctor kept saying things like, "When you're sixty-three, you must expect problems, Ida." Ida didn't believe that. The young fool just couldn't figure out what was wrong. She must stay well for the remainder of the trial, though. Wouldn't want to miss out on her jury duty. That poor Mr. Saunders. And that Sam Corbin was so adorable, just like Jimmy Stewart used to be.

The budget had been strained ever since Harry had been laid off at the Gallo warehouse. She missed not only his salary, but the occasional case of cream sherry. Well, they could still afford a bottle of vodka twice a week. It was cheaper than Geritol and worked equally well.

There was no one on the street. It was cold and late, but Ida had walked the familiar route every Tuesday and Friday night for years. Cross the alley, go to the corner, turn right, walk one block to Sepulveda, turn right again to the next corner. On Tuesday, they close at 11:00.

Ida shivered and her nose ran. She reached into her brown Naugahyde purse for a tissue. A giant of a man loomed out of the black alley, blocking her path. He had something pulled down over his face and carried a baseball bat. As the giant squared off and brought the bat back over his shoulder, Ida brought out her can of Mace. Ida thought he seemed to hesitate for just an instant. She sprayed him full in the face.

Stunned and retching, Sullivan stumbled back into the alley.

"Dammit, you're throwing up all over my new seatcovers," Doblonski muttered as they pulled away.

Shaken by her experience, Ida returned to her apartment. The latching door woke Harry. He saw she was wearing her coat. "What's it like out, anyway?"

"The neighborhood is going to hell." She went directly to the telephone and dialed. "Can you deliver just one bottle?"

53

"**G**ood morning, Lucrezia. This is Vanessa Armour. Isn't it a beautiful winter morning?"

Lucrezia picked a red rose from the vase on her desk. "Morning, Vanessa. I'm forced to be brusque. I have to leave for court in a few minutes."

"Of course. I'll get right to the point. We've been watching the progress of the trial closely, naturally. You're quite a way along now, and some of us were wondering when you intended to start developing the conspiracy aspects? You know, the industrial-government-complex thing."

"Vanessa, I thought we had resolved all that. There is no evidence to support a conspiracy theory."

"Lucrezia, I'm shocked to hear you say that. It's already obvious to anyone who has been listening to your presentation that Consolidated is covering up. They got the NRC to back off. The company and the FBI planted the plutonium in Gloria's house. They admit there are at least two pounds they can't account for. Lucrezia, are you aware that one pound of plutonium is enough to contaminate every single person in the world?"

"The married ones will certainly be relieved. I'm sorry, Vanessa, but none of that is evidence of conspiracy. All you have is innuendo. Believe me, if I don't buy it, the jury won't either." She held the rose close and inhaled deeply.

"Lucrezia dear, I know you're a wonderful lawyer with years and years of experience. But have you considered that perhaps you don't have the necessary social awareness to exploit the

177

conspiracy? Why don't you concentrate on the civil liability issues? We can bring in a marvelous man from the ACLU to take over the conspiracy part. He was fabulous at Wounded Knee . . .''

"No, Vanessa. Absolutely, unequivocally no. You are not slicing my case into separate pieces. Now, Peter is free to bring in Chief Big Court Mouth, or whoever the hell else he wants, but he will have to fire me first."

Tenderly, Lucrezia replaced the flower.

Sam had requested a conference in chambers with Judge Iverson. He was waiting in the corridor for Lucrezia and hoping she would be early.

"Sorry," she said, as if she weren't sorry about a damn thing.

"Were you stuck on the telephone?" Sam asked.

Lucrezia laughed. "Only the barest scratch."

Sam had not the slightest idea what she was talking about, but he enjoyed her anyway. "Let's go see the judge."

"And what new obstacle to the efficient administration of justice do you bring me this morning, counsel?" Judge Iverson turned to his court reporter. "For God's sake, don't put that down, Ava."

"Your Honor," Sam said, "based on the witnesses plaintiff's counsel has already called, we anticipate an attempt to make this trial into a nuclear power debate, and I'm requesting a ruling barring such evidence before any effort is made to expose the jury to it."

Too bad Sam couldn't have overheard the conversation I just had with Vanessa, Lucrezia thought. She said, "This is the third case Sam Corbin and I have tried against each other. He should know me well enough by now to quiet his fear about me trying to turn this into a political contest on pros and cons of nuclear power. I do insist upon putting on my entire case, however. I suggest Mr. Corbin could go a long way toward limiting evidence that could be construed as antinuclear by giving up his ridiculous position that plutonium is not ultra-hazardous."

Sam hoped his wince didn't show. Lucrezia had touched a tender spot. Sam knew as well as anyone that plutonium was one of the most lethal substances concocted by man, but he had been hobbled by explicit orders.

Contrary to Sam's advice, the late Larry Levenson, when in charge of the case, had initially taken the position that properly managed plutonium was not ultra-hazardous. To be fair to the deceased, that position had been foisted on Larry by the client. Consolidated considered it intolerably bad press to publicly admit that its nuclear power plant was in any respect less than totally safe. Sam thought it was a stupidly indefensible position, which could easily backfire if the jury thought so too.

"Your Honor," Sam said, "Lucrezia distorts our position. We merely contend that it is the plaintiff who has the burden of proving that radioactive materials, in the context of their industrial use in the Point Anacapa plant, are inherently dangerous."

"Well, I can appreciate the importance of the issue to your defense, Sam," the judge said. "I haven't seen your proposed jury instructions yet, but as I recall the law, if Lucrezia can establish that plutonium is inherently dangerous, she will be entitled to contend strict liability on the defendant. She won't have to prove that Consolidated was in any way at fault in letting the plutonium get away. As she said in her opening argument, it's their snake."

"Exactly," Lucrezia easily agreed.

"Unless, of course, the plaintiff contaminated himself with material he took from the plant without authorization." Sam was not enthralled with that argument either, but it had been forced on him when plutonium had been discovered in Peter Saunders's butter.

"On the other hand, I have to tell you," the judge continued, "that, although I understand why you take your position, I think you will have one hell of a time selling it. And by sticking with this defense, you open yourself up to all sorts of evidence about the inherent hazard of radioactive materials and nuclear reactors. And that, as I understand you, is the very thing you are asking me to limit. How can you expect to have it both ways?"

"Your Honor," Sam said, "may I bring to your attention the case of *Bromfield versus Exxon*, which was tried in your own courtroom—"

"Don't bother reminding me of that case. I remember it all

too well. Anyway, the supreme court of this state has reversed me so often I've lost all faith in their opinion. Jesus, Ava, don't put that down either. Your motion, if that's what it is, is denied without prejudice. I suggest we just deal with the issue as evidence develops."

That was probably a total bust, Sam thought, as he waited for Lucrezia's first witness of the day to be sworn. *At best, it might give me a leg up on another motion for mistrial if Lucrezia goes too far.*

54

FBI Special Agent Herbert Furness spent the rest of the morning testifying to his investigation of the anonymous allegation that two pounds of stolen plutonium 239 could be found in Peter Saunders's possession.

He had recommended the Saunders file be closed. It was his conclusion there was no substantial evidence of theft or any other criminal offense by Saunders. His supervisor had agreed.

On cross-examination Sam forced Furness to admit that, in spite of his opinion, it was possible for Saunders to have stolen the plutonium and placed it in his own refrigerator.

Yes, Furness admitted, Saunders had access to the material and the opportunity to remove it from the plant surreptitiously.

Sam hoped to imply a motive by getting Furness to confirm the existence of a black market for plutonium at a current market price of over $2,000 per ounce.

On Lucrezia's redirect examination, the FBI agent testified that only one-half gram was found in Saunders's butter, a speck compared to the missing two pounds.

Sam did not believe he netted any profit from the exchange.

The only possibility of gain for the day came from a telephone message Sam received during the recess.

"Mr. Pringle says you are to meet him and the Consolidated CEO for lunch at the Jonathan Club. He says this is for your benefit," Jean said.

What the hell is this all about? Sam wondered. *Pringle has never done anything for me yet that didn't benefit himself.*

From the courthouse to the Jonathan Club on Flower Street was only three minutes by taxi. Sam had been a guest, but had never liked the place, which was felicitous because he could not afford membership. The stark, high-ceilinged room raised the image of a cold, stone-castle dining hall. Well, the food would be good.

Sam gave his name to the eunuch at the door.

"Yes, Mr. Corbin. You're expected. This way, please."

As Sam approached, Bartlett Pringle actually stood up and put his arm around Sam's shoulder. He had never done either before. "Sam, glad you could join us. This is Randolph Champion, president of Consolidated Utilities. Randy, Sam here is our up-and-coming associate. I'm going to see that he makes partner as soon as he wins your case."

Randolph Champion was smiling, rugged, tan. A good-looking man, even without much hair. His handshake was more than firm, and apparently permanent. "Sam. Glad you could join us. What will you drink?"

"Nothing, sir. Thank you."

Champion dropped Sam's hand as if it were contagious.

"Only when I'm in trial, sir. It makes me drowsy. I'll have an extra one tonight, promise."

Champion's smile returned. "You don't have to call me 'sir.' "

Champion hadn't suggested what else to call him. Sam guessed that meant he had permission to substitute 'mister'.

Pringle and Champion ordered second martinis and rare steaks. Sam had a Cobb salad. Pringle gave him a reproachful look, but it didn't seem worth another explanation.

When the waiter brought the food, Champion asked Sam, "How does it look?"

"Pardon? Oh, our chances in trial. It's dangerous to make predictions in the midst of trial, Mr. Champion, but we've had some breaks our way. So far, I'm optimistic."

"Good, good. Bad press. We need that behind us." Champion

took a large bite of steak and chewed appreciatively. "Perfect," he said to the hovering waiter.

"I'm keeping my eye on him," Pringle said. "Sam is doing the best job possible. You may not have realized, Sam has taken over full responsibility for the case since we lost Larry Levenson."

"We'll all miss Larry," said Champion, with a heterosexual lack of enthusiasm.

"Yeah, I'll bet Whipple really misses him," snorted Pringle.

"Whipple Ewing? What does that mean?" asked Champion, suddenly interested.

"Oh, I was sure you knew. Larry and Whipple were buddies." Pringle broke out a sly grin. "I mean, bosom buddies."

"Well, Whipple's personal life is no concern of mine," said Champion stiffly. "He seems to be doing an adequate job for us."

"That's the least you can expect of any Tipson, Grumm & Nuttzer partner. But you always end up counting on us litigators, don't you?" Pringle lowered his voice to a confidential level. "You know, Randy, sometimes it's smart to talk to a litigator early, before you get sued. No one can practice preventive law better than a trial man." Pringle's voice came down another half-decibel. "You know, you might have avoided this whole Saunders mess if we had handled it right from the beginning."

There was no doubt in Sam's mind who "we" was. He wondered if Champion understood.

"Mmm. Yes," said Champion, as he trimmed away unwanted fat.

"Excuse me, gentlemen," said Sam rising, "but I'm due back in court at one-thirty."

"Oh Sam, almost forgot. We're in the process of distributing Larry's estate. As his executor, I'm supposed to give you this note." He handed Sam an ordinary business-size envelope. "Sam Corbin" was written on the face in Larry's handwriting. There didn't appear to be more than one sheet of paper in it. Sam slipped the envelope into his breast pocket as he said good-bye.

Sam was almost back in the courtroom before he figured out what luncheon had been about. The firm's distribution of profit depended on a sometimes complicated allocation between the partner bringing in the business and the one or more actually performing the work. The partner credited with getting the business always received some override, a percentage of the fees generated, even if he performed no service on that matter.

Whipple Ewing, a partner specializing in utilities law, had held the Consolidated Utilities account ever since inheriting it from his grandfather. A partner's claim to a long-standing account was rarely challenged. When it was, the executive committee resolved the dispute, deciding who was entitled to the override.

Pringle's insinuations of incompetence and homosexuality were designed to steal Consolidated Utilities away from Whipple Ewing. The greedy bastard was plotting to rob his own partner of the override.

What the hell did he need me for? Sam wondered. *Obviously I was being used, but for what?* Sam decided he was merely scenery. He added a touch of authenticity to the play.

The afternoon session was a parade of witnesses testifying to myriad defects in plant equipment, parts, and procedures discovered by Peter Saunders.

On cross-examination Sam established that each was a former Point Anacapa employee with a reason to be disgruntled.

Nevertheless, Sam had to admit the sheer volume of the occurrences was probably impressive to the jury. Undoubtedly, the day belonged in Lucrezia's column.

55

Sam was eager to return to the office. Estes Lousaire had located a new witness and was bringing him by for Sam to interview after court.

Maybe Estes finally had done something useful. Sam could accept an occasional miracle.

Sam's optimism was not long-lived. The instant Rush Hanson appraised him with those flat eyes, Sam knew in his gut the man was a liar.

"Saunders contacted me," Hanson said. "Told me he was the supervisor at the plant, something like that. Says he has something to sell I'm gonna be interested in. So I says sure. After all, that's my business, ain't it?"

"What is your business exactly, Mr. Hanson?" Sam asked.

"Surplus. I buy and sell. Could be anything."

"You don't mean stolen merchandise, do you, Mr. Hanson? You're not a fence, are you?" Sam would have bet a day's pay that was exactly what he was.

"Not if I can help it." Hanson's grin displayed unusual gaps between each visible tooth. "I'm not that stupid. The fuzz is always checking me. I get stuck once in a while with something hot, but I try to stay clean."

Sam thought that was refreshing.

"Saunders, he says, 'let's meet where we can talk,' so that's what we do. This guy has plutonium. He's got thirty ounces and he wants ten thousand dollars per for the whole package."

"Three hundred thousand dollars for all of it? Did he actually show it to you?"

"Jeez, no," Hanson said, looking at Sam as if he was a little dull. "Who's gonna walk around with plutonium in his pocket? He's gonna show it to me when I come up with a good-faith deposit. Three grand."

"Did you ask where he had obtained this material?"

"No, but shit, he'd already told me where he worked." Hanson looked at Lousaire as if to ask, "This guy's really your lawyer?" Lousaire smiled back pleasantly.

"Why did he come to you, Mr. Hanson, did he say?"

"Yeah, he says he heard I had contacts. He figured I could move the stuff."

"And what did you say?"

"I told him I'd think about it. And, to tell you the truth, I actually did. I mean it was kinda tempting, you know, like it coulda been a big score."

"But?"

"Yeah. 'But' is right. I start thinking, but this stuff is really hot." Hanson stopped long enough to determine if Sam understood his little pun. He shrugged and continued. "Then I think this isn't an ordinary bust for receiving I'm fooling with. This is a federal rap. So I pass. I tell him thank you but no thanks."

Sam asked a lot more questions. Hanson had all the answers. The times, dates, places. He was accurate about Saunders's appearance, his mannerisms, and his clothes. He even had Saunders's automobile license right. He had checked it, he said, to make sure Saunders wasn't a federal agent himself.

Hanson's story was entirely consistent and coherent. *Maybe,* Sam thought, *this time my gut just doesn't know what it's doing. Maybe lunching at the Jonathan Club was too unnatural an experience for my plebeian intestines.* Sam continued to dislike the man, but he was beginning to doubt his own instincts. Was this man just possibly believable?

And if the jury believed him? Christ. Rush Hanson could blow plaintiff's case right out of the water. Blam. The end.

Get Hanson a decent haircut. Put him in a gray pinstripe suit. Sam could sell him, he was sure of it. Wasn't that, after all, his job? Selling?

Even if he had doubts about Hanson, what he thought was not relevant. No, it was more than that. As a lawyer, he had an affirmative obligation not to judge. Judging was for juries.

"Is that it?" Sam asked. "Is that the whole story?"

"Well, yeah. Until I finally decided to call the FBI."

Sam stared.

Hanson gave him that hideous grin. "Yeah, I'm the guy who made the anonymous call. I didn't like the idea of blowing the whistle, but then I figure this guy could pulverize the entire goddamned planet."

"Mr. Hanson, are you aware the FBI has a tape of your telephone call, the exact words?"

"Well, I couldn't remember no exact words."

"Just tell me the substance of what you said and what the person answering said then."

"Maybe you better play the tape back to me first." Hanson's eyes were big, round, and sincere. "That should refresh my recollections, like they say."

Sam's gut alarm was ringing off the hook. *There's nothing wrong with my instincts. I almost let myself be conned.*

"Mr. Hanson, do you realize the FBI has voice print analysis equipment?"

"Voice print . . . what the fuck is that?"

"If you testify, they will electronically compare the pattern of your voice with the voice on their tape. No two voices make exactly the same pattern." Sam saw he was getting through. "Like fingerprints, Mr. Hanson."

Sam watched Hanson look to Lousaire for help. Lousaire smiled again. Sam saw Hanson's resignation. Lousaire was not going to be a source of inspiration.

Hanson shrugged. "I guess I better not testify I made the call, huh?"

"I guess you better not testify at all." Sam sighed. "Mr. Hanson, would you do me a favor, please? Wait out in the reception room for a few minutes."

Sam closed the office door behind Hanson and turned to Lousaire. "Where did you find this guy?"

"I don't know. Magnasunn's investigation uncovered him."

"Is there a lot more of Magnasunn's investigation I haven't heard about yet?"

"Certainly he would want to turn over anything favorable to you."

"That leaves one hell of a lot out, doesn't it?"

"I'm afraid I don't understand."

Sam tried to keep his voice down. "You don't understand Hanson is a phoney? You don't understand if we got caught creating perjured testimony it would be our asses? Jesus, man. We could both be disbarred. Don't you understand anything?"

"I had no idea. . . ."

Sam screamed and shook both fists. "*Aaaaaaaaaaah!*"

Lousaire left quickly. Sam's demeanor was shamefully un-professional.

56

What a crummy day it had been. At least the evening held promise. Sam stopped to pick up a bottle of Chardonnay for Susan and a six-pack of his favorite kind of beer. Cold.

Emily let him in. "Hi, Sam. When are you taking us sailing?"

"Kiddo, I'm working every weekend until this trial is over."

"When's that?"

"Oh, by the end of the year, I guess. Maybe even by Christmas."

"Okay, I'll wait."

Sam pinched her nose. "I appreciate that."

Sam walked into the kitchen and gave Susan the wine. She gave him back a kiss.

"I had lunch with your boss today. Ol' Randy Champion," Sam announced as he held his overflowing beer can above the sink.

Susan was impressed. She had only been in the same room with the man twice. "What's he like? Open this for me, please."

"Kind of a born politician," Sam said. "Where's the corkscrew?"

"I thought they were elected," said Emily. "It's in the dishwasher."

Sam was drafted to barbecue chicken in the backyard, while Susan and Emily made avocado salad and pasta. The early evening air was turning cold, but that felt good to him after being cooped up all day. Through the open kitchen window, Sam told about how Pringle had used him as window dressing at the luncheon and tried to steal the client from his own partner.

"That's some outfit you work for." Susan sipped her wine. "Crooks."

Then Sam told them about the phoney witness that Consolidated's general counsel had brought him.

"That's some outfit you work for, Susan." Sam toasted with his beer can. "Crooks."

"Fabulous salad," said Sam as he took a second helping. "Who's responsible?" Susan and Emily both had mouths too full to answer, but they both raised their hands.

"The thing that really burns me," Sam continued, "is that I almost got conned into suborning perjury."

"I understand perjury, but not suborning," Emily said.

"It just means procuring . . . getting someone to testify falsely. If I had been a party to putting that witness on, with the doubts I had, it would have been just as if I committed the perjury."

Sam rinsed dishes, Emily stacked the dishwasher, and Susan made coffee.

"Damn. I almost forgot. Larry's letter. Excuse me." Sam dashed off to find his discarded suit jacket. He opened the envelope and read the single typewritten page to himself, frowning. "Here, take a look." He handed the note to Susan.

To my friend, Sam Corbin,
As you well know, you started out as extremely promising, but you now
are nothing but a overripe associate attorney of thirty-five or more.
The chance of partnership in Tipson, Grumm & Nuttzer, Attorneys at
law, isin dire jepardy. After my death, which is now clearly
imminent, it is you who will undoubtedly inherit full responsibility
for handling of   Peter Saunders v. Consolidated Utilities because
it is only you who knows the case, its ramifications, strengths and
many, many weaknesses better than any one else in the firm. I'm sure
you know, this may be your absolutely last and positively without
doubt you last chance at your Tipson, Gumm & Nuttzer career, only if,
of course, that's your real desire. You, undoubtedly have more than
adequately potential to be one of the greatest trial lawyers in our
time.   Only the problem is that you have some sloppy sophomoric and
really too too romantic notions, which you should have outgrown by
now, regards some boyish scruples. You have foolishly allowed what
some might call a laudable morality to become a serious obstacle, too
very much in thee way. Certainly, I don't mean to minimize and I'm

```
not unawareof personal marital problems between yourself and Allison.
The only advice or key I have to offer you through these difficulties
is perhaps to simple  to be taken seriously at first consideration.
Regardles this is it:  There is nothing immoral  about money or
success.  It may be useful to read this over  a few times until you
really understand.  Twenty should be right.  Have a good life.


Larry
```

"Not much of a typist, was he?" Susan commented as she handed it back. "Not much of a writer either. Kind of overly wordy and pontifical. I thought you said this guy was really sharp."

"He must have been really in bad shape by the time he wrote this." Sam started to put the letter away.

"Do you mind if I borrow that and make a copy? I'd like to give it another look. Coffee's ready."

"It's yours. I'll have one cup, then I have to go. I still have an hour's work to get ready for tomorrow."

57

The Santa Monica City College auditorium was at least one-third full. Peter Saunders was gratified. This was the largest crowd he had drawn yet, clearly not entirely Mothers for Peace either. Many appeared to be students, some had every manifestation of yuppieness. Saunders smiled to himself. Maybe even an FBI man or two.

His audience had been slowly growing. He wasn't sure why. Was his message beginning to be heard? Could it be the publicity? The trial was getting coverage. Or was it merely that they wanted to see the freak, the walking, talking dead man?

He had given a variation on his standard theme. He was learning to cut it down. The maximum audience concentration period seemed to be about twenty minutes. That left plenty of time for questions.

"The nuclear-power industry is not dead," he said. "Even though future growth has been limited by reduced demand, we still have over one hundred nuclear plants operating commercially in this country.

"The nuclear-power industry is not about to die, in spite of its unpopularity. That is because demand for electrical power is again on the upswing and because we have no feasible alternative to nuclear. Yes, we have coal, oil, solar, tidal, wind, hydroelectric. None of these technologies will fulfill the demand projected within twenty years." Saunders went down the list and explained why that was.

"Nuclear power is unsafe," he said. That always restored attention. "But there are no inherent technical obstacles to resolving the safety problems. The only serious question is whether we have the political will to take the necessary actions."

There. He had done it again. It would never become easy. Standing before an audience and pulling out the first words was still torture. He could do it without notes now, though, and that helped. And he had actually enjoyed answering questions about the innovative modular, high-temperature, gas-cooled reactors. If only he could learn to enjoy his shirt sticking to his back.

"We're all going over to the Holiday Inn for drinks. Come on along." Gloria held out her hand.

"Thanks, Gloria. Not tonight, I have a date."

"At nine-forty-five? Aren't we working late?" She threw him a kiss as she left, but he knew she was hurt.

Saunders drove the short distance back to his apartment and changed into jeans, sweater, and sneakers. The Venice beach was cold and windy, but he walked rapidly, warming up. There were a few other strays and outcasts. Each kept his distance. Human contact was painful.

He still carried the anger, although it simmered and there were other feelings he had not analzyed. The anger was not directed at Lucrezia, though. He knew that was sadness. But how could he blame her for choosing life?

He felt a mass of contradictions. He needed immortality but he recognized the futility of the desire. He was desperate to justify his life. He was tired, too. He headed home. Rachel would be waiting. He knew Rachel was dead. He wasn't dreaming and he wasn't crazy, he told himself. Pretending just eased the pain. Besides, being dead didn't mean she wasn't real, did it?

58

La Fonda was only a tiny storefront restaurant at the rear of a neighborhood shopping center next to a laundromat. But the Enchiladas Mexico with sour cream was the best in West Los Angeles.

"I trust you found the wine amusing?" Cummings asked as he poured the last of the bottle.

"Hilarious," Lucrezia said, finishing off her Hearty Burgundy. "But we should head home. I still have to go over my notes for tomorrow's first witness."

Cummings took her hand. "You can get up half an hour early and review your notes. Let me stay over tonight, my love. I need you."

"Where are you supposed to be tonight, Congressman?"

"Fresno, but no one could be expected to really spend the night there."

He paid the check and introduced himself to the entire staff, shaking hands all around. His tip assured everyone's vote. Lucrezia shook her head, smiling. He insisted upon going where they would not be recognized, but could not stand being overlooked.

Cummings held the restaurant door open. "Let's take your car. . . ."

Lucrezia laughed. "I know. It's fun to drive." She could make herself tolerate the deception for a little longer. Paul's wife was recovering rapidly now. Soon, they would be openly together. Meanwhile, she did love to be needed.

"Tell me, will we feel like this when we're married?" The Lincoln's center console armrest prevented her from snuggling as close as she would like.

"Can you still doubt how much I love you? Very soon I'll prove it. The way Barbara is coming along, I'm confident I'll be able to leave by the first of the year, possibly even by Christmas. Wouldn't that be some happy holiday?"

"Paul, wouldn't that be unnecessarily cruel?"

"She has her whole family for Christmas. I'm traditionally in the way."

As they turned into Lucrezia's driveway, Cummings saw the parked white Nissan coupe. "Who—"

"It's Molly's. Must be something serious." Lucrezia hurried into the house.

Molly ran to meet her. "Oh, you're home. Carmen let me in before she left. Hello, Congressman."

Lucrezia looked at Molly's eyes. "You've been crying. What is it?"

"Oh, Lucrezia." Molly hugged her as she struggled to hold back tears. Lucrezia could feel Molly's chest heaving against her own.

Lucrezia gently pushed her back but continued to hold her shoulders. "Molly dear. You must tell me."

"Innes Balintin. Oh Lucrezia." Molly swallowed. "He shot his wife, his son, and the butcher. His son and the butcher are dead. His wife may make it."

Lucrezia's hand went to her mouth as she sagged. Cummings caught her and guided her to a couch.

"What?" Lucrezia had to know. "What happened?"

"Balintin says his wife was having an affair with the butcher. Claims he's been shadowing them sneaking around town for a week."

"Then that mousy little woman really was—"

"Lucrezia, the butcher just moved down from Bakersfield.

This was his first day."

"I feel sick." Lucrezia rushed into the powder room.

"Molly, when did this happen?" Cummings asked.

"Two to three hours ago."

"Damn. Media people will be swarming all over this place before morning. I guess I'd better call a cab."

"The driver might recognize you. Take my Nissan. You can leave it at the office in the stall next to Lucrezia's." Molly dug for the keys. "Here."

Lucrezia came out of the powder room carrying her shoes. She sank back onto the same couch.

Molly explained about lending Paul her car. Lucrezia tried to make a joke about it being fun to drive, but nothing came out.

Molly brought her a snifter of brandy. Lucrezia gratefully emptied it in one gulp.

She held out the glass. "More."

Molly took the glass. "No. You have to be in shape for court tomorrow." Molly put down the glass and took Lucrezia's hands. "Come, I'll help you get ready for bed."

"I can't sleep."

"I know, but you'll get some rest. We can talk if you want to, but you're going to lie down."

Lucrezia was in her white silk pajamas, sitting in bed, resting her head on her knees, when the tears finally came. "Molly, Molly. God. What have I done?"

Molly leaned over to hug Lucrezia's back. "It's not your fault. How could you know?"

Every time Lucrezia closed her eyes that beautiful, smiling boy shook her hand and said, "It's nice to have met you."

It's not my fault, kid. Sure, I turned your father loose to kill you, and an innocent stranger, too. Maybe even your mother.

But how could I know? How could I know that looney thinks every male in sight is making it with his wife? No, not merely thinks. He is utterly, completely convinced he is right. He is righteous, he is just. He is justified. Just like me. Like Sam, too. Even just like Consolidated Utilities?

I was so convinced I was doing a good thing. But, God forgive me, I was so wrong. How dangerous for a lawyer to judge the truth.

59

As soon as Sam saw Lucrezia, he knew what her problem was. All the morning news programs had the Balintin story. Of course, Lucrezia was named as the prominent criminal attorney who had managed, or engineered, or manipulated the maniac's release, depending on whether channel two, four, or seven was tuned in. KWLA carried an editorial advocating a bar against probation of defendants with known criminal tendencies.

Except for puffy eyes, Lucrezia looked striking as usual. Only her distracted air was new.

Sam came over to her end of the counsel table, offering his hand. "Lucrezia, you must not blame yourself."

She accepted and tried to smile. "Of course not. Neither one of us should."

Me? What the hell is she talking about?, Sam wondered. *I guess she means for what I'm doing to Peter Saunders. How can she be so damn cocksure what's right or wrong after Balintin? Damn her, I'm only doing my job. She knows that.*

The poor woman really is in shock. He caught himself hoping she made it through the day. Shouldn't he be wishing for a nervous breakdown? Thinking about Lucrezia Ferrara was confusing.

Judge Iverson climbed laboriously to the bench and studied her. "Mrs. Ferrara, are you ready to call your next witness?" He did not look too sure.

Sam watched her back straighten. Her chin lifted another fraction of an inch. "Yes, Your Honor. Thank you."

Sam wanted to walk over to the other end of the counsel table and hold her.

The next witness's credentials were as solid as his maroon tie and as impeccable as his white chambray shirt. Dr. Arnold Vandewalter. UCLA Associate Professor of Nuclear Medicine. Presidential Commission on Probabilistic Risk Assessment. Medical consultant to Department of Energy.

"Doctor, do you have a medical specialty?" Lucrezia asked.

"Two, actually. Oncology and cardio-pulmonary surgery." The witness smiled modestly. He glowed benevolence.

Sam's envy was unconditional. The man could not be more than a year or two older than himself. Undoubtedly, he also played first cello for the Los Angeles Philharmonic and was happily married to a movie star.

"Do you suppose he could be persuaded to adopt me?" Ben whispered.

"You're too ugly," Sam replied.

"He could fix that."

"Doctor," Lucrezia asked, "what diagnosis have you made of Mr. Saunders's condition?"

"The patient is suffering from undifferentiated small cell carcinoma with distant metastases—"

"Doctor, please," Lucrezia interrupted. "Just a moment." *Did the man think he was addressing the Union of Concerned Scientists?* She realized his language was cloaked in nervousness. Not unusual, even with the most sophisticated witness. But she had to make him talk to the jury in standard English. "What do you mean by undifferentiated?"

"A particular case can be classified as either a squamous cell carcinoma, adenocarcinoma, an undifferentiated—"

Lucrezia groaned audibly. "Doctor, do you think you could possibly put it in terms a Los Angeles lawyer might understand?"

When the jury laughed, that inexplicitly seemed to relax the doctor. "Oh, I see. I simply mean he has one of four main types of lung cancer, with metastasis."

Lucrezia wanted to pat him on the head. "Thank you, Doctor. Now, what does metastasis mean?"

"Metastasis is the process by which secondary deposits of tumors develop in organs distant from their original site.

Explicitly, in this patient's case, by the time of diagnosis, the tumor in the lung had already metastasized into the lymphatic system. These secondary tumors are the usual cause of death of most cancer patients."

The doctor described the primary tumor as a piling up of abnormal cells in the lung, gradually becoming a warty outgrowth eroding through the lining of the bronchial tree. He illustrated with vividly colored charts and a full-scale plastic model of the respiratory system complete with mucus.

Saunders was grim-faced. Eleven jurors were fascinated. One wouldn't even look.

"Doctor, can you describe the tests done to absolutely confirm this diagnosis?"

"Of course." Vandewalter started with pulmonary cytology and concluded with the flexible fiber-optic bronchoscopy.

Under local anesthesia, he explained, a flexible tube with lighting-magnifying devices and a small biopsy forceps was inserted through a nostril, then slowly advanced down the throat, into the trachea, and, finally, into the segmental bronchi in the lung's periphery. Only a tiny specimen of the abnormal area had been taken for biopsy. Saunders had hardly coughed any blood at all.

Lucrezia glanced at Saunders. This evidence was essential to an adequate verdict. She had warned him it was coming. He was pale, but nodded for her to proceed.

"Tell us, Doctor, what symptoms may Mr. Saunders be expected to develop as this disease progresses?"

"The symptoms are myriad and Mr. Saunders will by no means be expected to display all of these, but—"

"Move to strike, Your Honor." Sam stood. "The witness should be limited to listing only those symptoms he believes with reasonable medical certainty will be contracted by Mr. Saunders. It is irrelevant and prejudicial to catalogue every possible symptom that might hypothetically be experienced."

Lucrezia rose to respond but Judge Iverson waved her back. "Overruled."

Vandewalter's list seemed interminable. Fatigue due to anemia. External bleeding. The mucous membranes of the upper respiratory tract are especially vulnerable, he said. Alopecia, or sudden loss of hair, is a common side effect of therapy.

Chemotherapy also lowers the blood count, which leaves patients susceptible to infection. Loss of appetite is common, and the resulting protein malnutrition can cause sores in the soft tissues within the mouth. Many patients experience nausea and vomiting as a side effect of the chemotherapy. Pain can be chronic in about half the cases, in large part because of metastasis to bone.

Saunders whispered to Lucrezia that he would wait in the hall. Sam watched jurors' compassionate eyes follow him out.

Vandewalter described the almost inevitable shortness of breath, pleural effusion, chronic coughing, weight loss, skin reactions, taste alterations, constipation, and diarrhea.

He said metastasis to the central nervous system and brain is common. Headaches, blurred vision, dizziness, confusion, loss of muscle function, and convulsions are frequent early symptoms.

"Is any surgery or other treatment available to help Mr. Saunders?"

"Surgery is of no help to patients with spread of cancer to distant organs or lymph nodes. The treatment of choice is chemotherapy. Combination therapy consisting of three or four drugs on a trial basis to determine patient response is standard. Palliative radiation may be considered later, only to relieve symptoms."

He listed the pain-killing drugs from analgesics to narcotics and described the tedious rehabilitation that would be required to overcome lung scarring caused by chemotherapy.

"Doctor, what is the probable course of Mr. Saunders' disease?"

"Even with improved medical techniques lung cancer remains one of the most deadly of cancers. We can prolong life expectancy in 30 to 40 percent of patients. Complete remission rates of 75 percent have been reported for patients with limited small cell cancer. The duration of remission varies, but up to 32 percent live for more than thirty months. In this disease, long-term survival is defined as three or more years."

"Is there any cure?"

"Unfortunately, no. The survival rate remains low. Only 9 percent of patients with lung cancer are alive five years after the first appearance of symptoms."

"Do you have an opinion as to the cause of Mr. Saunders's lung cancer?"

"Yes. The mutagenic alteration undergone by the insulted cells—"

Lucrezia interrupted wearily. "Doctor, please."

"Oh, yes. Sorry. Based on the patient's history of inhalation of six nanocuries of radiation in an industrial accident, it is my medical opinion that was when and how the process that causes cancer began."

Lucrezia thought she had better end it while Vandewalter remained under control. There was little more to gain. "Thank you, Doctor. No further questions."

60

Sam thought Vandewalter was more than a little pompous, but nevertheless effective. Cross-examination must somehow tarnish that saintly image.

"You've testified that you are familiar with Mr. Saunders's history. You know then that he served for seventeen years in the nuclear submarine branch of the navy?

"You're aware that during his navy service Mr. Saunders was engaged in early experimental nuclear reactor projects?

"It's fair to say, isn't it, that during those years of navy service the dangers of radioactive contamination were not as well known as today?

"It's also accurate to say, isn't it, safety standards and precautions were not as stringent as currently?

"Mr. Saunders's history also indicates he was a moderately heavy cigarette smoker for almost twenty years, doesn't it?"

To all Sam's questions, Dr. Vandewalter could only answer, "Yes."

"Isn't it established, Doctor, that smoking is the leading cause of lung cancer?

"There is ample medical evidence that other carcinogens, such as asbestos insulation or charcoal broiled steaks, cause lung cancer, correct?

"There is also a scientific basis for the conclusion that lung cancer can be caused by genetic factors, isn't that right?

"There is even respectable evidence that lung cancer can be the result of nothing more than the aging process, isn't that right?"

Dr. Vandewalter had to admit all that was, indeed, right.

"And couldn't any one of those factors in Mr. Saunders's history have been the cause of his alleged lung cancer?"

"Yes, they could have been, but, in my professional medical opinion, they were not. The probable cause was the excessive contamination he suffered in the plant accident."

Win some, lose some. Sam thought he might do better on another tack.

"Doctor, in concluding that Mr. Saunders was subjected to six nanocuries of radiation in the plant accident, you have relied entirely upon the blood tests and other body counts performed on the plaintiff by Independent Biological Testing Laboratories, is that right?"

"They have an excellent reputation for reliability and accuracy."

"Move to strike the answer as nonresponsive."

"Sustained," ruled the judge. "The jury will disregard it."

"Weren't you aware the plaintiff was also tested for radiation by the Consolidated Utilities Lab, which reached inconsistent results?"

"Of course. I assume that is why he consulted Independent Biological Testing Laboratories."

Sam could have objected to that response, too, but let it pass. "You have never reviewed Consolidated's lab report, have you?"

"No, I saw no reason to."

Maybe he only plays second cello, Sam thought. "And you personally have attempted no determination of which of the two inconsistent reports is the more accurate, have you?"

"No, but I would be inclined to accept Independent's report."

"But if Consolidated's report turned out to be more accurate, that would change your opinion of the cause of Mr. Saunders's alleged cancer, wouldn't it?"

"I suppose it could."

"The foundation of your opinion is the assumption that Mr. Saunders has taken in at least six nanocuries of radioactive substance, isn't that so?"

"No, my opinion would remain the same even if the amount ingested were shown to be substantially less than that."

"Don't you agree, Doctor, that the question is still open as to how much plutonium exposure is required to induce cancer?"

"The precise threshold dosage has not been determined, if that's what you are getting at."

"You mean the amount below which cancer would not be caused?"

"Exactly."

"So you don't know how much plutonium you can take in without causing cancer, do you?"

"No, not the precise amount."

"And you don't know how much radiation is required to cause lung cancer, do you?"

"Nobody knows."

Sam liked that. "Nobody knows. And even the highest amount you've assumed Saunders might have taken in the accident is still way, way below the safe dosage prescribed by NRC regulations, isn't that a fact?"

"Yes, that is a fact. However—"

Sam did not think he could improve on that. "I think you've answered my question. Thank you, Doctor."

Lucrezia thought she might regain a few points with redirect examination. She could at least make a credible case that the Nuclear Regulatory Commission safety standards of permissible radiation levels were not adequate.

Vandewalter testified, "The NRC regulations provide that forty nanocuries of whole body or sixteen nanocuries of lung radiation is a safe dosage. These levels are based upon old Atomic Energy Commission standards issued almost two decades ago when sixteen nanocuries was about as little as we could measure with the instruments available. Today, many facilities can measure down to one nanocurie in human tissue."

"And since we now have the ability to measure smaller amounts of radiation, what is the permissible level?"

"It is meaningless to talk about any safe or permissible level of radiation. Any level increases the risk of cancer, even though we cannot precisely measure the risk. Therefore, the only scientifically justifiable conclusion is to assume that no amount is safe."

"Why then, Doctor, do the existing regulations specify these dosages to be safe?"

"In my opinion, the regulations are based upon political and economic considerations, not medical or scientific ones."

"Could you expand on that, please, Doctor?"

"What I mean is the industry and the government have simply concluded that a certain level of cancer in San Luis Obispo County is acceptable in order to deliver two thousand megawatts of power to Los Angeles."

Sam could see surprise, distress, and shock registered on jurors' faces. He was on his feet, objecting. "No basis in the evidence. Not within the scope of expert medical opinion. Inflammatory prejudicial propaganda." *Jesus.* With one sentence Vandewalter had devastated the defense. If the jury believed there had been a cynical disregard of public health and safety they would disregard everything Sam had so painstakingly established.

Judge Iverson granted his motion to strike and admonished the jury to disregard the statement, but Sam knew you cannot unring a bell.

After court, Molly drove the silver Mark VII back to the office as Lucrezia gratefully slumped in the passenger seat and struggled with the six-way control for a comfortable position.

As Molly pulled into Lucrezia's parking place, she noted that her white Nissan had been parked in the adjacent stall.

Upstairs, Molly brought tea, moved the daisies over, and placed the cup on Lucrezia's desk.

Lucrezia nodded thanks while continuing to talk on the telephone. "Thank you, Paul, that's sweet of you, but not this evening. I'm drained. Yes, I think I'll sleep tonight. Tomorrow then. Love you too."

Molly went through the agenda, selecting only that which was urgent. "Telephone messages," she said. "There is only one you have to deal with now." Molly cleared her throat. "Innes Balintin wants you to represent him."

Lucrezia shrieked, splattering tea over her gray cashmere sweater. "God, he must be out of his mind!"

As she realized what she had said, Lucrezia closed her eyes and laid her head on the desk.

61

"**D**o you think it's too cold to walk back to the office?" Sam asked.

"Let's do it. It will feel good," Ben replied. "I thought you did a really effective job on Vandewalter."

"Thanks. I'm not as sure as you are, though. He administered heavy damage."

As Sam closed the door to his tiny office behind himself he could not help but notice that Bradley Dillingham was seated at his desk. Sam thought, *I must have been fired.*

"I thought yours would be empty. The day sheet says you're in trial all day," said the recently named partner. "I hope you don't mind."

"Of course not," said Sam. *Not much I don't.* "I am curious, though. What's wrong with your office, Mr. Dillingham?"

"Call me Brad, please, at least when we're alone. After all, you're practically already a partner." Dillingham's voice shook. "Sam, I'm in hiding from the switchboard. But, Jesus, I've got to talk to someone. I can't talk to a partner. I can't talk to my wife. She would love to have something on me. Can I talk to you, Sam? It's all right if I call you Sam, isn't it? We were practically classmates, weren't we? Can I talk to you?"

"Sure, Brad." Actually Dillingham had been a year ahead of Sam in law school even though he was two years younger. Sam did not recall that they had ever even said hello. He dumped both briefcases on the floor and himself into the only other chair. "Only what the hell is it we are talking about?"

"Sam, I'm in trouble. I'm in big trouble. I can't talk to a partner. I can't talk to my wife . . ."

It took fifteen minutes for Sam to get just the first part of it. One of Dillingham's clients was Tectonico, a major real estate development company run by his brother-in-law.

"You know," Dillingham rambled, "Tectonico, 'Building a Better California.' " Dillingham's family owned 12 percent of the stock. That was how he brought in the account.

Last month, he had persuaded Tectonico to put up $200,000 to expedite a controversial hotel and condominium development through the Santa Barbara County bureaucracy and the Coastal Commission.

"Only, Sam, I didn't pay out any bribes to anybody. I was confident I could ram it through on my own. Well, with some help from . . ." Dillingham stopped and whispered the name into Sam's ear. "Only he couldn't even get himself re-elected. The bum. It's all fallen through. The permits are being denied. And now the client wants reports and accounting and receipts. Sam, what the hell am I going to do?" He jabbed one of Sam's pencils against a legal pad until the point broke.

"How much have you paid to . . ." Sam didn't think he was supposed to say the name out loud and didn't feel like whispering. "You know."

"The bum? Why, nothing yet. I've been stalling him off. Sam, you simply can't trust these people with payment up front."

"Well, fine, then. Just give it back. You can have accounting call it an overcharge due to computer error. Tectonico is not going to publicly scream that you failed to get their bribes accepted."

"Sam, you still don't understand. It's not Tectonico that scares me. I can handle whatever they come up with. I've got all that covered." Dillingham lowered his voice again. "I never turned the money in to the firm."

Oh. Dillingham was right. Sam had not understood.

It was not the theft from his own client, his family, or his accessory that concerned the young partner. He had all that covered. It was being caught not sharing the loot with the firm that terrified him.

"Right. Then turn it over to the firm now. You can dream up some excuse for the delay."

"Sam, I don't have it. You know what happened to the market in October. I dropped almost half of it there. Christ, in one day. Who could factor in that? I had almost all of it in Tri-Counties common. On margin with options. Another thirty-point jump and I would have controlled enough Tri-Counties to grab their legal account away from O'Malley and Byers. That would have increased my gross billings by as much as five mil. That's how you get someplace with this—"

"How much is left?"

"Left? The rest went into payments on the vineyard, except of course, the fifty-eight thousand for the Mercedes. I can't part with the Mercedes. Especially right now. It's my lifeline to reality."

"You spent fifty-eight thousand for a Mercedes?"

"Sam, that is an investment in my professional future. I'm not certain you appreciate the significance of image. Think about it, Sam. Success, performance—"

"Honesty. Brad, I'm trying to help you."

"Say, you wouldn't know where I could borrow two hundred thousand dollars, would you? I'd pay top interest and a finder's fee." He reached for another pencil and jabbed the point off.

Sam did not bother to answer. He reached over the desk and moved his pencil cup out of Dillingham's reach. "Brad, go out and get a little drunk. At least it will relax you."

"I don't drink, I don't smoke, and I don't do drugs. Nobody needs that kind of trouble."

"Brad, go for a drive then. I'll try to think of something useful for you, I really will, but first I've got urgent work to crank out, and, if you don't mind . . ." Sam nodded at his desk.

"The executive committee is going to skin me alive, you know." Dillingham stood. "I always do feel better in the Mer-cedes. I think better, too. Maybe if I drive around I'll think of a way out." He offered Sam his hand. "Sam, I really appreciate this, finally having someone to talk to I can trust." Doubt crossed his face. "Sam, I can count on you to keep this confidential, can't I?"

Sam shook his hand. "Sure, Brad. We'll talk again tomorrow."

Sam had no idea what he could do to help. He was appalled at Dillingham's twisted response to the pressure for bringing in new business. The dumb bastard had actually stolen from his client and his own firm for the purpose of advancing his professional career. Sam thought that had to be on the leading edge of perversion.

It was not until Dillingham left that Sam realized the significance of what he had promised, to keep a partner's embezzlement secret from the firm.

Jesus, this could jeopardize my own partnership. The executive committee would have no hesitation in deciding where Sam's loyalty and obligation lay. Two would be just as easy to skin as one.

62

Two hours and an equal number of beers later, Sam tried to grasp the edge of Susan's coffee table with his bare toes. "Well?" he asked.

"You shouldn't have promised, of course, although I can easily understand your doing it. Pass me that scissors on the table, will you?"

Susan was sitting cross-legged on the floor, fashioning Christmas tree ornaments out of foil, ribbon, gingerbread men, and unrecognizable objects.

Sam's toes grappled with the scissors, his leg swung it over, cranelike, to drop into Susan's outstretched hand.

"Thank you. It sounds as if his family has money. Why don't you persuade him to get the two hundred thousand from them, turn it over to the firm or back to the client, and make a full disclosure?"

"Yeah, if he came forward voluntarily, they would probably just let him quietly resign. At least he would be spared public disgrace. Not bad, Susan. I could use a clever wife."

Before the words were even out Sam felt like kicking himself. He had not intended another serious proposal, just a lame joke.

She looked up from her work and gave him a serious inspection. "At least you're not a thief."

Every time she heard any word related to marriage, Susan shied away. Sam smiled, but resolved not to raise the subject again until some hint of encouragement.

The door bell chimed.

Sam's back was to the front door. He heard Susan open it, say "hello," then stop abruptly.

The silence made him curious enough to turn.

Susan was saying, "You'd better come in," stepping aside and opening the door wider.

The blond young man in the neatly pressed, three-piece, blue, chalk-stripe suit stopped short when he sighted Sam. His face was a contradiction, self-assurance and uncertainty.

He pushed gold-framed, aviator-style glasses back to the bridge of his nose with his left hand and offered the other to Sam. "I'm Everett Schooling."

Sam stood up. Even barefooted, he was four inches taller.

Susan shook off her surprise. "Oh. This is Sam . . . my friend, Sam Corbin. Sam, this is Everett, my—"

"Former husband," Everett supplied.

Sam tried to smile. "Somehow I guessed."

Everyone stood, hesitant.

Everett turned to Susan. "I would like to talk to you," he said.

"Why didn't you . . . you know, call first?"

"I wasn't sure you would talk to me if I did."

Sam looked carefully at Susan. She wasn't frightened, just lost. He had never seen that in her before. It could not last.

Sam gathered up his shoes, socks, tie, and jacket. "I don't think this is any of my business."

Everett said nothing. Susan looked grateful. "Thank you, Sam. I'll talk to you later. Excuse me. I'll go get Emily."

She hurried from the room.

Everett followed Sam to the front door. "I'm going to steal her back, you know." Self-assurance had prevailed.

Sam threw his clothes into the MGB and climbed in after them. *Jesus, I've another thief on my hands.*

Inside the house, Emily was introduced to her father. She had no memory of him. Susan had taken her away when she was six months old.

Emily was polite, but aloof. She answered questions directly, but expressed no curiosity. Sitting on the floor next to Susan, she silently assisted in the manufacture of tree ornaments.

Susan was aware that Emily's presence made Everett uncomfortable. Obviously, he would have preferred to talk to Susan alone, but dammit, the child was entitled to know what was going on. Besides, Susan barely admitted to herself, there was some pleasure in his discomfort.

"Dad and I own the bank now. Fifty-one percent of it, anyway. He's retired, of course, although he's still on the board. I've been president for almost two years now."

Susan had little interest in the bank and less in Everett's father. "You seem so different from what I remember."

"I guess. The spectacles. A little myopia. And I wasn't wearing suits. Probably gained about fifteen pounds, too."

"I mean the way you act. You don't have . . . I don't sense the old . . . hostility."

That seemed to embarrass him. "The bank is doing good things, Susan. It isn't just a business like you might think. We have the lowest agricultural foreclosure rate in the district, lowest delinquencies too. We've helped make Emmet County into one of the strongest farming communities in the entire state of Iowa."

Well, thought Susan, *let me guess. He's attending a bankers' convention at the Century Plaza. Now that he's respectable, he feels remorse, and he wants to make up. He's going to invite us out for Chinese dinner with him and his wife.*

"Susan, the town's ready to grow, too. With the right financing and planning, we can make Estherville into the biggest little city between Minneapolis and Des Moines. Susan, do you hear what I'm saying?"

He wants to offer me a job in urban planning? Naa. "Everett, I hear you, but I don't have the slightest idea what you're talking about. Why are you here? Why are you telling me all this?"

"Susan, I want you back. I want to marry you again."

Susan's scissors slowed, stopped.

"Do I get a vote?" Emily asked.

"No," Everett and Susan chorused.

"Excuse me. I have homework." Emily left the living room.

"Susan, please. Hear me out. I was spoiled rotten. Arrogant. I know that now. I hurt you badly. I'm sorry for how you were treated by me and everyone else. But I'm not the same person. I grew up. Susan, I've been remarried. That lasted six months. You are the only one I ever cared about."

"Everett, I have a life too. You can't just—"

"Please. I'm not foolish. I realize I can't just walk in here and sweep you off your feet. I only ask you to listen and think about it. Okay?"

Susan realized how wound up he was. "Okay, Everett. I'm listening."

"I own four acres at the top of Half Mile Hill. You can see the courthouse, the library, everything. You could design our house. Whatever you want. I have the money. There's a syndication I'm working on for a shopping center on the south side. We're going to expand the junior college. I'm on the board of trustees. All that will need an architect too. Susan, there isn't one in the whole county. You can be your own boss. You'll have more business than you can handle."

"You're spewing all this out faster than a machine gun. . . ."

"All right. I know, I know. One more thing, then I'll leave you to think about it. I'm Emily's father. Okay, she's not too thrilled about it tonight, but she is my daughter too."

He leaned over to kiss her on the forehead, but stopped. "You cared about me too once. Think about it. I'll call you tomorrow. I'm staying at the Century Plaza."

Well, at least she got the name of the hotel right, she thought. After he left, Susan stayed on the floor, toying with tinsel and gingerbread men.

Who the hell did he think he was, waltzing unannounced into her life? Not even a goddamned telephone call. She didn't need that kind of melodrama.

Offering her the Frank Lloyd Wrightship of northern Iowa. Her, the next vice-president for planning, Consolidated Utilities of California. That would make her a pretty big fish in an awfully large pond. She would be on the leading edge of urban planning, not fooling around with junior college buildings, shopping centers, and country houses. Not that those projects couldn't be satisfying too, for someone who was interested. The freedom they offered. The opportunity to do her totally own thing.

And give up Southern California? Never. The climate, deserts, mountains, ocean. Take Emily to be raised in a strange land far from friends and everything familiar? For what? Green rolling hills over black soil so rich whatever you dropped grew on the spot. Pure fresh lakes you could fish and swim in the summer and skate in the winter. People who said "Good morning" and stopped to talk on the street.

Did he really think she would take up with him? After ten years of methodically cutting him up and throwing away piece after piece? The man who raped her. The man who helped drive her from her home . . . who gave her Emily. A man who was so changed from the one she knew. A serious man . . . who wanted to be a father to his daughter.

And was she supposed to just walk away from Sam? Sweet, bright, funny man. So he was being stripped bare in a divorce action. So his future with that law firm was precarious. They were all criminals there anyway. Unprincipled, ruthless con men. How could he aspire to be a part of that? Could she ever be married to a man who was?

Emily came out. "Mom, I'm going to bed. You're not even thinking about going back, are you?"

"Foolish girl. How on earth could you come up with a silly idea like that?"

63

As Sam drove home, he was plagued by images of Everett chaining Susan to a Victorian bedpost, inside a deserted farm-house, somewhere in Iowa. How on earth did he come up with such silly ideas?

He knew Susan was not about to pay the slightest attention to the man's pitch, whatever that was. She might not end up being Sam's, but she sure as hell would never be Everett's. Susan had put in too many years scrubbing the residue of that man out of every corner of her mind. *Right? Right.*

Sam pulled into the parking lot of the all-night convenience store on Santa Monica and Melrose boulevards. Inside, he selected a six-pack of Millers and a package of donuts. He figured no matter how serious his problems, a man needs nutrition.

Sam checked out his purchases and was heading back to the car. He turned when he heard his name called.

"Sam Corbin, I thought that was you. Bill Paulsen. Remember?"

At first Sam didn't remember at all. Paulsen was so shrunken and twisted with arthritis he didn't resemble the man Sam had met in a courtroom two years earlier.

The throttle linkage on Paulsen's two-week-old pickup truck had jammed open as he passed another vehicle. Paulsen had been wrapped around a steel lamppost, breaking bones Sam hadn't known existed.

Paulsen had filed suit against the truck dealer and manufacturer. Sam was retained to defend by their insurance company.

Paulsen's lawyer was uniquely incompetent. He hadn't even taken advantage of the distinction between negligence and breach of warranty. Sam had walked all over him.

With Paulsen's massive injuries, medical expenses, and loss of earnings, he should have been awarded at least half a million. But he hobbled out of that courtroom with a judgment against him for the defendant's court costs.

The claims supervisor was so impressed, he had given Sam and Allison an all-expense-paid week in Puerto Vallarta.

"Of course I remember, Mr. Paulsen. How are you doing?"

"Still running the garage. It gets a little tougher as I get older, though."

A little tougher? Jesus, the man was not even fifty and he could hardly move. "I'm sorry about that, Mr. Paulsen. I don't feel good about what happened to you in that case."

"Hell, you were just doing your job. I should have hired a better lawyer. Merry Christmas to you." Paulsen waved, and limped into the night.

Sam watched him go. *He sure as hell should have hired a better lawyer. I beat him down mercilessly. For what? To strengthen the quarterly statement of an insurance company?*

Sam recalled his final argument. "Of course, we are all sorry for Mr. Paulsen's injuries, but if he had just exercised reasonable care in the operation of his vehicle, as I've shown he could, this accident would never have happened. Mr. Paulsen will be returning to work soon, a wiser man for this unfortunate experience, but that isn't what he wants. He wants you to make him rich so he'll never have to go back to work. He wants the money."

A year after the trial, the manufacturer had recalled all forty-three thousand of Paulsen's truck model, replacing the defective linkages. Sam hoped Paulsen had never learned that.

What would Peter Saunders look like in a year?

64

Ingersoll Rawson addressed his fellow senior partners with understandable pride. "I have developed a formula for accurately projecting the annual net income per partner, NIPP."

The rest of the executive committee paid devout attention. Partners' income, gross or net, always deserved close interest.

Rawson approached the easel, marking pen in hand. "First, let me define the components."

"Somebody open the drapes a little so we can see."

Rawson wrote as he spoke. "NIPP, as I said, stands for net income per partner.

"L is for leverage, the ratio of associate attorneys, in other words, non-partner professionals, to partners.

"U stands for utilization, the weighted average chargeable hours per professional per year.

"BR is billing rate, the weighted average standard rate per hour.

"R is for realization, the percentage of time worked on client projects, valued at standard rates, of course, actually billed and collected.

"M is for margin, the ratio of net income to gross fees."

Rawson paused. "Are there any questions?"

The other senior partners tried not to show their annoyance. Why would there be any questions?

"All right," Rawson said, flipping to a blank sheet and writing rapidly. "The formula I have derived is:

"NIPP = $(I+L)(U)(BR)(R)(M)$."

The partners nodded appreciatively.

" 'I' is , of course . . ." one started to suggest.

"Yes, income," Rawson said.

"Admirable," said Bartlett Pringle. "And, please, do not misconstrue what I am about to say as in any way demeaning your accomplishment. Your formula is, as far as it goes, unimpeachable. However, it does point out what I am convinced is a serious flaw in our fiscal policy."

"Those are harsh words, Bartlett," said Rawson.

"Not at all, Sol. You've done the firm a great service by directing attention to this weakness."

"What weakness, for Christ's sake?" asked Morgan impatiently. He did not care much for even a suggestion of weakness.

"It is implicit in Sol's formula that rainmaking is a key to increased income. The more new business that is brought in, the more associates we can keep occupied, the more leverage we achieve, the more NIPP."

"Obviously," said Morgan.

"Obviously," agreed Pringle. "What is being overlooked, and could ultimately be fatal, is quality of product. Many clients perceive that we, not just us, but all lawyers have a license to steal . . ."

"Bartlett, please. That sort of gutter talk is not appropriate to an executive committee meeting."

"I am merely drawing your attention to a common perception, not vouching for its validity." Pringle continued. "In spite of such perception, clients continue to be willing to pay us substantial rates. And our clients are typically sophisticated business people. Now by substantial rates, I mean those rates considerably above the median fees charged by the legal profession generally."

"I hope you are not equating Tipson, Grumm & Nuttzer to the rest of the legal profession."

"Of course not. And neither do our clients. That is the point. They pay us higher fees because they believe they receive a quality of service from us they cannot get from the typical firm."

"And they do. We hire only the cream of each graduating class of the top universities. From the best families, men with invaluable contacts. We get them because we offer the largest salaries. We can afford that only because we charge high fees."

Pringle nodded. "That has traditionally been so, and still is. I simply want you to realize that continued quality of service, or product if you prefer, is the foundation of our success. This accelerated pressure for additional rainmaking cannot be allowed to continue at the expense of quality. I'm not talking about anything so naive as morality or fair value. I'm talking hard business survival tactics. If clients ever begin to suspect they can buy identical service elsewhere at half the price, that will be the beginning of our end. Hardboiled, ruthless talent, and quality. Winners. That is what we sell."

"Speaking of which, Bartlett, how is our young friend doing with the Consolidated trial? What I read in the *Times* makes no sense at all."

"The plaintiff is close to completing the case in chief. I've been monitoring closely. Predictions on the outcome of trials are foolish, but between us within this room, I will say it looks extremely encouraging. Sam Corbin is winning that case."

"Hardboiled talent, hmm? Is that what he is?"

Pringle answered. "Gentlemen, Corbin is already better than anyone else we have. Not that he is perfection. He still, for example, harbors some sophomoric ideals, and there are scruples he must shed that are inappropriate in a courtroom. But in ten years, gentleman, hand Corbin a decent case to try and he will be unbeatable."

65

Lucrezia knew jury curiosity concerning Peter Saunders was at its peak. That had to be satisfied if a substantial plaintiff's verdict was to be hoped for. Actually, it would take more than that. She had to create empathy for Saunders.

It was commonly held among her colleagues that if a jury liked a plaintiff, it would find a way to rule in his favor. Lucrezia had never quite believed that. The problem was more complicated. The jury had to be made to feel what Saunders felt, but it also had to attribute its own emotions and responses to him.

At least she didn't have to worry about anyone disliking Peter Saunders. She could not imagine that. The man was so scrupulously direct and accurate. But so goddamned reticent. If she could just get him to open up.

"I'd like the jury to hear about your background and experience first, Mr. Saunders," Lucrezia began. "Then we'll get into details."

Lucrezia took him back through his early days in the submarine navy under Rickover. Saunders liked to talk about himself least of all. Lucrezia had to pull it out, but Sam let her get away with it. It was innocuous stuff.

The entire morning was taken up with Saunders's catalogue of defective plant systems and unsafe practices. The subject was dear enough to cause him to finally warm up.

At the noon recess, Lucrezia took him up to the cafeteria. Neither was hungry. Lucrezia just wanted to keep him talking.

She wanted his motor hot and running when he returned to the witness stand.

"I don't know how you do this every day, Lucrezia," said Saunders as he forced a fork into a half-frozen tomato.

"You mean eat here?"

"I mean try lawsuits. Talk and argue all day long. I wouldn't have your job for a million bucks."

"And for two cents you can have all my rights to babysit a nuclear reactor."

Saunders reached out and pulled a shiny quarter from her ear. He handed it to her. "How about two bits?"

"Not enough. How did you do that?"

"A buddy in the navy taught me. They had him down in Leavenworth last I heard. Turned out to be a pickpocket."

Lucrezia laughed.

Saunders smiled back. "It's nice to hear you laugh."

Lucrezia looked at her watch. "Let's go get some more chuckles."

When Lucrezia resumed his direct examination, she had him describe each stage of the plant accident triggered by Bagdasarian. Lucrezia knew the jury would be moved by his modest, matter-of-fact presentation of the events that imposed his sentence of death.

"You were present in the courtroom during all of Michael Bagdasarian's testimony. Did he fully relate the orders given by you to him during that morning's events?"

"No, ma'am."

Lucrezia waited. *Come on, Peter, don't start running down on me.* She did not want to have to start prompting.

Saunders came through on his own. "Michael forgot to mention that after the pipe blew, I also ordered him to engage the turning gear on the turbine."

"You were injured, and you had the reactor back under control. Why was that turning gear so important?"

"Well, that turbine shaft is so massive that if you let it come to a halt while it is still hot, it will twist and warp. It takes hours to cool down. What you have to do is keep the shaft turning with an auxiliary motor even though the turbine is shut down. Otherwise, you would have nothing left but a huge expensive hunk of scrap."

Lucrezia thought the jury would appreciate a man who

would still be concerned about unnecessary company expense while lying in pain in a pool of contaminated water.

Lucrezia had Saunders go through all the representations Karrasch made about correcting defects and tightening up inspections.

"And did you believe him when he made these statements to you?"

"Sure."

Lucrezia folded her arms and resisted the temptation to tap her foot.

Saunders continued. "Because I figured nobody would risk workers' lives just to save money."

Lucrezia believed preparation was the key to winning lawsuits. A review of each friendly witness's version of events was essential before he was allowed to testify.

She was about to make her first exception. Peter Saunders was a special case.

Intellectually, the mental suffering of a person burdened with foreknowledge that he is doomed to a lingering, painful death is obvious. That was not enough for the jury to know. Lucrezia wanted her jury to feel that anguish twisting in their own guts, to project that feeling onto Peter Saunders, to know his horror. But the desired response had to begin with Saunders himself. He had to be made to tell of his desperation. They had to believe and feel.

On any subject the man was reserved. About himself, he was at best taciturn. Preparing him to discuss his own terror would merely increase his stubborn resistance. Lucrezia was gambling on Saunders's compulsion to testify truthfully and upon unrehearsed spontaneity.

"When you first learned you had been fatally contaminated, what did you feel?"

"Plum awful."

"Was this feeling like anything you had ever experienced before?"

Stubborn silence.

"Mr. Saunders, can you compare how you felt then with anything else?" *Come on, Peter, talk.*

Saunders stretched his neck. "When Rachel died . . . when I realized Rachel was dying."

"Rachel was your wife?"

"Yes. It was a long time ago. She—"

"I'm sorry to make you go over this. Did your wife die of cancer?"

"No. I mean, no one knew what it was. The doctors couldn't ... they didn't—that was part of what terrorized her. She knew she was dying but she didn't know why." Saunders stopped to stare back into time. "She was so afraid."

"I'm sorry. Was she in pain?"

"It went on for months. Months. Nothing helped much. They were afraid to put her under completely. They couldn't predict what would happen. I was with her all the time." He blinked as his faded blue eyes misted. "She was so ... alone."

"Mr. Saunders, is what you are feeling now like when you lost your wife?"

"Yes. No. Not exactly. I'm not so afraid of dying ..."

Lucrezia would not let him evade. "You're not so afraid of dying as you are of what?"

"The loss of dignity. The helplessness." He was with her again. "She was so helpless. . . ."

Lucrezia waited a few moments. "Thank you, Mr. Saunders. I have no further questions."

Judge Iverson cleared his throat. "I think this would be a good time for a brief recess before Mr. Corbin begins cross-examination. Ten minutes."

Saunders remained in the witness stand while the jury filed out. If he squeezed his eyes closed hard enough, he could make the images stop. Finally, he stepped down and walked over to Lucrezia.

"I had to do that," she said quietly. "For you."

"Goddamn you, Lucrezia." He stalked into the corridor.

66

"**S**am, be gentle with this guy," Ben whispered. "I think the jury feels for him. Hell, I feel for him."

Sam agreed the jury would not applaud if he handed Saunders his own head. But if he proceeded too cautiously, he would accomplish nothing. He could only deal with it step by step.

"Back in your days in the submarine navy, you worked with nuclear reactors constantly, didn't you?"

"The boats I worked with were nuclear-powered."

"And you frequently were involved in the handling of radio-active fissionable materials?"

"Usually not personally, but occasionally, yes."

"And in 1961 you were part of the U.S. Navy contingent at the Atomic Energy Commission testing grounds in Idaho?"

"Yes, I was part of the navy observation team. The AEC was testing a miniature experimental reactor in its laboratory there. They called it the SL-1."

"What happened there on January 3, 1961?"

"A maintenance worker withdrew a control rod beyond design limits. An explosion resulted. Three men were killed."

"And weren't you part of the emergency crew that entered the laboratory building afterward?"

"There were four of us."

"Mr. Saunders, after you were exposed to the radiation caused by the SL-1 explosion, were you tested for contamination?"

"Yes, we all tested negative."

"You were inside the building where a nuclear explosion of

sufficient violence to kill three men had just occurred, and you were not contaminated?"

"No, sir. We were only inside a few minutes, and we wore protective clothing."

Sam thought he had better try another front. "Mr. Saunders, isn't it true that you are a member of one or more antinuclear organizations?"

"No, sir. I've given lectures before Mothers for Peace and NOW groups, but I've never joined either organization."

"Isn't it a fact that Mothers for Peace is financing your attorney's fees for this trial?"

"No, that is not a fact."

"But Mothers for Peace is advancing your court costs, isn't that so?"

"No, sir. They did in the past, but all their money has been repaid. I'm paying my own court costs, and I believe my attorney has advanced some."

"But you've collected substantial fees from Mothers for Peace for your lectures, haven't you?"

"They paid my expenses twice to speak out of town, and I've had a couple of free lunches."

So much for Consolidated Utilities as an accurate source of intelligence, thought Sam. *I should have known better than to rely on Lousaire's reports. I've one more shot. If that doesn't hit something I'm going to walk away with egg on my face. Well, I'm not looking that good so far anyway.*

"Mr. Saunders, you are named after your father, is that right?"

"Yes, that's right."

"Peter Aleksandrovich, right?"

"My father had his name legally changed to Peter Saunders after he immigrated to this country. That was in 1933, two years before he even met my mother."

"Your father defected from the NKVD, the Soviet security police, isn't that so?"

"I was told he was running from them, if that's what you mean. I wasn't born yet."

"Wasn't he assassinated by the Soviets in 1938?"

"That was a rumor at the time. My father was shot walking home from work in downtown Boulder, Colorado. The police never identified the killer."

"Your Honor," Lucrezia asked. "May we approach the bench?"

"Your Honor," she began, "counsel's questions are ripe with inflammatory insinuations about spies and Communists, but no evidence supports this innuendo. This sort of smear tactic is highly prejudicial. I move that it be stricken."

"Sam . . . Mr. Corbin," Judge Iverson said, "I have to tell you I think your questions border on misconduct. What do you have to say?"

"Your Honor," Sam argued, "the facts are that plaintiff's father defected from Russia, changed his name, and was executed under suspicious circumstances. The fact is two pounds of plutonium are missing from the Point Anacapa plant. A significant amount was found in the home of the plaintiff, who goes around the country giving antinuclear lectures. I think certain legitimate inferences can be drawn from these circumstances, and the jury is entitled to have them for consideration. If the facts tend to discredit the plaintiff—"

"We haven't heard any discrediting facts yet," offered Lucrezia.

"All right, Mrs. Ferrara," said the judge. "I could strike this evidence now and admonish the jury. However, I think that would only serve to emphasize the insinuations already made and increase the risk of prejudice."

"I am going to order you, Mr. Corbin, to forebear from raising this subject again without first obtaining express permission, which, incidentally, you will not receive unless you produce hard evidence of substantiation. Mrs. Ferrara, I will reserve ruling on your motion until the close of all evidence."

Sam was getting hot. Would he be more ethical if he hung back and his client lost?

"Your Honor, I respectfully take exception to these remarks. As counsel for the defense I have the obligation to raise every—"

"Every red herring you can think of," Lucrezia interrupted.

"You always have to have the last word, don't you?" Sam countered angrily.

"I don't think so." She smiled sweetly, thinking Sam was so cute when he was angry.

"Please, please," interrupted the judge. "You can't keep arguing up here. This is a courtroom."

Lucrezia's style did not tend toward vengeance, but she

thought she owed Sam something for his last batch of tricks, and besides, he himself had created the opportunity.

"Mr. Saunders," she asked. "How did you happen to be chosen for the emergency team that went into the AEC laboratory after the SL-1 explosion?"

"Well, I volunteered, ma'am."

"And what did you find after you entered the building where this miniature reactor had exploded?"

Sam knew what was coming next. He stood. "Your Honor, may we approach the bench?"

Judge Iverson sighed. "Come ahead."

"Motion to exclude under Section 352. This is a flagrant attempt to exploit the gory details of the SL-1 accident for the sole purpose of unduly prejudicing the jury against nuclear power."

"Your Honor," Lucrezia replied, "on cross-examination, defense counsel sought to imply that Mr. Saunders had been contaminated by entering that building. I am entitled to show what it was like inside."

"Well, Mr. Corbin, you did open the door. Defendant's motion is denied."

"Now, Mr. Saunders," Lucrezia resumed, "you may tell the jury what you found when you entered the building where the explosion occurred."

"One man was on the floor, dead. A second was so hot with radiation, he was actually glowing red. He died within two hours. The body of the third man was pinned to the ceiling by a control rod which pierced his groin and came out his back."

"What happened to the bodies of these men?"

"Against regulations they hadn't worn complete protective clothing. Their uncovered faces and hands had been exposed. Their heads and hands were so hot they could not responsibly be buried in a cemetery. Those parts were, ah . . . removed and disposed of at a radioactive dump site."

Lucrezia looked at the jury. They seemed frozen. She hoped it was fascination, not mere indifference. She watched and waited. Juror number seven stared at the backs of her hands. Stefan Genik, number three, caressed his throat.

She had them. She knew it.

It was the end of the day and of the week. The jury had just heard impressive testimony that would have the entire week-end to sink in.

Lucrezia had no more new evidence to offer, only corroborative bolstering. This seemed like an ideal place to stop.

Lucrezia stood. "The plaintiff rests, Your Honor."

What an absurdly inappropriate phrase, she thought. She was wrung out. But now the defense would put on its case. Essentially, Sam's and her roles would be reversed. Some rest, she thought.

"Good," said Judge Iverson. This was measurable progress. "We will recess until nine-thirty on Monday morning then." The judge repeated all the routine admonitions, wished everyone a good weekend, and scampered off the bench.

Saunders helped Lucrezia and Molly gather papers. "What happens next?"

Molly answered before Lucrezia could. "The defense will probably make a motion for nonsuit. That's a common defense ploy even though the motions are seldom granted and are usually reversed on appeal when they have been."

Lucrezia tried not to smile at Molly's pontification. "It's an extremely tough motion to win because the judge has to determine that the plaintiff has put on no evidence to support a verdict in his favor, disregarding conflicting evidence in favor of defendant."

"So why," he wondered, "if the motions are so frequently turned down, does the defense bother?"

"A perfectly good question," Lucrezia answered. "Sometimes simply because it doesn't hurt to ask. Anyway, I'm confident we have covered all the bases. I'm only concerned about the sort of slimy witnesses Consolidated might put up against us. We can anticipate some extremely creative testimony, and there is always the risk the jury swallows some of it."

"The judge will break before Christmas, won't he?" Saunders asked.

"My guess is that he'll recess on Tuesday for the rest of the week, to keep the jury happy. Let them do their shopping and personal things." Lucrezia sighed. "I really won't mind either. Can you come up to the office about six-thirty or seven? I've got some fires to put out first, but then I'd like to go over some

of the defense witnesses with you. You'll get a cold beer out
of it."

"Sure. I'll hang around downtown. Give me a chance to do
some Christmas shopping myself."

"If you like, I'll give you a ride down to Broadway Plaza
now. You can walk back to the office from there when you've
finished."

"Appreciate it." He would have to buy her something red.

67

By the time Sam returned to the offices of Tipson, Grumm &
Nuttzer, Christmas decorations were in place. The largest tree
possible to stuff under the ceiling temporarily replaced one of
the reception room couches. The tree ornaments were obviously antique, delicate, and priceless. Sam guessed German
origin on loan from some senior partner.

The corridor was festooned with garlands of scented fir
boughs, punctuated by holly berries and satin bows.

The public address system discreetly played some Bach
cantata. Maybe it was Handel, he wasn't sure. He was thankful
it wasn't "Rudolph, the Red-Nosed Reindeer."

Each office door bore a wreath, identical except for a diffident gold-leaf-lettered placard. Sam's read, "Joyeux Noel!"

When Sam caught his first glimpse of his secretary, Jean, he
belatedly realized the entire place was pervaded by a distinct
absence of holiday joy. No one had wished him Merry Christmas on his way down the hall. Only curt, unsmiling nods.
Usually such atmosphere prevailed when someone lost a big
case, but Sam knew no other major cases were being tried.

Jean enlightened him.

"Bradley Dillingham. Automobile accident. Early this afternoon," she said. "Smashed himself into an abutment on the Cahuenga Overpass, doing a hundred five, according to investigating officers."

"Jesus. Dead?"

Jean clapped her hands together. "Just like that."

Sam nodded thanks for the succinctly colorful description as he closed his office door.

He couldn't face the stack of messages. His first thought was the poor bastard was probably better off. Imminent disaster probably awaited the disclosure, voluntary or otherwise, of Dillingham's malfeasance. Still, it was one hell of a Christmas present.

Then relief washed over Sam. The accident had taken him off his personal hook. There was no longer any dilemma regarding conflicting loyalty. No overhanging jeopardy to his future at good old TGN. *Tra la la la la. Lala, la la.* God, he felt awful.

Ben knocked and poked his head in simultaneously. He closed the door and sat. "Why do you suppose he killed himself?"

"Dillingham? What makes you so sure it was suicide?"

"I just guided Dillingham's widow down to his parking stall. She was anxious to pick up his Mercedes. Understandably, she would want to drive it to the funeral. Anyway, she peeled out of the garage like it was Le Mans."

"I don't understand."

"His filigreed platinum pen and the receipt from Hertz were on the passenger seat."

Sam was still confused. "Didn't he smash up in the Mercedes?"

Ben shook his head. "He rented a Chevy Camaro to do it in."

68

Peter Saunders rode the shopping-mall escalator feeling alien, as if he had just stepped out of his spaceship onto the surface of the third planet of a sun of a distant galaxy. The natives seemed vaguely humanoid, but they all spoke some unfathomable babble. The ones he supposed were female seemed driven, desperate, determined. Saunders had seen that look before, on men preparing to go into battle. There were obvious males in the throng, too. They had the glazed, hypnotized slave look, mere dull beasts of burden.

Hidden loudspeakers blared "All I Want for Christmas Is My Two Front Teeth." Music, the universal language. He knew then he would be welcomed to their planet.

He needed something red for Lucrezia and something quiet for Molly. Oh, and there was Gloria, too. He had been carrying her ring in his pocket for three weeks, intending to return it. But, somehow, whenever he had the time, he forgot. Or was it that he couldn't make himself go back there? He didn't know, and he was not in the mood for deep introspection.

He glimpsed broad, silver nylon-jacketed shoulders, already a hundred yards distant and moving away. Even at that distance, he could tell the man was a full nine inches taller than the median height of the crowd.

He had to see that man's face.

Saunders tried moving faster, but picking up headway in that sea of not-quite humanity was like rowing against a twenty-knot breeze. Twice, he lost the retreating figure and

226

spotted him again seconds later. Saunders blessed that silver jacket. It was a beacon.

When he finally did catch up, Saunders was sweating, even though the mall was air conditioned. Saunders got two steps ahead of the man and turned to inspect his face.

He recognized him instantly, and simultaneously swung a right uppercut with all he could pack into it.

Sullivan's head snapped back, he wobbled, but he did not go down. Maybe the crowd just held him up.

Sullivan was blank, puzzled. Then recognition dawned. He hesitated before turning to run. Running was not possible. Sullivan tried the breast stroke.

Saunders yelled, "Police! Thief!" and tackled Sullivan below the knees. The crowd parted and Sullivan went down.

A ring of enthusiastic, but uncommitted, spectators formed. Sullivan squirmed and attacked with roundhouse lefts and rights. He found it difficult, however, to inflict damage on a man holding him around the shins from behind.

Sullivan broke one leg loose and was preparing to use it to kick Saunders's head in when the white-haired security guard burst through the ring. He inserted the four-inch barrel of his Police Special .38 as far as he could into Sullivan's left ear, and said, "Don't."

At Central Division, a robbery-detail sergeant, who had hoped to get away early for some shopping of his own, listened impatiently to their stories.

Sullivan's grammar tended to deteriorate under stress. The best he could do was, "I ain't never seen him before in his life."

And it might have been enough, but his body search revealed, in addition to the usual wallet, keys, and bubble gum, a woman's ring, a small sapphire, surrounded by even smaller diamonds, in a gold setting.

Saunders identified the ring as belonging to Gloria Brewer, and part of the loot taken from her Hollywood Hills home. Sullivan denied that he had ever seen that before, either. He was promptly booked on first-degree burglary-and-assault charges.

After Sullivan was led away, Saunders asked the sergeant for permission to speak to the prisoner alone.

"Sorry, Mr. Saunders, but no way," the sergeant answered.

"Only visitors is attorneys and immediate family. Say, you're the Saunders who has that big lawsuit going against Consolidated."

Saunders did his shy celebrity grin.

The sergeant stuck out his hand. "It's a pleasure to meet you, Commander. You know, I was in New London in fifty-six. Were you there then?"

"No, just before my time. Were you in U-boats, too?"

"Hell, no. I was in the MPs. You couldn't get me inside one of those things. They could be dangerous."

"Sergeant, isn't there any way I can talk to Sullivan for a few minutes? I think he has information that can help my case."

"Yeah? Oh, what the hell." The sergeant yelled across the room. "Mick, find this gentleman an empty conference room and let him have ten minutes with Sullivan, the one we just booked." He turned back to Saunders. "Just talk now, Commander. No funny stuff. You could get me into big trouble. Okay?"

"Just talk, I swear. And thank you."

"Merry Christmas, Commander. Good luck."

The tiny interrogation room barely contained the two large men. Saunders didn't care about space. He was concerned with time.

"You are going to do five to eight on the burglary and the same again on the assault." Saunders was making it up as he went, but he thought it sounded pretty authentic. "And if they tie you to planting that plutonium, that's a separate federal rap."

"You planted that goddamned ring on me. We didn't take—" Sullivan stopped himself.

Saunders ignored the accusation and gave Sullivan time to digest the significance of his three-word admission. It took a minute, but Saunders felt it was worth the wait.

"Unless you are lucky enough to draw concurrent sentences on the state charges, you are looking at a minimum of six years with good behavior, with another four you'll do for the Feds."

"I can't do no more time."

Saunders believed him. Sullivan was visibly coming unraveled.

"Listen to me. I'm not interested in making you do time. I'm only interested in winning my case against Consolidated. Now you agree to testify at my trial on how you planted that plutonium in the refrigerator on Consolidated's orders. You agree to that, I'll drop the charges, and my lawyer will work you some kind of sweet deal. I've got the best lawyer in this state."

"I'll lose my job."

"Do you think they'll keep sending your paychecks up to Folsom?"

"Mag . . . They'll kill me."

"My lawyer will get you protection."

"It wasn't my idea, man. I was just doing my job."

"That's all I expect you to testify. I'm not trying to pin this thing on you. I've already told you. I want Consolidated."

"Zero time. Right?"

"Right."

"I guess I can handle the rest of it. Okay. Deal."

Saunders put out his hand. Sullivan took it.

"I'm going to call my lawyer now," Saunders said. "She'll know how to handle this."

"Hurry it up, will you? I've got to get out of here."

Saunders telephoned Lucrezia from the booth inside the station house. He told her everything that had happened from the time he spotted Sullivan in the shopping mall. Almost everything, anyway. He decided to leave out the part about planting Gloria's ring in Sullivan's pocket.

Lucrezia was incredulous. She kept saying things like, "What? You did what?," "I don't believe this," and, "You can't do that."

Within fifteen minutes, she walked into the station carrying her attaché case and a portable typewriter. Five minutes later, she was inside the interrogation room with Sullivan. Saunders was ordered to wait outside. Thirty minutes after that, she emerged, glowing.

She led Saunders to one of the hard wooden benches in the waiting room. "What you have accomplished in an hour and a half is nothing short of fantastic," she gushed like a schoolgirl.

"Peter, you have single-handedly wrapped up our case, and very probably gained us a verdict for substantial punitive damages. I have the whole story of how Sullivan and a cohort broke into Gloria's house, placed contaminated butter in the refrigerator for the purpose of framing you, and assaulted you when you surprised them in the act. All this on the express orders of a Consolidated Utilities official. He denies he stole Gloria's ring, but that's a detail. I have his signed statement. I have him on tape, and I've handed him a subpoena for nine-thirty Monday morning."

"Take a breath," Saunders suggested.

She gave him a hug.

"I still cannot believe this. You have overcome every one of the weaknesses in our case. There is no defense to this testimony that they can sell to the jury. Incredible. This sort of thing only happens on television. Peter, you are something."

"What about the fact that we've rested our case? Doesn't that mean you can't call another witness?"

"No problem. With new evidence under these circumstances, Judge Iverson will let us reopen in a minute. You did screw up somewhat with all those outlandish promises you made him, but I forgive you for that, and it's getting straightened out. I'm lining him up with another lawyer and . . ."

"Another lawyer? Why? I told him you were the best."

"Because there is an obvious conflict. I can't represent him while I'm representing you. It's taken care of. There is one more thing that isn't, though, and it's going to require your help."

"Name it."

"I tried to persuade Sullivan to stay in over the weekend. It would be safer. But he says he can't handle it, and I believe him. He had some kind of previous traumatic experience as a prisoner, and I can see this is making him crazy. If he is babbling by Monday he won't do us any good on the witness stand. I promised to obtain his release by tomorrow morning, and believe I can, although it will take some doing on Friday night. He's agreed to stay in our custody over the weekend. That's where you come in."

"You're right. We can't afford to have him running around loose. We can hire a couple of guys with shotguns and take shifts guarding him at my place."

"That sounds fine. I have the numbers of some security agencies at the office. You can start on that while I work on his bail and his new lawyer."

As they entered Lucrezia's suite, Paul Cummings was pacing furrows into her reception-room carpet. He started to glare at Saunders but turned it into a dazzling smile almost instantaneously. Lucrezia thought it was a remarkable performance.

"Hello, Saunders," Cummings said, extending his hand. "Nice to see you again. I understand your trial is going well."

Saunders nodded politely and shook hands. "Congressman."

"His trial is going spectacularly," offered Lucrezia.

"Lucrezia, we had a date for dinner. You're already an hour late."

"Oh dear, I am sorry." She explained what had happened. "I'm afraid I completely forgot."

Cummings understood, and he said the right things, but his expression suggested that even such inadvertent interference with his plans was not easily forgiven.

"Paul, we still have work that must be done. It shouldn't take more than thirty or forty minutes. Why don't you go over to the Windsor and have a drink. I'll join you as soon as I can."

"All right, but please hurry. We have important matters to discuss as well."

Even though he was frowning, Lucrezia could guess what they were. She kissed him on the cheek and let him out.

Twenty minutes later, Lucrezia and Saunders coordinated the results of their efforts.

"I've lined up twenty-four-hour armed-guard service," Saunders said. "I know one of them from the navy, and we couldn't get any better. I think I can rely on him to see that the others are suitable. They are ready to start tomorrow morning where and when we give them the word. It's going to cost three hundred a day."

"And well worth it. I've lined up Dalton as attorney. Excellent man. He understands our needs, too, and will cooperate. I had to guarantee his fee, but all this extra expense is a modest insurance premium if it helps us bring in a verdict of several million. Oh, bail is arranged too. They say they can't process him out before eight A.M., so why don't we all rendezvous at Central Division at seven-thirty. We will be waiting when he's released and we'll whisk him off."

Saunders agreed and said goodnight. He stopped at a Lincoln Boulevard liquor store and purchased a six-pack of Millers, a pint of Wild Turkey, and a package of salami.

Inside his apartment, he fixed himself a stiff boilermaker, drank half of it at one gulp, tossed the unopened salami into the refrigerator, and switched on the radio. He flipped the dial until he got John Denver, and downed the rest of his drink.

He rummaged through two cardboard boxes on the floor of his hall closet until he found the old fabric-holstered U.S. Navy issue Colt .45 ACP. He made himself another boilermaker and sat down to clean the automatic. It was an unwieldy weapon, clumsy, heavy, with the kick of a mule. But it would put Sullivan down even if it only grazed him, and Saunders remembered how to use it better than that.

He must remember to be gentle, though. His revenge would have to take the form of Sullivan's testimony, not blood. The bastards would be really nailed to the cross now. There was no way Karrasch or his Consolidated buddies were going to slither out from under this evidence.

He would have to get a couple of folding cots and some extra bedding tomorrow. Food, too. And he hadn't even bought presents yet. Saunders laughed out loud. It looked as if he was going to be a last-minute Christmas shopper after all.

69

Paul Cummings was on only his second drink when Lucrezia walked into the Windsor. He stood and let her slide into the red leather horseshoe booth. An ancient waiter in a rusty tuxedo appeared. Lucrezia asked for a glass of Fume Blanc.

"Let's order now," Paul suggested. "I am famished. How does abalone and Caesar salad for two sound?"

Lucrezia nodded approval.

The waiter approved, too. "With perhaps a bottle of the Fume Blanc, sir?"

Lucrezia nodded three more times. The waiter bowed as fully as arthritis permitted and shuffled off.

During dinner, Paul had dozens of questions about the development of the case. Lucrezia was so wound up with Sullivan's capture and anticipation of Monday morning she was delighted to discuss that exclusively.

She wolfed down the food, which was excellent as usual. Not until the end of the meal did she begin to realize Cummings was stalling.

"You said we had important matters to discuss." Lucrezia took her last sip of wine as the waiter appeared with coffee. "Does that mean you've told Barbara?"

Cummings delayed until the waiter left. "Yes, I told Barbara about us this morning, but," Cummings cleared his throat and braced himself. "I fear there will have to be a change in plan."

Lucrezia felt the anger rising and tried to put it down. She raised an eyebrow and sipped coffee. "I suppose Barbara has suffered a relapse."

"No, as a matter of fact she is recovering quite rapidly." He hesitated again. "Lucrezia darling, I know I can count on you to understand this—"

"Oh, for God's sake, try me already."

"Barbara's family has made me an irresistible offer. A two-million-dollar contribution to my senatorial campaign fund now and a pledge of an additional four million if I capture the presidential nomination."

Lucrezia knew he was watching for her reaction, but she was determined to keep that private. "On condition that you stay with Barbara, of course."

"Yes, of course. Darling, you are politically sophisticated enough to know how difficult it is to raise that kind of money. How can I refuse?"

"And that you cut it off with me, of course. Darling."

"That's what they are saying. But you know they don't really mean that. They'll expect us to be discreet and not cause embarrassment. Lucy darling, I love you as much as ever. There is no reason we can't keep seeing one another. . . ."

Lucrezia stood and carefully dropped her teaspoon into Cummings's coffee cup, splattering his fifty-dollar necktie.

"See one another? I wouldn't even vote for you, you spineless slug."

Lucrezia had always known Cummings's weakness. She was furious at her own. Why, she wondered, had she even thought the creep was attractive?

She smiled at the maitre d' as she walked out. "Superb abalone," she said.

Cummings looked over the bill as he got out his wallet. Dinner had turned out to be really quite expensive.

Lucrezia grossly overtipped the Windsor parking valet and drove the Lincoln back to Beverly Hills at a highly excessive rate of speed. Dolly Parton and seventeen members of her immediate family were singing something about the first day of Christmas. Lucrezia tried to hum along, but gave it up and punched Dolly in the off button. Lucrezia decided she already had her Christmas present. She was going to win a big one for Peter and for herself. There was a man who stood for something worthwhile. A decisive man who knew how to take action. Too bad she wasn't in love with him. *Too bad the poor son of a bitch was going to die. Too bad. Shit.*

Lucrezia found a half-full bottle of Chardonnay in her refrigerator, grabbed a wine glass from the cupboard, and climbed to her bedroom. They were all just different kinds of sons of bitches, she decided.

She toasted the photograph in the silver frame. *And if you had been careful, you dumb son of a bitch, I would be working a four-day week, tending my rose garden, and teaching my grandchildren to swim in my spare time.*

70

At 6:45 A.M. the guard shook Sullivan's shoulder. "Com'on, wake up. You're sprung."

Sullivan sat up and rubbed his eyes. "What time is it?"

The guard told him. "Your friend's waiting outside. Let's go."

"Great. I didn't think nothing was happening until eight."

The guard led him to a counter. The clerk was a person of indeterminate gender. "Here's your clothes. This is your property. Sign the receipt, here. No, not there. Right here."

Sullivan dressed and was released into the waiting area. Lucrezia was not in sight. He walked into the street and looked both ways. It was not quite dawn. No one was on the street. A white Buick swung around the corner and screeched to a stop alongside him.

Doblonski reached over and threw open the passenger door. He was grinning like a talk show host. "Come on, Dumbo. Climb in. I can't double park in front of a police station."

Sullivan hesitated, then got in. The Buick was doing forty before he had the door closed. "I didn't tell them nothing," he said. He looked Doblonski over carefully.

"I know." Doblonski sounded real friendly.

"Where we going?"

"First, I drive you home so you can pack some clothes. Then you and me is taking a little airplane ride down to Baja. Free, all-expense-paid fishing vacation."

"Hey, I get it. That's smart."

"There's a joint right up here. Want to stop and hoist a couple of belts first? We got time."

235

"At seven in the morning?"

"Hell, we're on vacation, ain't we?"

"Yeah. Why the hell not?"

Lucrezia and Saunders both awoke with surprisingly minor hangovers. They were looking forward to the day.

When Saunders and his friend, the armed guard, arrived at Central Division at 7:29, Lucrezia and Dalton were already standing outside the front entrance.

"He's gone," Lucrezia said. "Released on OR at six-fifty this morning."

Saunders didn't really understand. "How?" was all he could think of.

"Our guess is some papers were forged. There is no other way they could have worked his release this early on Saturday morning. Hi, I'm Dalton."

Saunders shook hands absently. "What do we do now?" he asked Lucrezia.

"We have Sullivan's home address and his friend's, Doblonski, on his statement. We also have their boss's name, Magnasunn. Let's check out their places first."

"If Sullivan's release papers are forged, he is technically an escapee. Maybe you can get the LAPD to issue an APB on him," Dalton suggested.

"I'll get Molly down to the office to run the switchboard. We can coordinate through her," Lucrezia said. "Let's go."

Three hours later, Saunders and Lucrezia met in her office. Saunders had released the guard. Dalton had gone home.

"As far as I can determine," Saunders said wearily, "Sullivan has not been home. The security service is staking his place out in case. Doblonski is on a leave of absence. He is reportedly in Warsaw finding his roots."

Lucrezia tried to smile. "And Magnasunn left on vacation yesterday. He is pursuing an archeological dig in the Yucatan. And if you believe that . . ."

"I walked through all the LAX terminals. That was hopeless. Will the cops help?"

"Yes, officially. But don't expect much. It's a big city and this is not exactly their most burning priority."

Saunders sighed and brightened. "Thank goodness you were

far-sighted enough to get his signed statement and the tape recording."

Lucrezia shook her head sadly.

"What does that mean?"

"Peter, what I mean is that neither the tape nor the signed statement is admissible evidence by themselves. We can't use either one."

"I don't understand." Jesus, he was getting tired of saying that.

"Well, for example," Lucrezia tried to explain, "if Sullivan were on the stand and contradicted something in his statement, we could use it to impeach him. To show he'd made a prior inconsistent statement. But you can't cross-examine a signed statement or a tape recording, so by themselves they are just inadmissible hearsay."

"It doesn't seem entirely fair, but okay. So where do we stand now?"

"At this moment, just about exactly where we were before you tackled Sullivan in the mall."

"What are you going to do Monday morning if Sullivan hasn't been caught before then?"

"Ad lib like hell. We do have him under subpoena. That would probably buy us a continuance and a bench warrant if we wanted it."

"How about a private investigator?"

"I've already done it. Here's his name and number if you think of anything useful."

Saunders took the information and stared at her. He was empty of ideas.

He looked so tired. Lucrezia supposed she did too. She offered cheer. "Remember the immortal words of Yogi Bera. It ain't over till it's over."

Saunders pulled the .45 from his waistband. He checked the safety and removed the clip, laying it on her desk. He ejected the cartridge from the chamber and slid it back into the clip. He jammed the clip back in with such a resounding thwack that Lucrezia jumped. He rechecked the safety and put the weapon in his jacket pocket.

"Right," he said.

71

When court reconvened on Monday morning, nothing new had been uncovered. Saunders had spent the weekend wandering secondary airports, bus depots, and train stations. He knew it was futile, but he needed the exercise.

He rested by watching the watcher stake out Sullivan's apartment. Anything was better than going home.

Lucrezia spent some of the time reminding people who were in a position to notice things that they owed her favors. The rest she devoted to planning alternative tactics. She knew she overdid it, but the alternative was sulking over her misguided attraction to that worm, Cummings.

Before she entered the courtroom, she had already decided that, in the absence of news concerning Sullivan's availability, she would not ask for a continuance.

Sullivan would have been a bombshell, but even without him, plaintiff's case was in reasonably strong shape. To delay the trial and lose momentum in the mere hope of locating him and bringing him in was not appealing.

Sam was already waiting. "Good morning, Lucrezia. Let's go see the judge. I have a motion."

Lucrezia was sure it would be a motion for nonsuit. She was prepared for that. Routine. May as well get it over with. She picked up her trial notebook and followed him into chambers.

"Good morning, Your Honor," Sam said. "The defense has a motion for nonsuit."

"Somehow, I expected you would put me through that. All right, let's use the courtroom. The facilities are better for everyone. Bailiff, tell the jury we have some questions of law to work out, so they'll have to stay penned up until we're finished. Don't say 'penned up.' "

"Yes, sir," the bailiff said and started for the jury room.

"And don't answer any questions," the judge cautioned.

Sam stood. "Your Honor, defendant moves for a judgment of nonsuit pursuant to Code of Civil Procedure, Section 581c. There is insufficient evidence to support a verdict in favor of the plaintiff on any available theory of plaintiff's case.

"The motion is based upon two grounds. Let me begin by summarizing them.

"First, if the evidence only shows that plaintiff's injuries arise out of and in connection with his employment, then workmen's compensation is his exclusive remedy. This lawsuit is barred.

"Second, to the extent that plaintiff's contamination arises from activity outside his employment, then, in the absence of evidence that such contamination was proximately caused by defendant, plaintiff is not entitled to recovery from defendant on any theory, including workmen's compensation.

"Starting with Labor Code Section 3600—"

"Forgive me, Mr. Corbin," interrupted Judge Iverson. "Rest assured that I intend to hear you out completely. But before you proceed you should know I am usually reluctant to grant nonsuit, since I still have the right to grant a new trial if I believe the verdict has been against the weight of the evidence. You are going to have to come up with something startlingly persuasive to turn me around on this. Now go ahead."

Lucrezia smiled at Saunders.

Sam resumed. "I understand your reluctance, Your Honor. If this were the usual case, I would agree. But let me point out, sir, it is the trial judge's duty in a proper case to grant the motion in order to eliminate unnecessary expense and delay. Why should the parties and the jury and the county be put through another month of trial if the plaintiff hasn't even made out his case?"

Sam merely touched on the elements of workmen's compensation doctrine. It was sufficient to remind the judge of the fundamentals.

Workmen's compensation laws were designed to protect employees and employers, he argued. The worker is permitted to recover for job-related injury without having to prove any fault on the part of the employer. The trade-off is that workmen's compensation benefits become the employee's exclusive remedy. The employer is protected against any lawsuit based on such injury.

"Given the most generous possible interpretation," Sam said, "plaintiff's evidence only shows contamination from two industrial accidents. In both incidents, plaintiff was performing services growing out of his employment and was acting within the course of his employment. This is the clearest possible case for application of the workmen's compensation procedure as plaintiff's exclusive remedy for his alleged injuries.

"The only other evidence of possible recent contamination in this case arises out of the plutonium found in the plaintiff's own place of residence. But there is no evidence at all even suggesting that defendant is in any way connected with that plutonium. With no causal connection between that plutonium and defendant, there can be no liability.

"Plaintiff has failed to produce sufficient evidence to support a verdict. The motion for nonsuit should be granted."

Sam sat down. Lucrezia stood.

"Your Honor, I must confess I am really impressed with the defense argument. I think it deserves the award of the year for *chutzpah*. I can't help but be reminded of the boy who murdered his parents and then pleaded for leniency on the ground that he was an orphan.

"Their argument is that Peter Saunders was not contaminated by their defective plant, so he must have gotten it from outside, but if it came from outside, you can't blame them. What shameless audacity.

"The Point Anacapa Nuclear Power Plant deals with one of the deadliest substances ever created by man, plutonium 239. Because of the extra-hazardous nature of that lethal isotope, the law imposes an extra responsibility on Consolidated. That is the doctrine of strict liability. That doctrine says that if extra-hazardous material escapes and injures someone, the owner of the material is liable, even if it was not at fault at all—"

"But," Sam interrupted, "there is no evidence that the plutonium found in the plaintiff's residence came from defendant's plant."

"Your Honor," Lucrezia continued, "I paid counsel for the defense the courtesy of listening to his flawed, contrived argument without interruption. I hope he can bring himself to allow me the same consideration.

"This is but one more example of their brazen insolence. In cross-examining one of plaintiff's witnesses, the FBI agent, defense counsel did his best to insinuate that the plutonium was stolen from defendant's plant. Now he argues there is no evidence it came from defendant's plant. What other sources of plutonium were there? The only commonsense inference is that the stuff had to come from the plant. But the plaintiff does not have to prove how the deadly stuff got out. That is irrelevant. The defendant has an unconditional legal responsibility for the safe confinement of that material and is strictly liable for its escape."

"Mrs. Ferrara," the judge asked, "do you have authority for the proposition that a cause of action based on strict liability is an exception to the exclusive remedy provision of the workmen's compensation laws?"

"Your Honor, my research has uncovered no California case on the point." She cited West Virginia and Ohio cases supporting her position, conceding they were not binding precedent, but arguing that their reasoning was persuasive. She passed copies of the opinions to the judge and Sam.

"There is a line of California cases, commencing with *Magliuto versus Superior Court* in 1975, holding that civil action by an employee against an employer for an intentional tort is an alternative remedy and an implied exception to the exclusive remedy provisions of the workmen's compensation statutes. The analogy is direct. If the employer's intentional misconduct constitutes an exception, then the employer's strict liability for ultra-hazardous substances must also constitute an exception, since strict liability applies regardless of fault." Lucrezia handed out a list of citations.

Sam argued that the cases cited by Lucrezia did not apply because they only dealt with aggravated intentional misconduct on the part of the employer, such as assault on the employee.

"Take a look at *Williams versus International Paper Company*," Sam argued. "This case held that where the employer's intentional misconduct did not go beyond knowing failure to assure a safe work place, workmen's compensation was still the employee's exclusive remedy."

Lucrezia countered that Consolidated's intentional misconduct clearly did go beyond failure to assure safe working environment.

Lucrezia said, "Not only did defendant intentionally fail to correct known defects in its system, creating a safety hazard, it fraudulently misrepresented that it had done so, suffering that hazard to continue, resulting in a catastrophic accident. Then Consolidated compounded its previous misconduct by fraudulently concealing the existence of the plaintiff's injuries."

Lucrezia was dying to add there was also a witness who would prove Consolidated even planted plutonium in plaintiff's home in its attempt to discredit him, but of course she could not prove that without Sullivan, damn him.

"All right, let me catch up here," said Judge Iverson. "Take thirty minutes while I read these cases. Bailiff, bring me the Labor Code, please. Make sure it has current pocket parts."

"Jeez," Molly said, "I'm worried. I didn't think the judge would give Sam the time of day for those arguments."

Saunders looked at Lucrezia. She did not appear happy either. Apparently she agreed.

"Remember," he said, "the immortal words of Yogi Berra . . ."

Lucrezia smiled. "Let's telephone around. Maybe there is some word on our missing witness."

Telephone calls to the office, the private investigator, the security service, and friends at LAPD produced nothing. Wherever Sullivan was, they were no closer to him than they had been Saturday afternoon.

Sam and Ben went down to the second floor snack stand. Ben had black coffee. He had been gaining weight since Thanksgiving. Sam bought a carton of milk and an enormous chocolate chip cookie.

Ben eyed the cookie with envy and resolved to start running. Soon. "Iverson may be buying it. You certainly have his serious attention. And why not? Our position is perfectly good law."

"Perfectly good law," Sam agreed. "Only it sucks."

72

Thirty minutes later, Judge Iverson resumed the stand. Lucrezia thought his demeanor was ominous. She could feel pressure mounting in her chest.

"I've read all your authorities and a few more I dug out myself. I'm going to give you a chance to respond to this, Mrs. Ferrara, but I have to say that I am disposed to grant this motion.

"I do not believe the plaintiff's evidence establishes an exception to the workmen's compensation exclusive remedy provisions of the Labor Code.

"Specifically, Mrs. Ferrara, I do not agree that the case law establishes an implied exception for strict liability situations. I don't mind telling you that I am personally not in sympathy with those cases. But even though I may not agree with our courts of appeal, I am obliged to follow them.

"If you have any further argument you wish to present on this issue, I will be pleased to consider it now. Perhaps even more to the point, if you have any additional evidence to offer that could avoid a nonsuit, I will allow plaintiff to reopen his case in chief. Is there anything more you would like to put in on plaintiff's behalf?"

Saunders sat stiffly, staring straight ahead. Molly was twisting her handkerchief beyond its limits. Lucrezia's mind raced through alternatives. She simply must not let this case flush down the drain.

"Yes and no, Your Honor," she said. "Yes, there is additional evidence we would like to put on which we believe would prevent granting nonsuit, but, no, we are not prepared to do so today.

"We have a crucial witness under subpoena who has failed to appear and for whom we are actively searching. In addition, Your Honor, I continue to believe that a case based on strict liability is an implied exception to the workmen's compensation law. For the law to be otherwise is a travesty. I would like the opportunity to do additional research and to file a brief on this issue. For both these reasons, I move for an immediate recess and a continuance until next week."

Sam was slow to rise. Obviously he should oppose Lucrezia's motion, but was having trouble making himself do so.

Sam thought Lucrezia was entitled to a chance to save plaintiff's case, wasn't she? If he was the judge he would grant that in an instant. But he was not here to judge, was he? And he sure as hell was not here to identify with Lucrezia's position.

Goddammit, Corbin, he snarled to himself, *do it right. She is a fine lawyer who surely understands you have your job to do. A fine, understanding, forgiving woman.*

Sam stretched to his considerable height. "Defense does not oppose a one-week continuance, Your Honor."

He sat down abruptly, wondering what the hell had made him say that. *What made you say that*, he told himself, *was compassion. Bullshit*, he responded.

Judge Iverson nodded. "Good. We will recess until next Monday at nine-thirty. Both sides have until eight-thirty on Monday to file briefs on the strict liability issue. Mr. Corbin, I realize that puts you at a slight tactical disadvantage on the briefing but, in view of the fact that you have a leg up, it seems fair enough. On Monday morning, I will allow plaintiff to reopen to present any additional evidence. If plaintiff has no additional evidence, I will consider any new arguments, but please, not a rehash. I intend to then rule on defendant's motion for nonsuit. Now, if there are no questions, I'll have the jury brought in and advise them of the recess. I'm sure they will be delighted to have the extra time."

Lucrezia stopped Sam on his way out. "Thank you. I didn't expect such compassion. I owe you one."

She loved to watch those lashes when he blinked. *Lucrezia,* she demanded, *what the hell are you thinking? And whatever it is, forget it.*

Sam grinned. "The judge would have granted your continuance anyway, Lucrezia. But since you feel so obligated you can tell me who your mystery witness is."

Lucrezia motioned for Saunders and Molly to go on. She took Sam aside.

"Can you keep a secret?" she asked.

"Sure," Sam said, puzzled.

"Good." She squeezed his hand. "So can I. Merry Christmas, Sam."

Saunders had parked his car at Lucrezia's office, so he rode back with her and Molly. Christmas shoppers were out en masse. It took three signal light changes for the Lincoln to squeeze through the intersection of Third and Figueroa. No one said a word.

Lucrezia parked and pushed the trunk latch button. She patted Saunders once on the shoulder and motioned for him to come along. He nodded and hoisted the attaché and exhibit cases out of the trunk, reserving the largest two for himself. It was silent inside the elevator except for the Mormon Tabernacle Choir singing Handel's *Messiah.*

Inside her office, Lucrezia finally spoke. "Molly, get yourself up to the Court of Appeal clerk's office and see if there are any fresh decisions not yet published that might help. Same for the Supreme Court."

She pushed an intercom button. "Mike, get Elaine and come in here, please. I need you both for rush research on a trial brief." Another button. "Sally, get me Wayne. Tell him I want to hire two more investigators and it's urgent. He's to call me as soon as they're ready."

She turned to Saunders. "We just got knocked on our collective ass. The judge's tentative ruling stinks. This should not have happened, but it has. But if we can just hang on and get your case to the jury, we'll be all right.

"Peter, I've got a list of things I can't ask investigators to do, things you can try to locate Sullivan. They are all long shots, but we are not going to quit. Right?"

"Hallelujah."

73

Ben was exuberant. "I've never seen anyone score on a motion for nonsuit before. You are about to, I can feel it. And you got us an extra day off. You're a goddamned hero. I'll buy you a beer."

"Don't count your chickens until the check for the egg money clears."

"That doesn't make sense."

"Neither does winning this case on a nonsuit motion. Anyway, I can't, thank you. Susan invited me for dinner."

Sam stopped first at the Central Market. He bought a pint of fresh Oregon wild blackberries and a quart of blackberry frozen yogurt. He hesitated over the CoolWhip, but what the hell. Christmas comes but once a year and sometimes not that often.

And not for everyone, either. It wasn't trampling Lucrezia that troubled Sam. Every time two lawyers went against each other, one lost. Just another day's work. Beating down Peter Saunders was something else. The man was taking a screwing because of an archaic technicality. Sam could not sustain much elation over that.

He couldn't do much about it, either. Was he supposed to blow the case and his career because he felt sorry for a plaintiff?

He'd already shown one flash of weakness by failing to oppose Lucrezia's motion for a continuance. If he had pressed he might have had the win already wrapped up under his Christmas tree. Naa, the judge would have given her the break anyway. Sam swept Lucrezia into the jumble of his subconscious. Too bewildering.

Sam dropped the ancient MGB into second gear, threading his way through a hole being closed by a converging Bentley and UPS van. They peeled away like jet fighters. Nothing intimidated like a battered $800 MGB.

Susan's Toyota was in her carport. Sam pulled in behind it. He wondered if Everett Schooling had returned to Iowa. Susan had not mentioned him, and Sam didn't think he was entitled to ask.

"I have something nice for you," Sam said as he presented the brown paper bag.

Susan peeked. "Oh, sinful calories. You shouldn't."

Well, pardon me, Sam thought. He didn't say anything.

"Let me see," said Emily. "Oh, yes you should."

Dinner was latkes, pork sausage, applesauce, sour cream, and marinated cucumbers, washed down with red Zinfandel. Susan kept frying and Sam kept eating potato pancakes until he and the batter were exhausted.

"I have something nice for you, too," Susan said. "I'll fix the dessert first."

Sam raised a palm. "Dessert later, please. Show me what I get."

"All right. Settle down in the living room. I have to get my briefcase."

Susan knelt beside the coffee table. " 'Nice' is not the right word, but I think it's going to be interesting. Remember I asked to borrow the note Larry Levenson left you?"

"I've been so busy I'd forgotten all about it."

"I told you I wanted to study it. There was something strange about it. Well, there is. Here's your original back. I made a copy. I think it's a code."

"It's a what? Come on. Let me see that again." Sam took the original note and read slowly.

To my friend, Sam Corbin,
As you well know, you started out as extremely promising, but you now
are nothing but a overripe associate attorney of thirty-five or more.
The chance of partnership in Tipson, Grumm & Nuttzer, Attorneys at
law, isin dire jepardy. After my death, which is now clearly
imminent, it is you who will undoubtedly inherit full responsibility
for handling of   Peter Saunders v. Consolidated Utilities because
it is only you who knows the case, its ramifications, strengths and
many, many weaknesses better than any one else in the firm. I'm sure
you know, this may be your absolutely last and positively without
doubt you last chance at your Tipson, Gumm & Nuttzer career, only if,
of course, that's your real desire. You, undoubtedly have more than
adequately potential to be one of the greatest trial lawyers in our
time.   Only the problem is that you have some sloppy sophomoric and
really too too romantic notions, which you should have outgrown by
now, regards some boyish scruples. You have foolishly allowed what
some might call a laudable morality to become a serious obstacle, too
very much in thee way. Certainly, I don't mean to minimize and I'm
not unawareof personal marital problems between yourself and Allison.
The only advice or key I have to offer you through these difficulties
is perhaps to simple to be taken seriously at first consideration.
Regardles this is it: There is nothing immoral about money or
success. It may be useful to read this over a few times until you
really understand. Twenty should be right. Have a good life.

Larry

"Well, it doesn't sound much like the old Larry, but . . ." Sam shrugged.

"Stilted language, full of cliches, superficial observations?"

"Yes, exactly."

"That's what first caught my attention. It didn't seem as if it could have been written by the man you described. Brilliant, articulate, witty."

"Yeah, I attributed it to his illness."

"Then I remembered that you'd told me he'd been a cryptographer in some war or something."

"Korea."

"Okay. Notice all the typos?"

"So he was a lousy typist. So am I."

"They are all on the left-hand side of the page. Extra spacing, no spacing, misspellings. Only on the left-hand side. Isn't that too much coincidence?"

"Susan, have you figured this out?"

She smiled. "I'll bring the coffee."

"You are making me crazy on purpose, aren't you?"

She ignored him and left, returning from the kitchen with two steaming mugs. "There are clues near the end. 'Regardles, this is it:' marks the end of the real message. And here, where it says, 'Twenty should be right,' is another clue."

"Susan, what does the damned thing say?"

"I deciphered it almost accidentally. I knew there was something hidden but I was getting nowhere. And I didn't dare show it to anyone else. It was on my drafting table weighted down by a straightedge. The straightedge was vertical, like this." She removed a flat metal ruler from her briefcase and placed it along the left-hand margin of the note. "Keep the straight-edge parallel to the left-hand margin, and move it to the right nineteen spaces."

Sam did it, counting out loud as he slid the ruler over.

"Now the twentieth space on each line is next to the ruler's right edge. Read down vertically, starting with the C in Corbin."

Sam read,   C
             o
             v
             e
             r
             u
             P
             k
             e
             y
             c
             o
             l
             o
             n
             b
             l
             a
             n
             k
             e
             t

"CoveruP key colon blanket? Coverup key: blanket," Sam repeated. He lifted the ruler and glanced through the note again. "Obviously referring to the case of *Saunders versus Consolidated*."

Sam got off the couch and paced. "Susan, how long have you known this?"

Well, you're welcome, Susan thought. "But what does it mean?"

"It must mean that Larry discovered that Consolidated had rigged some sort of cover-up of their culpability in the Saunders case, and that 'blanket' is the key to that."

"Then 'blanket' must be the code name for a—"

"—computer file," they chorused.

"Susan, you've got to find this for me. The client is never going to give it to me. If I ask for it, they'll just cover up the cover-up."

"Sam, I can't. Consolidated is my employer too. I can't spy on my own company. Let the other side do it."

"You mean Lucrezia? This is confidential, privileged information. I can't just disclose this to her. That would be unethical. If I got caught doing that I could be disbarred."

"And if I got caught digging into the data banks, I could get fired."

Sam's annoyance was evident. She poured more coffee, asking, "Want to watch the nine o'clock movie?"

"I guess. What is it?"

"To Have and Have Not."

Sam watched Humphrey Bogart fall in love with Lauren Bacall. He ate blackberries with frozen yogurt and CoolWhip.

His attempts to snuggle with Susan fell flat. All he could think about was how to uncover the secret file.

He didn't know what he could do with it when he found it, but he had to find it anyway. He had to know. There must be a way. With or without Susan.

74

By the morning after Judge Iverson's tentative ruling, almost the entire capacity of Ferrara and Associates was being devoted to the case of *Saunders v. Consolidated Utilities*. Only critically imminent other matters were allowed to interfere. With the sole exception of Lucrezia, everybody in the office was devoted to one of two aspects of the Saunders case, finding Sullivan, or some precedent to support argument that would defeat the motion for nonsuit. Lucrezia supervised those efforts, but permitted herself the freedom to also explore other possibilities for saving the plaintiff's case.

For the past hour, she had been reviewing deposition summaries and transcripts, searching for any bit of evidence she might have overlooked that might fill the gap. Dozens of Consolidated employee depositions, all uncommunicative, all worthless. If only she had found a way to make even one of those witnesses open up.

"Dr. Raskin on line three," her intercom announced.

Grateful for the respite from her tedious search, Lucrezia picked up the telephone. "Happy Chanukah, Morty. Discovered any new diseases lately?" The young doctor was completing his last year of residency in pathology at Los Angeles County General Hospital.

"Thank you for asking. It isn't often such profound questions are raised by a shiksa lawyer. Listen, I've got a John Doe here that matches the description you put out."

"Can't talk or won't?"

"You ask hard questions. This one is DOA. I suppose 'can't' is the right answer. If you can show up in the next hour, you can ID him here. After that, he moves over to the morgue. You might never find him again."

"Thanks, Morty. I'll be there." She hung up and called the receptionist. "Do we have any number for reaching Mr. Saunders right now? Good. Try it for me, please."

Three minutes later Saunders was on line two. "Peter, a body was brought into County General that matches Sullivan's description. You're closer than I am. Can you meet me over there now?" She gave him directions, told the receptionist and Molly where to reach her, and headed for the parking garage.

The basement of County General was fifteen degrees colder than outside. Saunders was already waiting. The undecorated green walls were clean but peeling. The sweet scent of formaldehyde combined with Lysol and denatured alcohol.

Dr. Morton Raskin had to stand on tiptoe to kiss Lucrezia's cheek. "If my wife weren't working two flights up, I'd have you right here. Nice to meet you, Mr. Saunders. I've read about your case. I wish you luck. Come on. I'll show you both the stiff. Why they brought him here God only knows. He's been dead since at least Saturday."

Lucrezia and Saunders looked at each other. Sullivan had not been released from custody until Saturday morning. They followed the doctor down the corridor. "Morty," Lucrezia asked, "have you autopsied him?"

"No, not our problem since he was DOA. The ME's at the morgue will do it."

"What can you tell us?"

"According to the report, the body was discovered in a dumpster behind a K-Mart on South Broadway. Stripped of all identification. Here we are." The doctor pulled open the drawer and zipped open the body bag. "As you can see, the cause of death was apparently one hell of an incision."

The face was bloated, gray, but unmistakable. Sullivan.

Raskin watched their faces. "You know him, huh?" He re-zipped the bag and slammed the drawer shut.

Lucrezia had to turn away and swallow several times before she could talk. "Yes, Morty. We can ID him. Anything else you can tell us?"

"Probably had a lot to drink just before he bought it. The weapon was a knife with at least a five-inch blade. Whoever did that to him had to be one awfully big, strong dude. And I would guess, since there were no signs of struggle at all, it was someone he knew."

IV

JUDGMENTS

75

Sam's next morning in the office after the recess had been declared was a gift.

He luxuriated in the extra catch-up time, although every twenty minutes, someone would stop in to congratulate him on having the Saunders case practically won. Sam told himself he was not the least superstitious, but that made him nervous.

Jean came in. "Here are letters to sign. I corrected your atrocious grammar in the top one. You used 'that' to introduce a nonrestrictive clause."

"A distinction which I find unworthy of preservation, but thank you."

"Very amusing. Oh, and there is a Constance Savin on line one."

Sam remembered Constance Savin from his Point Anacapa inspection trip and from her deposition. Isaac Karrasch's elderly secretary, the archetype of reticence.

At Mrs. Savin's deposition, Lucrezia had whispered to him how remarkable that a person of so little awareness could be secretary to the plant manager. And, as Sam recalled, her ignorance was matched by her memory. Whatever she had once known she no longer remembered. She had probably been given the Consolidated Witness-of-the-Year Award.

Sam picked up the telephone. "This is Sam Corbin, Mrs. Savin. Merry Christmas. What can I do for you?"

"Merry Christmas, Mr. Corbin. I wasn't sure you would remember me. It's about my testimony in the Saunders case. I must see you."

San Luis Obispo was a long way to go just to help an old lady correct some trivial error in her deposition. Especially a lady who never was going to be called as a witness by either side.

"Can't we do this over the telephone, Mrs. Savin? It's a little difficult for me to come up to San Luis right now."

She cackled. "I wouldn't expect you to. I'm retired now, living at the Casa Serena in Woodland Hills." Her voice turned confidential. "This is important."

Sam looked at his watch. He could afford a break. He had been given a whole extra day. He took directions, promising to be there in forty minutes.

Sam took the Ventura Freeway to the Topanga Canyon exit, then drove west on Ventura Boulevard, looking for the cross street. The Casa Serena was typical of apartment complexes designed for senior citizens. Single-story stucco. Unused putting green. Swimming pool too small to swim in.

Mrs. Savin answered the door. She was heavier than Sam remembered and used a cane now. "Come in, Mr. Corbin." You're very prompt."

The tiny apartment was spotless. The built-in bookshelf was crowded with Hummel figurines. A lilac scent filled the room. Sam was led to a rose-colored velour couch.

Mrs. Savin eased herself into a matching recliner. "I know how busy you must be. I'll come right to the point. I perjured myself at my deposition." She leaned back and waited for the reaction.

Sam was not shocked. He had observed attacks of testimony reversal before. The most interesting question was usually "Why?" That was what he wanted to know first.

"It must be obvious why I testified as I did. My job. A widow, ten months from retirement."

"Of course, I understand that, Mrs. Savin. But why are you turning now?"

"My son-in-law, Marvin, died three weeks ago. Forty-four years old. He had emphysema. He was an insulation installer.

Made good money, but all that asbestos and fiberglass. He smoked, too. It was probably all those things killed him. Such a good boy. He treated my Martha and my granddaughter as if they were goddesses, which was a good thing, too, because my Martha barely knows how to change a TV channel. I don't know what's to become of them. She has a lawyer, of course, but the insurance company is denying liability, and you know how long those lawyers take. I can't help them much on—"

"Mrs. Savin. Why now?"

"Oh, yes. I've been following the Saunders trial in the *Times*, and how the company is trying to wiggle out of responsibility to that poor man. I don't blame you, of course. You're merely doing your job, just as I was. But it's not right. When they destroy people's lives, they should have to pay. Besides, what can they do to me now?"

"So now you feel free to tell the truth?"

"These companies have to start being held accountable."

"I understand, Mrs. Savin, and I appreciate your calling me. Now tell me what the truth is."

She told him. She told him all about the confidential meetings in the Point Anacapa executive conference room. Always Karrasch and Magnasunn present. Usually a couple of department managers and the chief inspector. Once the executive vice-president, Mr. St. James.

The theme in every meeting about Peter Saunders was the same. How to get him out. It had to be done without strengthening his credibility. An accident or even a termination for incompetence if it could be made believable.

They called him an embarrassment, a thorn in the side, a nuisance, even a threat. They discussed every conceivable method for getting rid of him. Coercion, pressure, they even discussed the possibility of framing him for a crime.

"Such as planting plutonium in his refrigerator and claiming he stole it?"

"You know, I read that FBI agent's testimony in the paper, but no, I don't remember ever hearing that one considered."

But, Sam thought, *her testimony would be sufficient to permit the jury to make that inference.*

"You know, he handed it to them when he quit," she continued. "Karrasch had still not figured out how to fire him for incompetence and make it stick." She laughed her high-pitched cackle. "Even after they fixed the control-room gauges."

Sam was incredulous over that. "Are you saying that they sabotaged the instruments and risked a nuclear accident just to make Saunders look bad?"

"It wasn't that extreme. They talked about tampering with the instrument readings just enough so that Saunders would be misled into making a dumb move they could nail him on. But when the accident really happened, which they did not plan, of course, Saunders did everything more than right with virtually no instrumentation working at all."

"And all this just to save money on the plant safety requirements?"

"Oh my, no. If it had just been the existing plant involved, they would have made the recommended changes to shut him up, even though that would have cost several millions."

"I don't understand. What then?"

"The fifteen-year plan. They were projecting a 4,000-megawatt expansion. Four new reactors to be on-line before 2002. They estimated Saunders's requirements would add 3 billion to the cost."

"You were actually present at all these meetings?"

"They kicked me out when St. James came up. But I took notes on most."

Sam could let himself get really interested in that.

"There are notes? Where?"

"They were always destroyed. Karrasch's orders."

"Oh."

"But first, he always had me transcribe my notes to disk."

"Oh. And you have the disks now?"

"Then I would turn each disk over to him."

"Mrs. Savin, does the computer file or directory name 'blanket' mean anything to you?"

She shook her head, but it was clear she understood the question. "Mr. Karrasch always did his own encoding. He knows a lot about computers, you know."

76

Sam rejected the notion of putting up the top as he walked back to his car. Afternoon clouds were forming, but no rain was forecast.

Mrs. Savin recalled telling Larry Levenson nothing more than she had testified to in her deposition. Still Larry somehow had figured it all out.

Mrs. Savin's testimony would certainly defeat his motion for nonsuit. By the time Sam entered the inbound Hollywood Freeway, he still had not decided what to do.

Perhaps his cross-examination could discredit Mrs. Savin, perhaps not. But if the jury did accept her story, she might trigger an extremely large plaintiff's verdict, including substantial punitive damages.

Sam parked the MGB. The tired old machine gurgled, popped, and dripped, cooling down.

He would talk it over with Pringle. Not Sam's favorite person, but an analytical mind. Sam hoped he would catch him in. Partners had a custom of disappearing in the days before Christmas.

"Come in, Tiger," Pringle said. "They tell me you've been wiping up the courthouse floor with Lucrezia." Pringle recognized Sam's distaste. "Don't worry about her. She's been through it before. Lucrezia Ferrara was winning and losing cases while you were struggling to pass trigonometry. What can I do for you?"

Sam told him all about Mrs. Savin's vacillating heart.

Pringle grimaced. "Lucky she came to us. How do you see handling her?"

"That's what I want to talk about, of course. But I don't think we have a choice. It seems clear we are obliged to disclose this new evidence to plaintiff and probably to withdraw as defense counsel."

"Whoa, Sonny. What about BP Code, 6068?" Pringle swiveled and grabbed the blue vinyl-bound *Business and Professions Code* from his back shelf. "Every California attorney is required to, and I quote, 'maintain inviolate the confidence and, at every peril to himself, to preserve the secrets of his client.' "

"Come on, Mr. Pringle. The duty to preserve client's confidences doesn't authorize us to conceal evidence. But if you want to play 'quotations,' try Penal Code, Section 135. 'The willful suppression of evidence is a criminal offense.' So don't overlook what we have here is knowledge of commission of perjury. Are you saying we don't have a duty to disclose that?"

"Slow it down, Corbin. You don't even have a basis for concluding perjury has necessarily been committed. How do we know the old lady's deposition testimony wasn't true, and she's lying now?"

"That doesn't make sense. Why would she do that?"

"Hell, I don't know. Guilt over her son-in-law. Some real or imagined slight by Karrasch. Senility. Booze. Drugs. The point is, you don't know either."

Sam was silent. Pringle was right about that much. He could not be certain.

Pringle's tone changed to paternal. "Let's talk pragmatics, son. What happens if we disclose? One, we lose the case. Two, we lose the client. You know what that annual billing is worth? Three, the client loses public good will and credibility. Can you even imagine the cost of that? Four, Tipson, Grumm & Nuttzer will look like a collection of nerds. Every lawyer in the country will be laughing his head off. What do you think that will do to the effectiveness of your law firm?"

"Are you trying to say we can ethically suppress this?"

"Ethically? Get real, man. This is Los Angeles, California, USA. Late twentieth century. Tuesday. The sun does not shine all the time."

Sam looked past Pringle to the window. He was right again, it was drizzling.

"Corbin, do you believe that our client, or the world for that matter, gives one genuine fuck about our ethics? Have you ever heard a client insist we be ethical? All they want from us is success, just so it's cost effective. To win and not get caught. That is the highest ethic in this business."

"I sort of have this old-fashioned idea there is some distinction between the legal profession and a business."

"This is a business first. Don't you forget that. Without a profit base to provide livings for you and me, neither of us gets to practice our profession."

Sam thought of Susan's repugnance. "Maybe I shouldn't be."

"What are you, a visiting choir boy from St. Paul's? I can tell you now, confidentially, at the conclusion of this trial you are assured of your partnership. Are you seriously willing to blow your career over this?"

Sam did not answer. He really didn't know. He was certainly glad he had not mentioned the decoding of Larry's note.

Pringle returned to his usual commanding-officer mode. "I'm going to make this easy for you. This is a direct order. There will be no disclosure of Mrs. Savin's statements. I will take responsibility for the conclusion that Mrs. Savin is not a reliable witness. You will proceed with the trial on your present line. Let me spell this out. You follow these instructions or you are out. Do you completely understand, Corbin?"

"Yes, I completely understand." Sam was sure he did not completely agree though. He headed for the door.

"Tiger, just stay cool and trust me. I'm saving your ass."

Sam slammed the door behind him.

Pringle thought for a moment, unwrapped a piece of home-made walnut divinity left by his secretary, and picked up his telephone. "Get me Mr. Champion. Yes, CEO of Consolidated Utilities. Track him down if you have to. And hold the other calls."

Pringle thought the divinity was excellent. He tried the pecan fudge. His intercom buzzed. "Mr. Champion on line one." Pringle swallowed hurriedly and glanced at his watch. Two minutes. Not bad.

"Randy? Bart here. I am sorry to interrupt, but this may be urgent. It would seem evidence of the company's possible culpability in the Saunders matter is leaking out."

He told Champion about Mrs. Savin's desire to change her testimony and the potentially catastrophic consequences.

"Yes," Pringle said. "Karrasch's former private secretary. Yes, it is a shame. No, I don't know whatever happened to simple, old-fashioned loyalty."

Pringle reached for the last piece of divinity but found it difficult to unwrap while shouldering the telephone. "Yes, only a few minutes ago. From Sam Corbin. You met him at the Jonathan Club. Yes, he is the one that is going with one of your assistant vice-presidents, Susan. . . . Yes, Schooling."

Pringle almost dropped the telephone and gave up. Candy would have to wait. "No, Sam is all right. Yes, you can. Certainly I can vouch for him. Completely under control, I assure you. Merry Christmas to you too, Randy. I look forward to that also."

Pringle tore the wrapper open. My God, that was delicious stuff.

When Sam returned to his office a minor crisis awaited. Nordlund Dairies Inc. had just been cited for employing illegal aliens by the Immigration and Naturalization Service, which was threatening to shut them down pending a hearing. These little Christmas-week emergencies seemed to be a tradition in the legal profession.

"I've got Christmas orders to fill. What about due process and the presumption of innocence?" the client screamed. The guy was a natural-born lawyer.

There goes my afternoon, Sam sighed. Nordlund, one of the largest dairies in the state, could not be denied. They had major antitrust litigation pending.

By the time Sam had assured the unabated flow of low-calorie eggnog mix throughout the holiday season the afternoon was nearly gone.

Sam's thoughts returned to serious matters. Before making a decision he would talk to Mrs. Savin again. He had to make sure she was telling the truth now.

When Sam telephoned, she was incongruously evasive. "Did I say that? Are you sure?"

Something had happened. Something wrong.

"Mrs. Savin, I think I had better come out and see you again. Right now if that's not inconvenient."

She was reluctant, but did not know how to say no. "I don't really see the need."

"There is a need. I'm leaving now. I'll be there as soon as I can, Mrs. Savin."

He had been invited to Susan's for dinner. He called to warn her he would be late.

Sam got the MGB top up at the cost of only one skinned knuckle. Attaining Woodland Hills during a rush-hour drizzle was not recreational. By the time Sam reached the Casa Serena, he was tired, frustrated, and his left knee ached from depressing the clutch.

When Sam rang the bell, Mrs. Savin came to the door promptly, but left the chain secured.

"May I come in, Mrs. Savin? It's important."

"No. I've changed my mind. I mean, I made a mistake. Whatever I said in my deposition is correct."

"Mrs. Savin, you know that's nonsense. You've got to talk to me and tell me what has happened. I may be able to help."

Mrs. Savin looked away. "My Martha just got hired as a receptionist at Consolidated headquarters. I have to look out for my own. I'm sorry." She closed the door.

Sam was still shaking his head as he climbed into his car. Only three hours had elapsed since he had walked into Pringle's office. Man, talk about your corporate efficiency.

77

Traffic inbound was as bad as it had been coming out. Christmas shopping destroyed the patterns. Sam was an hour later than he had estimated.

As Sam turned the corner on Susan's street, Everett Schooling's rental Chrysler backed out of her driveway and headed in the opposite direction. Now what? Sam wondered.

"Hi," Sam said when Susan came to the door. "I was so late I didn't stop for dessert. I'm sorry. I'll take you guys out for ice cream."

Susan's lips brushed his cheek. "It's okay. Dinner's late too. I had company."

"I saw him drive away."

"He wanted to talk to you, but he couldn't wait any longer."

"Me? Can I have a beer, please?"

Susan got it out for him and pulled the tab. "Everett has invited Emily and me to Estherville for Christmas weekend."

Sam's elbow stopped in mid-arc. "Goddammit, Susan. I thought we planned to spend Christmas together."

Susan poured herself a glass of white wine. After what seemed like an hour and a half, she relented. "Relax. I told him that."

Sam brought the beer can the rest of the way and half-drained it. "So why did he want to talk to me?" Sam smothered his anger and tried to grin. "Am I invited too?"

She smiled. "He thought he could persuade you to encourage us to go. He claims it will be an invaluable lesson in psychodrama."

Sam felt his face getting hot. "I realize this is none of my business, but I can't resist the observation. What the hell does a banker from Estherville, Iowa, have to teach you?"

"So far it's been quite a lot, actually."

He started to say something, but she put her fingers on his lips. "Don't be angry. He doesn't even know he's doing it. If you toss the salad I'll give you another beer."

Sam wanted to ask a lot more, but it was clear that Susan was not yet ready to answer. He would temporarily settle for less. "I'll take it."

Sam's first bite of red snapper was a tranquilizer. "This is the best I've ever had."

"Thank you. It's the garlic butter and fresh lime."

"Does Consolidated have a fifteen-year plan to add four more reactors to the Point Anacapa plant?"

"How on earth did you know that? That's why I was up at Anacapa when we met. It's the deepest company secret."

"Not quite the deepest."

Sam told her about his two visits with Constance Savin and the session with Pringle in between. Susan was appalled, but fascinated. She made him tell it all again.

"Say," she said, pausing to gulp wine. "Should you even be telling me all this?"

"Of course not, it's just that I have to. Besides, compared to what Pringle wants me to do, telling you is as serious as overtime parking."

"My God, Sam. This is serious. What are you going to do?"

"Me? What am I going to do?" Sam paused. He would not permit himself anger. "For one thing, urge you again to break into that secret file."

"I want to help. I'm troubled by what you've been telling me. But I'm also repulsed by the idea of committing espionage against my own company. Besides, what good would it do if I found it?"

"I don't know. Don't know. Maybe none. But I have to find out. I guess the more I know, the closer I can come to the right decision."

"There isn't much time for indecision, is there?"

"No, there sure as hell isn't, Susan. Just one more thing I ask you to consider, and then I'll press no further. Is your position so much different than mine? And if it isn't, don't you have a similar dilemma?"

78

On Friday, Christmas Eve, the entire staff was shutting down early but Susan wanted to enjoy Christmas weekend free of concern over what had to be faced Monday. Now everyone else was drifting out, the telephone would stop ringing, she could concentrate.

She didn't even have to think about fixing dinner. Sam and Emily had promised to wait, however late. They would go for pizza, Mexican, or Chinese, depending on the majority vote. Tomorrow she would prepare a fantastic Christmas feast.

As her pile of unfinished work decreased, more and more room was left for Sam's argument to intrude.

If Sam was Consolidated's hired gun, then what was she? If Sam was defending the company's irresponsibility, wasn't she planning an expanded base for more of the same? Was what she did any more virtuous than what he did, or was she simply further back from the battle lines? If they were both abetting Consolidated's malfeasance, was environmental planning less reprehensible than lawyering?

Susan removed the copy of Larry Levenson's note from her briefcase. The code word was Blanket. There was nothing wrong in examining the file, was there?

She looked through the glass partition of her office. There was no one else on the floor. Who would know?

Susan did not presume to consider herself a hacker, but she had been taught how to use the computer. And her employee code number was high enough in the corporate hierarchy to permit her unlimited access to the data banks.

Blanket was probably the name of a document or file. First, she would have to be in the correct document or file directory. But what the hell was that called, DEEP, DARK SECRETS?

She took Volume II of the *Consolidated Utilities of California Operations Manual* down from her shelf. Back to school.

After a half-hour's studying, Susan slammed the book shut. Why was she fooling around? Sam was already annoyed, she knew. He would just have to handle disappointment as well. She had real work to do.

Fifteen minutes later, she was trying likely sounding file directories. Point Anacapa Plant. Nuclear Power Plants. Nuclear Power Systems. Nuclear Power I. Nuclear Power II. *Nothing.*

Okay. Litigation. *There was something.* Susan punched keys furiously. Litigation Federal. *Nope.* Litigation State. *Maybe.* Litigation State California Blanket. *No.* Litigation State California Saunders v. *Okay.* Blanket? *Nothing.*

Susan began to sense a challenge. That made her motivated. Motivation made her stubborn.

She decided to call up every file and document directory alphabetically. How long it took didn't matter. She refused to be blocked by mere chips on printed circuit boards.

Should she start with the A's or with the Z's and work backward? She decided to start with M and work backwards a few letters. Then she would return to N and work toward Q. Alternating made sense, didn't it? Susan laughed out loud. Her methodology had all the logic of a crapshoot.

An hour and a half later, her eyes were red and her back sore. Damn Samuel Corbin. What was she doing anyway, playing Jane Bond?

She got up and walked around her desk twice, then went back to accessing Operations files.

The next file opened was Operations Cleanup. Somehow that had the ring of euphemism. The document directory in that file listed documents named Blanket Conditions and numbered 001 through 999.

Susan felt the thrill of anticipated discovery.

She punched the key to open the first document. The monitor

screen flashed INVALID KEY. She must have fingered the wrong key. She tried again. INVALID KEY. Then she realized that each Blanket Conditions document name was preceded by a three-digit number. Of course.

She opened 001 Blanket Conditions. The monitor screen flashed OPENING DOCUMENT. It took a few seconds. Susan relaxed in satisfaction as the monitor displayed the document. Boring stuff. Deed restrictions or covenants, apparently.

It would take two hours to go through them all. Why hadn't Larry given them more of a clue? Then she remembered "Twenty should be right." The code words in Larry's note had been in the column twenty spaces from the left-hand margin, but he could have put them anywhere. Maybe the number had a double significance.

Susan held her breath and keyed to open 020 Blanket Conditions. The monitor screen flashed OPENING DOCUMENT. She waited impatiently. The last one hadn't taken this long. There. The monitor display changed.

SECURITY CLEARANCE ACCESS ONLY.
INSERT APPROPRIATE CODE OR CANCEL

All right, all right!

This had to be it. Susan entered her employee code number and waited. The screen displayed

UNAUTHORIZED CODE
TRY AGAIN? [Y/N?]

Susan punched Y. The display reverted to

SECURITY CLEARANCE ACCESS ONLY
INSERT APPROPRIATE CODE OR CANCEL

She entered her employee code number again carefully. She might have made an error.

UNAUTHORIZED CODE
TRY AGAIN? [Y/N?]

This did not make sense. When Susan had been promoted to assistant vice-president, she was told her code number granted unlimited access. She had never even seen a SECURITY CLEARANCE ACCESS ONLY restriction on the screen before. The manual listed no such classification.

Susan kept trying. She used every number that might be in the company records. Social security, residence address, office number, telephone extension, birth date, even her driver's license. Nothing worked.

She was at the goddamned gate, but it would not unlock. This had to be the file. Damn. She banged her desk top in frustration. The picture flickered, wavered, but stubbornly steadied.

TRY AGAIN [Y/N?]

Susan hated the idea, but she had to admit she was beaten. This was going to take the expertise of someone who knew a lot more about computer security than she did.

She would quit for tonight. Maybe she or Sam could find someone to help. They could try again, perhaps on Christmas night, or on Sunday. The place would be deserted all weekend. There would still be time enough.

Susan stretched her aching back and looked at her watch. Uh-oh. She called home but the line was busy. At least that told her where Emily was. Sam would be there by now too.

Susan threw her copy of Larry Levenson's note and two unfinished files back in her briefcase. She picked lint off her pleated tartan skirt, pulled on her camel blazer, and headed for the elevators.

Randolph Champion was in the elevator. He nodded vacantly.

"Merry Christmas, Mr. Champion." Susan stepped in, the door closed and the elevator resumed its descent.

"Merry Christmas," he replied. There was no recognition.

But by the time they dropped four floors there was.

Champion's mental processes churned. Susan Schooling, assistant vice-president, planning. Girlfriend of Sam Corbin, defending *Saunders v. Consolidated*. Telephone call from Bartlett Pringle. Leak of evidence of the cover-up. Information came from Corbin. What was she doing here so late on Christmas Eve?

Susan was doing the same thing. How much did he know? Was he behind the entire plot? Had he been spying on her? Could he guess what she had been doing? Spying. She clutched her briefcase close.

"Working unusually late, aren't you, Mrs. Schooling?"

"No, sir. Yes, sir. I just wanted to clear away a few details so I could enjoy the holiday."

Champion recognized the need to be abrupt in a descending elevator. "They wouldn't happen to be details in the Saunders case, would they, Mrs. Schooling?"

Jesus. He knew everything. She held the case tighter and backed up a step. "No. I mean, I don't know what you mean." *Why wouldn't the elevator door open?*

"Perhaps you had better show me what's in that briefcase." *Not Larry's note.* "No. I mean, it's only company papers."

"That's why I want to see them, Mrs. Schooling."

Susan squeezed through the opening doors and started running across the granite-tiled lobby.

A barely awake guard sat at the information desk.

Champion shouted. "Stop her! She's stealing secrets!"

The guard was grossly overweight. His gun belt was too uncomfortable to keep buckled when he sat. As he jerked to full consciousness and stood, his holstered weapon clattered to the floor. It was not easily retrieved.

"Fool!" Champion yelled. "Help me catch her."

Susan was out the door. She kicked off brand-new Dior pumps and ran in stockinged feet for her parked car. Thank God the skirt was short and full.

Champion was already using the guard's telephone.

The guard gave up trying to rebuckle, unholstered his .357, and let the belt drop back to the floor.

He waddled to the entrance.

Susan had to drive back past the front of the building to reach the street.

The guard cleared the front door just as her white Toyota passed. He spread his feet, took a two-handed grip, and led the accelerating automobile with his sights.

He couldn't run worth a damn, but he was still a good shot. The first round struck the right front windshield pillar. The second one went through the rear window, leaving a small neat hole and a spider's web of cracks. The spent bullet dropped harmlessly onto the Toyota's center console. Susan was doing sixty when she turned into the street. The third shot missed.

She was free.

79

As Sam turned onto Susan's street, it occurred to him that smoldering anger might be incongruous to the occasion. It was Christmas Eve. Gifts for Susan and Emily and two bottles of Chandon were on the floor of the MGB. There were three nights and two whole days to look forward to. Susan apparently had rejected Everett Schooling's proposal (hadn't she?), whatever that was. He would not dare say it out loud, but he knew he had the Saunders case won. Partnership lay within his grasp.

He was not even sure that was anger down there, maybe just confusion. Hell, didn't that prove how confused he was?

Susan had not said yes to him either. If that was what he wanted, he would just have to be patient, wouldn't he? Of course, why not?

He wasn't sure he wanted to play the kind of hardball that would insure victory in the Saunders case either. And the partnership's appeal was already tarnished. Was that really his idea of ideal?

If only he knew what was in the Blanket file. That might help him decide. At least he had three lovely nights and two days to think it through. That was when he got close enough to see that Susan's house was dark.

Her Toyota was not in the carport. What the hell? He was late himself, and even if Susan was later, where was Emily?

He tried the front door. Locked. Susan kept saying she meant to have a key made for him. Sam sensed that was a problem for her so had not pushed.

The telephone was ringing.

He brushed dust off the front stoop and sat down to wait.

Susan drove north on Beverly Glen to Wilshire and turned west. She had intended to drive straight home, then realized they could be waiting for her.

Isn't that strange? she thought. *Suddenly Consolidated is "they," not "us."* One of the things she had recently learned from Everett was how drastically her perception of a person could change. Why not of a company as well? *But surely, Consolidated couldn't get anyone there that fast. Anyway, Sam should be there by now. Nothing will happen if he's there. I'd better call and be sure.*

She pulled up to a telephone booth in front of a closed Texaco station. She slid her briefcase out of sight under the seat as usual. If only she hadn't panicked when Champion confronted her. There was nothing damning in that briefcase. Larry's letter would have meant nothing.

She let her home number ring for a long time but there was no answer.

She got back into her car and drove, unsure of where.

Sam sat, waited, and worried. *Susan would not just pick up Emily and fly off to Iowa with Mr. Cornfed. On Christmas Eve? After inviting me over? She wouldn't. Not without at least leaving a note.*

Sam brushed the seat of his trousers as he rose to search the mailbox and behind the screen door. He heard the telephone ringing again.

"Hi, Sam."

Sam turned back to see Emily strolling up the front walk. "Where in the hell have you been?" he shrieked, hating his shrillness as he heard it.

In one leap he took the three steps down, threw her up, caught and hugged her on the way down. "You don't know how glad I am to see you, Kiddo."

"Sam, you are totally weird. That's why I like you."

"But where have you been? Where's Susan?"

"I was down the street visiting Vernice. I kept calling to see if Mom was home. Then I remembered you might be waiting, so I came to see, and you were." She produced a key. "Come on in. I'll give you a beer."

Sam laughed. "You are a gracious hostess. Thank you. Do you know where Susan is?"

Emily shrugged. "She'll call soon."

Sam waited another twenty minutes and called Consolidated's administrative office number. The taped message said the office was closed until 9:00 A.M. on Monday, if you have a service emergency call the number listed in the directory for your area, and have a Merry Christmas.

"Emily, let's take a ride over to Susan's office."

"I'll leave a note."

Traffic was light. It was only twenty minutes from Santa Monica to Consolidated's Century City headquarters.

The heavy glass front doors were locked. Sam and Emily could see the guard sitting at the desk in the middle of the lobby.

Sam pounded on the door, but the guard waved him off. Sam kept pounding. Finally the guard forced himself erect and waddled toward the door.

"Boy, is he fat," said Emily.

The guard pointed toward the lock. "Closed," he mouthed.

"Jeez, we already knew that," said Emily.

Sam yelled, "I have to ask you a question. It's important."

The guard relented, bent painfully and unlocked the door.

"Thanks," Sam said. "We are looking for Susan Schooling. She works here. Could you possibly see if she is still in her office?"

"Sorry. Mrs. Schooling checked out about seven-thirty."

"Did she happen to mention where she was going?"

"No. She seemed to be in a big hurry though."

"Thanks. Merry Christmas."

"Merry Christmas to you too." The guard locked the door and waddled back to his desk.

Fat doesn't mean stupid. He reached for the telephone.

Champion's first telephone call was to Magnasunn. "You are in charge. Find her. But no more shooting. It is imperative that we find out precisely what she knows and who she's told. Report every hour."

"I may need more manpower."

"Pull in what you can from existing security stations. Most of them are sitting on their fat asses anyway. If you need more, get them. We have no room for failure on this operation, understand?"

Magnasunn understood in the context under discussion, "we" meant him. First he ordered a tap with around-the-clock monitoring on Susan's home telephone. Within a half-hour he had four unmarked radio cars cruising her neighborhood and four more on the way.

Before joining his units in the field, he took a moment to telephone Karrasch in San Luis Obispo. It was remotely conceivable she might head north. She knew people there.

"Thanks," Karrasch said, although he did not sound grateful. "It would be useful if you'd keep me informed."

Magnasunn agreed. The key to a successful search mission was to plug as many holes as possible.

80

Consciously or not, Susan's route was inching toward home. Surely Sam would be there by now. She would just drive by slowly. If he was there, she could safely dash inside. If not, then . . . what?

Staying home alone and waiting for someone to take another shot at her did not seem prudent. She could call the police, though. And tell them what? "They are after me. They've already taken shots at me."

"Who took shots at you?"

"The guard where I work."

"Oh, and who is after you now?"

"Them."

"Sure, lady, sure."

There was a street lamp on each corner of Susan's block, but they did not do much to light a moonless night. Susan turned on her bright headlights as she entered the street. Every house had a garage or carport. Usually, almost no cars were parked in the street at night. Tonight was different. Of course, on Christmas Eve there would be guests. As Susan approached her house, she could see it was dark. Sam's MGB was not in sight. She slowed with indecision.

Behind her, an engine started, headlights lit. A vehicle pulled out from the curb and rapidly, it seemed, began to close the distance between them. Susan jammed the gas pedal to the floor and executed a four-wheel drift into a right turn at the corner. Further behind her now, the other car turned right too. She made a series of turns through a maze of one- and two-block-long streets until she entered the heavier traffic of Montana Boulevard. She really was not sure whether she had just thrown off a tailing vehicle or was merely being paranoid.

She was frightened for herself and worried about Sam and Emily. Where the hell were they? And why weren't they home waiting for her? She was tired. But where should she go? There was a motel close by on Ocean Boulevard. Not one of the big, fancy places, the Ocean something. The name didn't matter. She knew where it was.

The Ocean Shores Motel was a half-mile from the shore, but the vacancy sign was lit. The old-fashioned motel consisted of two long rows of single-story buildings with parking in between.

Susan parked outside the office, paid with an American Express card, and received the key for number forty-eight. It was not until she was walking back to her car that she remembered she was shoeless and that the soles of her pantyhose were in shreds. The space in front of her room was taken so she parked in front of the opposite building. She locked the Toyota and started for her room. She turned back, opened the trunk, and removed pink and white sweat socks with matching running shoes.

Inside the room, she closed the drapes, locked, bolted and chained the door, and looked for the telephone. There was none. Damn, she had just assumed . . . well, she would rest just a little, then go out and use the pay phone. She hung up her blazer, shirt, and skirt. She threw the shredded pantyhose into the waste basket, grateful for cotton briefs. She threw back the covers and stretched out. It would just be for a few minutes.

81

"**S**am," Emily said as she climbed back into the MGB, "I'm getting kind of scared."

"I know, Kiddo. I think the best thing is to go back to your place. That's the first place she's going to call." *The first place the hospital or morgue will call too*, he thought. "Let's try to get some sleep. I'll stay on the couch." *In the morning*, he thought, *I'll report her missing. LAPD won't do anything until after twenty-four hours anyway.*

As they walked back into Susan's house, Emily asked, "Did you notice that man working on the telephone pole near the corner?"

Sam hadn't spotted him. Telephone lineman working at night on Christmas Eve? Strange. "Would you like to open a Christmas present before you go to bed?"

"Let's wait for Mom. Nite."

Outside the motel room, there were low sounds of men talking. Susan sprang up and went to the window. Without even opening the drapes she could tell it was dawn Christmas morning. She peeked through. Two men were standing near the rear of her Toyota. Their backs were toward her but one of them could have been Karrasch. God, she was getting paranoiac. They headed toward the front office. She threw on her shirt and skirt, grabbed the rest, and ran out in the opposite direction.

Three blocks later she stopped at a twenty-four-hour service station and asked to use the restroom. The attendant eyed her with disfavor.

"It's a jungle out there," she said, and handed him five dollars.

He grinned and gave up the key. When Susan returned the key, he looked over her combed hair, scrubbed face, and neatly tucked-in shirt under camel blazer. "Much nicer," he said. "But those shoes don't make it."

Susan went to the telephone booth and called home. Sam answered on the first half of the first ring.

"Sam, it's me. They've been chasing me and shooting at me. Sam, I found Blanket, but . . ."

"Stop. Don't say another word. Your phone may be bugged. We'll talk about it as soon as I get you."

"All right. What should I do now?"

"Just answer my questions. Nothing more. Are you safe where you are right now?"

"Y-yes, for now."

"Can you stay on this line for a few minutes?"

"Okay, Sam."

He started to yell for Emily, but she was at his side. "It's your mom. She is safe but in trouble. Someone is after her. I'll explain later. What I want you to do right now is get on your bike and ride to both ends of the block. I want to know if you spot anyone sitting in a parked car anywhere on the street. As fast as you can. Go."

Emily nodded and sped off.

"Susan, it's me again. We are waiting for some information." Sam continued to talk, saying nothing significant at all, just soothing and calming. He kept it up until Emily returned. "Hold on a moment, Susan."

Emily was breathless. "I rode to both corners. There's no one in any parked car."

Sam hugged her. "Okay, Susan, come on home. I'll be cruising the block with a shotgun to make sure you get in okay. No one is going to try a shot at you here."

After Susan hung up she wondered how he'd known to have a shotgun ready.

"What shotgun? asked Emily.

"I just said that in case the phone really is bugged. Do you have any black tubing or rod around here, about three feet long and an inch in diameter?"

"Give me a break. Wait. I've got an exercise bar in my room that I put up in the doorway sometimes to do chin-ups. But it's chrome-plated."

Sam took a look at it. He removed the white rubber crutch tip from one end. "Perfect. The top's down. We stick this end up between the seats, it will look like a stainless-steel gun barrel."

Susan started walking back to the Ocean Shores. Of course, Sam had assumed that she had the Toyota, and in the excitement of finally making contact she had overlooked the fact that she might not. Maybe she should walk home. It really was not all that far. But if the house was being watched by men in automobiles, she would be extremely vulnerable. Better drive. If she still had a car available.

She cautiously approached the rear of the motel and peeked around the corner. Her Toyota was still there, but so was a man in a business suit, lingering near the office. She walked away.

It was less than a mile's walk to the Holiday Inn. The Budget agency had a blue Grand Am immediately available. Susan thought it would be prudent to order full insurance coverage.

82

It had taken Magnasunn three telephone calls to trace Champion. He strove to remain patient. "Yes, Mr. Champion," he said. "Those were her exact words to Sam Corbin, 'I found Blanket.'"

"Shit," said Champion. "We are losing control. Bring her in this time, or we will all be up to our necks in it. Inform Karrasch." He hung up.

"She found Blanket? Shit," said Karrasch. He had been confident that the code was virtually unbreakable. He hung up and called another number. "Have the helicopter ready. I'm going to Los Angeles. Yes, I know what day it is. So, Merry Christmas." Everything was falling apart. He could no longer sit on the sidelines and leave it up to those clowns. They had screwed up damn near everything they touched. He got dressed.

Magnasunn replaced the cellular phone on its console bracket. He could see it coming. If this turned sour, the bastards would try to lay it all off on him. He had goddamned better well succeed. Either that or end up back in southeast Asia.

He picked up the microphone and keyed the transmitter. "This is Unit One to all units. Target is going to try to make it home. She will be coming in any minute. Stay off her street. Repeat, stay off her street. I do not want her scared off. Continue to circle and be ready to close off the north and south ends of the block as soon as she enters. Grab and run. Do not fire. Do not fire. MGB may be armed."

Susan meticulously adjusted the rear-view mirrors on the blue rental car. She would tolerate no blind spots. She closed the windows, locked the doors, and started driving home.

Sam and Emily were driving the length of the block, back and forth, making a U-turn at each end. Watching for a white Toyota.

The shiny chrome tubing stuck up between the seats and rested against the windshield, reflecting sunlight every time the MGB headed north. Sam altered its angle. "Hold it, Emily, so it doesn't fall over. Low down so they can't see your hands. That's it."

"All units. This is Unit Three. I think we've spotted target. Blue Pontiac heading east on San Vicente."

"This is Unit Two. I thought we were looking for a white Toyota."

"The driver matches target description. She's turning south on target street. We are right behind her."

"Unit Four. We'll close up the south end."

Emily yelled and pointed ahead. "Sam, I think that's her in the blue car turning the corner."

The sun was reflecting off the Pontiac's windshield. Sam squinted. "Are you sure? She's got a white . . ."

"It's her. It's her. See the black car coming around the corner behind her?"

Sam glanced in his rearview mirror. "Yeah, and there's another one coming up behind us."

Susan's blue Pontiac was headed southbound, the black sedan now close behind. Close enough for Sam and Emily to see two men in the front seat. Sam was heading north toward the Pontiac, with a second black sedan carrying two more men, close in his rearview mirror.

Sam accelerated, closing the gap further, and skidded to a stop that almost blocked the street. The car behind him hit its brakes hard and veered to its right, coming to rest inches from the MGB.

Sam waved Susan through. "Go. Go," he yelled.

Susan nodded, and squeezed the Pontiac around him, climbing the curb with her right wheels to do it. As Susan sped away, Sam backed the MGB to block the car following her.

As Sam started to climb out of the MGB, both sedans backed

away, and headed off in opposite directions. The Pontiac was already out of sight.

"This is Unit One. Does any unit have target? Does any unit have target in sight?"

"This is Unit Three. We made her license plate number."

83

Sam took Emily with him to the Wilshire station. It had occurred to him she was possibly tempting hostage material. Far-fetched, but he did not dare leave her alone.

Sergeant Liebowitz was polite, but noncommittal. After his questioning revealed Sam was a lawyer, he became downright cynical.

Sam sat on his displeasure. He knew displaying it would only compound Liebowitz's disbelief.

"I ain't sure she's exactly what you would normally consider to be your regular missing person. This sounds more like your private civil matter with variations. You know what I mean, counselor?"

Sam received Liebowitz's verbal assurance that a missing-person bulletin would be put out, but it did not ring with enthusiasm.

"Counselor, you can understand we're shorthanded, it being Christmas and all. Why don't you come back on Monday if this hasn't straightened itself out by then. Lieutenant MacNutt might be able to do something for you."

Outside the station house Sam allowed himself to fume. "Sonofabitchsonofabitch," he kept muttering. He grabbed Emily by the arm and almost threw her into the car.

Emily's eyes went wide. "Sam!"

Abashed, Sam touched her cheek. "Jeez, I'm sorry, Kiddo. I'm a jerk."

"It's okay. I know you're worried."

Worried was the understatement of the day. Susan was in mortal danger. Because of his coercion. He was such an asshole, volunteering to risk her life. If anything happened . . . this was entirely his responsibility. It was all up to him. No one else was going to do anything.

Sam veered over to a telephone booth. "Yellow Pages," he explained.

The closest was near Melrose and Hayworth.

GUNSMITHERY
"We sell peace of mind"
Major credit cards accepted.
Open Sundays.

Sam wondered if that included Christmas Day.

Sam had never owned a real gun. At twelve, his interest in air rifles was supplanted by his discovery of a girl named Daisy. He had fired low-powered rifles at carnivals with embarrassing lack of success. A friend once invited him pheasant hunting and lent him a shotgun. He had test fired the weapon once with only minor shoulder injury.

He was able to park directly in front of the small store. The street was deserted.

The door was locked. Damn. Didn't anyone care about customers anymore? He peered through the bars and glass. Someone was inside. Sam rattled the door. No one came. He rattled some more.

The wizened lady who reluctantly opened the door was at least thirteen inches shorter than Sam.

Eventually, she surrendered to his begging.

"You seem like a nice enough lad," she said, fingering the lace collar of her ancient silk dress figured with tiny pink pansies. "I'm Mary Perkins. Naturally, everyone calls me Ma. What do you want a gun for?"

To save Susan with? That did not seem like the correct answer.

Ma Perkins recognized his confusion. "Son, I've got sporting shotguns, assault rifles, competition pistols, self-defense automatics, etcetera, etcetera. We have to know what you intend to use the weapon for, *comprende?*"

"He wants a handgun," Emily said.

Ma led them to a glass-topped counter and pointed. "Uzi pistol, 9 mm., 20-round magazine. Adjustable sights. List $579. Our price $479. Here's a Linda Luger . . ."

It looked like Star Wars weaponry. "Something I can stick in my pocket," Sam suggested.

Sam had settled on a Desert Eagle .357 Magnum before learning about the mandatory fifteen-day waiting period until delivery.

Chagrined at his ignorance, Sam apologized and wished Ma a Merry Christmas.

"The want ads," Emily proposed.

Forty minutes later Sam owned a used Charter Arms Bulldog Pug 44 Special. For only $150 the seller included an almost full box of Federal 185-grain cartridges. He showed Sam how to load.

The 2½-inch barrel slipped easily into Sam's waistband. And it gave him the creeps.

84

After rendezvousing with Magnasunn and being briefed on the operation, Karrasch concluded he would be more effective investigating independently. His private assessment of Magnasunn was less than glowing. The man talked a good operation, but everything he touched turned to shit. Some sort of character flaw.

Karrasch took down the call number of Magnasunn's cellular car telephone and the operating frequencies of the radio cars before saying he'd be in touch.

By combining the license number of Susan's rental car with the services of a friendly San Luis Obispo Deputy Sheriff, Karrasch determined the vehicle was registered to Budget Auto Rentals.

The same deputy encountered no difficulty in securing co-operation of Budget's regional office, whose computer quickly ascertained the car had been rented out of the Santa Monica Holiday Inn agency.

It took Karrasch thirty minutes' cruising to find Susan's Toyota parked at the Ocean Shores Motel, three blocks from the Holiday Inn.

The car had to be searched. There might be a clue as to precisely how much secret information Susan Schooling had obtained, or even as to her whereabouts.

He was momentarily tempted to break the side window glass but dismissed that as a typical Magnasunn approach and an unnecessary risk.

It took another hour and a bonus to locate a locksmith who would come out Christmas day.

Karrasch told an incredible story about his wife losing both sets of keys.

The locksmith looked from him to the bullet hole in the rear window. Just as Karrasch had anticipated, the size of the bonus overwhelmed all doubt.

All the locks on the Toyota were changed and Karrasch had the keys.

The contents of the briefcase under the passenger seat were disappointing. Larry Levenson's note to Sam was interesting but of no apparent relevance. Karrasch replaced the contents and the case.

Then it occurred to him that the opportunity might arise for the car to be used as a decoy.

He left his own car in the Ocean Shores lot and drove off in the Toyota, searching for a shopping center.

Sears was closed, but in Santa Monica Place the Radio Shack was having its first annual Christmas Day sale.

The Arab manager proudly turned Karrasch over to his

eldest son, who willingly demonstrated a portable all-band receiver for $159.95, batteries included.

Karrasch turned the tuning dial until he heard Magnasunn say, "This is Unit One to all units. Units Two and Three patrol the area bounded by Wilshire, Seventh and—"

He flicked the off switch. "I'll take it. Don't bother with the box."

85

Susan drove aimlessly, trying to decide where to go. Tired of that, she parked and walked among window shoppers in Santa Monica Place. Almost every shop was closed.

As she approached the Radio Shack she again saw a man whose receding back looked exactly like that of Isaac Karrasch. This time he was carrying some sort of portable radio. She really was becoming paranoiac.

The line at the replica old-fashioned popcorn wagon was not overly long. She bought a bag of roasted cashews but made amends with a Diet Pepsi.

Walking back to the car she again considered going to the police. Would she receive protection if she asked for it? She wasn't sure. Perhaps Consolidated had filed some sort of complaint against her. Could she be released to them? That didn't sound right.

If she could only talk to Sam. He would know.

Poor Emily. Some Christmas. At least she was safe with Sam. Although, come to think of it, wasn't he the one who got us into this mess?

Wouldn't a shower and some clean clothes be grand? Can't buy clothes today. Everything closed. Another motel room? No, I can't go through that again.

She got in the car. Where? Elena? Sure. Of course. Her friends, Elena and Orlando Espada in the Valley. That had to be safe. Elena had been dying to do Susan a favor ever since Sam had settled her case without charging a fee.

Susan took the northbound San Diego Freeway. She would take Victory Boulevard, and head east for Van Nuys.

She remembered the cross street but not the address. That was all right. She would recognize their bungalow when she saw it. It was the smallest on the block.

Elena and Orlando welcomed her wholeheartedly. They listened to her nearly incoherent explanation without interruption.

Elena brought coffee mixed with Mexican chocolate and cinnamon. It was the best thing Susan had ever tasted.

But in spite of her hosts' gracious welcome, Susan had second thoughts about staying. "I just realized they could take your name and address off the Rolodex on my desk. They could be checking. It's too dangerous. They actually shot at me. I can't jeopardize you."

"Don't worry," Orlando said. "I have the solution. First, give me your car keys."

Susan was too tired to ask why.

Orlando returned a few minutes later. "I parked on the next street south. No one will connect your car with us."

"But they could still come here looking for me. I shouldn't stay."

"You're not going to stay here. There is only one bedroom anyway. Come, I show you." He pulled Susan to her feet and led her to the back door. "Come, Elena."

Orlando led them through the small backyard to the alley. He worked the combination padlock securing the door of a detached garage on the opposite side of the alley.

"We rent this garage for extra space, as you will see. Your car is parked in front of that house," he pointed, "but on the opposite side of the street."

He gathered them in, closing the door behind and switching on the light.

Susan was standing before a pristinely restored dark green Indianapolis race car. "Miller Special 27" was painted on a large yellow circle on the cowling.

"You want me to drive this?"

Orlando and Elena laughed. "No," Orlando said. "It's not even finished yet. Your guest house is behind you."

Susan turned, her nose almost touching the metallic red and gold van. Orlando slid the door open. The entire interior was upholstered in red and gold velour.

"Bunk with foam rubber mattress. Air conditioning. Stereo. Color TV. Refrigerator." Orlando demonstrated. The van had every comfort.

Susan sighed. She was in love with an altered Dodge.

"First you come back to the house," Elena said. "Have a proper hot shower. Then back here and sleep. You look exhausted."

Susan could find nothing to argue about. Her hair must be permanently matted to her head.

As Susan dried, Elena brought her clean underwear, a white sweat suit with blue stripes, and socks.

"This should fit you well enough for sleeping anyway. I'm washing and pressing your clothes."

Susan started to protest, but Elena shoved her out the back door. "Sleep. When you awake, you will have Christmas dinner and we figure out something. *Felices pascuas.*"

86

Sam hated to let Emily out of his sight for even an instant, but he had to know definitely whether Susan's phone was tapped or not. He felt confident there would be no shooting. They could easily have shot Susan, Emily, or him yesterday if they had wanted to.

"Be careful, Kiddo. Any questions before you go?"

"No. This is kid stuff." Emily knew that she could safely make it home over backyard fences if that became necessary. She hopped on her bike and waved.

"Don't forget the donuts," Sam yelled from the front stoop.

The tiny neighborhood convenience market was only around the corner and a block and a half away. Not only did they sell donuts, but they had a pay telephone inside the store.

Emily bought the donuts before calling home. "Sam, this is Susan. I don't care if the phone is tapped. I'm coming in. You'll have to figure some way to keep them off me. I simply can't take this anymore."

Emily munched donuts on the way home. "I hope you didn't want chocolate-covered, Sam. There were only two of those."

"I don't remember rehearsing, 'I simply can't take this anymore.' "

"Yeah, maybe that was too melodramatic. The powdered sugar aren't bad."

Sam took a donut. "Let's go run a check."

The rapping on the side of the van half-awakened Susan. She heard her name being called. Karrasch was chasing her down a beach. It was only a frightening instant before she remembered where she was.

She swung her legs down and slid open the door.

"I was getting worried," Elena said. "You missed Christmas dinner but you can still make Sunday breakfast."

Susan stretched and shook her mane. "Then I have to call Sam. Help me figure out a way to tell him I'm here without saying so."

The Espada family was impressed with Susan's appetite. Three scrambled eggs. Countless sausages. Sliced tomato, whole-wheat toast, buttered tortillas with guava jam, half a mango, and a leftover Christmas cookie.

When Susan telephoned home, Sam answered and interrupted as soon as he heard her voice. "The phone is definitely bugged. Don't say where you are."

"Okay. It was a minor case anyway."

Sam frowned. She said minor, not miner, didn't she? Minor, small? Minor, unimportant? Minor, under legal age? Of course. Susan's friend. He had settled the collection agency suit against her. Elena. Elena Whatshername? Elena Espada.

"Susan, I think I understand. If you don't hear from me, check back, okay?"

He remembered Elena Espada lived someplace in the Valley. "Emily, do you have a San Fernando Valley Directory?"

There were twelve Espadas, none of them Elena or initial E.

Maybe she didn't have a telephone. *Naa, everyone has a telephone. Unlisted? No, Susan would not have been so quick to agree. Of course. It's listed under her husband's name.* Sam could not remember what her husband's name was. He would have to get it from the file at the office. "Come on, Emily."

Sunday-morning traffic from Santa Monica to downtown Los Angeles was virtually nonexistent. Sam was certain they could not have been followed.

The Tipson, Grumm & Nuttzer offices were empty.

"This is where you work, huh?"

"Yeah," Sam said, thinking Emily was impressed.

"Pretty stuffy, isn't it?"

Sam found the Espada file quickly. There was probably no danger in calling from the office, but he used a pay phone in the lobby.

"Elena? Hi, this is Sam Corbin. Is Susan—yes, great. Thank you." Sam grinned and nodded confirmation to Emily.

"Oh Sam, you got it," Susan said. "Is it all right to talk now?"

"Yes, I'm in a pay phone downtown. First, are you all right?"

"Yes, Elena and Orlando are taking marvelous care of me. Is Emily all right? Can you get me out of this mess?"

"Yes and yes. Emily and I are coming out to get you. I have a safe place in mind for all of us tonight. Tomorrow, I can put an end to this nightmare."

"Oh Sam."

He waited for her to say "I love you," but she didn't.

He continued. "I'm going to rent a car as a precaution. I'm sure we were not followed here, and it's doubtful the MGB would be spotted on the freeway, but I want to be sure. We'll be there as soon as we can."

87

The National Car Rental counter at the Bonaventure Hotel offered him a blue Pontiac Grand Am. "Anything else," Sam pleaded. He reluctantly settled for a red Buick.

"Unit One, this is Unit Two. That was a good guess. Subject went into his office building and came out twenty minutes later. Target's daughter with him. Drove to Bonaventure Hotel. We put a man inside. Subject is now renting a car at the National counter. We can cover the National lot as he exits."

"I copy, Unit Two. All units. This is Unit One. Prepare to execute staggered loose surveillance, Plan B. No unit in place for more than five minutes. Do not allow subject to spot you. Unit Two, take the first leg."

"This is Unit Two. Got him. It's a red Buick Skylark, heading north on Grand."

"Keep a sharp lookout now, Kiddo," Sam said. "We can't afford to be tagged."

"There are quite a few cars out there now."

Yeah, Sam thought. *LA traffic lulls are short-lived.* They would have to be doubly careful. If there was even any suspicion they were being tailed, he would abort until he was certain they were clear. He didn't care if it took all day. He would not lead them to her.

"Susan, here are your clean clothes." Elena handed her the folded bundle. "I got the spot off your blazer. I wish I had some shoes to lend you, but I'm a five."

Susan wiggled the toes of her size sevens. "Thank you, friend. I'll take these back to the van to change. My purse is out there anyway."

Sam took the Victory Boulevard exit. "Spot anything?"

"I thought I might have, but he got off at the last exit."

"Okay, I'm going to take Victory in the wrong direction first to see if we attract anything."

Sam took every precaution he could think of. He drove two miles in the wrong direction, backtracked, parked twice, even got out of the car and waited once.

"We must be clean."

"I think so too," Emily said. "I haven't spotted a thing."

Sam parked in the Espada driveway and waited. There were no vehicles moving on the street. The house was set well back from the street. Someone was peeking through a curtain.

"Let's go in." He and Emily got out of the car simultaneously and started up the front walk.

They were within ten feet of the front door when it burst open and Elena appeared. "Cars! At both ends of the block!" she yelled.

Sam looked back. They were blocking off the street. A beige Oldsmobile screeched to a stop behind his parked Buick, cutting off its escape.

Sam dashed into the house, Emily close behind. "Susan. Where are you?" He ran through the rooms. All four. Where the hell was she?

He sprinted back through the front door. Emily was still searching rooms. Three men were hurrying up the walk.

Sam wasn't sure he could hit heads. He aimed for their chests.

At first sight of the 44 Special, the men scattered.

Each time he fired, Sam roared "Cocksuckers!"

He emptied the revolver at the retreating vehicle, then sprinted into the street and threw the gun after it. The weapon fell thirty feet short before bouncing off the curb.

Sam walked slowly over to retrieve it. Shit. He couldn't even hit the side of an Olds 98.

*   *   *

Orlando was already out the back door. As he crossed the alley he saw a dark sedan start to turn in. He threw open the van door. Susan was dressed and tying her shoelace.

"Let's go. They've been tailed," he yelled. "Grab your purse."

They heard shots.

The two ran through a backyard to the next street, Orlando leading.

"There is your car across the street. Go quickly. This street is clear."

Susan jumped in and drove off.

88

Sunday was the second day in a row Everett met disappointment at Susan's house. Yesterday, there had been no one home either. On Christmas Day. He could hardly conceive it. He considered leaving the two gift-wrapped packages behind the screen door, but that did not seem prudent. It would have been safe in Estherville.

He would try again later. As he turned to go, he was confronted by Magnasunn hurrying up the walk, flashing his San Luis Obispo County Reserve Deputy Sheriff's badge.

"Will you identify yourself, please," Magnasunn ordered.

"Everett Schooling. Is Susan in some sort of trouble with the law?"

"What is your relationship to Mrs. Schooling?"

"I'm her former husband. What's the problem, officer? Maybe I can help."

"Do you know her present whereabouts?"

"No. She hasn't been home the last two times I've called. Are you going to arrest her?"

"Nothing like that, Mr. Schooling. We are Consolidated Utilities Security. Mrs. Schooling is a material witness in a pending case, and we have information that she may be in danger.
We are here solely to protect her. You can do her a service by
calling this number if you learn her whereabouts." Magnasunn
handed him a card. "Thank you for your cooperation."

Magnasunn returned to his car and watched Everett Schooling get into his Chrysler. "This is Unit One to Unit Two. Subject
leaving target residence in white Town and Country. Follow
him."

Susan knew she needed help. She felt on the verge of hysteria. Another day of aimless wandering was intolerable. She
had a vaque idea she might catch Sam at his office. After all,
he had called from a pay phone downtown. She headed for
Bunker Hill, she needed Sam.

It had been a mistake to let Orlando shove her out the back
way. *Of course he meant well, but I should have stayed with Sam
and faced them.*

As Susan cleared the Harbor Freeway interchange it dawned
upon her that if her phone had been tapped they would know
to watch Sam's office. *Now I need someone else they don't know
about. Someone who can safely contact Sam. He is the only one
who can help me out of this. Everything will be back under control
when we are brought together.*

*Everett can do that. Consolidated cannot possibly know about
him.*

She headed for the westbound Santa Monica Freeway interchange and the Century Plaza Hotel.

"This is Unit Two to Unit One. Followed subject in Chrysler
Town and Country to Century Plaza Hotel. He left vehicle with
valet at front drive and entered lobby."

"Unit Six to Unit One. I have target in sight. I have target
heading westbound Santa Monica Freeway, now approaching
Normandy."

"This is Unit One. Units Three through Six execute Plan A,
tracking target. I'll join the pattern within ten minutes. Unit
Two, check with desk clerk for possible registration of Everett

Schooling." *Damn*, Magnasunn thought. He was going to have to circle back east to get behind her.

Karrasch adjusted the squelch knob on the portable all-band radio. *Good*, he thought, *I'm almost exactly in position.* He swung Susan's white Toyota into a tight U-turn and headed for the westbound Santa Monica Freeway entrance.

When Magnasunn spotted the white Toyota ahead of him, he recognized the bullet-damaged rear window even before he could read the license plate.

The spider-web-cracked window prevented him from seeing the driver, but it had to be Susan. She must have switched cars again.

He tried to pass and cut her off but traffic prevented it. He accelerated and gently tapped the Toyota's rear end with his front bumper, waving for her to pull over.

The Toyota accelerated too. Damn her. Stubborn bitch.

Magnasunn put his throttle to the floor and struck her bumper hard.

The Toyota veered off, its right wheels digging into the soft shoulder. The speeding car rolled as it flew over the embankment. It had already turned ninety degrees when it skimmed the chainlink fence, laying it flat.

The Toyota glanced off the concrete wall, rolling twice more before coming to rest.

Magnasunn pulled over and ran down the embankment.

He had seen Karrasch and death often enough to recognize both immediately. What an unpleasant surprise. Karrasch's head was at an anatomically impossible angle. He felt the carotid artery. He was right. Real dead.

Magnasunn felt ambivalence. At least he hadn't killed the target.

He dashed back up to his car and took off. He would have to deal with this later. He was not about to let her slip away again.

"This is Unit Three to Unit One. I have target in sight. Looks to us like she's heading for the Century Plaza too."

89

Susan was conscious that several women in the hotel lobby raised eyebrows at her pink and white running shoes.

She went to the nearest house phone and asked for Everett Schooling's room. Of course he would be delighted if she came right up. Suite 1215.

Susan was so relieved when he opened the door. "Everett, it's so good to be here."

"At last," he sighed, kicking the door shut and hugging her close.

She was surprised at how comforting that felt. "Everett, I really need you—"

"I was sure you would." He was exuberant as a boy with a new scooter. "Excuse me. We have to celebrate."

Susan decided to let him calm down before she tried again.

"Room service. This is Mr. Schooling in 1215. Will you please send up a bottle of champagne? Right away." Everett turned away and lowered his voice. "Dom Perignon '37? No, the Paul Masson will be fine. Thank you."

He turned back to her, grinning with the joy of accomplishment.

She held his shoulders. "Everett, I don't want to burden you with details, but Sam and I have had problems communicating, and—"

"That doesn't surprise me, Susan."

"No, Everett, we've had trouble reaching each other."

"It's obvious he is really not your type."

"What I mean is that it's impossible for Sam and me—"

"What you mean is you've finally come to your senses."

"Don't tell me what I mean. Let me figure it out for myself."

There was a knock at the door.

Susan jumped. "Be careful."

"Don't worry, it's only room service." Nevertheless, Everett cautiously opened the door just a crack.

It was Magnasunn. Everett opened the door the rest of the way. "Oh, please come in—"

Magnasunn saw Susan in the corner. He did not wait for the rest of the invitation.

He shouldered past Everett and drew his Smith & Wesson Airweight .38. "Close the door," he growled.

"Now, just one minute," Everett protested.

Magnasunn barely had to turn in order to backhand him on the temple with the barrel. Everett collapsed without a sound.

Magnasunn faced back to Susan as she swung her purse at him. He slapped it out of her hand. The contents spilled across the carpet.

Magnasunn moved behind her, squeezing her left arm hard as he jammed the .38 into the small of her back. "You've given me a lot of trouble, lady. Now just shut up as we walk out of here and you can stay alive."

He prodded with the gun and Susan moved obediently to the door.

The elevator was empty. Magnasunn shoved her in without letting go, pushed the down button, and faced them both to the front.

By the time they had stopped at the eleventh, tenth, eighth, and fifth floors, the elevator was packed and they were jammed to the rear.

An enormous Hawaiian woman stood in front of them. She was nearly as tall as Magnasunn and wider. Susan almost smothered in her muumuu.

She watched the red light read 4, 3, 2, L. As the doors opened and the elevator started to empty, Susan pinched the woman's ass as hard as she could.

The giantess bellowed as she pivoted. The force of her left uppercut snapped Magnasunn's head against the elevator wall. Susan broke loose, running fast.

Magnasunn tried to shove his way around the hulk, but the woman pinned him to the wall with enormous breasts and punished him with another left and a right cross. He raised both hands in surrender.

She tweaked his nose until he whimpered, then stalked off.

Magnasunn ran through the lobby to the entrance. He burst through the doors and stopped at the doorman, flashing his badge. "Black-haired girl. Tan jacket. Plaid skirt. Did you see her?"

The doorman pointed south toward Olympic Boulevard. "Running fast," he said.

Magnasunn ran to his car. As he opened the door, two sport-jacketed men approached from each side.

"Police. Hands on the car roof. Spread your feet," said the one on the left, as he assisted him into position.

"You are under arrest," said the one on the right, as he applied handcuffs.

"Looky here," said the left one as he removed Magnasunn's .38.

"I have a right to carry that. The permit is in my wallet."

"You have the right to remain silent." The left one gave Magnasunn the rest of his rights as they walked him to their unmarked car.

As Magnasunn's head was pushed into the rear of the vehicle, he said, "I don't understand. What's the charge?"

The driver answered. "Two witnesses on the Santa Monica Freeway saw the whole thing and got your plate numbers. I think vehicular manslaughter and hit and run at least. Maybe if we find a motive we can make it murder one."

90

Randolph Champion paced the study of his pink stucco Bel-Air mansion.

The place had been purchased by his father from the estate of the British actor Ronald Coleman. It had been such a serendipitous discovery, his mother never tired of exclaiming. God, he had learned to hate that word.

It had been a fortunate find, though. Irreplaceable brass door knobs, carved wall panels, priceless china, crystal and silver, all pre-monogrammed RC.

He was delighted to have inherited the place, but he was vaguely uncomfortable with the thought that he had been named to match a house and furnishings.

Champion had to face the possibility the search for Susan Schooling might fail.

He took the gold-plated putter from the monogrammed umbrella stand and began to practice on the forest green carpet. He concentrated on better putting.

He had to deal with potential consequences. It was already Sunday afternoon. The trial would resume the next morning. All the news had been devastating. Karrasch was dead. Magnasunn had been arrested. The entire operation was in shambles.

He knew that Susan Schooling claimed to have discovered the Blanket file. He had to assume she had stated the truth. After all, she'd said it to Sam Corbin in what she believed was a private telephone conversation.

Why had she uncovered it, though? What possible motivation could she have had? Champion could not bring himself to believe she would engage in industrial espionage. He had just reviewed her personnel file. That was digression. He must stick to the point.

The point was he had no handle on what, if anything, had really been disclosed. Had Susan even passed her information to Corbin? There was a chance the two of them hadn't had enough contact to exchange any detailed information. At least that had been so until this afternoon. After Magnasunn's arrest, she'd dropped out of sight again.

And even if Sam Corbin had received the information, it wasn't at all clear what he would have done, or would do, with it. Would he be unprincipled enough to blackmail the company? At least there was no reason to conclude that he might disclose it to the other side, or even the judge. After all, Corbin was working for Consolidated Utilities. And Pringle had assured him that Corbin was under control.

Still, Champion did not have enough data to project comfortably. Better be prepared for the contingencies.

Champion punched 22 on his telephone console. The automatic dialer obediently called the residence of his executive vice-president, Jesse St. James.

"Jess, this is Randolph. I'm sorry to disturb you on Sunday afternoon, but we have to avert a crisis. Listen." It took ten minutes for Champion to fill him in.

"Christ," St. James said at the end. "She apparently has copies of all the Blanket file data. That could be devastating."

"That's why I want you at the trial Monday morning. I'll have Pringle there too. We cannot predict what will happen. Consider that you have full authority. Use your discretion, you understand. We're counting on you, Jess."

St. James understood he would be counted on to take the fall if things turned sour in the morning.

91

Sam was furious at Orlando. He remained polite, though. The young man was only trying to help.

Sam was no longer merely angry, he was mad. He hated himself, goons, guns, Consolidated Utilities, Tipson, Grumm & Nuttzer, and the practice of law, although not necessarily in that order.

Had he failed the law or had the law failed him? Or did he give a fuck? Failing Susan seemed more imminent.

He detoured to Marina del Rey, where he and Emily walked to the end of the empty breakwater. A light fog rolled in. Sam wound up once and threw the 44 Special out to sea. That helped. They drove in silence.

Before leaving the Espada home, Sam had taken the names of all Susan's friends Elena could remember.

At the Santa Monica house Sam called them all. Some were suspicious. He understood that. No one told him anything remotely useful.

"I've telephoned myself hoarse. I can't think of another one," Sam said.

"May as well try Everett," Emily suggested.

Everett Schooling answered the phone only because the ringing made his head throb. After Sam identified himself Everett started to describe what had happened, but Sam interrupted with multiple questions about Susan's whereabouts. Everett decided his head ached too much for extended conversation.

"Yes, Sam, she was here, but I have no idea. You caught me packing. Oh, give her a message from me, please. Tell her I'm going home. She knows where to reach me. Her purse will be at the front desk."

Susan kept to side streets, walking toward the ocean. She was becoming apprehensive. No car, no purse, no credit cards, no money. She could not even make a telephone call now without begging.

Damn. She wanted her self-sufficiency back. She was entitled. Hadn't she spent years earning independence? Before she met Sam Corbin she had needed no one. Look at her now.

It was dusk when she reached Pacific Avenue. Between the ramshackle buildings, she watched the orange glow spread over gray fog. The wind had died. Still, it might be a bitterly cold night.

Tonight in Estherville she probably would have been in front of a fireplace roasting chestnuts and sipping brandy.

She looked at her watch. No wonder she was exhausted. She had walked for three hours. Where could she hock a watch on Sunday night?

She thought she felt a raindrop on her nose. Please God, not now.

The priest was lounging against the wall of Our Lady of Sorrows Mission, smoking the largest meerschaum Susan had ever seen. He wore a clerical collar under a navy-blue cardigan with leather elbow patches. Wisps of white hair protruded from his LA Dodgers cap.

A light rain started to fall.

"Father, I need to rest," she said.

"Come use the cot in my office, child. We'll talk later."

As Susan entered the Central District Courthouse, she felt conspicuously disheveled. Actually, in the kaleidoscope of Monday-morning bustle, there was nothing about a beautiful woman wearing expensive, although slightly rumpled clothes, with pink and white running shoes, to attract undue attention.

She had thought she was early, but failed to anticipate the massive volume of the place, a full city block.

Then she realized she did not know in which department the Saunders trial was being held. She had to get directions to Department 1, then stand in line to find out.

Susan knew what she wanted, but had only a half-formed idea of how it should be accomplished. Where the hell was her intuition when she most needed it?

As she passed the second-floor snack stand, she remembered she did not even have her briefcase. That had been left in the Toyota about a hundred years ago.

She wove through clusters of coffee-sipping attorneys, dipped to pick a nice, black calfskin case from the floor, and kept walking. No one turned a head.

It was only 9:33 when the Consolidated Security plain-clothesman grabbed her at the entrance to Department 101.

That was when she started screaming for Sam.

92

On Monday morning, Sam rose earlier than usual. He had to make sure Emily was properly dressed. Then they had to go back to his place for a suit and tie.

He installed Emily in his office together with a book, a Sony Walkman, and a box of Cheez-its, her choice, not his.

He assured her that he would return from court as soon as possible, but at latest, noon.

He took a taxi to the courthouse, resolving on the way to press immediately for the granting of his motion for nonsuit. Not that he now thought it deserved to be granted. It was simply the fastest way for him to get out of there and continue the search for Susan. Lucrezia would forgive him. He was only doing what he had to do.

When Sam walked in, the jury was not yet in the box.

Lucrezia, Molly, and Saunders huddled at their end of the table, so engrossed they did not even notice his entrance.

Ben, St. James (whom Sam did not know), and Pringle were at the other end of the counsel table. What the hell was Pringle doing here? He dreaded courtrooms.

Ben nodded, Pringle introduced him to Consolidated's Executive Vice-President Jesse St. James, but before anything more could be said, Judge Iverson called the case.

"*Saunders versus Consolidated Utilities.* Are we ready to proceed outside the presence of the jury?"

Lucrezia was first to respond. "Your Honor, I urge you to deny the motion for nonsuit. I have—"

Pringle spoke at the same moment, but handicapped by his stutter. "Your Honor, I am Bartlett P-Pringle, a senior p-partner with T-Tipson, Grumm & Nuttzer. At the request of our . . . client, I move to substitute myself as attorney of record in p-place of Mr. Corbin for the p-p—"

Lucrezia was simultaneously saying, "—filed a supplementary trial brief with your clerk this morning, which I would like to—"

Judge Iverson was pounding his gavel. "Please, please. Mr. Corbin, don't you have anything you want to say at the same time?"

"Yes, Your Honor, I do." There were suddenly a lot of things he wanted to say.

He wanted to say that he had reconsidered and was withdrawing the motion. He wanted to disclose Mrs. Savin's admission of perjury. He wanted to complain about Susan's ordeal. He wanted to ask to be relieved as defense counsel so he could go find her.

There was a lot of noise out in the corridor. Voices yelling.

Sam was certain one of them was Susan.

"Your Honor, could we take a recess? I've got to go help Susan."

Sam was already half out the courtroom door before the judge could respond.

"Of course, Mr. Corbin. Take five minutes," the judge said to Sam's rapidly disappearing back. He scratched his head. Was he supposed to know who the hell Susan was?

Sam burst through the door and ripped the security man away from Susan. He tried to hold her tight, but the black calfskin case was between them.

The security man was about to try for a comeback when St. James, Pringle, and Ben came into the corridor. "I've got her, Mr. St. James," he said.

"So I see," said St. James, noting that Sam Corbin seemed to have her even more. He also noted the briefcase she clutched so tightly.

He waved the security man off, and nodded at the case. "Why don't you hand that over to me, Mrs. Schooling. After all, it is Consolidated property."

He reached out.

Susan recognized St. James, and had an immediate, although somewhat general, idea of why he was there. She held the case tighter. "No, I want Sam to have it. It's evidence."

"C-come now," Pringle said. "We don't even know what's in there."

"020 Blanket Conditions." Susan said it as if she was announcing a lottery winner.

St. James paled. *She had it all.* He was absolutely certain. They were all going down the toilet. He could hear it flushing.

"Susan," Sam said. "I can't use stolen evidence against my own client."

"He is indisputably right about that," Pringle said without stammering. Once he was outside the courtroom his muscles began to relax.

Susan's eyes flashed, and she spaced her words. "The documents are Consolidated property. They are in the possession of a Consolidated officer, *me.* Therefore, they are not stolen. Sam, as an officer of Consolidated Utilities, I am handing these documents over to you and authorizing you to disclose them to the court."

She shoved the case toward him.

Sam hesitated.

"Damn it, Sam. You owe it to me."

Sam was a little slow in accepting.

"Goddamn you!" Susan yelled. "You owe it to yourself!"

Sam took the case and started to grin.

St. James momentarily toyed with the effect of a countermanding order from a higher-ranking Consolidated officer. He concluded this was not the time for legal subtleties, and turned to the security man.

Sam stepped forward, holding the case in both hands. He came toe to toe with St. James, and smiled down. "Mr. St. James, could I speak to you alone for a moment?"

St. James was startled, but nodded. The security man halted.

Pringle started to stutter again. "Now just a d-damn—"

But Sam was already leading St. James down the hall, speaking softly and rapidly. St. James kept nodding. They came back.

"Let's go in and see the judge," Sam said.

Lucrezia, Molly, and Saunders were still huddled at the table trying to figure out why Pringle wanted to substitute himself for Sam.

"Where is Emily?" Susan whispered. Sam told her. She relaxed.

Sam sat Susan where he could keep an eye on her. He placed the unopened case on the counsel table but kept both hands on it.

"Your Honor," Sam said, "could we have an extended recess? The defendant has a settlement proposal to make to plaintiff."

Saunders started to smile. Molly put her hand over her mouth. Ben was fascinated but could think of nothing to say. Lucrezia stared at Sam. Susan stared at Lucrezia, whom she had never seen before.

Judge Iverson appeared confused. "Mr. Pringle," he asked, "do you concur in that request? Mr. Pringle?"

Sam was smiling at Susan, and St. James was glaring at Pringle. Pringle appeared completely tongue-tied. He managed a nod.

Judge Iverson sighed. Perhaps soon someone would let him know what was going on. "Mr. Corbin, can you report the progress of negotiations to me in an hour? Mr. Corbin?"

"Oh sure, Your Honor," Sam said without taking his eyes off Susan. "Whatever."

Judge Iverson sighed. He understood the futility of competing for Sam's attention. It was either accept Sam's temporary distraction or hold him in contempt. "Fine. Then we'll decide what to do next." The whistled first phrase of "Love Is in the Air" could be heard as his chambers door closed.

As the judge disappeared into chambers, Sam tore his eyes

away from Susan and whispered to Pringle. "Just stay cool and trust me. I'm saving your ass. Tiger."

Sam took Lucrezia to the empty jury box where they sat next to each other. Sam talked too quietly for anyone else in the courtroom to hear. Lucrezia seemed to be mostly listening.

After listening to Sam's opening offer of settlement, Lucrezia took Saunders to the cafeteria for coffee and a conference.

She did calculations on a yellow legal pad before offering it to Saunders. "After deduction of my fees and reimbursement of costs advanced, you would net slightly over $1.7 million. I'm sure we can get that offer raised."

Saunders brushed the scribbled figures aside. "The money is already more than I need. I couldn't think of ways to spend that much in—" He smiled. "Anyway, do whatever you want about that. I do have other demands, though."

Outside the presence of a judge and jury, Pringle regained the power of speech, and used it to advocate the stingiest possible settlement terms. In spite of Pringle's transparent attempt to ingratiate himself with the client, Sam insisted that fair compensation to Saunders was only good business. The alternative disclosures could be devastating.

Settlement negotiations took less than an hour. In addition to a cash settlement higher than originally offered, Saunders received Consolidated's public apology and written promise to correct the most dangerous plant conditions. The corrections were short of everything he thought should be done. But he deemed the agreement an excellent foundation for his responsible nuclear power campaign.

St. James considered the settlement agreement a bargain. Although the overall cost of Saunders's compensation and the safety corrections would total more than any potential punitive damage award, a plaintiff's verdict would have carried other even more costly consequences. The public disfavor would affect future licensing and undoubtedly cause a wave of stricter regulation.

Besides, St. James thought the settlement was a sure win for him. If the Consolidated board disapproved, he could easily create the inference that the settlement had been necessary to save the company from the consequences of Champion's irresponsible policies. If the board applauded, he was a hero. Either way he strengthened the position from which he would eventually make his bid for the CEO position.

Ben whispered to Sam that the settlement was a frustrating anticlimax on the verge of victory. Sam responded that he could live with getting Saunders a fair deal instead.

After the settlement terms had been entered in the record, St. James repeated his request for the black briefcase.

"You won't have any use for that now," he suggested to Susan.

"I'd like to see it first," Sam said as he started to open the case.

"I'll tell you about it later," Susan said to Sam, taking the case back and handing it to St. James. "You must promise to return the case and whatever contents do not belong to the company."

"Of course, I'll have it back to you tomorrow."

"No, not me." Susan smiled. "You'll see. Can we go now, Sam?"

St. James did not see, but was not going to quibble over details required to gain possession.

When St. James opened the case in the privacy of his office, he gained some understanding. The contents were the probate file in the Estate of Karol Wyszynski, Deceased, half a cheese Danish, carefully wrapped, a bottle of Excedrin, and a stack of business cards of Cohen, Kan and Cain, Attorneys at Law.

Taped to the inside lid of the case was one of the cards with the handwritten notation, "Please return to . . ."

St. James's understanding was complete later in the day, when he received a copy of the report of the computer security expert hired to re-encode the confidential data banks.

The expert had proved electronically that the 020 Blanket Conditions file had not been opened on December 24 by anyone.

93

Susan borrowed forty dollars from Sam. She had to go to her office and to the bank. Sam would get Emily and they would all meet at her house as early as possible.

As Sam entered the offices of Tipson, Grumm & Nuttzer, the receptionist flagged him down. "Mr. Morgan wants you in his office the moment you come in."

Morgan kept Sam waiting in his outer office only about five minutes, which was ten minutes less than usual.

Morgan glared as he entered. *At least,* Sam thought, *he's looking at me now.*

"Corbin," Morgan began, "I've just been on the telephone with Bartlett Pringle. He's been telling me Consolidated is delighted with the settlement and the way you've handled the crisis. Bart says the only trouble was caused by your lady friend going out of control, but he has persuaded Consolidated you could not be responsible for her misconduct. Bart thinks we ought to give you your partnership and three weeks leave with pay as a bonus."

Morgan stopped to watch Sam's reaction. None was visible.

He continued, "Personally, however, I think we should fire your ass. Now what do you think we should do about your position here?"

Sam looked at Morgan's hunting prints as he reflected on his last time in this precise spot. Almost three months ago, when he'd told himself, *Be assertive, man. Say something brazen. Oh, what the hell.*

Sam realized his suggestion about what Morgan should do with the position was not only anatomically impossible, but defied the laws of Newtonian physics.

Nevertheless, Sam thought his description had been extraordinarily lyrical, with Zenlike, conceptually irrational overtones.

On his way out, Sam decided there was nothing in his office worth going back for. He was so euphoric he reached the lobby before remembering Emily.

Susan's finger poised over her office telephone, unwilling to press the requested numbers.

Her gaze shifted from the brass sailboat paperweight Sam had given her to Emily's photograph. She had never before fully recognized Emily's resemblance to her father.

And would her daughter thrive on a four-acre site overlooking the Estherville Public Library? Country house designed by resident architect, Susan W. Schooling? Indeed.

Susan punched the numbers. "May I speak to Everett Schooling, please? This is Mrs. Sch—" That sounded strange. "—tell him Susan is calling. Thank you. I'll wait."

"Yes, Everett, it's me. Happy New Year to you too. I want to apologize for what happened to you. Yes, I'm fine. Yes, it's all over. Yes, I will tell you the whole story later."

Susan explained all the reasons she could not once again be Mrs. Everett Schooling. She was more polite than candid. She was proud of Everett for asking, and honored, but no.

Of course, he could visit Emily whenever he liked.

Susan hung up. There was still so much to do before she met Sam.

Sam was childishly proud of his valediction but could not repeat one word of it to Emily. He was bursting to tell Susan as soon as they were finally alone in Susan's living room.

"Me first," she insisted. "My news will not wait another minute. I just quit Consolidated. I want nothing more to do with Con U."

"So it's Con U now?"

"Perhaps it should be Con U Cal. That has broader connotations."

Sam laughed. "I'm glad you quit. You probably just beat them to the draw."

"They don't deserve me. Now tell me your news."

"Tipson, Grumm doesn't deserve me either."

Susan came to him. "Oh Sam. Does this mean we can't afford a church wedding?"

94

Lucrezia spent most of January catching up. It was always that way after a prolonged trial. Everything that could be put off, was put off.

Not only was there the backlog, but new cases were pouring in daily. Lucrezia supposed the publicity from the Saunders settlement was doing it. She had even been asked to do an interview for the 6:00 news. She had declined, so they used ten seconds of her walking down the courthouse steps with voice-over. There was nothing she could do to prevent that.

It seemed there was only time for morning laps in the pool, work until her mind grew fuzzy, something to eat, and sleep. Lucrezia thought that was healthy. It left no time to dwell on Paul Cummings III, or anyone else, but she knew she would have to find some help.

She had only spoken to Peter Saunders once this month. He had telephoned from Houston to ask her opinion about a certificate of deposit in a Texas financial institution paying 15 percent. He had sounded content. The settlement publicity had created so many lecture and television opportunities, he'd said, that he could not accept them all. He was averaging only one or two nights a week at home in Venice.

Lucrezia stepped out of her high heels in the middle of the kitchen floor. The tamale pie appeared to be as represented by Carmen's note, and she was hungry, but not hungry enough to eat alone. She put the casserole dish back in the refrigerator and selected the white Zinfandel instead.

She poured the wine. What she needed was a vacation. New places and faces. No, that was not for her. She knew she was incapable of relaxing for more than one day.

She was tempted to call Saunders. That wasn't fair. She would never . . . Hell, that didn't mean they could not have a friendly dinner, did it? This just might be one of his nights home. She picked up the kitchen telephone.

It was damn cold and Saunders was too tired to walk the beach anyway.

He'd had to hire an agent to deal with the flood of offers. He was actually being paid to lecture. And people were paying attention. He was reaching them, he could tell.

He would unpack later. He threw his overnight bag on the bed, put his shoes in trees and placed them on the closet floor rack.

God, he was so tired. This was the first night he'd been home all week.

The appearances were getting easier, but harder too. The words flowed more smoothly but the exertion seemed more fatiguing each time.

He reached into the refrigerator for a beer. As he bent forward, the sudden pain in his chest stabbed with such intensity he dropped the can.

That was the third time this month.

He leaned against the refrigerator, waiting for the burning to subside. Taking shallow breaths seemed to help.

When he could move, he rummaged blindly in the cardboard box on the closet floor until he found the Colt .45.

He removed a fleck of dust from the barrel with his handkerchief. He flicked the safety catch a few times. The pain subsided.

He returned the weapon to the closet.

There was too much more to do. Next week he was invited to testify before a joint congressional subcommittee.

He would fight as long as he could hold out. He had to get something back for being killed.

He didn't feel like answering the ringing telephone. Rachel would not be calling this late.

Paul Cummings III had known for weeks he'd made a terrible, terrible mistake. It took until tonight to admit it, however. Of course the money was important but he should have tried to get it some other way.

He was already late for a scheduled photo opportunity but would take time to dial the old, familiar number just once more.

Damn. The line was still busy.

95

Susan had been looking for a job all month. Sam found one almost instantly. A former client had offered him the job of supervising the renovation of *Fidelity IV,* a classic sixty-foot Sparkman & Stephens yawl. The pay was one-third of what he had been earning at TGN, but he got to live aboard rent free, and the owner provided the telephone for his own convenience. Besides, he was enjoying working with his hands and getting a tan in January.

When Susan came down the Marina del Rey dock, it was already dark and cold. Sam had turned on the spreader lights to guide her. He wore a wool fisherman's sweater and was on deck waiting.

Susan slipped off her shoes and accepted his hand to be helped aboard.

"I'll have the dock steps done tomorrow," he said. "Come below. The fireplace is lit. I'll give you a glass of cheap Chablis and a kiss."

Susan hurried down the companionway ladder and warmed herself by the tiny brass charcoal stove. Except for the blue ceramic-tiled bulkhead behind the stove, every vertical surface in the salon was glowing, hand-rubbed teak. The overhead was tongue-and-groove enameled glossy white.

Susan turned around to face Sam. "That feels so good. I'll take the kiss first."

When Susan did sip the wine, she tried not to make a face. "Sam, I've got an exciting prospect. Tell me what you think. Dorman and Associates A.I.A. are on retainer to do this huge two-thousand-house tract in Orange County below Newport. They believe that the development is so big, it requires an urban planner, and they have persuaded the developer of that too."

"So they've offered you the job? Great."

"No, they haven't. They don't want to hire a planner on staff because they don't have an ongoing need. Hiring means fringe benefits and pension plan, you know. But if I submit a preliminary plan the developer approves, they can get me a one-hundred-thousand-dollar fee to do the project freelance. That's a year's work. It can set me up in business, give me a chance to pick up more clients. If I work out of my home, my overhead is zip. . . ." She paused for breath. "Well?"

"Terrific. Of course you do it. Listen, I have a report, too. The owner was down today. He wants me to have this monster ready to skipper to Hawaii in the spring. I get all expenses paid, so I should be able to throw the whole delivery fee into the kitty toward the day."

"But how long will you be gone?"

"Only about three weeks if I leave *Fidelity* in the Islands. But he is talking about taking it on to the South Pacific. I'm sure I can have that job, too, if I want it. It would be a year, but I'd save a bundle of money."

"Oh, Sam, that is so long."

"Honey, with me dependent on boat jobs as they come along

and you starting a new business, we had better have some cash in the bank before we take on marriage."

The telephone rang. Sam picked it up. "Yacht *Fidelity*. Sam Corbin."

"Sam, this is Lucrezia. I got your number from Ben. Sam, I'm getting too old to run it all alone, and I need a partner. Perhaps you would like to come over to the office tomorrow and talk."